THE
BIG BOOK
OF
BIZARRO

**EDITED BY
RICH BOTTLES JR.
GARY LEE VINCENT**

Burning Bulb
PUBLISHING

The Big Book Of Bizarro

Edited By **Rich Bottles Jr.** and **Gary Lee Vincent**

Burning Bulb Publishing
P.O. Box 4721
Bridgeport, WV 26330-4721
www.BurningBulbPublishing.com

First printing.

Edition ISBN

Paperback 978-0-61550-203-8

First edition.
Printed in the United States of America.

Library of Congress Control Number: 2011934290

This book is dedicated to the many authors whose work did not make the final cut for The Big Book of Bizarro. *We appreciate you taking the time and effort to submit your work and encourage you to continue pursuing your writing goals.*

CONTENTS

About the Illustrator
vii

Foreword
viii

HORROR

Daniel In The Lion's Den
Kai Miro
3

Wet
Mark Gallagher
15

The Whore of the Dartmoor
Rich Bottles Jr.
28

The Fall
David J. Fairhead
38

Glory Holes
Gary Lee Vincent
54

Channel 666
John Russo
64

Forever Ago Sunshine
Wol-vriey Jesuto
70

i

Honey-do
Nikko Lee
84

Every Bite
Matt Smallwood
92

Nothing Really Satisfies
Kelly R. Martin
99

Decorations
Nelson W. Pyles
106

Karnivali
Jesse J. Saxon
112

Front Page
Michael A. Migliore
124

Into The Night
Heather Lin
130

Hades on Ice
Kimberly Bennett
138

His Own Worst Enemy
Laird Long
147

Writer's Block
Ryan J. McBriar
153

Every
Charlie Kirby
173

City of the Dead
Clare de Lune
180

Want
Meself John
186

SCI-FI & FANTASY

Alien Apocalypse
Zmortis
190

Saved
Thomas Fuchs
201

Pearl
Scott Emerson
203

Worms
George R. Galuschak
209

In Cocoon, I am Embryo
Kenzie Mathews
216

The Only One To Save
Derek Tabor
233

Scotomization
D. Harlan Wilson
241

False Idols
Sean Martin
245

I'm Going To The Moon
Christy Leigh Stewart
264

Diethylamide
Michael C. Thompson
267

Their Quiet, Bookish Life
Chadwick H. Saxelid
285

Gloriana
Angela Caperton
291

Bleedin' Hearts
Salvatore Buttaci
299

The Image of the Lord
Jon Judy
309

Punch and Jesus
Anonymous Christian
320

Jumpers
Michael Bracken
327

Nude Sushi with a Twist
Keith Dugger
334

Talking Heads
Nicole E. Peffer
339

BOOM CLICK CLICK
William Pauley III
348

Succor the Child
Mercy Loomis
355

She Who Cleans: A Dung Sticker's Shitty Tale
A.D. Spencer
363

Tiffany's!! It's Get Even Time!!
George Kosana
372

Cotton Mouth
Christopher Danaher
377

InBox
Brennon ThompSon
387

Losing Control
R. Scott Steele
392

EROTICA

One Hell of a Band
J.T. Seate
404

Lester's Ominous Gift
Eva Hore
415

The Gathering
Madeleine Swann
431

Womb With a View
Reina Sobin
439

Love Bites
Andrée Lachapelle
447

Pomegranate Moth
Richard Godwin
460

Sonata for Insects and Violins
Peter Baltensperger
463

Frosty
Alice Jacobs
469

Fun House
Kimber Vale
474

Butterfly Kisses
Duncan Meece
484

Sexual Madness
Rose de Fer
497

Terra Cupidus
Robin Tiergarten
506

ABOUT THE ILLUSTRATOR

Jon Towers is the writer and artist of *The New Apocrypha* comics books. He is also the co-writer and artist of the upcoming *WZWA – World Zombie Wrestling Association* comic books. He is also an independent pro wrestler, and has his own podcast called **Red Horse Radio**. For more information, visit:

www.jonnyaxx.com

www.stigmataverse.blogspot.com

www.redhorseradio.podomatic.com

FOREWORD

We were somewhere around Mink Shoals on the edge of Charleston when the drugs began to take hold. I remember saying something like "What's that crappy book you purchased…"

Gary Vincent and I were returning from the annual West Virginia Book Festival last year, where we were suspiciously denied a vendor's booth "based on availability." Although denied booth space, we decided to check out the festival anyway and let the organizers know of our intent to apply for a booth as early as possible for the 2011 event.

Gary had purchased some kind of Appalachian folklore anthology from a local publishing company for twenty bucks. The damn thing only had a couple hundred pages and the cover looked like it was designed using free clip art from the Internet. The book contained a hodgepodge of poorly constructed poetry and shamefully short stories - all mish-mashed together to represent the Appalachian literary experience. Of course, the over-priced book was only available for purchase directly through the publishers.

I remarked that the anthology reminded me of those national honor roll publications where the company will print your student's bio in exchange for the purchase of the book. Gary then revealed that he'd like to create some type of genre anthology through Burning Bulb, but wanted to do it the right way. The Appalachian anthology was to serve as sort of the Bizarro World opposite of what he intended to do.

Thus, *The Big Book of Bizarro* was conceived on the long drive back to north-central West Virginia from the 2010 West Virginia Book Festival. Looking at the Appalachian anthology for our anti-inspiration, we decided that we would do the following: Use a theme that would be fresh and have universal appeal; make the book available through a wide distribution network, including Amazon; ensure that the book looks professionally designed and edited; actually read the submissions and judge them according to the submission criteria; and (this is the kicker) pay the authors for their submissions.

My god, were we crazy? We were actually willing to put our own personal writing projects on hold, endure the stress of reading and editing scores of eclectic submissions, and use our own money up front in order to create something unique - or at least really special in the publishing industry.

Almost a year later, you now hold in your hands the product of our endeavor and you damn well better appreciate it. Granted, you are not going to like every single piece of prose included in this anthology, and I'm sure purists of the Bizarro genre will find that some of the stories do not live up to their personal definitions of "Bizarro" literature; but we hope most of you will agree that there's a lot of interesting, captivating, entertaining and fun reading ahead for those who enjoy perusing transgressive fiction.

According to Goodreads, "Bizarro fiction is a contemporary literary genre, which often utilizes elements of absurdism, satire, and the grotesque, along with pop-surrealism and genre fiction staples, in order to create subversive works that are as weird and entertaining as possible."

I believe it was Carlton Mellick III, who once said on an Internet discussion board, "The genre is still in the fledgling stage and not quite established yet, so the authors/publishers who have a lot invested in the genre want to protect its growing reputation." Sorry, 'bout your luck, Carlton.

Rich Bottles Jr.
July 4th, 2011

Horror

DANIEL IN THE LION'S DEN
By Kai Miro

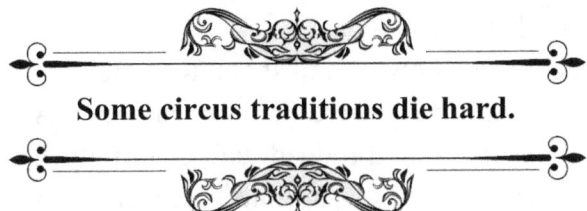

Some circus traditions die hard.

Kai Miro lives in her family's hundred-year-old farmhouse in Washington State. She loves cats and manga. When she's bored, she gives herself tattoos and walks in her Dad's old zen maze. According to Kai, "I write crazy lies that I half believe about the wasted fields and woods around the house. I like to hunt ghosts. I've seen stuff. I write a lot of dark stuff but this is my first sell. I wrote this story 'cause racism, cruelty, inhumanity, abuse of any kind really pisses me off."

Maria must have come up with the plan shortly after watching the old circus lions eat her latest baby. This was the third child served up to the animals and she would have been Maria's only daughter. Yeah, she probably had the plan already in her head because she wouldn't even look at One-Eyed Daniel, not once, while she flirted with the Knife Man, aka Bernard aka El Cabron. Knife Man paid Pit Boss extra to cut the girls. Girls got better drugs if they let it happen.

Maria just waited patiently as Bernard fed her his dick until the knife came out. Then, she bent his wrist in so he could get the first

3

taste of it, swinging his fat arms sideways with the blade until his stomach spilled yellowish blubber in a wet red greasy smile. Knife Man screamed like a new girl in her first gang-bang.

Daniel and all the others in the cages howled, screaming Maria's name to encourage her. Maria smiled briefly as Knife Man fell away, weeping desperately and struggling to pull his intestines back into the gaping wound of his body. The Pit Dogs came running, bearing their spiked baseballs and electric prods but it was too late. Tears in her eyes, Maria pulled Knife Man's razor one last time, opening her throat to release her soul.

In his cage, Daniel howled and shook the bars.

Girls who fought back were bad for business. As punishment, everyone in the cages were prodded with electricity. Then, the other girls were forced to cut Maria up into small pieces and feed her to the crocodiles. The girls wept until one of the scarred ones, a former fighter, both of her legs gone to the animals, started singing "Ava Maria." Silence reigned then and Pit Boss returned to his mobile home, not able to do anything about the mood.

Daniel went silent with deep thought.

By dinnertime, Daniel'd come up with a plan closer to reckless death and senseless degradation than actual revenge and redemption. But, it was something and that something looked better and better as evening fell. Experience had taught Daniel that for every minor rebellion in the camp, Pit Boss hit back with an iron fist. The dark man had gone angrily into his mobile home to brood. Now, hours later, Daniel was sure the payment for Maria's rebellion and body loss was going to be their blood for his money.

Now, as the other fighters in the cages scooped up cold greasy stew from the ground, Daniel gave an upwards nod towards Mark and Matthew, the blond American boys. Mark grinned, his white teeth sharpened into canine butcher knives. Matthew just ducked his head back in an animal nod before whoofing softly like a chimpanzee. Daniel could always count on those two.

Daniel focused his one-eyed glare on Black Jude. She cocked her dreaded head as if listening to his thoughts. What she found there, she liked, her mouth slightly open and drooling. Tomas had his back to everyone. Daniel racked his brain trying to figure out how to get his attention but then Tomas shouldered the bars of his cage to a rattling. Tomas was in, then, and that was a good thing. Tomas was big and he didn't seem to care much about pain. By the time Daniel got around to checking in with Zeke, he found the small intense boy already staring at him. That was good then, there were fighters he could rely on. Fighters who'd cross the Pit Boss with him.

Ruthie came up to Daniel's cage, one hand curving around her softly rounded belly, the other wrapping fingers around the cage bars. She whispered, "Where you go, we will follow," and walked back to the other party girls.

Daniel examined them. Magdelina, the party girl who used to be a fighter until she lost her legs, she was tough as hell. Maria may have actually been Ruthie's sister. Addicts would sell all of their kids to the Pit Boss. Daniel was sure his mom would have but instead, after her mouth, her ass and some of her better working organs, all she had was him. Lucy, Catrina and Agate just had the dumb luck of being pretty and alone. They were kidnapped. It would be good to have outside help. He nodded his thanks. The party girls simply stared back with their dead black eyes.

Daniel took a nap to gather his strength. He would need it all when night fell and the floodlights roared on, announcing Showtime.

In the dream, Daniel stood alone and unarmed in the center of the pit. The old circus lionesses circled while the sickly Bengal tiger bided his turn on the outskirts with the scarred up Lion male. In nature, it is the females who hunt while the males fight for harem control.

Now, as Daniel watched, the lionesses wove hypnotic patterns of hunting songs they barely remembered their mothers telling them as their father roared forlorn and lonely in his cage far away. Daniel could follow the hunting lines the lionesses danced, those haunting songs predators sang to their prey.

Behind them, and past the two males watching and waiting, packs of hyena gathered, their yellow teeth and golden eyes bright as urine. Beyond the packs of hyena, narrow-headed jackal gathered, followed by a flock of vultures. Then, a murder of black crows descended. Rainbow-colored flesh-devouring beetles poured out of the ground, quickly over-run by small black ants.

And finally, in the far away distance, past multitudes of animals, and past the last crumb of land and sea, the red hot sun ate itself, leaving behind only a cool darkness that promised stillness but smelled of rain.

Daniel no longer wanted to fight. He wanted to give in instead. To become part of something bigger, wilder. Something liberated and free.

It hurt at first when the lionesses came but the tiger and lion had dull teeth and that kind of tickled. The hyena and jackals were quick while the vultures and crows took their time. By the time the beetles and ants came, Daniel wasn't really feeling much of anything but peace and timelessness. He wished desperately he could offer his face to the sunshine, his soul to the cool still darkness but there wasn't anything left of Daniel that was Daniel by that time.

Everything he had been had now become everything else instead.

Daniel woke in the harsh flood lighting, more sure of his mission and confident than he'd ever been in his life. When Pit Boss screamed to release them all into the pit, Daniel laughed out loud. It was as if all of reality was aiding his plan. Maybe the old childhood nuns had been right. Maybe there was a God who listened to the prayers of one-eyed pit boys with acid scars, beating welts, and half-healed animal wounds on their bodies. Maybe a little suffering sweetened the deal.

If that was so, Daniel thought, God could take his other eye and all the rest of him, even take all of the others. Just give them one night of grace and miracle.

The Pit Dogs prodded all of them into the pit where they stood in a circle, backs to each other, facing the paying audience.

"Tonight," Pit Boss sang, "We have a Special Treat. A One Time Finale to the Pit Show Extravaganza. Tonight, for one night only, we offer up all of the warriors together in a grudge match war. Never seen before. Never to be seen again. Anyone with less than one thousand marks must leave the arena. Only big spenders here to watch the show. Only big spenders may stay."

Pit Boss waited. No one in the audience wanted to leave. Pit Boss pointed at a few audience members he knew didn't have one thousand marks. The Pit Dogs carried them out of the arena kicking and screaming. The Pit Dogs walked among the remaining audience members, collecting the fee for watching a massacre.

Daniel tried to focus his breath, to control his racing heart. Black Jude took his icy hand in her thumb-less hand. Daniel returned her reassurance gently so that he wouldn't crush her remaining three fingers. On Daniel's other side, Mark and Matthew crouched like animals. Beside them, Zeke swayed back and forth, humming his half tongue between his cracked teeth. Tomas stood beside Zeke and on the other side of Black Jude. He centered his weight, digging in with his heels.

"What's the plan?" Black Jude whispered. "What are we doing?"

Daniel shook his head. It was a stupid plan. It wouldn't work. They were going to die like dogs. Black Jude squeezed his hand. Daniel peered at her with his one eye. When he'd lost it, it'd been Black Jude who'd got him through the first rough nights. Her husky voice singing to him in the dark. Her hands, scarred and missing fingers reaching out to comfort him through the bars. Daniel wanted to back out now. He was going to give her a meaningless death, her flesh torn by animals and men, her bones scattered to desert and wind. He was going to give the same to the others, too. His name would be burned into their souls for all eternity, marking him their Murderer.

Then, all lingering doubt fell away as Daniel saw the party girls weave their way into the crowd. Pit Boss probably thought it was their last chance bid for life. Daniel grinned. Pit Boss was going to choke on his assumptions. Along with all those bad, bad men with their one thousand marks. From a fat man's lap near the arena wall, Ruthie blew Daniel a kiss. The rest of the party girls followed her example: they sat near or on the men closest to the arena wall.

"We're bringing the fight back to them," Daniel said hoarsely.

Pit Boss stood up, his arms raised upwards for attention. A hush fell over the audience then. Daniel and the others stiffened, waiting to see which weapons they would be given. The minutes stretched. Finally, one of the Pit Dogs threw in a spear made by attaching a thick bladed knife to the wood shaft of a gardening tool. No other weapons were given.

Daniel stepped forward and picked up the spear, glaring up at Pit Boss. Had Pit Boss expected them to open up the games by fighting each other for the spear? His face hard and cold, Daniel turned and faced the other fighters. They were kind of his friends now. This was as close to friendship any of them had ever gotten. And they were going to follow where he led.

Smiling, Pit Boss opened his arms as if throwing roses and gifts into the pit. Then he clapped his hands. Doors opened in the arena. The Lionesses poured through first, taking the pit in a leaping run. The lionesses stopped a few feet short of the fighters. Warily, they circled. Experience had taught them that the fighters usually carried weapons. A cautious if hungry lioness was better than being a quick dead lioness. The male cats, lion and Bengal tiger, walked leisurely behind them. Then, the bears came from the other side: one grizzly mother and three sub-adult males blinking in the spill of floodlights. The mother grizzly stood, straining to see the others in the pit.

Daniel looked up. In the sky, vultures circled. It was time. How he could interpret angels from vultures was a mystery even to Daniel, but a sign was a sign.

Daniel sighed, passing the hand-made spear to Tomas. Tomas raised an eyebrow and Daniel nodded, pointing at the fat man Ruthie sat on. "Feed the animals, Tomas."

Tomas hefted up the spear and after a few seconds of scan found his target. The handmade spear whistled thickly, the strapped metal singing in the air before it thudded to a wet stop in the center of a fat hook-nosed man sitting next to Agate. She jumped up, giggling wildly, and shoved him towards the edge of the pit. He fought her, one hand striking at her, the other desperately pulling on the shovel handled spear in his belly. Then, Catrina quickly joined in, kicking the man in the head until he fell spear first into the pit. He slid slowly down the wooden shaft, screaming the entire way.

Matthew whooped, running alongside one of the younger lionesses to get to the body and the spear. She fell on the man first, spinning him before sitting fully on him. Ravenous, she dug into the meaty flesh of his left leg and thigh. Matthew howled, arms waving until he just gave up on trying to scare her off. Warily, he jumped on the man and tried to pull the spear out of him. The lioness turned to growl at him briefly but hunger won out. She ignored Matthew for the most part, eager to tear her pound of flesh from the dead man instead. By the time another lioness joined in, Matthew had pulled the spear free. He threw it towards Mark just as the other lioness decided to make a live kill. She took Matthew down quickly, his screams ending in strangled laughter. Daniel turned away sharply at the first crunch of teeth on skull, Matthew's sudden gush of blood squirting black in the bright floodlights. Matthew was his first cross.

From then on out, everything else happened so quickly, all at once.

Mark ran to the spear just as one young male bear rushed towards him. He swung the spear wildly, dancing just past a swipe of long black claw. For the longest moment, Daniel was afraid it wouldn't hit out of the arena but wind like a finger of grace spun it upwards at the last instant. The spear found its way true, breaking into the bodies of two men, taking one in his skinny chest and the other behind him in his fat groin.

Lucy had been entertaining the both of them and when the spear hit, she jumped up naked, clapping and squealing with glee. Agate and Maria came running to help Lucy push the bodies into the pit. On the other side of the arena, legless Magdelina was crawling from man to man, cutting throats and balls, before feeding the animals. One of the young bears followed Magdelina's carnage, licking the blood up from the seats, sharing the kills with the older lion. At one point, the old lion even took meat from Magdelina's hand. She laughed cruelly, her witches' cackle raising goosebumps on Daniel's arms.

At Daniel's side, Black Jude growled darkly before she ran towards Mark. The yearling had pressed its attack and now Mark pounded on it fiercely, trying to free his leg from the bear's mouth. The mother bear roared angrily from across the pit and she charged.

Daniel screamed out: "NO!" his voice harsh and husky.

Desperately, he tried to grab Black Jude's hands, to slow her down, to stop her. Black Jude broke free, sparing only a quick determined look for him.

But Black Jude leaped forward, meeting the mother bear head on, her arms lifted together over her head like a mighty fist. Black Jude cracked her fists down on the grizzly's nose, breaking it with force and weight. The mother screamed, blood pouring into her open maw and she rushed, roaring into Black Jude, her jaw open to accept what her paws pulled in. Black Jude screamed back: anger, fear, and pain. Again and again, she pounded her broken hands on the mother's skull as the mother tore her flesh, rending her to pieces, her giant head turning side to side. Then, Black Jude flopped like a rag doll, her arms and legs weak as knotted string, her face quickly matting and caking with dirt and blood. The grizzly settled down to devour, her final child joining her in the feast.

Mark continued to pound weakly at the bear eating him until the old Bengal tiger came up and bit the back of his head. Then, it was just a tug of war between white tiger and brown bear.

Daniel dropped to his knees, screaming brokenly, his sight narrowing to a small dark tunnel. Tomas lifted him up with one hand. He shook Daniel roughly, Daniel's toes barely touching the ground before shoving him away. Daniel whirled to drop some of his anger onto Tomas but stopped just as abruptly, the anger dying in the face of Tomas's calm accepting eyes.

"Someone must survive," Tomas said in a deep rumble, nodding at Daniel.

It was a question. Daniel nodded back finally, accepting. Tomas lifted Daniel then, pushing him out of the arena and into the audience. From the pit where the animals still roamed, Tomas stood, looking up at Daniel but not making a move to join him. Daniel put out his hand to help him if he wanted to come but Tomas grinned and turned his back on him. Tomas roared, charging the other animals. As calm and accepting of their fate as he was, they came running. Tomas took many companions into the dead lands.

And all around the pit, the bodies of the watching audience fell as the party girls slaughtered their way through their customers. Daniel took a step. Then, another. Men screamed around him, running, desperate to get out, to get away. Some were customers, others pit dogs. Lionesses roamed, killing indiscriminately, taking a bite here, tearing a part there. One of the young male bears grunted wetly, its muzzle black with blood and gore before passing Daniel in the stands and leaving behind it the scent of raw savage death. The vultures came down, squawking at each other, fighting over the bounty.

Zeke was already there in the stands, stabbing Pit Boss in the throat as Maria held him down, her hands wrapped around his fleshy arms, her legs crossing over his fat belly. Zeke shrilled with his half-tongue, singing madly a song Daniel nearly recognized from childhood. Something about all the pretty horses.

11

Then a sharp loud sound silenced Zeke in mid-song. Smoke drifted up from Pit Boss's pistol. Maria shrieked. She climbed on top of Pit Boss, choking him and banging his head on the wooden stands. But Pit Boss was already dead. The pistol had gone off in his death spasms. Growling lazily, the old lion came up and started eating Zeke.

Daniel picked Maria up, dragging her away as he kept on walking. At first, Maria sobbed quietly. Then, she fought against him. Daniel dropped her, staring intently at her, trying to understand. Her mouth was moving but he couldn't hear a thing over the wet tearing sound of teeth and claw on flesh, followed by the scraping sound of teeth on bone. Then, sound came but it was like she was jabbering in a foreign language. Finally, he made out the words: something about Magdelina. He stood up and looked around. A few rows down, Magdelina stood on her bloody stumps, one hand still cradling the razor knife.

Beyond her…there were just bodies and animals roaming.

There was only blood and stillness. And when the wind picked up, the smell was sweet decay, copper sweetness, and the earthy rich scent of feces.

Magdelina waved a bloody hand but the dead never left her eyes.

"OK," Daniel muttered, leaving Maria behind as he went to fetch Magdelina, "OK."

After Maria's weight, Magdelina didn't seem to weigh anything at all. Daniel carried her the entire way, Maria following behind them as they left the arena, the cages, the compound. In cool darkness, they moved through the wet forest, finally finding the sandy long highway under the bright cruel sun. No one asked for water or food. No one complained or talked about anything. When night fell again, they cuddled together for warmth. Maria cried for all of them, Daniel shriveled up inside at the loss of Black Jude and Magdelina too dead inside to feel any loss for long. The stars remained cold and distant, silent in their judgment.

Daniel didn't dream. When he closed his eyes, he was still awake. Still alive.

Maria dreamed, though. Nightmare after night-mare. Magdelina slept like the dead. By morning, she seemed better, healthier somehow, like a well-fed vampire. Daniel couldn't stop watching her. She scared him just a little.

They crossed the border at dawn one day, leaving one country of night to come into another at daybreak. If there hadn't been yellow territory signs, none of them would have realized that boundaries had been trespassed. They kept walking, stealing water and food from cars and houses along the way, never taking so much that it would matter. They'd all lived on so little for so long. This was paradise in comparison. They were finally free.

By the time the blue car came, Magdelina had licked her skin and clothes clean of blood and gore. A smile had entered her face and never left. There were three white men in the blue car, all of them robust and healthy. It was a tight squeeze for all six people in the car but no one mentioned it. None of the men asked for money. Daniel thought it could be because they didn't need any. Later, when night fell and the darkness outside the blue car had ridden so long with them, Daniel realized that money had never been an option.

It started with the white man in the passenger seat turning around to face them with a gun. He waved his gun at them happily, telling Daniel in great detail what they were going to do to Maria and Magdalina. Then, he went on about what they were going to do to Daniel. It must have annoyed the white man when Magdelina started laughing. He made the driver pull over so they could shut that bitch up first.

When the blue car stopped, the Driver with a knife took Daniel to a tree and handcuffed him with a plastic tie. Back at the blue car, Maria started screaming. Magdelina didn't though, not even when the passenger seat man began punching her in the mouth with his gun. After a while, Maria stopped screaming and then, there was just the muffled sounds of fists and flesh.

The Driver snickered, flicking a cigarette at Daniel, "Welcome to our country, wet dick."

Suddenly, the sounds stopped and the night was silent and peaceful again.

Even though she'd lost some teeth, Magdelina's voice was still sweet and strong. "Ava Maria" rang out into the darkness, clear as church bells. Daniel nodded as the door to the blue car opened, spilling black blood, pale flesh, and a whole lot of dark promise.

Magdelina stopped singing mid-verse, slowly rolling forward on her bloody arms and stumps, her smile a bright knife cutting across her shattered face. Beside her, Maria stood, the gun held at her side. She lifted the gun, pointing it at the Driver. The Driver snorted in disbelief. Maria shot his left knee. The Driver went down, whining. Pain was not something he knew how to deal with. He stared at the girls, as if trying to figure out how this had happened to him. If this was really happening to him. Maria started laughing. Licking her lips, Magdelina rolled closer.

"You're just animals," Daniel said, looking down at the writhing Driver. "We know what to do with animals."

WET
By Mark Gallagher

**An unhappy suburbanite finds a unique way
to wash away the effects of depression.**

*Born and raised amongst the horrors of cows and cornfields, **Mark
Gallagher** has pursued careers as an actor, model (you may have
seen me on Japanese television), computer whiz, and finally writer
(his latest screenplay, **SATURNALIA**, was selected as a finalist in
the Paranoia Horror Film Festival in LA, and the Pittsburgh Horror
Film Festival). With over two dozen short stories (published in
Abberations (RIP)), screenplays (including a spec/hire adaptation of
Kiss Them Goodbye by Joseph Eastburn), and novels under his belt,
he continues to write about the one thing that has been his
inspiration throughout his atypical years: horror.*

*From the earliest days of Creepy, Eerie and Vampirella magazines,
through HP Lovecraft, Poe and King, Mark's undying thirst for
works of the macabre continue to provoke and propel his
imagination to ever higher (or lower) depths.*

I like the way it feels, running through my fingers, dripping off
my hair, splashing against my chest. I don't know why, exactly, I

just do. I was never molested, never abused, had average grades, an average job, an average family. Even my name, Steve, reeks of normalcy. I just love getting wet.

I don't mind who I get wet with, or what, for that matter. Solo, group, men, women, children, dogs, cats. Christ, even fish, I don't care.

As long as it bleeds.

I wasn't always like this. Before my first, well, I guess we can call it a "dip," I was pretty much the opposite. Miserable, a real Mopey Mike. I didn't understand what part I was supposed to play, couldn't see the opportunity life presented me every day. I was blinded by the universal, self-absorbed morbidity of a man striving to be what the slick advertising bastards on Madison Avenue told me I should be. I thought I needed the perfect house, the perfect car, the perfect body, the perfect family, the perfect life. When all I really needed was what was inside me all along. What's inside all of us, every man, woman, child, every animal on this planet. But I didn't know that. Not then.

Not until my first dip.

***

Sunday afternoon; August; hot; humid; sitting in my favorite leather recliner in front of the large picture window watching the grass wither on my three-quarter acre backyard that I had just spent over five hundred dollars re-seeding and paying the goddamn Weed Doctor another three hundred to kill anything that was not genuine Grade-A Kentucky Blue Mountain Grass. And it was all dying.

I didn't even have the energy to get off my sweaty ass and turn on the hose. I felt like I was dying, too, with my lawn, out there, shriveling and withering and dry as death. My wife, Chrissy, had left with my daughter, Caitlin, taking the minivan to her sister Marsha's house for the afternoon. I had to practically push Chrissy out the front door. Today we were supposed to go to the lake together, the three of us, the perfect little family frolicking in the sun and showing the whole goddamn world how fucking perfect we were. Well, today I just didn't feel so perfect.

What I felt like was dying. Just like that lawn. I leaned back, wondering, trying to imagine what it would feel like to die, right here, in my chair, bake in the sun until my skin bubbled off my bones and my eyes burst. Chrissy would have a sight when she came home, one hell of a mess to clean up. Not that she would. With me reduced to a greasy pudding, she'd have no one to tell her what to do. She was incapable of performing even the most basic tasks, like cleaning, making dinner, washing Caitlin's piss-stained sheets. Chrissy had to be constantly reminded to do the things a woman was supposed to do. I tried like hell to remind her as gently as I could, but it was getting harder and harder. Like teaching a dog over and over not to shit on the rug. Chrissy was shitting on me, it seemed, on purpose, just to make me want to die.

I was more than a little puzzled to see the van pull back into the driveway. I was downright amazed to see Chrissy get out without Caitlin. Just Chrissy, in her bathing suit, a skimpy spandex thing that showed off her figure and made the most of her long, incredible legs. She could lift those gams clear over her head if she wanted to, or if I wanted her to. I watched her skip over the hot tarmac and disappear around the corner to the front of the house.

I realized I hadn't budged an inch since they'd left. I glanced at the clock. It was 2:30. They'd been gone for almost two hours. I thought about running to the bathroom and jumping in the shower, try to put some life back into me, but I didn't. I couldn't. I just sat there, listening to her open the door and call my name.

"Steve? Stevie? Honey, where are you?"

I almost answered, but held back. It was dark where I was sitting, dark and hot and the air smelled like sweat and despair. I wanted her to find me this way. Wanted her to see how miserable I was and how useless my life had become. Wanted her to feel the same way I did because she was a part of it, of my life, of my dying.

I'd worked so damn hard for her and Caitlin, for this house, for the damn lawn. It wasn't right that I suffer alone. I wanted her to suffer too.

I sat there until she found me.

"Oh, Christ! Honey, you surprised me!" Her hand flew to her chest. I heard the wet slap as it struck her sweaty tits. "Are you okay? It's so hot in here! Why isn't the window open?"

She meant the picture window, of course, the one I'd been staring out of for the last two hours. She walked around me, close. I could smell her skin, it smelled like coconut and sex. Her feet made soft shushing noises on the carpet, as if she were walking through fine sand. Her arms swung by her sides, long pendulous motions that brushed against the golden moons of her breasts. I reached out and caught her arm before she reached the window.

"Wait," I said.

I don't know if it was the sound of my voice, or maybe her eyes had become accustomed enough to the dimness so that she could really see me, but when my hand touched her arm, she gasped. As if instead of my flesh against hers, her husband's flesh, the man she slept with and fucked, some scaly, slimy thing had slithered out of the darkness and circled around her wrist.

"Let go of me," she said. Her voice was too bright, too quick.

I didn't let go. I pulled her toward me. She came unwillingly, her heels digging in the carpet.

"Steven, let *go* of me!"

"I wanna tell you something, Chrissy, something important."

Chrissy stopped trying to resist, she became almost limp, just the slightest trembling in her fingertips belied her nervousness as I pulled her onto my lap.

I looked into her blue, blue eyes. She was looking into mine, too, and I could tell she saw something she didn't like, something that made her clutch the sides of the recliner and take short, rapid breaths. Like she was getting ready to bolt, like she were inhaling something foul.

There was something in her eyes looking back at me. Not her soul, surely, not hers. It felt too familiar, too close. A vague, cloudy thing that pulsed and shimmered like a distant star in a smog-choked night. My breathing had become very deep and very relaxed. I was seeing the reflection of *my* soul. The depression which had almost crushed me vanished. My voice was level, almost velvety as I spoke to her.

"Chrissy, I'm losing my mind."

"You're what?" Her voice held just the tiniest trace of panic.

"I'm losing my mind. Everything I've ever worked for means nothing to me, nothing at all."

I heard two quick "pops." Looking down for a moment, I noticed that two of her fingernails had punctured the upholstery.

"Steve, honey, you're -- you just need to get out. It's too dark and hot in here. Why don't you come back with me to Marsha's house? Her pool is perfect and Caitlin keeps asking for you. Come on, honey, the sun will do you good. Here, let me help you."

She tried to climb off my lap, but I wrapped my right arm around her waist and squeezed.

"I don't want to go to Marsha's. Didn't you hear what I just said? I don't feel like going out, I don't feel like taking a swim in Marsha's fucking perfect swimming pool, and I don't feel like playing with Caitlin. I don't feel like -- anything." I loosened my grip around her waist, but placed my left hand behind her neck, entwining my fingers around her thick auburn hair. I drew her head closer to mine, until our eyes were inches apart.

"You're beautiful. The most beautiful woman I know. You're all I ever thought I cared about, but now I realize I don't care about anything at all."

As I pulled her closer still, her eyes seemed to change from the calm blue of an autumn afternoon to the violent slate-gray of a thunderstorm and I lost my soul's shifting reflection.

Chrissy reached behind her and tried to pry my fingers from her hair. "Steve, I -- I just don't know what to say. Not now. Let go of me, please? You're starting to hurt me. Honey? Please?"

My soul had left me. That's exactly how it seemed. I had lost my soul and I couldn't fight anymore, so I did as she asked. I didn't want to hurt her. I let go. What happened next may have seemed like an accident to a detached observer, but I know in my heart that this was the moment my whole life had been waiting for.

Chrissy was still reaching behind her when I let go. I guess the momentum of her efforts to escape combined with the sudden lack of resistance propelled her backwards as if she had been shoved. She had no chance to protect herself. A cat maybe, but not my Chrissy. I watched it all, like a home movie, frame by frame in slow motion.

She arched her back and reached up above her head as if a trapeze would magically appear and carry her to safety. Instead, her fingers curled around air and despite her backwards fall, she leaned her head forward to look at me, her eyes growing so wide that for a moment I thought they would explode and show me the lightning behind those thundering orbs. Instead I saw my own reflection return. A reflection of a man watching his destiny unfold before him.

Her eyes didn't explode, but her skull did as her head struck the corner of the coffee table with a sound that reminded me of cracking a walnut. The meat inside Chrissy's shell was not just white, but red and gray and white and blue, a rainbow of gore.

I sat there in my chair, my hands clutching the armrests as a torrent of blood washed over me. As Chrissy's life rained upon my face, I felt something come alive within me. It was almost as if her life were flowing into me, replacing the cold maddening emptiness with a fiery sweetness I had never known.

I got off the chair and kneeled down as close as I could get to the wound in my wife's skull, letting the remaining blood pump onto my chin and into my mouth. It wasn't the *taste* of the blood that was making me dizzy with excitement, it was the *feel* of it -- the thick, syrupy weight of it as it trickled down my neck and soaked through my t-shirt.

I found myself giving in to it, like a delirium of pure euphoria. My ears filled with rushing sounds, my body shuddered. And then I must have lost consciousness entirely.

I woke up some time later (only about ten minutes when I finally checked the clock) and saw Chrissy lying next to me. Her skin was white, so white I though she had covered her body in cold cream. Then I saw the still glistening wound above her ear and the blood which was everywhere. I started to cry.

I wanted more.

***

I stripped out of my t-shirt and underwear and took a shower. As the blood was rinsed from my body, I was struck with a great sense of sadness; of loss, as if something precious were being taken away from me, denied me. This feeling was immediately followed by an uncontrollable fit of anger. My body trembled with it, my vision blurred and my heart raced until it felt like it would sever itself from its cavity and burn its way through my ribcage. I quickly turned off the water and pulled on a pair of jeans and a fresh t-shirt. The simple act of covering up my naked flesh seemed to lessen the rage. It enabled me to focus on the task at hand.

I found a pair of work gloves and got a heavy lawn bag from under the sink then went back to Chrissy. I removed her bathing suit and soaked up as much of her blood as I could. I put it in the bag and hastened out the side door to the driveway. Chrissy had apparently expected that I would not be long in returning with her to Marsha's because the keys were left in the ignition. See? I can't count the times I asked her *never* to do that.

Anyway, I got in and drove the van around the opposite side of the block to a deserted movie theater where I parked behind the building. I left the keys in the ignition and took out the bathing suit.

I smeared Chrissy's blood on the front seat and the windshield and threw the suit on the back seat. I left the driver's door open and walked back calmly to my house, rather pleased at how I felt. I even managed to whistle, "Raindrops Keep Falling On My Head," which is one of my favorite schmaltzy songs from the sixties. Chrissy never liked it, but her disapproving days were pretty much over.

I got back to the house and began cleaning up the living room. Luckily, most of Chrissy's blood had gone into the area rug enabling me to get the majority of the job done in one quick roll. It was long enough to cover Chrissy's beautiful, long legs and thick enough so that the blood hadn't soaked through. I took the rug to the garage and left it by the table saw for later.

I did a quick mop-up and wiped down the recliner and the coffee table and made sure that nothing was too obvious. I would do a more thorough job after Caitlin got home.

I called Marsha's house and made up some lie about Chrissy having to go buy some kind of steak roast and asked if she would mind bringing Caitlin home. Marsha was very understanding and said she would have Caitlin home in ten minutes.

I waited for Caitlin by the front door. Fifteen minutes passed before Marsha finally pulled up in front of the house in her shiny new Mustang convertible. Marsha had always fancied herself something of a perpetual babe. She could still turn heads in bars, but only the ones that were hazy with smoke and inadequately lit. In the bright afternoon sunlight, her Jackie Onassis sunglasses and Courtney Cox pressed-hair only accentuated her haggard desperation.

Caitlin hopped out of the passenger side and raced ahead of Marsha to the door. With her golden hair bouncing around her sunburned cheeks and her Pool Side Barbie towel flapping around her shoulders, she resembled an angel from a heavenly Toys 'R Us ad. I opened up the screen door and let her inside, closing it after her. I remained just inside the screen door as Marsha climbed the steps.

"Hey, Steve," she said, weaving her hips back and forth like she were balancing on a row boat. "Chrissy home yet?"

"No, Marsha, she's not," I said, keeping the screen door between us.

Marsha came up to the door and pushed her sunglasses on top of her pretty brown hair. Marsha was prettier than her sister, my wife, Chrissy, but she had the hard lines around her eyes and mouth that spoke volumes of an unhappy domestic life. Although, to look at her simply as a piece of meat, she had a very fuckable ass. I'd always wondered if that was what attracted her husband, Stewart, to her in the first place.

Stewart sure did have an eye for ass. He left Marsha a little less than a year ago for an eighteen-year-old boy from his high school social studies class. The "scandal" wasn't pretty and the only headlines were the poorly spelled ones in the local rags, no National Enquirer, never even made it to Jerry Springer. Just enough to utterly annihilate Marsha's eggshell existence.

"Well, I'd invite myself in," she drawled in her affected southern accent, "but the sun's just too perfect to pass up. Sure you won't change your mind? You could leave a note for Chrissy and come for a splash with Caitlin and me." Marsha stepped close enough to the screen to actually flatten her perky nipples against the mesh. "You look like you could use some sun. Whaddya say? A little sun, a little Coppertone and a whole lot of frozen daiquiris?"

She was coming on to me again. Ever since I'd known Marsha, she'd been a bit of a flirt. With Stewie out of her life, and rum his replacement, her boldness was increasingly annoying.

"No, Marsha, thanks, but I'm getting the grill ready and besides, Caitlin looks a little too rock lobster as it is. Maybe tomorrow."

"Well, okay, Steve," she answered, poking her finger into the mesh against my chest. "But don't come crying to me if you wake up tomorrow and there's no sun. Seize the day, and all that, right?"

"Yeah, right," I said and managed a small smile. Marsha really looked good, in a carcass hanging from a meat hook kind of way.

Maybe I would pop over tomorrow for a splash. "I promise I'll seize tomorrow, how's that?"

"That, Stevie, sounds wonderful. Give Chrissy my love. Bye Caitlin!" she yelled into the house patting the screen door (and my chest) one more time before returning to her car.

I closed the door and stood there a minute watching Marsha drive away. For a moment, as she opened her car door, I imagined I saw a wave of blood spill from the Mustang and wash over her, leaving her shrieking and beautiful. The most beautiful I've ever seen her. Then the vision was gone and Marsha was waving as she drove back to her lonely life. Her loneliness would be temporary. I promised myself I would take care of that.

A small gasp from the living room alerted me to the fact that I had almost forgotten my daughter was home. I hurried from the door and entered the living room to find Caitlin standing in the middle of the room staring at the floor where the carpet had once been.

"Daddy," she said, her voice small and clear like a tiny bell. "How come the room looks so big?"

I looked at her and smiled. In the gloom of the fading afternoon light, she appeared as a revelation among the shadows, a bright flame in my eyes and in my brain. And like a moth, I was drawn to that flame with my arms outstretched and my smile widening as I picked her up and held her close to my heart.

"Daddy had to take the rug to the cleaners, honey. Now, let's go upstairs and Daddy will fix you a nice, hot bath before Mommy gets home."

"With lots of bubbles?" she asked, already squirming out of my arms and running up to her room.

"Lots'n lots of bubbles!" I called after her. I took my time climbing the stairs, listening to the familiar sounds of Caitlin opening her drawers and watched her race across the hallway into the bathroom just as I crested the last stair.

"Come on, Daddy!" she cried, her voice urgent with anticipated pleasure and yet strangely hollow sounding as it echoed off the floor-to-ceiling blue bathroom tiles. "I wanna use the purple bubbles!"

"No, I don't think so," I said as I entered the bathroom.

"Why not?" Caitlin whined, her little nose crinkling and her brow furrowing together in an altogether convincing expression of genuine dismay.

"Because," I replied comically, making my voice obscenely exaggerated like Caitlin's favorite purple dinosaur, "Daddy's got a surprise!" Caitlin had her own separate bathroom. Caitlin had insisted, and I, as always, went along. Now I was glad. I didn't want Caitlin's surprise to be spoiled by the sight of her mommy's and daddy's bathroom.

Caitlin clasped her tiny hands to her chest and jumped up and down. "Gimme, gimme, gimme!"

"Okay, but first you gotta say, I love my daddy more than anything else in the whole wide world."

"I love my daddy more than anything else in the whole, wide world!"

I picked Caitlin up and squeezed her to me and began to tickle her bony little ribs. "Say, I love my daddy more than a whole truck full of vanilla ice cream with hot butterscotch syrup!"

"I love my daddy more than a whole truck full of vanilla ice cream with hot butterscotch syrup!" she repeated, giggling and squirming as I carried her to the tub.

"And with a cherry on top!" I added, to prolong the delicious feeling of this sweet, delicate life hammering me with her fists and laughing so hard tears were running down her apple cheeks.

"And with a cherry on top!" Caitlin squealed, just as I drew her into my chest with a convulsive hug that cut the air supply to her lungs and left her suddenly gasping and rigid with shock.

"Tell daddy you love him, baby," I whispered fiercely into her reddening ear. "Tell daddy you want to bleed for him, tell daddy, honey, tell daddy you want to bleed."

Her fists began to beat my arms and her legs kicked violently against my thighs, once or twice connecting painfully with my groin before I lifted her high in the air and in one motion turned her upside down and plunged her headfirst into the tub.

I would not have believed she was capable of such a loud scream had I not heard it crash off the tile walls and ricochet into my brain. Even under water, her cries were almost unbearable. They quickly, blessedly, died down as her lungs filled with water and her thrashing body soon relaxed into my arms once again.

I wasted no time, but gently rolled her over on her back and wiped the long strands of hair from her face. Her cheeks still puffed in and out with the weakest hint of a breath, but with every watery exhalation, her body grew weaker and I knew I had to act quickly.

I reached over behind the toilet where I had placed the cleaver and withdrew it in one hand, keeping my other firmly on Caitlin's chest. Raising the cleaver over my head, I brought it down just between my daughter's delicate blue eyes and watched as her flesh unfolded before me and the tub exploded with cherry-red froth. Abandoning all restraint, I threw myself on top of her and began to hack furiously at her body until I could no longer recognize her. All was red, warm and wet. After a series of ferocious orgasms, I lost consciousness.

***

The authorities have a name for me. They call me "The North Country Butcher," but that's not really what I am. It sounds too destructive, too insane. I create, I do not destroy. I release that which is within all of us and within its candy red current I find the only true passion that is man's alone to know.

The house was put up for sale a month later. That was over eight years ago. Chrissy and Caitlin have not yet been found. At this point, there wouldn't be much to find, and besides, I wasn't foolhardy enough to forget to remove their teeth before I ran them through the table saw and disposed of the several dozen pieces in various rivers, lakes and ponds throughout the wilderness that had always frightened me as a boy.

Now, the wilderness has become my accomplice and protector. I live in the woods, enveloped in its infinite seclusion, in a simple, yet very comfortable cabin that I had built with the money from the sale of the house and, much to my surprise, the substantial life insurance policy Chrissy had taken out completely unbeknownst to me. It took seven long years before they were officially ruled "deceased" and the insurance company reluctantly paid up, but everything has worked out beautifully.

Except for one small thing. I'm not really sure how to describe it. It's just a feeling I get while I wait for the "latest" furor to quiet. I shop. I read. I ride my bike. And wait some more, until my flesh feels like its shrinking so tight my bones will snap. And the air becomes so dry I can no longer breathe. I take showers, five, six, ten times a day. The hot, steamy water scalds my skin until it turns pink and soft like the cheeks of my once beautiful daughter. And as my fingers stroke my fevered, soap-slicked skin, I find it harder and harder not to open up my own flesh and swim in my own eternity.

THE WHORE
OF THE DARTMOOR
By Rich Bottles Jr.

An aspiring writer finds that copyright infringement is frowned upon on both sides of the pond.

*Although much maligned for his handling of **The Big Book of Bizarro**, **Rich Bottles Jr**. is best known for his genre-defying novels **Lumberjacked** and **Hellhole, West Virginia**. After an unillustrious print journalism career in southwestern Pennsylvania, Rich moved to West Virginia at the age of 32 to pursue a career in technical writing. He spends his free time visiting and hiking at the many state parks in the Mountain State, which is also where he develops the concepts for his novels. He plans on producing a trilogy of WV-themed 'humorrorotica' and is currently working on a story set in the vicinity of the infamous West Virginia State Penitentiary. His only regret in life is that his out-of-state secondary school education prohibited him from earning West Virginia's prestigious Golden Horseshoe Award.*

Stephanie could never decide whether she was a literary whore or a literal whore. The readers of her fan fiction on deviant art dot com probably considered her the former, while the people she met through adult friend finder dot com probably considered her the latter. The only thing she knew for certain was that she needed to earn some cash from the former to take care of a medical condition resulting from the latter.

But how could an unpublished writer create and market a best seller in as little time as possible? After all, the itching and inflammation were becoming unbearable.

Working from home, in her underpants, as an underpaid and underappreciated customer service rep for the online bookseller amazon dot com allowed Stephanie to understand that the popular trend in fiction was the horror genre, especially stories involving vampires and werewolves.

Unfortunately, eighteen-year-old Stephanie was used to writing about giving blowjobs to celebrities and her recreational reading included very few horror novels. Her personal entertainment budget was also limited, which is why she had to do all of her reading online, predominately the stale ancient fiction available at gutenberg dot org.

It wasn't until she finished reading the serial novel *The Hound of the Baskervilles* by Sir Arthur Conan Doyle that she had her epiphytic epiphany. She began drooling as she read the legalese located at the bottom of the text file.

"Nearly all the individual works in the collection are in the public domain in the United States. If an individual work is in the public domain in the United States and you are located in the United States, we do not claim a right to prevent you from copying, distributing, performing, displaying or creating derivative works based on the work as long as all references to Project Gutenberg are removed."

Edit – Select All; Edit – Copy; File – Exit; Microsoft Office Word; Paste – Paste Special – Unformatted Text; Replace – Find what: Holmes – Replace with: Vampire Hunter Holmes; Replace – Find what: Stapleton – Replace with: Count Stapleton; Replace – Find what: hound – Replace with: werewolf...

After the initial auto-rewrite, Stephanie forced herself to read through the manuscript, correcting some of the inconsistencies that MS Word inadvertently created. She also added some gothic flourishes and supernatural tidbits to enhance the story and make it appear as if some thought had been put into the process. It took her about an hour.

Once the format of the document had been ported to a portable document format and the absence of a cover had been covered by the selection of a generic cover, Stephanie uploaded her slavepiece to wepublishanything dot com and awaited approval. Approval can take up to forty-eight hours! What the fuck?!

Frustrated by the lack of instantaneous gratification to be derived from the wepublishanything website, Stephanie decided to retire to her nearby bed, where she had more control over her desire for instant gratification.

Before climbing into her perpetually unmade bed, Stephanie stripped off her bra and panties and stood in front of a full-length mirror, which interrupted the wall space between her computer desk and her double-sized bed. Sometimes the lack of food available in her double-wide trailer drove her crazy with hunger, but she appreciated her economically-induced diet plan every time she admired her slender naked body in the mirror.

Her shoulder-length, greasy, red hair actually contrasted with the wiry flame-like red bush between her legs, which she patted down like she was putting out a small brush fire. She then massaged and caressed her fun-sized breasts, just like one of her favorite celebrities would do if he were in the room with her at that moment.

A sense of guilt overcame Stephanie as she continued to watch herself in the mirror. Was it because of her current role as a self-satisfying voyeur? No, because she had express written consent from the author to watch herself naked. Was it because she was masturbating yet again? No, because she wasn't Catholic. Was it because she was trying to profit off of someone else's hard work and creativity? Maybe, but that dude was dead. Regardless, when her none-on-one physical relationship moved to the bed, she was going to have to make sure she was properly disciplined for her transgressions.

Prior to stretching out on the bed, Stephanie sat on the edge of the mattress and collected two spring-activated clothespins and a couple of elastic hair bands from the bed stand. And before she turned off the lamp to darken the room, she patiently wrapped the bands around the business ends of the clothespins, making them difficult to open.

Covered in darkness as she reclined onto the bed, Stephanie pretended it was someone else who was cupping her left breast and clamping a banded clothespin onto her erect nipple. While she was still wincing from the pain encountered by the initial assault, the second clothespin was snapped shut onto her right nipple.

As pangs of anguish shot deep into her beleaguered breasts, Stephanie's oxygen-starved breaths became quicker and shorter, almost to the point of hyperventilating, and she instinctively directed her right hand to the burning wetlands between her legs. Skillfully spreading her labia with her index and ring fingers, she then began feverishly rubbing and circling her swollen clitoris with her middle finger.

Stephanie felt a climax building almost immediately, but knew that she must maintain control over her affliction if her body was to experience the true retribution it so richly deserved. Her middle finger skimmed smoothly and effortlessly across the moistened playing field, but somehow Stephanie managed to slow down the maddening pace of the circling strokes that stoked the flames of her desperate desire.

As the fingers of her right hand began to neglect their disciplinary duty, like the guardians of a red-headed stepchild, the fingers of her left hand began twisting the clothespin imprisoning the left nipple. Every nerve ending within the throbbing nipple seemed to erupt in a fury of boiling, blood-engorged, short-circuitry. Tears began squeezing out through Stephanie's tightly closed eyelids and muffled cries started pouring from her trembling lips.

When the torqued and tortured flesh of the tormented tit was twisted to 180 degrees (Fahrenheit *and* Radial), Stephanie knew that the slightest touch of her right middle finger on her locked and loaded clitoris would trigger her body into a series of uncontrolled convulsions. Still she tried to still her hand. But soon the climax began building without any clitoral stimulation, so Stephanie resigned herself to finish the job by flicking the last bit of oil on the out-of-control brush fire.

"Ugh!!!" she screamed out as her body bounced upon the bed and she simultaneously yanked off the clothespins, one at a time, immediately increasing the waves of passion that violently shook and overtook her senses.

Completely exhausted, emotionally and physically, and breathing deeply through her mouth to maintain consciousness, Stephanie unclenched her left hand atop her chest and allowed the clothespins to drop down between her overheated breasts. She then delicately removed the sticky fingers of her right hand from the depths of her vanquished vagina.

Swamped in sweat, Stephanie knew she should get up and shower off, but she didn't seem to have any energy left in her paralyzed person. Soon her breathing normalized and she was able to close her mouth in a smile and drift off to sleep.

Until the voice woke her up…

Stephanie knew she was alone in the trailer that evening, so was she dreaming and violating the first rule of bizarro story-telling - or was the voice coming from outside her bedroom real? Stephanie covered her head in her blankets, but still tried to listen.

"Aye, I've finally cornered me the daughter of the yeoman!" shouted a man's gravelly and grave voice from just behind the door (before the door was kicked in by the man's heavy riding boots). The parenthetically busted door swung inside the room and crashed against the wall, knocking off various framed posters of harmless-looking male celebrities, who were probably gay but still fancied nonetheless by Stephanie.

Stephanie sat up in bed with a blanket pulled up to her terrorized eyes as the intruder fumbled with a light switch inside the doorway. Soon yellow energy-saving light bathed the scene in all its horrific glory and a stocky crazed-looking man, overdressed in severely outdated formal garb, approached her bed with a black riding crop in his gloved hand.

"Do you know who I am, young maiden of the Dartmoor?"

"You're trespassing?" stammered Stephanie through the blanket.

"My name is *Sir Arthur* Conan Doyle," replied the man with a heavy British accent, lifting his hand and pointing his index finger at her trembling head. "Perhaps you recall removing the name Conan Doyle from my manuscript this very evening!"

"You're not him," Stephanie cried out. "He died a long time ago. Get the hell out of my house, whoever you are!"

"But I am he!" shouted the man straight back at 'er. "If you'd done your research on me, you would know that I was good friends with fellow spiritualist Harry Houdini. We both studied spiritual materialization and we both made a pact that we would assist each other in avenging any injustices to our character even after death."

"You're fucking nuts!" screamed Stephanie, throwing down her blankets and revealing her naked torso, which the man immediately slashed with the crop.

When Stephanie felt the sting of the crop cutting across her bare chest, she immediately curled up in a ball, hiding her face in her hands, as the Englishman circled around to the side of the bed where he'd have a clearer shot at her back and arse.

"Fucking nuts am I?" he yelled as he started to slash her fetal body with the whip. "Was Roy Horn (*slash*) fucking nuts (*slash*) when Houdini (*slash*) materialized (*slash*) as a white (*slash*) tiger and (*slash*) attacked him (*slash*)?!"

Stephanie tried to escape the enraged onslaught by rolling off the bed away from her attacker. After she slammed onto the floor, she quickly crawled toward the open door of the bathroom, which was only a few yards away from the bed. The man then jumped up onto the empty bed to see where his victim was going.

"Get back here, you thieving whore!" he commanded, slicing the air with crop. "I'm not near done with you! I plan to ravish every inch of your body, like you ravished every page of my book! I plan to assault and tear apart every filthy orifice that I can find, just as you assaulted almost every word of mine that you could find!"

Stephanie successfully crawled into the bathroom and quickly shut and locked the door. Knowing that her aggressor could easily kick in the bathroom door, she quickly threw on a terry cloth bathrobe that was hanging on the inside of the door and then ran toward a small window above the toilet. She climbed onto the toilet seat just as she heard the man's boots hit the floor beside the bed. As the heavy boot stomps approached the bathroom, Stephanie pushed open the small opaque window and began squeezing herself out head first into the cool night air.

When the bathroom door crashed open, Stephanie's body crashed onto the cold ground outside of the trailer. She hit the ground hard, but still managed to leap up on her bare feet and dart toward the moor. Her feet sloshed through the icy mud of the moor as she tried to get as much distance between her and her pursuer as possible.

She kept looking back as she ran, hoping that she would see no tall shadows approaching her from behind. The dim light of the diminishing trailer gave her eyes no indication that she was being followed, but she thought she heard a faint growling coming up behind her.

When the growling erupted into a sharp barking, Stephanie quickly increased her pace, even though she was already out of breath. Now Stephanie was afraid to turn around.

As happens in all outdoor pursuits of females, the victim eventually trips and falls to the ground. In Stephanie's case, her foot got finagled in some foliage and her forward momentum forced her face first into the frosty moor.

With the front of her terry cloth robe now thoroughly soaked and soiled, Stephanie resigned herself to rolling over onto her back and using a moistened sleeve to wipe off the remnants of her *au naturel* facial.

As soon as Stephanie scooped the caked mud from her eyelids, she looked up to see a massive wolf-like beast straddling her midsection. Its red eyes stared directly into hers like lasers cutting through thick cataracts. From its snarled snout came a steady growl and clouds of steam emanated from its dilated nostrils.

With the front of her robe now pinned open by the sharp claws of the beast, Stephanie felt hot saliva dripping down onto her bare breasts like melted wax from a dominatrix's candle. Stephanie had no choice but to lay still under the crushing weight of the animal and sob uncontrollably.

The moonlight provided just enough illumination for Stephanie to watch the beast slowly open its mouth, revealing razor sharp canines that glistened through the darkness. She could also see its tongue curled back inside its mouth as if it was going to speak.

"You're mine now, bitch," it snarled in the most non-human evil voice she had ever encountered.

Stephanie managed to break away from the beast's hypnotic glare, but as soon as she turned her head to the side she unknowingly offered her pulsating jugular to the predator. The beast instantaneously struck its prey, tearing out half the girl's throat before she even had time to gasp. Blood gushed from the open wound and the beast lapped it up like a dog being sprayed with a garden house.

Can't this please just be all a dream? Stephanie thought as she drifted into unconsciousness.

Indeed, the horrific scene taking place in the small West Virginia town of Dartmoor turned out to be exactly that – a dream and nothing more. But the nightmare proved so unsettling and disturbing to the dreamer that sleep was no longer possible.

Waking up from the nightmare, drenched in sweat and screaming in terror, the conscious mind took a few moments to adjust to the stark reality of a darkened bedroom. Or was adjustment even possible when one reality suddenly switches to another - and both seem equally absurd?

"My god that was horrible!"

The loud voice even startled Louisa, who woke up in a coughing fit, which was a symptom of her secret East End opium-smoking excursions. As soon as she could get the coughing under control, she angrily replied, "What's wrong with you, you old fool? I finally get some sleep and you start screaming like a crazy bastard!"

Sitting up on his side of the bed with his back now turned to his wife, Sir Arthur apologized as he wiped the cold sweat from his brow. "Forgive me, Louisa, but I'm afraid I had another one of my bizarre dreams. This time I was in a strange land and I was acting like Hugo Baskerville from the Hound novel."

"Ask me if I give a damn," was the response from Louisa's side of the bed.

"Louisa," begged Sir Arthur. "Why must you always be so disagreeable towards me? I understand that you are (supposedly) ill, but you are still my wife and I would appreciate some level of basic respect. I have never once complained of your coughing, which has kept me awake for many a night."

"Go to hell and let me sleep!" yelled the woman, who immediately broke into yet another coughing fit which shook the entire bed.

Sir Arthur felt his anger rising to unchartered territory as he rolled back onto the bed and got onto his knees. When he looked down on his hacking spouse, he was suddenly overcome with a pounding headache and his blood seemed to boil inside his skull, causing his vision to be tinted in red and his mouth to become dry and sticky.

"You want sleep?" he rhetorically asked, suddenly grabbing the pillow from his side of the bed. "I'll help you sleep, you ungrateful junkie!"

Soon Sir Arthur found himself sitting on top of his coughing wife, who desperately wanted to curse him but could not gain control of her vocal chords. The hate and scorn in her face seemed to penetrate Sir Arthur, even in the dark room, but he quickly found solace once her face was completely covered by the pillow.

"You're mine now, bitch," he snarled in the most non-human evil voice she had ever encountered.

Sir Arthur held the pillow forcefully in place as the woman pathetically struggled beneath him and he did not let up until her body was completely still. He knew she was dead when five minutes had passed without a cough or a gag emanating from her drug-starved lungs.

Pleased by the sudden silence within the room, Sir Arthur threw the murder weapon back to his half of the bed, making sure the side of the pillow containing her last breath was not facing up. Still panting from the thrill of the kill, he then rolled off his prey and onto his pillow. Soon his breathing normalized and he was able to close his mouth in a contented smile and drift off to sleep.

In the morning, Sir Arthur awoke to the sudden reality that his poor wife must have passed away in her sleep. Since he was a well-respected and dutiful London physician, he felt compelled and obligated to immediately draw up his wife's certificate of death and give "Tuberculosis" as the cause of death.

Later that day, after screwing his mistress in neighboring Hampshire, the grieving widower had a good laugh at his dead wife's expense.

"What do think the great Sherlock Holmes would make of this day's events?" asked Jean Elizabeth after she finished licking Sir Arthur's cock clean of her vaginal juices.

"Unfortunately for Louisa, her case is one that Mr. Holmes shall never take up!" laughed Sir Arthur.

THE FALL

By David J. Fairhead

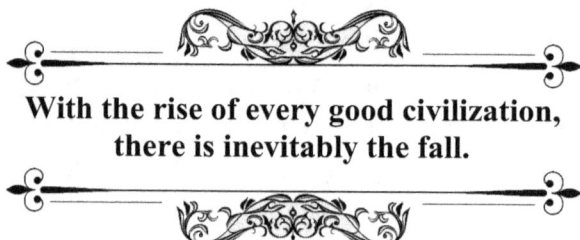

**With the rise of every good civilization,
there is inevitably the fall.**

*David J. Fairhead is the author of the romantic fantasy/science fiction trilogy, **Worlds Apart** and currently touring with his comic book series **WZWA (World Zombie Wrestling Association)** in association with Jon Towers and Stigmata Studios (**www.jonnyaxx.com**). The creative force behind Fairly Dark Productions, David is also the artist and writer of twenty-eight issues of his own comic series. Finding his passion in writing contemporary fiction, he has two horror novels in development (**CHARLIE, A Child's Tale of Terror**; and the demon zombie epic **IN THE DARK**), as well as this current work in progress: **THE FALL**. He grew up on Long Island and currently resides with his wife in Pittsburgh. Contact him on Facebook.*

We had been running for weeks. You will truly never know how to run until you've been chased for your very flesh, blood and bone. I had run my whole life, whether in a soccer game, street hockey, even from the cops with my friend Eric on a Friday night binge-drinking episode. None of this was real relentless running.

Not until you have to run or face a horrific death by mutilation, do you know the meaning of the word fear.   In the dark, you forget who was with you at different intervals.   Friends, family, old and young, they just became fellow runners from the dark itself.

In the first few weeks it was chaos abound.   Like ants raiding mounds of sugar, humans were plucked from their beds, from their cars, pulled down sewer drains and dragged to the sky by dark feasting claws, and calloused hate.   Eric told me it had been months already but his little sister Drea said it was longer.   The sky had turned a dark turquoise on her sixteenth birthday, she reminded me. Girls, even in duress, seem to remember anything associated with their young birthdays.   The last memory I have of safe daylight, real daylight without being hunted, was in the beginning of it all, right after Drea's birthday party.   High school girls dressed up in their newest jeans, party dresses and blouses from expensive department stores, smelling pretty, looking happy in the sun of Eric's backyard picnic party.   It went to shit in twenty-four hours I think.

I found Eric and Drea in the basement of an empty warehouse in Pittsburgh's Strip District, down the road from our neighborhood a couple of days after.

"They took our mother…" Eric said, his thinning blond hair plastered to his forehead, jawbone protruding with despair.   Drea held his hand tight.   She too was drawn and thin with grief.   They had a canteen with them and shared some water.

"We are heading to the Midwest.   There's talk of more people and a light…"

"Nowhere is safe Eric.   You know what this is…"   Something in me just wanted to pound out any hope Eric had.   This was selfish of me, but I did not care.

"Fuck you…we're going.   We're going to our camp, and from there I'll get the Jeep.   Come with us Kyle."   His deep brown eyes practically ordered me.   I shook my head and watched them leave up the dusty steel stairs to the street above.   Pale sunlight shone down those stairs from the building's giant industrial windows.   That last bit of pale and ailing sunlight seems so brilliant now.

I waited. Surely they were in the street by now. No screams.

"No screams. It might be safe..." Darrell Peck, an older co-worker of mine at the bank, just months before all of this, stepped from the shadows. His black face and curly hair riddled with the dust and asbestos of the basement haven we called a temporary 'place to sleep' during the day. Shany McCocklyn, his much younger girlfriend, stepped into the dusty light. I could smell their sweat from across the room.

"You shouldn't have let them go out there...." Shany tried to guilt me.

"How else would we know it was safe for us?" I asked my old college drinking buddy. "Now, we know we can go out there. I do not want to stay down here one more night. That slithering sound was only one floor up last night...something we may not have seen yet..."

Shany glared at me as she always did when she felt guilty, and I felt nothing, about anything wrong we did. And we did a lot wrong. But those days of stealing quiz papers at school and robbing the pizza joint that we worked for to get us through school, by tapping the register now and then, just really did not matter any more.

Yeah, I loved Eric and Drea, but these were the days of the fall. Numbers meant there was less chance of you being dinner for some crouching predator that looked half goblin and half wolverine. I'm not exaggerating about that description, except that those furry beasts inhabited the woodland regions, not the cities. One ate my neighbor's kids while I stood in their living room in horror. It happened so fast... I was babysitting... I don't know... I guess it snuck in through the basement flap windows and ran up the stairs, passed me ...straight to the kids' bedrooms. There was a sidelong glance at me while the galloping ball of teeth and fur ran past me. I swear it was smiling.

Those sounds...

We eventually came out from the warehouse basement when the sound of other voices seemed to be gathering. It was daylight, if you want to call an amber haze of heat, daylight. The night came earlier and earlier and the turquoise and blackened sky lasted longer and longer. That afternoon, the city of Pittsburgh stood like a cemetery in the sunlight. The Ohio River was still brownish green at that time. One side of the street was empty, but then the other had a crowd of fifty some people of all races and ages. I knew this was bad. This many folks should never feel this comfortable in the light of day making such a racket.

"Let's move…" I said to Shany. Darrell nodded in agreement.

"But there's others…came out from hiding too?"

"YES… that's the problem…"

No sooner than I said that had the swooping black giants fell from the sky. They made no noise, only the cacophony of their beating raven wings swooshed overhead. Their heads were burrowed so deep in their chests that you could never really focus on the faces. Eventually I would.

The familiar fray began. People scattered, blood spattered wetly on the blacktop, screams gargled, dying cries. We ran. I made the two of them keep tight to the buildings, running through alleyways that we were familiar with on our old lunch breaks together. I remember wondering if Eric and Drea were among those people being cut down and slaughtered, and tried not to care. One woman's screams just never seemed to stop. Four blocks away we could still hear her screaming. Why were they taking so long to kill her?

"…Oh God oh God… that woman…"

"Shany, there is NOTHING we can do for anyone against those things…guns barely have an affect…" Darrell used the butt of his 45 to smash our way into a department store on Smithfield Street. Guns were still good for that.

As we climbed through the glass, avoiding shards, Shany cried insistently, "I can still hear her…why do they do *that*?"

41

"Because THEY CAN, Shany… Because they can… now move inside!" I rasped, spitting my own hair from my face.

The final wisps of sunlight disappeared that afternoon behind clouds of permanent turquoise. We did not know we had witnessed the last of our Sun through the barrier of bleakness. The three rivers of Pittsburgh now glowed red too. Red water was one of the early reports we heard over some radio shows and news blurbs in the beginning. Further inland now. That's where the running would continue.

***

I ran toward the thinning blue light. Our deadening world's darkness lashed at my heels. Most were dead. Others were enslaved or dying in the bellies of winged soundless demons with diamond eyes. Faithless hearts on the rise in the final years…. We opened the doorway.

There were many others. Soon, the three of us became five and then ten, and I welcomed it. More pickings and less chance it would be me the next raid.

Trees had black bark. All the trees. The leaves were gone for the most part and tentacled shrubs and vines threatened to engulf your every step. On more than one occasion it did. No longer could you tell the difference between a branch and a black slimy tendril that just…

Numbers dwindled. Then we came across a camp of families, or bikers. Numbers went up. A raid. The running continued as numbers disappeared repeatedly.

One night walking through the woods, still heading west (but never really knowing where we were, just where not to go due to screams of the tortured and dying in the distance) all the woods seemed to come alive. I had my hunting knife, and so did some of the others. We were able to cut our way out.   Darrell was by my side, I had to grab him as we watched Shany's pretty brown face elongated into a scream while she was dragged through the dead leaves. A blackened tendril that had wrapped around her leg tugged and dragged her relentlessly. We gave chase, and then her screams faded into the putrid ashen woods.

Nights later, one of the bikers, a man by the name of Mason, first, last name... no freakin' clue, became sort of a leader for a bit. He claimed to know the woods and his barrel chest and shotgun gave him that right. I didn't like him though; he breathed too heavy and smelt of tobacco. I wondered if that smell would give us away.

Those first days, or more distinctly, on the same night that I ran from my neighbors' house where I was babysitting, I learned just how well these creatures relied on more than their sense of smell. Their taste for destroying all you hold dear, ripping all your beloved memories right in front of you was their glee.   Terrified I ran out of the house and ridiculous as it sounds I feared for myself, and how the hell I was going to tell these parents that there was something upstairs eating their six and eight year old daughters. Would they believe me? A dumb college kid with a pot smoking habit and long hair that worked part time at a bank and delivered pizza at school? No... I would get the blame first...

That's when I found Mr. and Mrs. Kindrick on the lawn. I should say, half of them. They were still alive as I was backing down their front steps, looking up at the girls' bedroom window. Literally I backed into them, being chewed up by some ungodly thing underground. Briefcase, purse, VHS tapes and a pizza lay on the ground in front of them in a pool of mud, blood and their own torn clothes. Under my feet, the ground shook and sounded like a lawn mower that took breaks to swallow chunks. The Kendricks still had their glasses on and stared wide-eyed in shock as they were slowly being pulled under ground in short bursts of crunching and horrid rumbling. Their arms reached out for me, and I took Mrs.

Kindrick's thin hands in mine. She went under in no time and I had fallen on my back in the grass. The kids were still screaming in the house. Three ribbons of blood had striped their bedroom window. Mr. Kindrick saw that, looking up at his house, from the middle of his lawn right smack in the middle of DOWNTOWN USA, Suburbia, affluent neighborhood... sunny day... pizza for the babysitter...watch movies with the kids....get eaten on my front lawn... but first let me watch my kids being slaughtered.

He disappeared under the shredded mulch and blood-soaked sod.

I had no idea, outside of strange news reports what was happening, but I knew I had to get home to my family. So I ran down the block four houses to the Cape Cod I grew up in.

Mom was there and so was my older sister Tammy. They were at the dinner table.

"What is it Kyle? What's wrong..." My mother's hair was wet from the shower. She was getting ready for the nightshift at the police station where she was a clerk. Tammy was dolled up like a slut, ready for her date with Peter Glitchen (that was IF the rich prick from New York even showed up). Don't get me wrong, Tammy was pretty, but also so much more naïve in her mid twenties than this swinger from the Bigger city. He was a dick, and I didn't like him.

She made me sick with her tight black pants under a sundress, and her curls all falling to her shoulders and her "cum–fuck–me" boots. Smelled of desperation.

"What? The Kindricks kick you out? You have like three jobs... what the hell! Just stay at school and party! You're such a freakin loser..."

"SHUT UP Tammy...not now... not now." I turned to the other side of the table to my mother behind her make-up mirror. "Mom... it's not safe... something..."

Maybe the sirens were first, maybe the screeches of the winged creatures, or perhaps the agonized shrieks of those taken by surprise, like the Kindricks, stopped me short. The noises were the immediate answer to my shouts at the two of them. Soon, the lights went out. Cars in the distance smashed. More screams, and some gunshots. "To the basement!" I shouted.

The front door was bashed to a million splintered shards and something clawed its way through and poked into our foyer. If you have ever seen one of those brown stick bugs that they have in the Amazon or some shit... that's what was pulling into my foyer now with four extended arms, each with pincers. It tap-danced its way in to our hallway like a giant grasshopper. Down came the head into my face. One yellow eye with a black pupil and two sets of mandibles made up the face. It had tentacles too, coming off its back where it had none other than Peter Glitchen, stock broker from New York, the young go-getter, wrapped and dangling. I guess he showed up after all. I would have a laugh about this all to myself in later weeks, alone in the dark.

The thing smelled like shit roasted over hot coals. Tammy was screaming but she grabbed me and hurled me down the hall. "Get the bat...Kyle...get the bat..." I'm not sure if it was shock coming out of her mouth or not, but the next thing I saw was that tall elongated mass of legs, tentacles and head of mandibles grab my sister from behind. My mother ran to her side with a chair raised. They were both screaming when the tentacles and claws snatched them and pulled them into our guest room to the right of the foyer. Peter Glitchen was pulled in as well, though he could not scream. It seemed his mouth had a tendril running directly inside it and down his throat.

Trying my damnedest to get inside that room to get to my mother and my sister, I felt desperately deflated. I'm not even sure if I was screaming while I bashed my entire body against the door. That thing must have blocked the door with its own body. Tears poured helplessly down my cheeks almost as fast as the blood pooled under the door, yet the screams of my mother and Tammy persisted for what seemed hours. I had collapsed at one point, facedown in the warm blood of my family. It was night when the door opened and that thing stepped over me and threw Peter's body at me in bits and

45

pieces, shredded and diced like a fish, it had actually scaled the rich stock broker from New York who wanted to fuck my sister. The giant stick bug seemed to laugh a chittering buggy laugh while it pelted me with bits of the filleted man and his loamy suit.

I got a glance back in the room. On the floor and very much alive was Tammy, and my mother. My mother had her back against the wall, her eyes open in shock. Her black hair turning gray as I looked at her. There was nothing in her eyes resembling the person I knew. My mother's mind was gone, but she lived. Tammy lay there, naked on the floor, her head turned to face me, her blue eyes filled with dreaded despair. It took all of her strength to reach out her hand to me, for me to take hold.

The chittering creature scoffed at this, and swatted me aside, returning to the room and closing the door.

I would pound and plead for hours. At one point I know I had my baseball bat. They screamed the whole time and the floor pounded in the room beyond the door. Eventually I went outside, not caring what else waited for me, but aware of the chaos spreading about the city beyond. My throbbing head, boiling with blood drowned everything out except the fact that I had to get to the window on the side of the house. It was high off the ground, but I had to try something…

With a CRASH, the window exploded as if the creature knew what I wanted to do. Trampling over me, bruising my legs and chest the creature emerged. Shards of glass shattered around me and the side of our yard. The creature held my mother's limp body and Tammy, who was still whimpering. She reached for me when the creature's praying mantis-like wings opened up and it took to the sky.

***

Now, months later, with this turd biker, Mason in charge I just waited for death, wondering which of the assorted horde would get to me first.

The beating wings followed us till we reached this wooded seclusion that seems to be a Midwestern squatter's dream. Survivors, runners, like me, cheating death by the skin of their teeth for months. Woods engulfed our tribe of survivors. Dark hunger surrounded our clearing of blue light that emitted from an unknown source. Some say it is **HE** that they pray to. Yes, some still prayed.

Why me, why us? Why all those dead people who ran with me through the shattered cities and rivers that run red, filled with beasts of the netherworld, sinewy and dead things....

How we got here was amazing in itself. I only know my story, and a few others that came from the ferry.

Mason and some others knew about this abandoned ferryboat, that, ironically, would get us the furthest in our journey to this part of the Midwest, and this so-called light in the woods, we'd come to find.

Thoughts of the secret ferryboat make me shudder now, but it was big old Mason with the lumberjack beard who knew where to find it. Darrell was for it and soon we would commandeer it in the quiet eternal night. I wished Shany had made it this far.

Hope lit anew for me when we climbed aboard and found other survivors. Over a hundred people had met here and waited because they knew others like ourselves were coming. Some kind of miracle right?

My own Uncle Richard and Aunt Lisa were aboard (we were somewhere in Mississippi, who knows anymore) with my cousins, Keith, Talayne and Jacob. I remember at one point me and Darrell had run into them as we fled from Jersey... so much death... so much rustic blood on the pavement in Jersey and Philly. We lost them on our return back to Pittsburgh when we found the East Coast to be hopeless. But our destination was the same.

The skies, still an ethereal turquoise, just light enough for the creatures of legion to see their quarry, and yet it blanketed the woods on the riverbanks and to the horizon of the red river. Not all relied on smell. Most did need the scent of flesh on bone to swoop out of the sky and split the tender bone of a child with their needle teeth the size of …

The ferry was a double-decker. This was by far the most covert of vehicles to use under these circumstances. Still I had to disagree with Mason and the two men piloting the thing when he said we should take it as far as we could. I saw this as a liability and it was only a matter of time. Besides, what likes to swim in a river of blood?

No one had seen anything the first day of our river boat ride, this hardly making me feel any better. There were splashes and bumps. My cousin Keith, the fourteen year old pointed at the water once in front of us when he claimed a hump rose up. I missed it, but I did not doubt the kid. Aunt Lisa was holding little Talayne in her arms, straining back the child's tears as well as her own. Jacob, only six, stayed by his older brother's side, visibly shaking but having no idea that his was a permanent vacation from normalcy, not just one of Uncle Richard's day trips to the Delaware Water Gap.

"Kyle, come with me." My Uncle, a stoic man, lawyer and self-made, was always a bit serious and over the top, unless it had to do with watching the Three Stooges or giving tips on the perfect pool game. He grabbed my shoulder and we went to the top deck. Keith and Jacob followed.

"If anything happens to me…"

"I got it Uncle Rich, I got it. I'm going there." We looked out over the woods as if the blue light could be seen from here. "And I'll take them …"

He just looked at me sternly. No tears, no smiles, just understanding.

"Hey Kyle …I found your friend Drea…!" Darrell came running up to me from the steps on the lower deck. "She's here ..." He had Eric's sister Drea by the hand. Both were smiling. She jumped and gave me such a hug. I think this is when I became more frightened than ever. Thinking on that night, listening on the other side of the door, to whatever horror was taking place in our guest room. Now, I had people to care about again.

The sky had been clear of those winged horrors. They were Sentinel type beasts that calculated strikes on thousands of humans at a time. We had heard of their pin-like needle teeth, diamond eyes, but until that night, I never got that close. Saw many other horrors... that's for sure. Yet, that night on the top deck of the ferry, is what came down on Jacob and Taylane, snatching them up into the night. Taylane was swiped from Aunt Lisa's hands with such a grip and force, that her left arm was ripped from its socket and she fell to the deck. I went to her but the boat shifted to the side and people were thrown into the water. There were shouts of surprise below deck and all about us on the top deck. I got to my feet in time to see Keith jumping overboard into the sludgy lava-like brackish river when one of the giants swooped down on him. He had avoided the Sentinel by diving headlong. When I looked down into the red water, Keith was pulled under by something green with jaws like a vice full of iron maiden spikes. Oh God the boy's eyes were so wide when he looked up at me....

The chaos of another attack was unraveling again, at a maddening pace! The boat had struck something, or something had struck the boat from the bottom. It did not matter because my boat trip was over now anyway...Where was Drea? Darrell? Uncle RICH!!

He had run to Aunt Lisa, while the boat listed again.

I lost my balance and fell to the side of the boat, hitting my back and then going over the rails. Breaking my fall was a black crisp branch. I hung there for a bit and then made my way down a bit using branch after dry dead branch.

I was on the shore, dangling from the black swirls of crusty brush, no longer reminiscent of earthen foliage. Still, it broke my fall and kept me from going into the red river.

In front of me the grisly show unveiled itself.

In front of the boat, a leviathan of a tentacled head of some unnamable creature rose from the river and proceeded to pick off folks from the top of the ferry. I heard Uncle Rich scream and crunch like a cartoon character would…this did not look real before my eyes, but the smell of the burnt woods, the coppery river and foul beasts reminded me to focus.

I saw Drea up on the top deck, looking down at me. Her wide eyes agape in terror and her blonde hair matted and mopped about her as she shook. "NO."

I was motioning for her to jump.

"DREA!! NOW… You have to…"

She half jumped half fell. And I half caught her, and half fell with her further down the thorny tree branches.

Grabbing a sooty tree branch overhead, I hauled myself and Drea up, and then down, the tree as the howls and thunderous roars of the feeding proceeded down that red river. The screams were almost comical. One every three seconds as the long tentacle with the cavern of teeth for a head, continued to pluck people off the boat.

I climbed down the tree (the woods not only smelled of soot now but left you marred with the stuff) and hit the charcoal earth with my boots. Drea followed carefully. Wiping the knotted hair from my face, I knew we had to run… the relentless run again. The kind you learn by fear of being eaten alive, you know? Yeah, now you know what I mean.

The boat moved down the river, and there were other creatures attacking it now… some with beaks, some with flippers like dinosaurs, and some unspeakable spider crab, which ran from the shore to the frenzy of people swimming toward the shore, only to be met with more atrocities.

The winged black demons were the hoarders and the Sentinels. In the light of the bright red water I finally got a better look at them. Their wings converted to horrific stilted legs when they landed on the boat decks. I could smell those flying overhead, passing Drea and me on the shore, heading to the real kills. Those Sentinels and their scent of melted coppery blood, and seeping hate in black liquid through pores the size of baseballs; it was those that were most common. I had seen them weeks ago, corralling humans down the streets in Pittsburgh to walk to whatever slave work was planned (or more than likely to whatever feasts and blood orgy of the damned they were preparing for HIM and his creations that had now taken our world).

"They're all dead... Any family I had was on that boat...dead..."

"Not necessarily." Drea spoke with a deep voice of a woman, not a young girl of sixteen. Of Knowing.

We ran that night in the woods, with the screams echoing down the river. Aunt Lisa and Keith, well, I never saw any of them again. I was close now, and the ferry was to take us there, or at least a close proximity.

***

I'm here now, and already, the blue shield of light grows in radius every day that one of us makes it to the clearing. There is food, and precious wine. I watch the people arrive. Eric had made it as well. We hugged when I first arrived. Shelters were being built and we helped. I'll never forget the tearful hug that Drea and Eric shared that day we arrived. He thanked me deeply. He now helps me with my drawing of lines in the new Earth. The lines I carve outside the cabins grow farther away from the blue shield of protection. It expands, is expanding. Soon our light will engulf the black woods and soon we will re-inherit the Earth, some say. More must come.

Sometimes others come. The damned horde shows itself beyond the blue border into the black of the woods. Shany came one night. She called to Darrell, and Eric and myself ran to hold him back. They like to tease with familiar comforts and they know how to torture, but this night was different.

While Eric held Darrell back, the slithering beast that was Shany stood before us in the glow of our protecting light. Her body now a mesh of black tendrils, and quills of tentacles that flew back with her hair, while she elbowed up on imitation arms seeping with an open wound of black ooze. Shany's ebony skin was gray, cracked and wilted.

Her eyes were empty sockets with a brackish fluid. Her teeth smiled like a gar's needle grin. "Do not hate us. We merely want what you had. We intend to get just that."

"SHANY!" Darrell screamed through tears.

"I'm not her." The creature rasped, and raised its snake-ribbed body higher than any of us stood. "I'm her child, like many others you will come to find. We want ..."

The creature's voice reverberated around me, as another's chimed in.

"...Beauty. Life, love, warmth and beauty that we were so cheated..." It was Drea, who came up from behind us and in no time was wrapped in Shany's tentacles.

"NO!" Eric wailed.

I knew it was too late. Drea was gone the same night that the rest of Eric's family died. I just knew it, as the same happened to mine. Drea was gone in mind, as she was raped in body.

Drea's eyes turned to puddles of silver black and she stared and smiled at us.

"I understand now Eric. I will go be with my family. They only want to be like us...and they are merely learning...as the humans once did."

The two disappeared, creeping backwards into the forest, never unlocking their stares from us, and the other people who came to see what transpired.

So here I stay, for now; the blue shield of light grows daily when another here and another there arrives. We realized that very few women ever made it to our haven (those that were still capable of reproduction, especially). One for every fifty men or children who showed were female. So, in the end, we also know why they did not always kill the women. God, were my mother and sister still alive and becoming like Drea? Were there slithering siblings of mine on the crest of these woods, watching me, even now? There were nights that I felt their eyes.

Well, like I said, there is food, and precious wine. Our numbers grow. Our blue shield of protection expands. How soon our light will engulf the black woods and we will re-inherit the Earth, I don't fuckin' know. But I do know, we better get cracking because if the horde of the damned get it figured out before we grow in numbers, beauty will have a whole new meaning.

For now it belongs to **HIM**. But his time will be short too.

GLORY HOLES

By Gary Lee Vincent

**Unfortunately, some Asian massage parlors
do not offer happy endings.**

*Gary Lee Vincent (born 1974) is an American author and musician. As a fiction writer, his credits include **Passageway** and the West Virginia Vampire Series: **DARKENED** (featuring the standalone novels **Darkened Hills** – winner of Foreword Reviews Magazine's 2010 Book of the Year Award for Best Horror Novel, **Darkened Hollows** (Fall 2011), and **Darkened Waters** (Summer 2012).*

*As a musician, his albums include **100 Percent**, **Passion, Pleasure, & Pain**, and **Somewhere Down The Road**. For more information, visit **www.DarkenedHills.com** and **www.GaryVincent.com**.*

Jerome Thachet lived his life like most people do – obliviously. In fact, that fateful Wednesday morning was like any other day of the week for Jerome. Each morning, he would wake up, get dressed, and walk through a sleep-haze to Wagner's Grocery, where they served fresh coffee every morning at 7:00 a.m.

He would stumble in past the old timers who where always there, mumble something to them, grab his coffee, and go about his business. Jerome's 'business' was a few blocks down the street where he worked at a hardware store that dubbed as a farmers' co-op.

Yes, there was not much exciting for Jerome to do but wake up, get his coffee, and go to work – day in and day out. That was, until he found the token.

After leaving Wagner's, Jerome had made it about a block and stared at a newspaper vending machine reading the headlines. He rarely bought the paper, but every now and then would find something worth reading about. Of course, there was not much crime in sleepy Melas, West Virginia, and all the news came from over in Clarksburg.

As he stood reading about the disappearances of two female hikers, his eye caught something glistening on the sidewalk in front of him. *My lucky day*, Jerome thought as he reached down to pick up the coin.

At first, he thought it was some new kind of quarter because it had an eagle on one side. Upon closer examination, he realized it was a token. Written above the eagle was an Internet web address – www.sexco.us. Below the eagle were the words, "The Sex Company." Flipping the coin over, he saw a torso of a shirtless woman revealing a nice rack with the words, "Heads I win," written on the left and right sides of the woman's ample breasts.

Interesting, Jerome thought. He was a little bit disappointed that it wasn't money; at least he could spend money. What the heck could he do with a token?

Placing his new found treasure in his pocket, he continued on to work his oblivious day at the hardware store, forgetting to even mention it to his co-workers. In fact, Jerome didn't even mention it to his wife, Missy, when he came home later that night.

"How was your day, honey?" Missy asked as Jerome walked in.

"Fine," Jerome replied. "Yours?"

"Fine."

Like many couples, the Thachets were in a sexless marriage

where every day was routine and they simply lived their lives in blissful ignorance and co-dependence. They ate supper with little conversation and mumbled about work.

After he ate, Jerome had planned to take a shower. Missy had already left the dirty dishes in the sink and had retired to the living room to get her daily four-hour fix of sitcoms before zoning out to sleep for the night. As he emptied his pockets, he noticed the glistening token in his hands. *Humm, I wonder what's on that website?* he thought, curiosity driving him wild.

Instead of going into the bathroom and taking his shower, Jerome headed into the spare bedroom where they kept a computer. He brought up the website and saw that it was an advertisement for a chic adult novelties store and massage parlor. A cute Asian woman with abnormally large tits that reminded Jerome of Elvira in a strange kind of way was standing next to one of the tables. "Come try our Glory Holes," was a caption written underneath the lady.

Jerome laughed so hard he almost fell out of his computer chair.

"Something a matter honey?" Missy yelled from a room away.

"I'm fine," Jerome yelled back. "Pay no mind."

Looking back at the screen, he noticed the store's physical address was over in Parkersburg, West Virginia, which was not too far from Melas. He grabbed a pen and jotted it down. *Might have to check this out*, he thought. This was especially true since it had been over eight months since he had last done the horizontal belly dance with the wifey.

The following day, Jerome asked his boss at the hardware store if he could leave half a day early for an appointment. That was not a problem and by noon, Jerome was on U.S. Route 50 heading for Parkersburg.

When he pulled up to the address, it was in the rear of a truck stop. Jerome liked this arrangement, because the large trucks concealed the cars that parked at the store. Jerome expected to see large signs announcing "Adult Books, Videos, Etc." but there weren't any. In fact, the entrance was a bit understated and had a quaint brick façade. A small sign was affixed above a doorbell that simply said, "Please ring for service."

A tinge of nervousness mixed with excitement filled Jerome as he pressed the button. He did not know what to expect, but knew that if it were a queer bar or something, he would be out the door and back down the highway in no time. To his surprise, the door was answered by the Asian woman from the website.

"May I help you?" the lady asked.

"Yes. I saw your website and want to know about your glory holes."

"Of course." The woman gestured him inside. "Please come this way."

Jerome was led through a small adult novelty shop and through a doorway that had beads dangling from the frame in place of where a door would be. *Very Seventies,* Jerome thought to himself as he passed the threshold. It reminded him of a hippie set-up and he quite expected there to be longhaired folks smoking the old Mary-J somewhere in one of the rooms beyond.

"You said you found us on the web?" the Asian host asked.

"Yes," Jerome replied. He then added, "Actually, I found a token with your website on it."

"Do you have the token with you?" she asked.

"Yep," Jerome said, pulling out the coin to proudly display it to the woman.

"Well then," she said. "It is your lucky day!"

She led him into a small room with a six-inch hole in the wall and shut the door. She lowered her voice to a whisper and asked, "Are you with law enforcement?"

"No," he replied.

"Good," she said. "Let me have the coin."

Jerome obediently handed her the token.

"You are going to get a freebie for having this," she said as she took off her blouse. Jerome stared at her with his jaw dropped as she unfastened her bra and revealed the most perfect set of D-cups he ever laid his eyes upon. He instantly felt himself getting hard as he watched her undress.

Next, she provocatively took off a pair of blue jean shorts she was wearing to reveal pink thong panties. Jerome could tell that her pussy was shaved and it was a good look for her.

"Now to keep things legit," she said, "I am going to go over to the room next door and you can fuck me through the hole."

"Okay, I get it!" Jerome exclaimed excitedly. "Now I know what you meant by 'Glory Hole' on your web site."

She grinned and winked at him. She picked up her jean shorts that were on the floor and pulled out a condom from the front pocket. Handing it to him she said, "Be sure you use protection."

"Sure," he agreed as she left the room.

"I'll be on the other side," she said. "Don't keep me waiting!"

Within seconds, Jerome took his pants off and was over at the wall. He hurriedly put the condom on his erect penis and pushed it blindly into the hole on the wall. Instantly, he felt himself penetrate a wet orifice that – in Jerome's mind – was the Asian woman's mouth. The sensation was tight and as he began to thrust his hips at the glory hole, he found unbelievable pleasure.

As the pleasure built, his speed increased and he thrust harder at the wall. Within minutes, the pleasure was so intense he felt his knees growing weak and he put his entire body against the wall to steady himself. At some point, the condom came off and his engorged shaft was met with warm wetness that caused him to go at the hole with even more force than before.

Jerome no longer cared as he fucked the hole. Twenty seconds later, he came. As he pulled out of the hole, he was shocked to see that his genitalia were covered with a green slimy film. In shock, he stumbled back and touched the substance, bringing it to his nose.

The goo stank with a heady, pungent aroma. Jerome quickly dressed and ran out of the establishment, not even wanting to know what in the world he had just fucked.

As he drove away, he was a nervous wreck – at least for the first couple miles anyway. However, as he began to think about how much pleasure he found in the glory hole, the initial remorse slowly faded and was quickly replaced by arousal.

Missy had never felt like that before, he thought. If she had, Jerome was sure their marriage wouldn't be sexless. *Hell, I'd tap that every day if it were that good*, he imagined.

Suddenly, he realized he was so aroused that his penis ached. Without even pulling the car over he unzipped his pants and masturbated. The horrible stench of the green goo that repulsed him before now did not seem to smell as bad. In fact, it had a pheromone effect that he liked as he stroked away. He brought himself to orgasm quickly, shooting cum all over himself and his steering wheel.

"Wow! Fuck yeah!" Jerome exclaimed in his car. His penis throbbed and glistened with a tint of green and cream.

Unlike the normal plateau effect when a man ejaculates, where the sensation goes away, Jerome had quite the opposite effect -- he had become hornier. It was almost as if his penis was growing as he drove. In fact, Jerome could swear it looked like it had grown two inches!

The drive back to his house was about forty minutes and the entire time, he left his hardened manhood out. He couldn't wait to see Missy this evening. He didn't care if she wanted to fuck or not, he was going to have his way. *The cock wants what the cock wants*, he thought.

As he pulled into his driveway, he found that his erection was getting so big that he could hardly fit it back into his pants. It actually pained him to walk with the constricting clothing.

When he came into the living room, it was roughly the same time that he usually returned home from work. To Missy, she did not know of Jerome's escapades and to her, it was just like any other day. "Dinner will be ready in a few, hon," she yelled from the kitchen when she heard him come in.

"Baby, I can't wait for dinner," Jerome said. "I want me some dessert!"

"My God, man," Missy exclaimed, looking at Jerome disheveled look and hardened sex organ. "What is going on?"

"I don't have time to explain, only fuck!" was Jerome's reply.

She started to protest when he brought his hand to her nose. The horrible smell made his wife recoil in disgust. "Ooh! What on earth do you have on your hand!" she shrieked.

Her rear hit the kitchen counter-top and suddenly her head began to spin. Somewhere deep in her loins, she felt herself getting wet. *Something just ain't right*, she thought to herself. But then, on second thought, she found herself reaching for Jerome's hand, bringing it up to her face and inhaling a deep sniff of the green substance that was caked all over it.

After the second sniff, she reached for Jerome's engorged member with her other hand and brought him to her. "Please, come inside me."

She didn't have to ask twice. Jerome pinned her against the kitchen counter-top and hiked up Missy's dress. His penis had grown another two inches and by now was almost a foot in length.

Somewhere deep inside Jerome's mind, he could feel sheer pain from his skin breaking away as his penis grew, but at the same time, it also felt incredible. So much, in fact, that he no longer minded that his penis had turned entirely green and resembled an octopus's tentacle more so than a man's penis.

Missy screamed as Jerome entered her love cave. "Damn!" she cried. "It is so huge!"

Within seconds he drove the tentacle deep into her vagina and ejaculated about a pint's worth of green jism.

"What the fuck!" Missy cried, as the green goo seeped out of her. "I've got to clean this up!"

She retreated to the bathroom and began douching her vagina to get rid of the green substance. Much like Jerome, she found herself growing more aroused as she tried to clean the goo. In only a matter of minutes, she was deep inside of an empty bathtub with feet hiked high, playing with herself. She was like that for most of the night.

After twenty minutes or so, Jerome decided he was still horny and could no longer wait for Missy to come out of the bathroom. In fact, he always wanted to give one of the prostitutes that hung out over in the Melas railroad district a try.

He ran into his bedroom, changed from his jeans to a pair of loose gym pants and headed out the door. "Honey, I'll be back!" he yelled as the door flung shut behind him. He didn't really care if she heard him or not.

Fifteen minutes later, he pulled his car up to a man standing inconspicuously near a street corner. Jerome recognized the man as Owens, a local pimp whom he had seen from time to time in the hardware store. "Owens! How goes it, my man?"

"Yo, Homie, whatcha doin' over in this side of town this fine evening?" Owens asked.

"I need me some action, if you know what I mean," Jerome replied.

"Yeah, I hear ya," Owens replied. "He leaned into the window and said in a hushed voice, "Gimmie fifty bucks, and I'll hook you up."

Jerome quickly handed Owens three twenty-dollar bills and said, "Keep the change!"

Owens instructed Jerome to park the car in a nearby alley and come with him into an adjacent building. Owens led Jerome to a door and motioned for him to go inside.

Inside was an attractive blonde about 5'7" in height, kind of skinny, but definitely fuckable. Owens nodded to her and left the two alone.

"What's your pleasure," the blonde asked as she helped Jerome out of his gym pants.

Her eyes got really big as she looked down at him. "Boy, you've got a horse cock! I don't know if I can handle that!"

By now, Jerome's tentacle cock had grown over two feet and was

61

the size of a small baseball bat. It was an accurate description that Blondie applied when she labelled what she saw as a 'horse cock.'

"I am so horny!" Jerome exclaimed, moving towards the prostitute.

"Wait!" Blondie protested. "You gots to getcha a rubber on ya!" she said with a ghetto-like slang.

Suddenly, the two-foot tentacle sprung to life like an alien appendage and shoved its way towards Blondie's vagina, not waiting for her to find a condom.

"Stop!" she screamed, but it was too late.

The tentacle cock pulled Jerome across the room at lightening speed and plunged all two feet into the woman's vagina.

"Aaaah!" she yelled. "Please, don't!"

Suddenly, the tentacle grew another two feet and Jerome pressed her arms down against the bed. He thought he was going to black out, but the pleasure was just too good. The tentacle continued to fuck her even without Jerome being consciously present.

As the whore screamed, her sounds were muted by the tentacle as it pushed completely through her organs and out her mouth. It pulsated and erupted in an orgasm that shot the woman over five feet across the room, where she landed in a heap. Green goo ran down her chin.

Owens, who had heard Blondie's first screams, entered the room just in time to see Blondie soaring through the air with Jerome in a half-standing posture with a tentacle cock whipping madly around in the air.

"You're killing my hoe!" Owens screamed. With a knee-jerk reaction, he pulled out a Glock 9mm and shot Jerome, killing him instantly.

Meanwhile, Missy had started to grow tentacles of her own, only hers were tinier and looked similar to the appendages on a jellyfish. As she fingered her labia, the tentacles sent pulses of pleasure all over her body.

Suddenly, there was a knock on her door. She covered herself the best she could in a nightgown and went to answer it.

On the other side of the door stood an Asian female.

"How may I help you?" Missy asked.

"My name is Mei-Lien," the woman replied. "I work at Sexco over in Parkersburg."

"And what does that have to do with me?" Missy asked.

"I'd like you to come and work for us," Mei-Lien replied.

"In what capacity?" Missy asked.

"We have hundreds of men wanting to fuck. Would you like to fuck them?"

Missy grinned. The tiny tentacles pulsated with shockwaves of pleasure at the thought. Yes, she would like that very much.

The two headed into the night towards the other town. When they arrived, the Asian showed Missy to a room with a hole in one side.

"See that?" Mei-Lien asked, pointing to the orifice.

"Yes." Missy replied.

"Bend over and put your ass against the wall," Mei-Lien commanded.

Missy did as she was told.

It was only a matter of minutes before she felt the first penis penetrate her from the other side. The tentacles like this. They liked it a lot.

CHANNEL 666

By John Russo

**Isn't television a marvelous invention?
It brings good news and bad news into our living rooms. Some
say it stimulates our imaginations. Others say it pollutes our
minds with images of sex and violence. If you could step through
your television screen the way Alice stepped through her magic
mirror, would you be entering a land of wonder or a land of
horror?**

*John A. Russo (born 1939), sometimes credited as Jack Russo or
John Russo, is an American screenwriter and film director most
commonly associated with the 1968 horror classic Night of the
Living Dead. As a screenwriter, his credits include Night of the
Living Dead, The Majorettes, Midnight, and Santa Claws. The
latter two, he also directed.*

*He has performed small roles as an actor, most notably the first
zombie who is stabbed in the head in Night of the Living Dead, as
well as cameos in There's Always Vanilla, The Majorettes, and
Santa Claws. John Russo is also the founder and one of the co-
mentors along with Russell Streiner of the John Russo Movie Making
Program at DuBois Business College in DuBois, Pennsylvania.*

Thanks to the strange-looking converter box he got by mugging and robbing a strange-looking old man in an alley behind a video arcade, Spenser Katz's TV was bringing in programs that nobody else could get.

The box was wireless; no cables connected it to Spenser's TV. It sat on top, glowing softly, pulling in fabulous shows. Spenser figured the shows must be beamed in by satellite from somewhere.

Funny thing, but all these great shows were hosted by the same creepy guy, a guy named Nasta. He opened each show with a chuckle, saying, "Welcome to Doc Nasta's Wacky Far-out Medicine Show!"

Nasta certainly looked like a snake-oil salesman. He also bore a weird resemblance to the old man Spenser had mugged to get the converter box. But uglier. Much uglier. His face was bruised and burned, oozing yellowish fluids, the skin stretched tight, exposing teeth that grinned perpetually as if in rictus, under his black, heavily waxed mustache.

On one of his shows, Nasta said he was a serial killer who had died in the electric chair forty years ago, which couldn't be true because there he was on TV, live, not prerecorded. They certainly didn't have these cool, far-out programs forty years ago - all they had was square, boring pap like AMERICAN BANDSTAND.

Last Saturday, Spenser had brought his friends, Gary Parsons and Elena Holmes, into his bedroom to show them some of the great stuff he'd been watching lately. But all he could get was static. The converter box perversely decided to go on the blink at exactly the wrong time, just to make him look like a fool or a liar. He blushed and stammered furiously in front of Elena because he had a mad crush on her even though she belonged to Gary: they were engaged.

Spenser had trouble getting dates. He was gawky and shy in most situations. But underneath his shyness lurked a nasty, violent temper that he turned loose in dark alleys when he was mugging people like the old man with the converter box.

Because of the anger locked inside him, Spenser was addicted to MTV and its weird, angry, erotic imagery. He envied the rock stars, the rap stars, and pictured them in a constant orgiastic swirl with the voluptuous groupies who permeated the music videos with their red, sneering lips and pulsatingly perfect hips, breasts and thighs.

Spenser's favorite rock group starred on Doctor Nasta's

Medicine Show, a group called Triple Six with a dynamite song called *The Devil Made Me Do It to Ya.* Spenser tried to tape Triple Six, but got nothing but static. He hunted for their stuff in music stores and video stores. He asked about the group, but nobody seemed to have heard of them.

He got mad at Gary and Elena when they told him there wasn't any such group, maybe he dreamed it all up, including Doc Nasta and the Medicine Show. But Spenser knew he wasn't going crazy. This shit was *real,* goddamn it, even if he couldn't figure out why he could only tune in to the stuff that really turned him on when he was in his room all by himself.

One day Nasta read some of his fan mail out loud. Spenser didn't know how people could be writing in, since he had never seen the station's logo or address onscreen. The fan letters asked Nasta to satisfy various whims, urges and desires. Some wanted exotic vacations, some wanted expensive cars, others wanted jewelry or furs or love or sex.

Nasta gave out "prescriptions." He told the people exactly what they must do in order to satisfy their wildest whims and urges. He prescribed sins for them to commit. Sometimes the sins were venial: little white lies or tiny acts of malice or spite. Other times they were mortal: rape, robbery, murder or worse. These sins had to be "taken" like doses of medicine.

Spenser figured it was all a gag. Nobody really wrote in. Doc Nasta just had a weird and maybe slightly evil sense of humor - because of whatever kind of accident that had caused his disfigurement. It certainly wasn't an electric chair, or he'd be dead. Maybe he got burnt by a hot wire in his own basement. He was so ugly it was easy to see why he couldn't get a job hosting a regular network show.

With a chuckle, Nasta announced that one of his fans had sent in a homemade videotape to prove that she had "followed doctor's orders." The tape looked amazingly real, but Spenser figured it for a fake. No way could anybody get away with showing such a thing on TV, even on a cable channel. Some fat guy in loud pajamas was being stabbed over and over by some skinny gray-haired old woman. The fat guy was groaning and screaming, blood flying all over the place, splashing the walls and soaking the mattress.

Triple Six started singing The *Devil Made Me Do It to Ya,* as the images got wilder, crazier, sexier. Spenser was riveted to the TV, horrified yet enthralled. Not only the band members but everybody in the music video began copulating with each other - right on the air!

Then Elena appeared on the screen, wearing something flimsily transparent. She smiled seductively, undulating to the beat of the music.

Spenser cried out her name, "Elena...Elena!"

She beckoned to him. He got to his feet.

He found himself in the TV screen. Suddenly, unaccountably, he was a part of the music video...the beat wilder, crazier...people copulating all around him.

They fell into each other's arms, kissing passionately, their bodies writhing hotly together.

She pulled away. She kissed her fingertips and touched them to his lips.

Then Nasta's voice intruded. "Spenser Katz?"

Spenser sat up in bed startled. He still had his clothes on. His forehead was beaded with sweat. He gawked and stared - Nasta had come into his room. Behind him the Triple Six video still blasted on the TV screen, its denizens continuing their orgy.

Nasta said, "Spenser Katz, you have just had a brief trip into my world, a special treat reserved for my disciples."

"But I'm not one of them," Spenser blurted.

"Not quite yet, for you have not fulfilled your initiation. But soon you shall do so. That is why I have allowed you to sample the delights that await you once you join my Medicine Show."

"You're kidding! This can't be happening!"

"It can be, and it is. And now I have a prescription for you."

"What... sort of... prescription?"

Nasta emitted a sly chuckle, his waxed mustache twitching, his face wounds oozing. "You want her badly, don't you? Well, take my prescription, and she shall be yours."

"Elena?" Spenser murmured incredulously.

"None other."

"What do I have to do?"

"Kill her."

"Never!"

"Oh, but you see," Doc Nasta said soothingly, "in giving her the gift of death, you both shall become more alive. Both of you will join my show. Eternally you will feel and understand a level of ecstasy that is unknown to mortals."

"Who *are* you?" Spenser cried.

"Never mind," said Nasta, and his oily laugh reverberated as he dematerialized on the TV screen and the screen rapidly dissolved into static.

The very next day, Spenser got Elena to come to his room by telling her he had gotten the box working.

It turned out to be true! The box *was* working!

Elena sat on the edge of the bed next to Spenser, her short skirt hiked up, her creamy thighs showing. He didn't say, "See, I told ya, Doc Nasta is real," he just smiled and smiled, watching her take it all in.

Nasta said, "A new disciple will join us today, along with his lady love. I have given him a prescription that he is bound to follow."

Spenser got goosebumps, partly from fear of what he was about to do, and partly from the thrill of being mentioned on the television.

Triple Six blasted into the first chords of *The Devil Made Me Do It to Ya.*

Soon the orgy started.

Elena jumped up, covering her eyes, yelling, "Turn it off! Turn it *off!*"

Spenser pounced, seizing her throat and squeezing hard. She barely made a gurgle, but she pounded and scratched at him, her eyes bulging. He choked her harder. Her tongue came out between her perfect white teeth, oozing spittle and turning purple.

He kept choking even after she went totally limp and sagged at the ends of his achingly weary arms. Then at last he let her sink onto the bed, half on and half off, till she thudded to the floor.

He looked at the screen. Triple Six was blasting. The orgy was in full sway.

He looked at Elena's dead body, shuddered, and closed his eyes.

Suddenly the music was surrounding them both and they were *in* the TV. He was more alive than he had ever felt. And Elena was alive, too - gorgeously and nakedly alive in his arms - and he reveled in an orgasm that overcame him, sweeping him to a pinnacle of erotic delight...

But something was wrong.

Elena's skin was burnt and oozing like Nasta's, peeling away from her face.

He touched his own face, which suddenly felt as if it was on fire, and a huge gob of burning, oozing flesh stuck to his hand. He stared at the gob, then frantically tried to paste it back where it belonged and pat it into place.

Elena laughed. Her breasts were flat and rotted, her abdomen split wide open, stinking of decay.

Nasta chuckled. Standing over Spenser, he said, "Welcome to the Medicine Show!"

He wished he would wake up. But he didn't. And now he knew from where the show was broadcast. And he understood who Nasta really was.

FOREVER AGO SUNSHINE
By Wol-vriey Jesuto

Always be sure to read what you're signing.

Wol-vriey Jesuto is Nigerian and quite tall. He currently resides in a state of uneasy stalemate with his threatening-to-thin-beyond-redemption hair, and believes there actually are things that go bump in the night. As you will see in this tale, Wol-vriey recycles the ridiculous into reasonable reality for the reader.
His WEIRRRD fiction philosophy? WEIRRRD = Warp/Write Everything into Realistic Ridiculous Readable Distorted Dream Dimension Descriptions.

*A free PDF of his WEIRRRD book **Invasion Of The Ass Chickens** can be downloaded from his blog: **oddityfarm.wordpress.com**. A number of his other assaults on polite literature can be read online at **newfleshmagazine.blogspot.com**. He's also the agent provocateur behind the band Rocksurface (www.myspace.com/rock.ng).*

1.

You're seated at the table, as always. There was once upon a time when you weren't seated there, but that was forever ago--seems way back before you were born even.

You're a prisoner. Your wrists are shackled to the table facing you, your ankles to the sides of your metal chair. Both table and chair are bolted to the floor.

Your right wrist shackle is separated from its table restraint by a foot of chain so you can move your hand to your mouth when you need to eat.

Seeing as you never alter your posture, you're now adept at sleeping sitting upright.

You've just woken up.

The door opens and Ms. Sexy minces in, bearing her tray of medicines and breakfast. You look at her in learned apprehension, dread concerning what's about to happen to you now. Again, for the nth time.

Ms. Sexy *isn't* sexy in the least, you think, though her cute white nurse's uniform is cut way too high for a nurse, its hem more than halfway up her thighs. In addition, and you think intentionally, she's popped several buttons off its top, so she appears to be wearing a low-cut party dress. Her breasts are small, almost invisible, and her legs are scrawny, in addition to which, she has over-large feet.

Her face is passable, a handsome spinster's--a wide fleshy mouth, small nose, calm blue eyes, and black hair done up in a bun.

She never wears makeup.

You like her bunned hair, but it doesn't make Ms. Sexy any sexier.

You've always assumed that's her name: 'Ms. Sexy' is what's written on her white nametag.

"I'm the only game in town, as far as you're concerned," she says, answering your unvoiced question.

She walks over to your table, and puts down her tray. As usual breakfast is a bottle of cola and a Huckleberry Finn sandwich. You poke the Huck Finn with a finger, to make sure it's dead. They played a trick on you once, serving you a doped Huck Finn which woke up screaming when you bit through its legs. Shit, you couldn't eat anything for two days after that.

You satisfy yourself however that today's Huck Finn *is* dead, and relax a little.

"So how do you feel today Andy?" Ms. Sexy asks with a professional smile.

Her smile creeps you out, her teeth are perfectly even, and her canines project just that bit too far down. You always have the feeling she'd love to bite a chunk out of you.

You don't reply, rather point to your left forearm, from which a half-grown hairless rabbit projects. The result of yesterday's shot.

Ms. Sexy smiles. "Oh, we'll take that off tomorrow. I know it hurts a little, but don't worry Andy, I've got just the thing for you." She picks a large syringe full of green liquid off her tray and swabs your arm.

You look at her startled. "What?"

"Just the next test."

You slump back in your seat, already feeling unwell with a capital 'U' as the drug begins taking effect.

Ms. Sexy reaches below you and removes your chamber pot. She gives you a sponge bath, smiling with amusement at your wormlike penis. "So you still don't find me attractive? That's a real shame: I've told you: I'm the only game in town."

You make no response.

Ms. Sexy spits in your hair and rubs the spittle into shampoo lather on your scalp, working it into a foam, then she finishes your sponge bath.

She towels you dry, then after cleaning and disinfecting the underside of your chair, exits the room, taking the chamber pot with her.

She's back in three minutes flat with a fresh commode, which she replaces beneath your seat.

"You're nice and clean for today now," she says. She pushes your breakfast tray at you, and then minces off again. "See you this evening."

She *always* minces.

Once she's gone, you stare at the overhead lamp in its metal bracket, and wish you'd never signed that damn petition.

***

"Please sir, can you spare a minute?"

The girl had been young and pretty, nothing like Ms. Sexy. You'd listened to her because you liked the sound of her voice, not because you cared about stopping animal lab testing, which was what she was proselytizing.

You'd signed the petition, appending your signature after that of a Mr. Lionel Jackson.

"Thanks sir," she'd said when you handed her back her pen, her smile dissolving, and promptly walked off to proposition the next person.

Afterwards, you'd felt cheated by her attitude; there had been something professionally perfunctory about the way she'd broken off your brief social interaction, as though from the offset, all her friendliness had been camouflage, and she'd simply intended using you to achieve her own selfish ethical ends and discard you afterward.

Like a hooker who was only after you for your money, she'd romanced you for your signature and left. You'd felt dirty, like tissue must feel after its been used in the toilet.

Well screw her, you'd thought and promptly forgot both her and the lab animals she was campaigning for.

But you wouldn't forget her for long. Signing that petition had been the biggest mistake you ever made in your life.

Its 'substitution clause' had read: 'all signatories to this petition accept that they will be compulsorily used for laboratory and other miscellaneous experimental procedures, in place of all animals they succeed in freeing as a result of the success of this petition.'

No shit.

2.

You're seated at the table, as always, remembering that series of distant yesterdays when you weren't seated here, that forever ago sunshine.

Your skin has turned bright green from yesterday's injections. You look like a plant mutation, the sort of 'anti-radiation treatment' example protesters show during campaigns against using irradiated seed. Your dinner tray reflection has blood red eyes, like those of a rabid wolf.

Yesterday's rabbit had grown to full size now and hopped off your arm. It has skis in place of paws. It's a major distraction to you, hop-sliding around the room in endless stop-start motion. The noise of its metal runners scraping over the floor is worse than fingernails on a blackboard.

You feel you're about losing the little amount of your mind you've still got left.

"Shut the fuck up!" you yell at it. The hairless rabbit glares back at you. It bares its teeth and twitters. You're startled--its teeth are sharp and pointy, those of a carnivore.

You resolve not to annoy it until Ms. Sexy comes.

To mollify it, you throw it the Huck Finn in last night's leftover sandwich; better it have your dinner, than you for breakfast.

The rabbit makes the Huck Finn disappear with a rapidity you find sickeningly astounding. The dwarf is gone in three bites, only the rabbit's blood-stained muzzle shows that anything out of the ordinary has happened. Its whiskers now look like the 'positive' wire in an electric cable.

The rabbit resumes skiing around the room. The grating noise gets so bad you start praying Ms. Sexy comes soon.

3.

"Oh, it's so cute," Ms. Sexy says, when she finally does come. "You too, your skin's so . . . green . . . you're like a begonia without the flowers."

"It's a carnivore," you point out. "It ate my leftover Huckleberry Finn."

"I'll get you another," she replies curtly, "and one for the cute bunny also."

"It's driving me up the wall with its skiing, take it away, will you? Please?"

"No--it has as much right to this room as you do. Relax will you! At least you look like a plant--it's not going to try eating *you*. I'll work something out."

You concede defeat.

She removes this morning's breakfast from the tray and sets it before you--Huck Finn sandwiches and cola as always. Then she picks up a syringe filled with a silver compound off the tray and says: "Please stick out your tongue."

You refuse. She smiles evilly, then reaches between your legs with her left hand and grabs your testicles. She fondles them lovingly, savoring the pain she's about to give you. "Now don't be a prick Andy, stick out your tongue, or you know what I'll do."

You know what she'll do, so you stick out your tongue and take your medicine--a spike deep into the meat of your tongue, which makes you think about death and dying.

"Good boy." Still holding the hypo, Ms. Sexy minces over to the rabbit. It waits for her, allows her to pick it up. You see that she's kept a little of the silver liquid in the syringe.

"Aren't you supposed to be against animal testing?"

She ignores you. "And a little shot for the cute bunny too," she says, stabbing it in its right ear.

The rabbit squeaks, but make no effort to escape. She puts it back on the floor, where it promptly falls asleep.

She bathes you and sanitizes you as usual, then leaves.

4.

The effects of the shot become evident the next time you relieve yourself in the floor pan beneath the table.

Your urine is silver in color and thickens into a stinky black sludge once it's out of your body. You're thankful the sludge isn't *moving*--like it happened that time she gave you that red strawberry liquid to drink.

In addition your veins all turn silver, and your head aches like you've two separate migraines waging the headache world war for control of your pain centers.

Also, you seem to have developed a slight magnetic ability; the edge of your breakfast tray lifts above the table when you place your hand above it. You already know it's nothing really useful--using the ability seems to amplify your already amplified dual migraines further, but maybe Ms. Sexy will be impressed.

The effects of the chemical on the rabbit, are much more mundane. It just sleeps and sleeps and sleeps and sleeps, snoring like an overweight human being.

It snores so fucking loud, its nasal emissions sound like the Hollywood soundtrack to the migraine war in your head.

You start screaming at it to wake up and start skiing again.

5.

"We're in luck," Ms. Sexy says, when next she visits you. "I've been able to kill two birds with one stone."

You've no idea what she's tattling about, but you know it's bad. *It can't be good*; nothing has been good since you signed that damn petition and wound up here.

Your warring migraines have now declared a ceasefire, though you're still peeing the same silver-urine-turning-to-black-sludge, and you're still magnetic.

The rabbit is also awake again; it's been skiing round your cell for the past two hours, a blur circle. Thankfully it both stopped and made itself scarce the moment Ms. Sexy arrived.

Ms. Sexy pokes her head outside for a moment. "You can come in now Marcie."

Marcie's here? Shit, no!

The door opens wider behind Ms. Sexy and your wife Marcella walks in.

You gasp.

Her eyes are as vacant as a parking lot after closing hours. In addition, she's been shaven bald and has a brown goat growing out of the left side of her head.

She's also butt-naked, and has finally gotten the breast implants you always wanted her to. She's now a 36C.

"Marcie," you gasp, "are you okay?" You already know this is the world's most stupid question before you ask it: it's obvious she's not okay, not in the least bit.

In response, she bleats. Marcie bleats. You see her head-goat not-moving its mouth like a ventriloquist, and Marcie bleats.

She's totally fucked-up. Even worse fucked-up than you are.

You lose it big time.

"What have you done to her, you psychotic bitch?" you scream at Ms. Sexy, your sanity beginning to fracture.

Concerned for your mental stability, Ms. Sexy brings you back to both docility and seamless sanity immediately, by reaching between your legs and squeezing your balls soprano-hard. Your growl dwindles to a comic-opera whimper. "Now Andy, what have I taught you about using bad language?"

"I'm sorry Ms. Sexy," you gasp/whimper/plead.

She smiles, lets go of your testicles. "Good boy." And my name's not Sexy, it's Lovely."

You look at her like she's joking, then you see her name tag's been changed; 'Ms. Lovely', it now reads.

"But your name's always been 'Sexy'," you gasp.

She smiles at you. "No it hasn't. I've always been this version of myself."

You smile your best castrato smile, realizing you're wrong after all--her name *has* always been Lovely, how in hell did you forget?

Your wife Marcie hasn't moved since she's entered the room. She just stands there, a Statue of Liberty expression on her face.

Ms. Lovely notices you looking at her. "I was saying I've killed two birds with one stone. But first I'll explain. Just like you, she signed a 'Stop Animal Testing' petition."

Shit, you think--how could Marcie have been so dumb? Then you remember how easily you were taken in yourself, preyed on by that pretty girl with her toothpaste ad smile.

But that's different, you reason; Marcie should have recognized her scam a mile off--women's intuition, or just plain feminine suspicion of other females.

Whatever, you're both equally fucked.

Ms. Lovely has stopped speaking so you could digest her bad news that your wife is no smarter than you are. Now she continues: "I thought it would be nice to put the two of you together. No sex is permitted, but it's the thought that counts . . ."

"You said *two* things," you venture tentatively, certain you're not going to like the other, "What's the other?"

"Your wife can resolve your rodent trouble."

This is obvious bullshit. How can fucked-up Marcie, with a goat growing out the side of her head, blank-eyed bleating Marcie, resolve anything? You're not sure she even has a personality anymore.

Ms. Lovely looks around for the skiing rabbit. The rabbit is now seated on its haunches in a corner, its fore-skis held up before its face as if it's VERY scared of Ms. Lovely.

You think the rabbit is VERY smart to be VERY scared of Ms. Lovely.

"I've got a present for you cute bunny," she calls to it. "I've got you your very own snow machine. Now you can ski all you want." She turns to Marcie: "Start snowing Marcie."

You wait, unsure what will happen, and definitely aren't expecting what does.

Marcie lifts both hands to her breasts and begins to squeeze them, like she always does when she comes when you give her cunnilingus. Clouds of fluffy white snowflakes spurt from her nipples.

Her face is as expressionless as a corpse's. On Ms. Lovely's command, she paces the cell, spraying a thick layer of white frost everywhere.

It takes the rabbit a while to cotton on to what the snow is for. Finally however, after Marcie's third round, when the ice crystals are a foot deep, it takes its first tentative steps onto it. Soon it's skiing like a pro, zipping around the room, between both Marcie's and Ms. Lovely's legs at speeds which make you dizzy to watch.

Thankfully, it no longer makes the horrible nails-on-blackboard noise.

"Okay Marcie, that's enough for now." She points to a corner and Marcie marches into it and positions herself there, turning to stare blankly at you. "Top up the ice occasionally Marcie."

Marcie bleats her response.

Ms. Lovely now attends to routine matters. She serves you your unvarying Huckleberry Finn sandwich and cola breakfast.

"What's that?" you ask, pointing to a wrapped food pack which smells better than your sandwich. She unwraps it. "Roasted Tom Sawyers for the bunny."

You stare at the cooked dwarfs hungrily. "May I *please* have one?--they look delicious."

"No, I said they're the *bunny's*--it needs to keep its strength up." She walks over and drops the package in the bunny's favorite corner.

You know Ms. Lovely better than to ask her again. To get your own back at her you don't tell her that the last shot made you magnetic.

When Ms. Lovely lifts and examines the contents of your chamber pot, you discover you were VERY wrong about its contents inertia. Your last poop is a copiously quivering silver jelly. When Ms. Lovely prods it with a fork, it opens a pair of cow-eyes and blinks at you both. You're very traumatized by this.

"Nice, nice," Ms. Lovely says as if vibrating silver poop with cow-eyes really is nice.

She cleans you off as usual, disinfects you, draws some blood from your silver veins into a syringe, gives you today's shot, nods, and leaves with the blinking poop.

After she's gone, you stare at Marcie for a long time, while she bleats back at you.

Suddenly, you can't take this shit anymore and you burst into tears.

6.

This latest shot melts your brain. It mugs you with a psychic cosh. Everything becomes larger, more vivid, more intense. You are suddenly able to interpret non-existent meanings.

Marcie is THE sex goddess, more beautiful and desirable than any woman should be legally permitted to be. You want to strip her skinless so she'll be really naked, and then fuck her to death a million times over. You'll incinerate the world in the blaze of your cumulative joint orgasms, and then you'll both pee on the flames together to put them out.

Put out humanity's fire with freezing golden showers.

The snow is COLD. You're in a fridge shivering, and this motherfucking skiing rabbit will most definitely win the Olympic Slalom gold medal if it keeps with this current training routine.

Damn, this bunny's good.

You pick up your sandwich, and take a bite, and yeeeeessssss, it's the meal to end all meals. And even though Ms. Lovely's tricked you again, slipping a doped and alive Huck Finn inside your bun instead of a cooked one, you don't care, you eat that sucker, turning it round and biting its head off when it starts screaming. It tastes better than a roast Tom Sawyer or Mark Twain even.

You chew and chew on its tiny brain, crunching its bones, relishing both the taste and feel of blood-soggy bread between your lips.

Afterwards you see your reflection in the breakfast tray. There's red dribbling down your chin. It matches your eyes. You dab it away with a crust of bread.

Sheeeiiit, now *that* was a meal.

The world is fucking fantastic. You feel like masturbating, but your wrist chain means your hand can't reach your penis, so you simply shit and piss yourself instead.

After a while you calm down and watch Marcie walk round the room spraying a fresh layer of snow. You are now able to accurately count the number of snowflakes she's ejecting from each nipple with each spurt, as well as correctly predict the number to come.

You're certain Ms. Lovely, bless her ultra-sexy ass, will be really pleased.

7.

Tonight, you're unable to sleep. The rabbit is still skiing maniacally around your cell, your wife Marcie still stands in her corner, spurting ice flakes from her breasts, squeezing them for all she's worth.

You wonder if her head-goat is making her malfunction. It's HUGE now.

The rabbit occasionally stops below Marcie to bask in the snow. It sits back on its haunches and bows to Marcie, letting her snowflakes pour over it, till it's half-buried in them. You can see it clearly thinks she's a goddess.

Though extremely grateful that the damn rabbit no longer makes noise while locomoting about, you're growing more scared by the minute.

Then there's a noise above you.

You look up, see a trapdoor has opened in the ceiling, a three-foot-square concrete flap dangles down, swinging delicately as though concrete is paper.

Through the flap you see a spaceship hovering above your cell. It's a replica of those 'golden age' sci-fi movie ships--all brass and tin spheres and curlicues. A bright light shines out of its bottom.

A ladder descends through the light in the ship's bottom. Four tiny figures descend the ladder, dropping into your cell.

They're all totally clothed in white, and have totally white skin. In addition, they have long white beards and eyebrows, and look like wise gnomes without the wisdom.

They look so much like Huckleberry Finns or Tom Sawyers that you're glad you've finished dinner before they arrived.

"Greetings Andy," they say. "We're the Great White Hunters from the planet Jazz . We're here on a hunting expedition, collecting unique specimens from all over the universe."

"Me?" you ask in horror, too scared to even wonder how they know your name.

"No, we've already caught enough green-skinned people. We'd considered taking you regardless, but your magnetic powers will screw up our starship's steering mechanisms."

He shrugs at you. "It's your skiing rabbit we want. It's a great curiosity to us. We're sure it will be a major attraction in our zoo."

"You're welcome to it." You're relieved--Ms. Lovely isn't the only one able to kill two birds with one stone.

Three of the Great White Hunters stalk and corner the skiing rabbit in a corner of the cell, holding a table tennis net before it.

The rabbit leaps at them, decapitating one with its skis, using a kung fu move the likes of which you've never seen before. While it's busy eating its victim, the other two wrap it up in the table tennis net, along with their dead comrade. They drag the bunny across to their rope ladder and begin hooking it up.

The fourth Great White Hunter nods his approbation and returns his attention to you.

"That's done. Also, we need to take its snow maker. Jazz is a very hot world."

You stare at Marcie, now standing silent in her corner, her head-goat almost ready to drop off her. The goat is now precariously balanced on her head. It's still attached to her skull by its rear hooves and will end up dangling upside down if it slips.

82

"No," you say. "She stays."

"Sorry Andy, but she's coming with us."

"You can't have her," you scream. "She's my wife! Let her go! Let Marcie GO!!"

You're hoping your screaming will alert Ms. Lovely to your danger, but you know this is futile--Ms. Lovely has never responded to your shouting about anything. She probably thinks the last shot she gave you is taking effect.

"The rabbit will be less of an attraction in our zoo if it cannot ski," the little white man says amiably. "Therefore we must have the snow machine woman. From what we've seen, Earth is *half-full* of women--marry another one."

You stare in horror as they tie Marcie up in a sling and lift her up out through the ceiling-hole. She bleats at you.

The last Great White Hunter ascends after her.

A few moments later, the rope ladder descends again, with a laden sling. The brown goat from Marcie's head steps out of it and bleats at you.

A dread worse than any you've ever known falls on you through the ceiling along with the goat.

You throw it a bread bun, are relieved when it eats it. You both stare at each other. You're inexplicably very scared of this innocuous-seeming animal, certain it'll shortly morph into a T-Rex or demon or sabre-toothed goat and eat you.

Above, there's the hum of engines. The brass-tin spaceship dwindles to a pinpoint in the night sky. The ceiling flap closes over its departure.

The goat lies on its side and chews the cud through the night hours. You don't dare sleep. Whenever you look its way, you always find its yellow eyes fixed on you.

Scared out of your wit's wits Andy, you pray for morning, pray for Ms. Lovely to quickly come give you your next shot.

It seems like forever ago since her comfortingly familiar evil presence was last here.

HONEY-DO
By Nikko Lee

The family that preys together stays together.

*Nikko Lee is a scientific curator who enjoys writing paranormal fiction. She was born in Canada and moved to Bar Harbor, Maine, after completing a PhD in Zoology and post-doctoral training. Her erotic fiction is published under the pen name Nikko Lee, and she blogs at **nikkolee.squarespace.com**.*

The warning siren droned in the background as Josh Connolly pulled up to the ten-foot, reinforced steel gates of Green Orchards. Three men in full-body Kevlar armor approached the leaf green Prius with measured steps, semi-automatic assault rifles locked on Josh. An unexpected sneeze was as likely to be met with a triple tap as a God-bless.

"Hey, Thompson," Josh greeted the point guard with a familiar but slow wave. "Sounds like there's trouble by the river."

"Another day, another killing rampage." Corporal Steve Thompson's tone was friendly, but the assault rifle's red laser guide danced on Josh's forehead. "ID, arms, and trunk, Josh. You know the drill."

Josh popped the trunk release then dangled his Green Orchards' residence identification badge out the car window. His sleeves were pulled back to show the unmarked skin of his arms. Another corporal aimed a square-nosed sensor at Josh's car while his eyes remained fixed on the read-out screen and the third checked the trunk.

"Heart rate elevated, but within normal parameters. Temperature normal. Infra-red scan normal." The corporal didn't even look at Josh as he spoke. One reading out of range meant a strip-search for bite marks at best and a bullet through the brain at worst. "No sign of infection."

"You going to Jim's for poker on Saturday?" Thompson asked as he peered into the car for his customary inspection.

Josh's briefcase and a grocery bag topped with a bouquet occupied the passenger seat.

"Only if I get June's honey-do list finished," Josh replied with a semi-defeated shrug and pointed to the drop clothes piled in the back seat. "She's wants all the upper rooms repainted this weekend."

"She's a real ball-buster, isn't she?" Corporal Thompson joked as he waved towards the tower ringed in tinted, bulletproof glass. "Open the gates."

"Yeah, but I would be lost without her," Josh said then he pulled away from the gate, slow and steady.

The gated community was nearly half an hour commute from his downtown firm, but it was the only place June would consider raising a family. Every house in the community was built according to one of three floor plans. Everything from the length of the grass in the front lawn to color-themed flowerbeds was regulated by Green Orchards' owners association. They kept the world within their guarded gates clean and polished no matter how messy the world outside got.

Josh waved to a neighbor who tended her red, white, and blue flowerbeds while her daughters played hopscotch in the driveway. She returned Josh's cheerful wave before turning her attention back to her garden.

Down the near identical streets, Josh drove until he spotted the red, white, and blue flowerbeds and perfectly manicured lawn June was so proud of. She had fallen in love with the gated community the first time she'd seen the brochure. It was a little out of their price range, but Josh could never deny her anything. All the late nights and weekends at the office had been worth it to give June the home she wanted to raise their children in.

"Honey, I'm home," Josh called as he entered the house and locked the side door to the garage behind him.

The sea breeze blue house with a pristine white door was as quiet as a graveyard. He hung his coat in the front closet and exchanged his work shoes for the slippers June insisted he wear inside. Even though he rarely did more than venture from the house to his car to his office and back again, June didn't tolerate her floors and carpets being anything less than spotless.

In the kitchen, Josh's weekend honey-do list hung on the fridge written in June's flowing and looping letters. Regardless of how many hours he devoted to it, there was always some chore he needed to take care of. Not that he dared overlook a single item on it. There wasn't a speck of dust in the house or a dirty dish in the sink that escaped June's keen eye.

Josh didn't mind. June knew what she wanted and was never shy about getting it. When she had decided they should get married, he had been over the moon with joy. When she had told him that it was time to start a family, Josh had been more than happy to oblige her crazy ovulation schedule and the specialized positions that would have made a contortionist blush.

The far-off sounds of children laughing and birds chirping drifted in through the open windows.

"June, I have a surprise for you," Josh called.

From the grocery bag, Josh picked up the bouquet of fresh cut daffodils and snowdrops. Their delicate, sweet scent reminded Josh of early spring evenings spent working the flower beds with June. Under the other arm, Josh clutched a wrapped parcel the size of a roast to his side as he turned the series of deadbolt locks on the basement door. When the last lock clicked open, the parcel slipped from his grasp and landed on the floor with a dull thud. Crimson liquid seeped through the waxy paper. Josh quickly scooped up the package before a single drop landed on the floor.

A blast of floral-scented hot air struck Josh as he opened the basement door and peered down the long staircase. Below him, only a flickering fluorescent bulb lit the basement. The creaking of the stairs beneath his weight was greeted by a soft, low moan. At the bottom, Josh's eyes focused on the canopy bed that June had spent months searching every specialty furniture store in the Twin City area for.

On top of the stripped mattress, June was splayed out. Her wrists and ankles chained to the bed frame. Josh drank in the sight of her.

June's body undulated like a dreaming snake, eyes half-open. Her tussled auburn hair tumbled around her face. Piercing green pupils rimmed in crimson were surrounded by a sea of red. The blood-sweat sheen on her ashen skin gave June an almost life-like appearance, and the heated basement always kept her flesh warm and pliant.

When she caught his scent, her undulations took on an urgent rhythm. Her eyes locked on the package he carried. Delicious, guttural moans bubbled from June's throat. Her whole body reacted to her hunger. Lips reddened. Nipples hardened. The soft skin of her inner thighs made a silky sound as she slid her legs together and apart. The mattress beneath her butt darkened from her growing wetness. June's hunger for living nourishment was insatiable. It consumed her body and mind until she became pure want.

At first, Josh had tried to sate her hunger with her favorite foods. They only reduced her to a howling, sobbing wreck. If she went without sustenance for too long, her body started to digest itself. The only thing that satisfied her was meat, raw and as close to living as Josh could manage without presenting her with living prey. He had already decided he'd be willing to do that if it came to a choice between June and the life of another.

He placed the package on the dresser and replaced the withering flowers in the vase.

"How was your day, honey?" Josh asked. "I landed the Patterson account today. Don't worry, I already told them that I wouldn't work late nights. Family is my priority, and they respect that."

Josh eyed June's ruby lips streaked with cuts from her incessant gnawing. Behind them were razor-sharp teeth that could strip flesh from bone in a matter of seconds. As much as he missed the feel of June's lips on his or her playful tongue dancing across his skin, Josh had learned to keep his distance from her mouth. June's tongue darted suggestively over her lips as if she could hear his thoughts. Although maybe she had spotted his thickening erection in his pants. June's hunger did something indescribable to Josh. He wanted to feed her, to protect her, to give her anything and everything she craved.

First, he needed to make sure she was clean and comfortable. June had always been meticulous about her appearance, and now it was up to Josh to care for her. She had already torn to shreds the clothes Josh had attempted to dress her. With the basement as hot as a sauna, she didn't need to wear anything to keep her warm. There was no one else to appear respectable for. June had once admitted to Josh on a hot summer night that she actually preferred the feel of air against her skin. Josh would wash June's body and keep her hair brushed. She would tolerate that much, if only because it brought him almost close enough for her to bite him.

"You are so beautiful." Josh admired June's writhing body as he cleaned the blood-sweat from her brow.

The damp cloth cleaned her skin and drew a tremulous sigh from June. Her eyes were riveted on Josh's wrist, inches from her gaping mouth. A few near bites were enough to make him cautious about getting anywhere near that hungry mouth of hers. If anything happened to Josh, there would be no one to look after June.

"I hope you weren't too bored today." Josh continued to recount the mundane details of his day as he washed her.

Josh dragged the cotton washcloth down the length of June's body, pausing only to rinse it in a basin of fresh water. The throbbing of his erection grew painful if he lingered too long on her supple breasts, lithe arms, or powerful thighs.

The gentle motions of the cloth on her skin seemed excite June. Her indecipherable moans and gurgles grew impatient with each stroke.

Setting the washcloth and basin on the dresser, Josh unwrapped the package he had picked up at the butcher's on his way home. Fresh meat drove June wild. It had taken Josh nearly a month to find a butcher that catered to his peculiar requests for meat killed while he waited. Josh never asked where the meat came from, and the butcher never asked whom it was for.

"Just a little something to tide you over until the main course," Josh said as he sliced off a hunk of warm, marbled meat.

June lurched off the bed as far as her chains would allow. Her head strained at the sight of the meat. Blood ran from Josh's fingers and dripped into her waiting mouth. His heart broke at the need in June's fierce and frustrated cries even as his member stiffened at the knowledge that he could satisfy her. He knew exactly how to ease her hunger, and he had no intention of making her wait. He dropped the piece into her waiting mouth. June swallowed it whole. Delight shined in her crimson-rimmed eyes and it was breathtaking. Sometimes Josh was tempted to unchain her, and let June consume him whole.

"Are you ready for me?" Josh asked as he stroked her cheek.

He pulled his fingers away just in time to miss one of June's fatal love bites. Her desperate moans turned into a demanding and insisting groan. Josh stripped down until he was as bare as June. His erection arched towards his belly as he knelt between June's spread legs. Her swollen sex glistened in the fluorescent basement lights. The sight was enough to make Josh say a prayer of thanks for the beauty before him.

As Josh inched towards June, she lifted her hips to meet him. Her thighs spread and tightened in anticipation. Josh slipped inside her in a single thrust. Her hungry sex tightened around his cock and milked it as he attempted to pull back for the next thrust. He always tried to start slow. The first time, June had been so hungry for him that she had brought him to release upon the first penetration. Josh was always conscientious about his lovemaking and wanted to make sure she was as satisfied as he knew he would be.

June's hips swiveled wildly as he struggled to hold on. His hands locked onto her hipbones. Her sex suckled his cock by rhythmically contracting around it. Her frenetic bucking was wild and uncontrolled. He tried to hold back and make it last as long as he could manage for her. But what June wanted more than anything was the living fluid that accompanied his release. It fed her hunger just as well as the freshest meat.

"June, I'm going to come," Josh warned his wife. Her eyes glistened with a need that urged him to abandon his last strand of self-control.

The slick slapping sound of their bodies merging filled the basement, but all Josh could hear were June's undead moans and his erratic grunts. When his eyes opened, he marveled at the change in his wife. A peaceful look of satisfaction replaced her pinched and starved expression. The frenetic want of her body settled into a stillness that assured Josh that he was doing what was best for June.

Josh supported his weight on rigid arms. He had to resist the urge to lie down beside her and melt his body to hers. June had nearly ripped out his jugular the last time he had tried to rest his head on her chest. Before long he pulled out and replaced the water in the basin. Most evenings Josh spent caring for June and doing the chores on the last honey-do list she had made before she had been infected.

"I have one more surprise for you, my dear." Josh smiled as he spoke. He would do whatever it took to hold on to some semblance of the life he once had. "I'll be right back."

With a sheet draped over June's calm body, Josh dressed in his clothes and headed back upstairs. Josh returned to the basement with a small, limp body in his arms. The tranquilized boy let out a soft moan as he started to come around. Josh set him down on a chair ten feet from June's bed. Her eyes were riveted on the boy while Josh locked a shackle around the boy's ankle.

"June, you remember Billy?" Josh asked as he checked the other end of the chain fixed to the wall with an iron bolt. "Eric and Tina's son? You met him at the company party last summer."

A gargling sound burbled from June's throat. Josh couldn't tell if June remembered the boy or not. He had hardly recognized Billy when he had first spotted him at Eric's abandoned house. Josh had gone to check on Eric when he hadn't been to work in a week, and no one had heard from him. Josh had found two bodies ripped to shreds and the five year old boy huddled behind the sofa. It was hard to tell how long the boy had been on his own, but he was as dirty as the torn clothes he wore. Everyone would assume that the boy had shared his parent's fate or worse. No one would be looking for him. This was his chance to give June what she truly wanted.

"Time to wake up, Billy." Josh shook the boy gently by the shoulders until his eyes fluttered open. "There's someone very special that I want you to meet."

The boy's mouth opened and an ear-piercing scream erupted from his small lungs.

Josh scrambled backwards as the boy raged towards him. Billy didn't stop until the chain attached to his foot reached its full length. The boy's momentum jerked him backwards to the ground, but he didn't stay there for long. Billy jumped to his feet and lunged again.

"He's going to take some looking after," Josh said to June.

They finally had the family that June had always wanted.

EVERY BITE
By Matthew Smallwood

Chef Hoy goes the extra mile to see that your dish is seasoned just right.

Matthew Smallwood is a native of West Virginia and a graduate of Buckhannon Upshur High School where he majored in lunch. He has worked for West Virginia Radio Corporation writing ad copy and has spent some time as a pro-wrestler and a correctional officer.

When not sleeping he writes and occasionally works but not very hard. Matthew is a fan of most fantasy and horror books and is working on a novel about the mountain state.

Apple pie, peach cobbler and Bavarian crème... Had he forgot any? Yes, strawberry. It slipped his mind because it was seasonal. "What's happening to me," he thought. In ten years of waiting tables he'd never forgotten a special, never stumbled when someone asked about the wine selection.

"But why today?"

"---Hey, Hoy, this is my steak here...since when do we top it with raspberry sauce?" Courtney was the newest server. She was young and pretty and stacked in all the right places. It was simply a matter of time before the new owner was giving her what he called 'the chef's selection' in the freezer. Hoy didn't turn around; he didn't say anything. It was loud in the kitchen - too many plates rattling.

Effram the dishwasher had his radio cranked on as high as it would go, filling the kitchen with Spanish rock and roll. Back when Hoy was a server, the chef ruled the kitchen. But anymore, he felt like he was second in command to the screeching guitars and snare drums. When Hoy was a lonely grunt waiting tables, there was a rule about no radios in the kitchen or the dish room, but somewhere along the way the rules stopped being important.

As the leader of the kitchen, Hoy blamed himself. His grandmother said, "God made men strong because they have to be able to lift the burden He sets upon them." Hoy always felt his burden was a boulder among pebbles, but so is the way of things. He also thought the new owner pranced around like a butterfly among bees.

Twelve-ounce steak, charbroiled chicken, creamy shrimp Alfredo…no ma'm, no artificial thickeners - our Alfredo sauce is made from scratch.

"Where am I?"

The room was darker - less bright. The color was fading like a red shirt machined washed to a dull pink. The sound carried all wrong - too much volume. Things were too loud.

"What's wrong with me?"

Cholesterol-friendly omelets, blueberry pancakes, and buttermilk biscuits with homemade apple butter – you also get a choice of either sausage or bacon. You see it costs more, because of our guarantee that the meat is one hundred percent hormone and steroid free. We don't like to brag, but you can trace the pig farm where we get our bacon all the way back to the Mayflower. That's right, the ship with the pilgrims.

"Hoy, my main man, I'm going to step out for a smoke. You

holler if you need anything okay?" Hoy set the cleaver down and gave Effram the thumbs up. "Hot in the dish room (whew!), like an oven. Hoy, what you think of that Courtney? Pretty senorita. And that Coolo?" Effram whistled and then he was gone.

Hoy's leg hurt, the room spun, and somewhere someone was laughing. It was hot, but he was shivering; and he thought he could see his breath. Hoy worried he was going to faint. Years ago when he was still taking culinary classes all day and waiting tables at night, he used to have dizzy spells. The doctor said it was stress and told him to relax. Easy to say, like telling the guy stuck on a roof not to look down. But gradually the spells passed, and after he became a chef they vanished all together - or so he thought, but it would seem they'd only gone dormant.

Lamb curry, veal cutlets in a light spinach sauce, swordfish and three-bean soup…Napoleon buried his son in a dress. Liars go to heaven 'cause hell hates the truth. It shouldn't make sense, but it does - perfectly clear.

There was blood and bone-gristle on the cutting board, and a bloody stump where his thumb should have been. He saw a trail of droplets and a red smear on the blender lid. Without a second thought, Hoy hit the puree button and watched what was left of his thumb dissolve into a gooey liquid mush.

As a boy, he would fall asleep watching the flames leap around his grandfather's fireplace. Staring at the shapes in the flames soothed him like a lullaby or a nightlight. He was thinking of the fire and the smell of his grandfather's cologne when he clicked off the blender and poured the contents into the tomato bisque. Hoy stirred it with his good hand and tasted it to make sure it hadn't been over-flavored. Success! The flavor was perfect. He added a dab of cooking salt and brought the cleaver down on his index finger, or what his teachers in culinary school called his pointing finger. Surprisingly, there was very little blood and no pain. There was a heat, which was something he didn't expect. Wasn't blood loss supposed to make your body temperature go down? Hoy was anything but cold. It felt like his stomach had turned into an oven running on high. He knocked off the tip of his already severed finger, leaving it in two meaty hunks - one with a fingernail and one without. The clean part went into the cake batter for the evening dessert and the rest went into the disposal.

Pulled pork with apricot dressing, Mediterranean pizza and stuffed green pepper soup... He forgot dates and couldn't remember how many miles before an oil change, but the specials were always right there. Temperature, recipes, and what was going bad, these he never forgot.

A server came in, muttering under her breath. She grabbed a bottle opener and left without sparing him a single glance. Hoy flicked his hand toward her back, splattering blood across the kitchen door.

He preheated the oven to four-fifty and greased a baking pan, while servers came and went - some of them speaking to him; some of them not. A cook is only as good as his ingredients, and taste is never something you want to sacrifice. True flavor knows nothing of compromise. While waiting for the oven to heat up, Hoy stepped into the freezer and pissed on the most expensive cuts of meat. He smeared blood on the wall and was admiring his work when he heard the oven's timer go off. Everything was almost ready.

Ingredients - it's all about using the best to assault the taste buds.

Passion goes into each dish. Every order is a torrid affair where nothing but the best will be tolerated. It can be infuriating to find yourself failing after trying so hard, but it really drove him to madness to see a customer shamelessly give up at the table. Before taking a single bite, they heap on the salt. They complain until the server brings out some hot sauce (which no self-respecting restaurant should have). And then, after all these injustices, they scrape off the garnish and leave a pile of veggies on the plate, just to shovel the food in without enjoying it. Pigs eat slop much the same way.

Hoy wanted to go out there and tell them there are no accidents. He could sit across the table and relieve them of their knife and fork.

If they didn't want to listen to what he had to say, then they could use their hands and eat like animals. He would pull their head up from the garlic potatoes and tell them everything is on that plate for a reason. The taste of tomato is there because it brings out the fullness of the meat. It's a delicate balance, worthy of appreciation - not something to be torn to pieces. You can pick an onion off a fast food burger, but you don't, *and he would repeat himself here*, "You don't eat around the mushrooms when you come to my kitchen!" Would they take the overtures out of Beethoven's fifth?

Hoy took a steak knife out of the dish tub and, with a firm grip on the handle, he drug it across his belly. The blade was dull and the cut barely broke the skin, but it was satisfying nonetheless. He did this with every knife in the tub. By the end, his stomach looked like a spider's web of red slashes - most of them still dripping blood.

All together kiddies: how can disease get spread? Come on, don't be shy... "Through blood," Hoy said to the empty kitchen. "Through blood, and not washing your hands." He spit on all the forks and put the spoons down his pants.

"From under cheese," he said. It was the idea of cheese that made him cuss. "Shit." He'd forgotten about the oven. A slip of the memory, even for a few seconds, and you could pull out a tray of burnt cornbread or smoldering piles of bones that use to be fish.

Baked ham smothered with brown sugar, fried clams (seasonal) with potato cakes and pineapple upside down cake.

Hoy had a cyst just above his belt line. It was as big as the eraser on a pencil and bothered him a great deal. A knot of flesh serving no purpose but to embarrass him - could even kill him if the news was to be believed. It only took a second to separate him from the cyst. With barely a flick of his wrist, the fleshy bump was in the pan already lost among the cloves of garlic and bay leaves. There was blood - more than he would have ever imagined. He felt his underwear filling up with it. He tried to ignore the pain, but the blood was running down his leg. His white pants were turning red.

Hoy prided himself for having the steady hands of a surgeon, but now they shook and had no strength or dexterity. He took a deep breath and tried to relax, but his good hand wouldn't stop shaking. He was tired and his legs were screaming for him to sit down. Hoy cut a long slash down each calf and dropped the knife into the kitchen sink. He'd need something else for the larger chunks.

Cibatta bread with avocado spread, shepherd's pie drizzled in pepper gravy with peach pit soup and Boston cream cake made with pure unbleached flour.

If my mother is related to your brother's uncle, but not your dad, then what is she? Eat is the only English word that can form the past tense of itself by moving the first letter to the end of the word.

Hoy helped himself to a long draw from the cooking wine. It was like drinking oil, but he hoped the alcohol would steady his nerves and his good hand.

"---Of a bitch," one of the servers said. It had to be the new girl, because the others knew how Hoy felt about swearing in the kitchen. He glanced over his shoulder, hoping to see her leaving, but she stood on the other side of the large cooking table, her face nearly hidden by stacks of plates, pots and pans.

"What's all over the door?" she asked. "It looks like blood. Did you cut yourself? Not very sanitary."

Hoy kept his back to her, using his good hand to hold the other one against his chest.

"Did you need something?" He wondered if she'd hear the trembling in his voice.

"Counseling!" she shouted, and then she giggled and dropped her voice. "Sorry, didn't mean to shout. It's just that guy; he's a real a real…a-hole."

Hoy said nothing. He put the cutting board in the kitchen sink and rinsed it off with cold water. Courtney was still standing there looking at him through a window of plates and breadbaskets.

"Hoy, this guy's complaining about the steak I took out. He says he ordered it well done and it was still bloody. Don't get mad, but he wants you to cook him a new one."

Hoy froze. His entire body went rigid. He turned off the water and cocked his head so she could hear him. "What did he do with the other one?"

"He ate it," she said. "He ate every bite and he didn't complain till I brought him the bill. He's talked to the hostess and refused to pay until we do something to make it right."

"What can we do?" Hoy asked, his lips moving just enough for the question to come out.

"I just can't face that jerk again," Courtney said, covering her face with her hands. "Hoy could you talk to him…?"

"Every bite," Hoy muttered, moving his hand across the knife rack till he found the cleaver.

"Hoy?" Her voice sounded weak and maybe scared.

He grabbed the cleaver and spun around trying to point at her with a bloody stump. "Tell him I'll be right out."

Courtney's eyes took in everything and she opened her mouth to scream, but nothing came out. Her mouth kept moving, but nothing escaped except a weak cry.

"Never mind," Hoy said, taking a practice swing with the cleaver. "I'll tell him myself." His head still shook, but he wasn't complaining. All you need in life is a good eye, the right tool and, of course, the perfect ingredients.

NOTHING REALLY SATISFIES
By Kelly R. Martin

Some addictions you just can't shake.

*Kelly R. Martin lives and works a day job for the US Government in West Virginia, USA. His night job is as the owner (and sole employee) of Myth/Logic Press (**www.mythlogicpress.com**). His published works at the time of this writing are **The Lucky Cricket Tales from the Reading Dragon Inn Book 1** and **Thomas the Poisoner Tales from the Reading Dragon Inn Book 2**. He is working on the third book of this series.*

It's early morning as I pull my car away from the drive through window. I've got a cup of black coffee in one hand, and a breakfast sandwich in my lap. I take a sip of the still too hot coffee and think this is good. This was what I had been wanting since I woke up this morning. This would satisfy my desire.

I pull into work at the free clinic. There is a line of people already waiting by the front door. Some of them just poor, many of them junkies, and even a few of them crazies who live on the streets.

Welcome to the world of socialized health care, now hurry up and wait. As I step out of my car and approach the employee only side entrance I see what looks like a junkie approaching me.

I move a little faster, and he does too. I think, "Shit, not again," as I make a run for the door. Another robbery attempt, or possibly worse – it could be a hopped up crazy looking for a fix. The junkie collides into me just as I hit the entry buzzer at the door. I push us both away from the side of the building, and we both start struggling and screaming as we roll around on the ground.

The crazy son-of-a-bitch bites me in the right forearm even drawing blood. I punch and pound him while yelling and screaming. I fight for all I'm worth, but he's clearly hopped up on something, crazy strong, and not feeling any pain at the moment.

Then I feel the unpleasant jolt of forty two thousand volts coursing through the crazy junkie's body and into mine. I spasm in the pain of unwillingly contracted muscles.

Phil the security guard from the clinic comes up with a look of regret plainly in his eyes, "Sorry about that Bob. You know how these junkies are, you just can't fight them one on one. You should be able to walk in a couple of minutes. The police should be here soon. Let me get some twist ties on this twist."

Later that morning I'm still sitting down at the local precinct looking into the beady eyes of the detective in the interview room. I'm hating being in this place again. It's nothing but unpleasant memories after all. The detective has a look like he knows I just have to be lying to him.

"Look that guy just came and jumped me. He's a junkie hopped up on who knows what kind of shit. I don't know why you think I can tell you anything more."

The detective has a little sneer, "Why are you working at the free clinic Robert?"

I look up at him, "You know I've got a record. What other kind of job do you think I can get? It's only shit jobs like the free clinic out there for a guy with a record you know."

The detective shakes his head, "How do we know you weren't dealing?"

I look down at the table, "You know I've never done that right? They won't let me anywhere near the methadone anyway. It's too tightly controlled. I just mop the floors and clean the toilets for junkies and crazies all day. That's all."

The detective looks at me, "Isn't it a condition of your release that you stay away from the criminal element?"

I get angry, "Go fuck yourself. You damn well know by now that my parole officer got me that job. I don't like the fucking junkies or crazies any better than you do."

The detective's brows bunch together, "We all know what you like, don't we creep? I'd rather deal with junkies than sickos like you. They're just pathetic, you're something else."

I glare at him, "Unless you've got some reason to hold me, we're done here."

The detective gets a wicked cop grin on his smug cop face, "That arm looks pretty bad, possibly infected. You might want to get that looked at. Try the free clinic if you can't afford a hospital."

I stand up to leave as he says, "Don't forget to report to your parole officer first."

***

Early that afternoon I'm sitting in my parole officer's shitty office in the shitty building in the shitty part of town. I can tell by looking at him that he's hating his shitty job, and hating to see my face once again two weeks early for our regular appointment. I try my best sheepish look.

"You know I wasn't part of this mess right? I'm just the victim here."

John blows smoke in my direction, "Yah, you're all just a bunch of victims here. Look son, I haven't got time for this bull shit. Were you dealing?"

"You know I don't deal."

John gives me a skeptical look, "All I know is that you've never been caught."

"Then why am I here then if I'm so damn careful?"

John nods, "That's true. You're a disorganized fuck when it comes to that. Nothing but chasing that monkey on your mind huh?"

"I take my meds like I'm told by the docs. I haven't offended for four years. Four years of monthly check-ins with no problems. Four years of that shit hole free clinic, and being robbed or assaulted twice now."

John took a long drag on his cigarette and blew out the smoke again, "Four years of satisfactory work reports without any significant complaints. I'll read the police report when it's done, but I don't see any problem here. Now get out and tell the next sad motherfucker outside to come in here to tell me his sob story."

Later that afternoon I'm sitting in the corner bar three blocks down from my house. It's the only bar I can go to because it's a close enough walk. I don't want the fucking pigs having any excuse to pick me up on a "driving while" charge. The place is a hole half filled with other pathetic losers, all regulars, but it's where I can get a cool beer to calm my nerves.

What a fuck awful day. The three things I hate the most: fights, cops, and my asshole chain-smoking parole officer all in one day. I wave the bartender to send another beer over my way and look at the fellow patrons. The usual old whores and hardcore alcoholics. Pickled livers in plenty. My arm is beginning to ache like a screaming banshee. That fucking hopped up junkie. I hope he's feeling worse than me wracked with withdrawal symptoms.

I pull my med bottle out of the jacket pocket and pop a little pill in my mouth as I take it down with my beer. The bottle label says not to mix with alcohol because it may cause drowsiness. Fuck that noise, it's only three blocks back home, and I'm not driving.

The old jukebox which still plays forty-five RPM singles kicks in with some music in the corner. It's some old Rolling Stones tune, but I can't quite remember the name. The song gets to the chorus before I recall it's Satisfaction or something like that. Well the song is right about that, this beer is satisfying shit about now.

***

Early that evening I stagger into my living room feeling like twenty pounds of wet concrete has been dropped over me. I think back to my pill bottle label. Fuck, they weren't kidding about mixing this shit with alcohol. My arm is throbbing and sore, my stomach is roiling with nausea. I push for the kitchen and toss out the contents of my stomach in a mighty heave into the sink. I turn the water on, to rinse out the sink, and another wave of powerful nausea hits. Fuck, it's going to be one of those evenings.

I wait a while dry heaving for a period before the nausea subsides. I've never used but I have a suspicion that this is what severe withdrawal must be like for a heroin junkie. Fuck, that junkie motherfucker must have had raw heroin on his teeth or shit. I'm coming down pretty hard. No wonder the cops thought I was dealing or something. I must have been already pretty high or something without realizing it.

My body is starting to cramp up in a painful manner. I look out the kitchen window across at the neighbor's house. Sally lives there. Sweet Sally as I think of her. Innocent, pretty Sally, just starting out on her own. On her own and all alone. The nausea hits again, and all thoughts of Sally flee my consciousness. There's nothing left to vacate from my stomach, so I grab the small garbage can and move back to the living room to lie down on the couch a bit.

Later that evening I wake in a chill sweat. My breathing is labored, and every nerve is singing a chorus of agony. How do junkies ever use knowing this is what is waiting in the wings? I wish Phil had shot that fucker in the head. I feel like I could be dying. My heartbeat is irregular, and my muscles are weak.

I frantically think about what to do. If I call emergency then the police will respond, then they'll insist on testing me for drugs. Fuck I don't even use. Fucking asshole junkie. What did you do to me? Ride it out or jail? Not just jail, but likely prison too once John gets his teeth into me. Fuck, I don't want to die. Even jail is better than dying.

I try to rise from the couch and tumble gracelessly onto the floor dumping over my empty kitchen garbage can where I left it next to the couch. I start crawling painfully over to where the kitchen phone is hanging on the wall.

***

The next morning I'm still lying on my living room floor. I'm somewhat stiff and sore from the night before. I momentarily fear the withdrawal sickness is stronger now than it has ever been. Yet I'm not quite as much in pain than I was half expecting though. I tentatively raise my head and shoulders up off the carpeting. No dizziness and better yet no nausea anymore. Maybe just maybe the withdrawal sickness has retreated some. I struggle to awkwardly rise looking out the window at the sun rising toward the East.

Then the desire strikes me. That hard to reach itch, that want, that need, that craving. Knowing I just can't get me no satisfaction. I lurch over toward my kitchen and start randomly peering into the cupboards and refrigerator even though I know what I hunger for isn't there. I hold out hope anyway since I've got nothing better to do at the moment.

I catch a glimpse of movement through the kitchen window. Someone walking past the window in the house across the way. Sally's house. Sweet, sweet Sally. She's got just what I want. I smack, smack, smack my lips in anticipation as the stirrings of excitement begin. I just want some girly action.

I shuffle over to my kitchen door, and I fumble with the handle. The sickness has left me uncoordinated, and even something as easy as opening a door becomes difficult. I try. I try. I try try try try try.

The door handle finally gives in to my persistent attempts and the door opens for me.

I think back trying to remember the number of times I've warned Sally. Sally still doesn't lock her back door no matter how often I've told her about the junkies, and worse, who live in this neighborhood. Sally's still young, and sweet, and unspoiled. She just doesn't understand. She's got just what I want.

I walk the short distance across my back yard into her back yard. I approach her door, and struggle to think about how I'm going to do this. I move as slowly as I can, and my hands obey me without too much shaking. I manage to turn her doorknob on the first try. Good Sally always reliable, still not locking your back door I see. Let me just come in to borrow that cup of sugar I need.

I step into her kitchen and everything is clean. I can smell baking muffins in the oven, but they aren't what I'm hungry for now. Sally has what I want. I can see her round the corner from the hallway and looking at me – a moment of shock and confusion. I don't belong there, and her mind hasn't caught up to the disconnect yet.

"Bob? What's going on? You look unwell. Is something wrong?"

I rush her. I press my forearm savagely against Sally's throat as we tumble in a tangle on her kitchen linoleum. Sally screams weakly through the pressure I'm placing on her neck. I tug and I pull viciously until I get the restraining cover out of the way. Sally's sweetness is revealed before my eyes. Sally stops struggling and I know she has accepted what is to happen now.

I grunt and moan as I satisfy my unquenchable craving. I think to myself as I look down into her emptied skull for any remaining morsels, licking blood from my lips, that nothing really satisfies quite like, "Brrraaains!"

DECORATIONS
By Nelson W. Pyles

**It's just not a family Christmas Tree unless
everyone joins in on the decorating.**

Nelson W. Pyles was born and raised in New Jersey. He currently resides in Pittsburgh, PA where in addition to being an author, he is also a performing musician. He just completed his first novel and is working on his second album. You can find more information about Nelson at **www.nelsonwpyles.com**.

Riley walked out of her kitchen and into the living room. There was a small tree with lights and tinsel. No ornaments – she hated them in spite of the urgings of her boyfriend to at least have a star on the top.

"It'll just look better, baby." He said that every year. Of course, what he usually said was much worse. Things that were terrible and demeaning. The worst thing he said though, next to "You know I love you," was the bigger lie.

"I won't hit you anymore."

That hurt worse than the actual hitting, because she knew it wasn't true. Of course she'd get hit again. Worse than the last time.

It was always the case. But she never, ever bent on the tree. It was the one thing that was hers and hers alone. Once a year she decorated it as she saw fit – lights and tinsel. Period.

But this year would be different.

She was wearing an apron and thick black rubber gloves. The floor around the Christmas tree was lined with plastic.

It had been six years since she first met Parker. He was handsome and funny. And, oh Christ, he was charming. She had never gone to bed with someone after knowing them only a few hours, but Parker was different. There was a connection – an almost instant attraction that she'd never had before, and she knew, he was it for her.

Four months in, he had hit her for the first time. Not a slap, but a punch, right in the stomach. She crumpled instantly – she was a very petite girl and Parker was over six foot three. He had played football in college (a lie, she later discovered) and had kept his physique. Riley had spilled a glass of wine on his white canvas hi top sneakers and he had gone through the roof.

"Oh Jesus, I'm sorry," she had said as the rich, merlot covered his left shoe. Parker's face distorted into a knot of fury and punched her as she stood up to get a rag to start the clean up.

"Sorry," he said sarcastically. "There, does that make it all better? Look at my fucking sneaker!"

From that moment on, she told herself that it was a fluke – they had been drinking, and well, she needed to be careful. Every punch since then, she had gone down the list of excuses for him because as much as she feared him, she loved him. She was still attracted to him. Still wanted him. He was the one and only after all.

And then, when enough had been enough, she realized she didn't love him. She hated herself for staying and had told him she was leaving. When she woke up in the hospital a week later and opted to not press charges, she began to formulate her plan.

She had seen him cry after that one.

"Oh baby," he sobbed. "Never ever again. You'll see. I love you so much. I don't know why I do it..."

She lay in bed looking at him and she kind of liked watching him cry. She knew it was the same old lines. The same old bullshit. She knew what she had to do, but needed to wait for a sign, and then, right after Thanksgiving, she knew.

The tree went up the day after. The smell of turkey and bread hung in the air like a cloud. It was eight thirty in the morning when Parker came down stairs and saw the tree as Riley threw on the last bit of tinsel.

"Another boring ass tree huh?" he asked. "Just try a fucking ball or a star. It'll just look better." And then he slumped off into the kitchen.

And now, it was Christmas Eve. They had blown off all invitations for a surprise Riley said she had for Parker. She'd been working on it all day, so he should go out for a few hours. She smiled at him and he left without a word.

She was ready. Riley turned the tree lights on and waited patiently for Parker to come home. Hopefully, he'd be home before Midnight, and he did not disappoint.

She heard the car door slam and she sprang to life. Darting into the kitchen, she hid behind the door that led to the basement. Most of the lights were off, and the only lights in the front of the house were the tree lights. She smiled.

The door was flung open and quickly slammed behind him.

"Fuckin' cold," muttered Parker. He was drunk. Perfect.

"In here, babe." Riley cooed and coiled herself.

"Got anything to drink?" he asked as he lumbered toward the kitchen. He walked in and turned the light on. He had a full three seconds to register that everything was covered in plastic – the stove, the counters, the floor – even the little swinging tail cat clock. He was about to speak, when Riley exploded from the basement door and caught Parker behind his right ear with a swing from a pipe wrench. He fell sideways and landed hard on the floor. She looked and saw no blood. He was out. She put the wrench on the plastic covered counter and got to work.

As Parker came around, he experienced several things at once. The first thing he noticed was that his head hurt very badly of course. The next was that "Holly Jolly Christmas" was skipping on the CD player that ran through several speakers all though the house. It was stuck on the "Somebody waits for you, kiss her once for me" line of the song, except it was only saying *"Somebody waits for you, kiss..."* over and over.

Then the pain from his hands came next. And, oh Christ, his legs. He was still on his back from the fall. He'd have to think about quitting drinking he thought as he tried to stand. He couldn't move. He opened his eyes and looked around. He was still on the floor of the kitchen and the lights were really bright.

"Babe," he croaked, "Baby, I fell. I don't feel..." He turned his head and started to vomit. He opened his eyes and blinked after he'd finished and saw the cabinet under the sink. It had red lines running down both doors.

"What's that?" Riley called from the other room? She padded brightly to the doorway to the kitchen. He moved his head up and saw her there in her apron and gloves. She was holding something wet.

"I think I fell...and I just yacked," he said.

"You did yack and you didn't fall. Just relax for a minute. Kay?" And she went back to whatever it was she was doing.

Parker started getting angry despite the pain. He was going to yell, but he was sweating. He reached up to rub his forehead and saw that there was a thick rubber tube like they have in hospitals tied around his elbow. The rest of his arm was missing. His eyes went wide. He lifted his other arm and saw a similar scene.

"What the..." he started to say and threw up again. He spat and tried to sit up using his legs. He looked down and saw that the same thing had happened to his legs. His head dropped to the floor and he passed out.

Somebody waits for you, kiss…

When he came to, he saw he was in the living room. That made him feel better for about three, maybe four seconds. Then he heard the CD was still skipping in the same spot.

Somebody waits…

"Merry Christmas, Parker." He heard Riley say, pleasantly. "I'm almost done with the tree. Do you like it?"

for you, kiss…

Parker couldn't speak. He turned his head and saw it for the first time.

She had put ornaments on the tree.

Somebody waits…

There were eight of his fingers with hooks through them, hanging off of the branches. His two hands retained the thumbs and were straining the branches they were on. His hands reminded him of the Fonz for some reason.

…for you…

Ten toes were also sporting their places on the tree, although the pinky toes were hard to see. He began to sob. His arms and legs had been cut into chops and hung with wire instead of hooks. The branches were bent nearly down, but the chunks of flesh were cut thin, so the branches held. His feet were nowhere to be seen.

…kiss…

Parker tried to scream, but couldn't. He couldn't do anything but look at the tree and sob. He turned his head and saw Riley. She was smiling and holding an ax.

"You always said it would look better and you were right," she said. She moved next to him and sized up the ax to his neck. He looked straight up.

Somebody waits for you

"Too bad you won't get to see the tree topper," she said, genuinely sounding sad by the prospect. "Merry Christmas, dear."

She swung as hard as she could and the ax found its mark. The last thing Parker registered and heard before it all went silent was the CD finally catching and finishing the line.

...kiss her once for me.

KARNIVALI

By Jesse J. Saxon

There's never a dull moment when the carnival comes to town.

Jesse Saxon lives and works in the zombie capital of the world, Pittsburgh, PA with his wife, daughter, and their cat. He has written various macabre short stories ranging from zombie fiction to dust bowl horror, and a full-length zombie novel. Jesse graduated from California University of Pennsylvania in 2006 and has been writing semi-professionally ever since.

The dusty breeze of the Oklahoma plain bit through the Friday afternoon so sharply that if you stood in one place for too long your exposed skin would get a brush burn. Men and women alike were accustomed to wearing scarves around their necks in, what the newspapers were calling, "The Dust Bowl" so that the small dust storms were nothing but a nuisance.

The production of Karnavali wouldn't slow down for the small dust devils and tumbleweeds, and carnival barker Simon Barns wouldn't stop his practicing either. "Step right up, step right up! Boys and girls of all ages, step right up! Come and see the mysteries of the world! The Human Blockhead – able to pound railroad spikes through his nose! The Wolfman – raised among the wolves and wild as they come, able to bite right through meat and bone! Step right up and see the Painted Lady Athena, a face as beautiful as God could make but skin that only man could color. Come one, come all to see the wild side of life, the underbelly of the human world, the lost and forgotten souls rejected by our society put on display by the wonderful Maximo Coliusi for this production!"

Outside of Simon's train car the tents of the carnival were being erected. The dirty brown and yellow striped tents became the trademark of the Maximo Coliusi Karnavali and wherever the brown and yellow striped tents were seen, townsfolk flocked to time after time. The unmistakable sound of metal on metal pounding rose through the air as strongman Bruno Schultz swung the sledgehammer down onto the spikes held by the midget mentalist and snake charmer only known as Olt.

The two close friends had been in various vaudeville and freak shows from Coney Island to New Orleans and in addition to sharing a train car they were very efficient at raising tents. Romanian magician Lucian Radu had the most elaborate tent. Lucian wasn't a part of the freak show and didn't need Simon's barking to bring in the crowd. By all means Lucian was what people came to Karnavali to see, he sold the tickets where the freak shows made the extra money.

Lucian was from the old world and dealt in old world magic. He made a small name for himself in the New England states and the New York City metropolitan area, but when the crowds marveled at disappearing acts and underwater escape, Lucian's brand of slight of hand and mind manipulation became more and more ignored – that and his affinity for making God-fearing Christians feel uncomfortable on various levels and that they were paying a sorcerer for wicked acts. Lucian was marvelous to take in.

When Maximo saw him hypnotize an aristocrat's bride-to-be into taking her clothes off, and the sound of applause, Maximo knew that

Lucian was someone he would need to have in his array of talents and convinced the man to give up trying to beat out the other magicians of the area and come with Karnival. The allure of the road and seeing the great America was something that interested Lucian but the promise of a place to stay, and pay without having bills, was all that he needed to be convinced.

In the short two years that Lucian had been with Karnival he had become well liked among his counterparts. He ensured a crowd, even in those tough economic times, and crowds always meant pay and hot meals. In addition to all of that, the carnival folk liked that Lucian kept to himself. He was around enough not to be creepy, but he was always a pleasure to have around and always a welcome sight and never over-stayed his welcome. He was always well-dressed, smelled like fine oils and potions, and was the picturesque gentleman of worldliness.

When the Karnivali train pulled into Simmons Oklahoma the day before, Maximo's wife Izabella went into her routine of strolling through the town from the train station posting flyers for the carnival and giving every man every bit of true information they wanted to know about the carnival and false information about her. She didn't lie when she told them she was a contortionist and that she'd like to see them come on out. She did lie about her age, her relationship status, and her loneliness being on the road all year. Her blonde hair, brown eyes, and ruby red lipstick made her irresistible to the dirty men used to looking at their dirty wives. They had almost forgotten what a clean woman looked like since any water they came across there was used for drinking first and bathing later. Izabella didn't care if she needed to give a wink and a smile to get crowds, she didn't even care if she had to get a little dust on her lips by kissing a man on the cheek if it meant just one more person in the crowd – which made her perfect to get people to come. The women of the towns obviously despised her, but they also would never object to the man of the house and quite honestly didn't mind the carnivals anyway.

The flyers for the carnival read:

KARNIVALI Elveszett Sufletele!

Brought to you by MAXIMO COLIUSI!

Featuring famous magician and mastermind

LUCIAN RADU!

And MAXIMO COLIUSI'S FAMOUS FREAKS!

Below the headline was a drawn picture of either Maximo himself, face hidden by shadow, with his arms stretched out over the carnival below; or of Lucian. Lucian's picture was more insightful and captured almost exactly his personality of mystery and invitation. What could be confused as a smirk was drawn for his mouth and his right-gloved hand was extended as if asking for yours to join it. His left hand held back the left side of his cape showing the fine clothing he always wore. Izabella put the flyers in strategic locations that every town had: post offices, bars, general stores, and the train station.

Carnivals were always set up just outside of towns. After Maximo's train would pull in, the train cars would be unloaded and the carnival would be set up just about a half of a mile from the train station. The train itself wouldn't leave the location and never presented a problem because the down economy didn't mandate much train traffic and the rails were mostly restricted to traveling carnivals and random supply trains that maybe came once every six or seven weeks. And if ever the event came that there was a backing up of the trains, they never much minded when they saw a good carnival.

***

In a day's work Bruno and Olt could have the freak show tent and stage assembled and ready with Lucian's tent operational as well. Athena the Painted Lady would have the popcorn stand ready for her younger brother Rusty to work in. Simon had erected his barker's podium in the afternoon and that evening the carnival would be ready to go.

Maximo knew the men came to see his wife scantily clad bending for their pleasure, the freaks and oddities, and the wonderment of Lucian. He knew the women came along with no objection, but he also knew kids were a hard sell – especially those whose parents wouldn't allow them to see the freaks; so Maximo had clowns to roam the grounds and mind the petting zoo. The bands of clowns Maximo had on staff would dress the carnival with what the carney-folk called "flash" or the oil lamp lights, the colorful posters, the prizes hung from the games of skill, and the ambient carnival music.

The children typically were excited to see the clowns at first, until they got close enough to see the bad wigs and five o'clock shadows poking through whatever make-up they could scrape on their faces. Maximo never asked too many questions for anybody who wanted to be a clown in his show. If he was in need of one and someone happened to ask then they were essentially hired on the spot. Most carnivals were like that and quickly became a refuge for criminals giving credo to the hobo clown paintings.

Friday evening at dusk the oil lamps were lit signaling the carnival was open for business. Entry to the carnival was twenty-five cents a person or one dollar for a family of five. Guests, as they were called, were greeted by the button box music and organ grinding chimes, with clowns doing whatever appealing trick they knew to earn their keep in the traveling band of freaks and outcasts. Food always sold well at the carnival. Maximo demanded that the food be priced well below typical prices because as he said "a well-fed guest is happy, and a happy guest is more inclined to pay extra for the freaks!"

The guests filled the grounds and Karnival went to work.

As the guests walked about, Maximo's front office, band of freaks, oddities, and Lucian did their tasks, while his backroom team of pickpockets and thieves went among the crowds and into the town itself. On the first night the band of thieves went out to case the properties that Izabella reported back to the Back Hand as "places of interest." She always marked them with the flyers of Maximo in case there was confusion. While the entire town was out at the carnival, Maximo's team of thieves were out plotting entry points and looking through windows for fast grabs of items to sell in the next town.

Guests of the carnival were promised by Lucian for more feats of amazement and better magic from the old world the following nights to lead up to his greatest trick on Sunday night. The men were always quick to lead their family to the sound of Simon's voice projecting the oddities of the freak show to see the beautiful Izabella they had seen earlier in the day. Simon of course would never bark about Izabella but her large carnival poster hanging outside of a tent was assurance enough that she was behind the curtain. Outside of the freak show, Simon would typically call out for various acts to come out onto his stage and give a sample performance of their act, typically led by Bruno lifting anyone willing to come on stage over his head and bending metal bars in his mouth. Athena would typically tease the crowd from under a robe by pulling some away to reveal some of her tattoos. Like any side-show, just past the curtain entry way the walkway was separated into two with a wooden arrow sign indicating men to go to the left and women to the right.

The women were met by the first oddity of a half-man half-woman, which was always just a very skinny, attractive man with padding and make-up on one side of his body. Next the women would see the Wolfman: a man inflicted with a condition known as hypertrichosis – the growth of body hair at abnormal places and length, typically covering the entire face. While the women were gawking at the Wo-Man and Wolfboy, the men were taking in Athena and Izabella.

Athena was always first. Her area was well lit to show off the many tattoos she received from different towns and countries. She wore no clothes but her tattoos covered up any free space of what was once milky white skin so that now the only pieces of uncolored flesh she had left was her face and nipples. The men would try to get a peek at her womanly parts and giggle like children at the nakedness of Athena while they tried to decipher her shape through the blue, red, black, and green ink. She would turn cautiously so as not to excite the men with rapid movement and let them take in her very well crafted markings.

Past Athena was Izabella. Her area was not as well lit as Athena's but men hardly noticed. She also wasn't nearly as naked as Athena but any complaining of it stopped shortly after she did a handstand and her gluts flexed tight. Her costume was minimal, but covered all of her like a one-piece bathing suit except with the stomach cut out.

She would bend her body into amazing and provocative positions, making many of the men anxious, but the men behind them kept the line moving enough that no one ever got to see as much of Izabella as they would have liked to, or thought they would, if only they could have stayed just a moment longer.

When the men were reunited with their families, they saw Bruno bending metals, breaking objects made to look like real-life counterparts like safes, and lifting false dumbbells. They would move past Snakeboy, a boy with a skin affliction that caused his skin to crack and peel so that it appeared like reptile scales. They saw the bearded lady, which was always a farce of some sort, but always portrayed very well.

At the end of the freak show they were met by Olt, who would select someone from the crowd and perform acts of psychic ability and mind-reading, and would try to sell potions and Snakeoils. Since many of the town had much of the same problems, it made Olt's job very easy; and his stature added to the creepiness prompting one child to say, "Momma, God must'a given him the power to make up for him being so little." No one ever disagreed.

All of that was just a prelude to Lucian's show. Lucian's legend was beginning to grow among the guests. Some of Maximo's implanted "guests," and sometimes even Maximo himself, would walk among patrons talking up Lucian and his ability. Making up stories about feats that he's done and once convincing a cripple that he could be healed if he could pay one hundred dollars, which he couldn't.

Maximo and Lucian always allowed for about two hours of carnival before Simon would announce Lucian's show starting in twenty minutes. They would always allow the crowd to gather into the larger tent that was about two sizes smaller than a typical big top. Izabella would have a costume change into a ticket taker and gladly sell admission to anyone willing to pay to get in, although no one in Karnival would stop anyone from sneaking in under the tent. The focus was to get as many people inside as the place would allow.

When the music of the carnival stopped, it was cue for Lucian to begin his show and for the Back Hand thieves to either finish robbing the assigned location or get back to the carnival, depending on which night of the carnival it was. This dance lasted Friday into Sunday. But Sunday was always when Maximo Coliusi's Karnival made their bones.

The first two nights of the carnival were always meant to sell the Sunday performance. The Saturday and Sunday afternoons always involved Athena and Izabella making trips into the towns to coerce men to come back for Sunday (with whatever promises they needed to make and sealed with smiles and occasional gropes). If townies were not able to make it to the performances on either of the previous nights, word through the town and the sight of Athena and Izabella, ensured a trip for the Sunday showing.

Just as the last two nights, and all of the weekends prior to this one, the carnival became alive at dusk. The crowds began the exodus from town to the carnival grounds and the Back Hand found their way to the vacant homes and stores of the Oklahoma town. Simon at his podium was preacher-esque and captivated guests with a "Last night in town and gone till who knows when, do NOT miss your chance to see the wonders of Maximo Coliusi's Karnivali!" It was at that point where the implanted guests of Maximo would befriend real guests and sell them on Lucian. The male implants would entice the females and the male guests didn't need anything besides Izabella and the promotional sign in her area telling males to see Lucian.

The Back Hand broke into the homes taking family heirlooms. They broke into stores taking a few dollars here and a few there; just enough so no one would question carney folk of looting. The music would stop and they would make their way back, sneaking through the night like fog off of a river.

Outside, the lights of Karnivali were slowly being extinguished by the clowns and the carnival itself was being broken down. But inside of the tent, Lucian was captivating the guests with feats of amazement and magic. The implanted guests of Maximo would always sit to the left of a vulnerable woman indicating to Lucian that the woman to their left was young, single, and already entranced by Lucian's reputation. Those were the women Lucian would always perform his hypnosis on.

"A volunteer from the audience, please," Lucian would say. One of the implanted guests would elbow his new date and suggest her to go. The anxiety would build in that second and she would always whisper a disagreement. And then Maximo's agent would pinch her side, making her shriek, and the attention of the audience, and Lucian, would be drawn to the woman, who was promptly invited on stage as the volunteer.

"A round of applause for the young lady," would always overcome her, and before she could point out that she didn't volunteer, Lucian's gloved right hand was in front of her, inviting her on stage, which the naïve young woman would always accept.

In walking to the center of the floor, Lucian would always assure them they will be safe and "if you wouldn't disagree I'd like to invite you back to my staging area after the performance to offer you a formal thank you with a cup of tea and perhaps a gift of your choice."

The young woman smiled and Lucian went to work. He would amuse the crowd by making the young woman purr like a kitten or bark like a dog. Sometimes he would make them kiss the men he'd pull on stage or make them pretend they were doing housework around the tent while he continued his magic act. It never failed that the women would do whatever he asked. By the time the woman was being hypnotized, the Back Hand would be back in camp and the spoils were secured.

As the show came to a close and the guests began to file out, Maximo's implanted guests would do as boys do with girls of that nature and attempt to convince them to spend a little extra time together before the night ended.

Lucian would find his volunteer and as promised have a cup of tea with her and satisfy her with mostly made-up stories of his travels and experiences. Shortly into whatever story he began to tell, the sleeping elixir he put into every cup took its effect and the girl fell into a state of lucidity.

Before she could think about screaming for help, Olt, who was hiding somewhere in Lucian's staging area, bludgeoned the poor woman over the head – either killing her or knocking her out completely.

Lucian never checked for either outcome, but instead took a knife and cut the girl's throat, bleeding her out before sectioning her off at the major joints. By that time, the implanted guests had also struck out or had their dates unconscious or dead, bringing them back to Lucian's tent to be dismembered. Bruno would help out and carry two or three women himself.

"This one's going to make a beautiful rump roast for tomorrow Izabella," Lucian said.

"Glorious! The bitch's ass is nearly as succulent as Athena's. Had it not been for all of that ink I'd have cut into yours long ago!" Izabella said laughing.

"I'd cut you down before you even smelled my perfume," Athena said back smugly but with a smile.

Rusty, Athena's little brother, was already at work cutting the dismembered body parts into presentable cuts of meat. He'd wash the blood away and throw the fatty pieces to the animals in the petting zoo.

Bruno and Simon would work grinding the bones to be additives to Olt's Snakeoils. The blood soaked down into the dusty ground and was easily concealed by either the sifting of new sand or the next dust storm on the horizon. The women's bodies were cut up and gone faster than any processing plant could cut a cow. Nothing was left when Lucian was finished except a wet spot where the butcher did his deed.

"How I long for the taste of beef again," Simon said.

"Soon, Simon. Roosevelt's gotta have something planned," Rusty said.

"He's a shit that Roosevelt! He doesn't give a damn about any of us. As far as he's concerned we're already dead and this part of the country is a loss," Athena said.

"Eat the meat, do your job, and shut your mouth. Like you said, we're all as good as dead anyway. These people are our cows, this is our beef, and here's the door if you want out," Lucian said as he held up his knife.

Bruno and Simon bagged the bone dust, and whatever Olt didn't need disappeared with the wind only adding to its sting.

When the clowns finished packing the camp, one poked his head into Lucian's tent, asking if they were just about ready to go. Lucian nodded in agreement.

"Another successful Karnivali I trust?" Maximo said.

Lucian nodded.

"Fantastic. The train leaves momentarily."

Lucian nodded.

"Oh what's wrong Lucian? Don't the crowds love you anymore? Do you not have a full belly everyday? Do you no longer have the finest attire and finest magic?"

"I do."

"Then why so sad?"

"I- I'm not sad boss."

"What then?"

"Soulless."

"Of course you are Lucian. But the show must go on."

FRONT PAGE
By Michael A. Migliore

Celebrities always say that any publicity is good publicity.

*Michael A Migliore is one of the founding partners, along with Jenn Thomas, of **ColdFront Productions**. Currently in pre-production for an upcoming film, "**9ers**," ColdFront is the premier film making company in Pittsburgh. Michael is a disabled veteran who served in the US Navy from 1977 until 1993.*

In addition to film making, Michael is a photographer for a local sports magazine and co-hosts a sports talk television show.

Wilbur Canton woke early, drenched in sweat. As he sat up in bed he looked at the portrait of his mother that hung on his bedroom wall. How he hated the bitch. Sure, she was good to him on the surface. She gave him everything he needed or wanted. She appeared kind and loving. On the surface. But, she had committed her atrocity on the day he was born. She named him Wilbur. The Curse.

It had held him down his entire life, no matter what he did, no matter how he excelled, his accomplishments went unnoticed. Someone else would always get the credit. Even in sports, in college he piled up impressive rushing statistics, but the other idiot in the same backfield won the Heisman trophy. The quarterback was drafted number one. Wilbur went undrafted, unnoticed, always unnoticed.

Until today. Oh, how he wished that bitch was still alive to see his work on the front page. The front page of the city's biggest newspapers. As he rolled out of bed he glanced at the blood soaked clothes on the floor and the bloody knife on his dresser.

Fifty times, he had counted carefully. His arms got tired, but it had to be a lot. It drew attention that way; one stab wound would be on page six. Wilbur had to be on the front page.

The girl had been a pretty little thing, she probably would have been worth the fifty dollars she asked for. But sex was the last thing on Wilbur's mind.

He killed her fast, with the first thrust. Under the sternum up into the heart. She probably never even felt it. He then stabbed her forty-nine more times to make it an even fifty. Switching hands as his arms tired. He left her body in a spot where it would be found quickly. He was not concerned with being caught. There was no way to link him to the hooker's murder and, of course, he would never do something like this again.

Wilbur ran to his front door and swung it open. The newspaper lay on the porch. His hands sweating, he grabbed the paper and stared at the front page.

His hands began to tremble, then his entire body.

"You bitch!" he cursed his mother. "You lousy, filthy bitch!"

The headline read:

Man Mauled By Werewolf Killer

The story covered the top half of the page. Under that some bullshit about a summit that nobody cared about and a story about a tax increase.

Wilbur opened the paper. On the bottom of the second page was a one column article about an unidentified prostitute found stabbed to death. She had suffered multiple stab wounds.

"Fifty!" Wilbur yelled out as he shredded the newspaper. "Fifty, fifty times you assholes!"

Wilbur stormed around the room, kicking things and cursing his mother.

The second page? That was unbelievable. He had counted right. Fifty times! It was his name of course. The curse that his mother had given him. That bitch. How could anybody take him seriously when his name was Wilbur?

"No!" He screamed as he threw himself on the floor. He began kicking his feet and pounding his fists. "Bitch, bitch, bitch!"

The tantrum lasted almost ten minutes, until Wilbur was exhausted.

Again!

It came to him suddenly. He would do it again. Exactly the same way, the same knife, everything the same. The media loved serial killers. They would see the connection right away. He just had to make sure to count fifty times. He would not only be on the front page, he would be the headlines! He would be famous! Everyone would be talking about him. They'd probably call him the Phantom Slasher or something like that. Yes he would do it again. Only one more time naturally. After he was on the front page he'd go back to his usual daily routine.

He was calm again. He walked to the pile of bloody clothes. He obviously couldn't wear them again. He found a new set of clothes and put them on. He took the knife from his dresser, then sat on his bed and stared out the window, waiting for it to get dark.

***

Wilbur pulled his Cadillac to the curb. A pretty young girl walked to his car and leaned in through the passenger side window.

"Hey baby," she said. "You dating tonight?"

"I sure am." Wilbur smiled at her.

"That's going to cost you seventy-five," she informed him. "That ok?"

"No problem," Wilbur told her, and the girl got in the car.

She slid next to him and rubbed her hand over his crotch.

"Just pull into one of these alleys," she purred. "And we'll do something freaky."

***

Wilbur stared into his mirror as he stripped off the bloody clothes. The whore had tried to fight him, scratched his face, but he killed her right in his car. He stabbed her the mandatory fifty times and dumped her body on a main road. Wilbur quickly showered and went to bed. He slept well and dreamed of his headlines.

"You slut!" Wilbur screamed as he threw down the paper. "I hate you, you no good witch. I hate you!"

The headlines:

Werewolf Killer Claims Another Victim

The story covered most of the front page. Then another story about the summit meeting: on page four was a two-paragraph story. Hooker Brutally Murdered.

Wilbur ran around his house smashing everything he could get his hands on. The fit lasted fifteen minutes, until Wilbur collapsed.

"Again," he whispered to himself. "Again and again until I'm on the front page".

Wilbur thought about that. Maybe he needed a gimmick.

Something like this other guy had. Maybe he should bite his victims too. Maybe he should cut off an ear or something. Wilbur found a new set of clothes and cleaned off his knife. Tonight would be the one for sure. Tomorrow he would be on the front page. His life would be starting new. He would get the recognition he deserved.

Wilbur drove around for almost two hours, looking at the girls on the street. He saw many that would be easy. But then he saw one who would be perfect.

She had long black hair. She was beautiful and she wasn't dressed like the rest of the hookers. Wilbur pulled his car over.

"Hi," she said, smiling. "Can I get in?"

Wilbur nodded. She climbed in and Wilbur drove away, quickly.

The girl looked around the car. She ran her finger along the dried blood on the dashboard. She looked at Wilbur quizzically, but she still smiled.

"Are we going to have fun together?" she asked.

"You are just like her," Wilbur said. "Just like the one last night and just like mother. You are all the same."

"Yes." She smiled and nodded. "I can be whoever you want me to be, let's play."

"I've always worked hard," Wilbur said, as he pulled into a dark alley. "And never got on top, always second best. Because of the name!"

He stopped the car in the shadows, the only light coming from the moon.

"I've done perfect murders. Front Page murders. But someone else gets on the front page, not me. Never me! Never Wilbur!"

The girl looked at the dry blood on the seats and floorboard and at the knife that Wilbur pulled from under his jacket. She suddenly realized the situation.

Wilbur flung his door open and ran around the car, knife in hand. He yanked the passenger side door open and reached in to pull the girl out. The claw that grabbed Wilbur's forearm was covered with course black hair. Wilbur screamed as he was dragged into the car.

"Cheer up." The beast snarled as it tore out Wilbur's throat. "Tomorrow you'll be on the front page."

INTO THE NIGHT
By Heather Lin

Sometimes visiting relatives outstay their welcome.

__Heather Lin__ obtained a degree in English Literary Studies from York College of Pennsylvania in 2010. Although her erotica can be found in various anthologies and on several bawdy websites, this is her first venture into the realm of erotic horror. For updates on all of Heather's steamy publications, visit her blog at __heatherlin88.blogspot.com__. Her non-erotic prose and poetry can be found under her given name, Heather Smith.

Roselyn first met Michael when she was eighteen: young, pretty, and new to the city. She'd moved there from her hick town in an attempt to make something of herself. With her glowing skin, dark hair, and striking brown eyes, she'd been sure she could make it as a model/actress. Instead, she'd ended up as the manager of the burger joint where they'd worked together.

But Michael was lucky. Michael had gotten out of there before the trap of monotony could close in on his life. As she stared out the window of her third floor apartment into the smoggy night sky, she thought about calling him.

But the challenge for Roselyn did not lie in dialing the seven familiar digits on her cordless phone. The challenge lay in having to accept the fact that, once again, this would only be a booty call. As usual, her body would get what it wanted, but her heart would remain empty and unsatisfied. Her shaking hands dialed the number, and the phone rang three times.

"Hello?"

Roselyn jumped, startled. The voice on the other line was smooth, incredibly masculine, and completely unfamiliar.

"Hi, I'm sorry. I...I must have the wrong number."

"Who are you looking for?"

She ran a hand through her short hair, unnerved by the way his words reverberated through her body.

"Michael O'Mally."

"What's it regarding?"

Sex. She wanted so badly just to say it—to come clean. She needed anyone, even a mysteriously sexy stranger on the other line, to tell her that she was crazy, she would never be anything more to Michael, she needed to forget about him. But she held back. Besides, at 3 am, her intentions and desperation must be obvious.

"I'll try back tomorrow."

"Maybe it's something I could help you with."

Roselyn felt her face flush. Heat rushed through her body. The way he said it—sultry, seductive—he had to know.

"How...how do you know Mike, exactly?"

"Why don't you come over? I'll let him know you're on your way."

There was a click on the other end of the line, but Roselyn continued to hold the phone to her ear. Was it possible she'd misinterpreted? It had to be. He was a friend of Michael's. Maybe he was just teasing. Maybe the edge of sexual frustration that the man's voice contained had only been imagined. She finally put the phone down and decided to at least walk by Michael's apartment and see if he was expecting her.

She checked her appearance in the cheap, full length mirror that was tacked onto the back of her bedroom door. She hadn't changed out of her work clothes. Grease spattered her polo, and her hair was a mess. She told herself she wasn't changing to impress Michael. Cleanliness was a necessity, not a come on—and the little black dress she chose was just the first thing she came across. She fixed her hair, dabbed perfume on her neck, and walked out the door.

Ten blocks later, Roselyn arrived at Michael's upscale townhouse. Except for the occasional flicker of headlights as a car zoomed past, the building was dark and quiet. Even the streetlight outside was broken, providing no comfort for the eerie feeling that suddenly overpowered her. She looked back over her shoulder, senses alert, debating whether or not she should just go home. Before she had a chance to decide, a familiar voice startled her.

"Come inside."

Roselyn's head snapped back around to Michael's doorway. A strange man stood at the top of the steps, leaning casually against the doorframe. He was handsome, but at the same time he seemed surprisingly ordinary—the glasses perched on his nose and the tousled brown hair that settled around his face didn't quite justify the sudden attraction she felt for him. Her knees went weak, and she felt a rush of nervous excitement pulsing through her veins.

"Is Michael home?" she asked, her voice barely above a whisper for reasons she couldn't explain.

"This is his house, isn't it?"

His black eyes settled on her brown ones, calming her, convincing her, and drawing her in. Before she knew it, she was climbing the steps toward him, and he was stepping aside, letting her enter the dark hallway.

"How do you know Michael?" she breathed for the second time, her voice a quivering violation of the stillness and silence.

His footsteps stopped behind her, making the hair stand up on the back of her neck and blood rise to the surface of her skin. She heard him breathe in deep behind her. Even if Michael wouldn't find her perfume appealing, his friend did.

"My name is Reggie. I'm a distant cousin."

His breath brushed softly against the skin of her neck as he spoke, almost making her forget that she'd asked him a question in the first place.

"He's never mentioned you."

"Hm."

She turned, suddenly remembering that being in such close quarters with a man she'd just met should be awkward. But even when she saw the way his eyes raked over her body, admiring the way the dress hugged her curves, she couldn't put the expected force into her next words.

"Don't look at me like that."

Her soft tone begged the opposite, and she realized the contradiction it had created immediately. Her cheeks flushed, and Reggie—if that really was his name—brought his fingertips up to touch the heated skin. A soft groan escaped his lips, sending a shock of carnal sensation through Roselyn's body. She shivered, and he smiled. Her mind was a fog of confusion and intrigue as his eyes held her gaze from behind the clear lenses.

"You make it so easy," he murmured.

She couldn't think of anything to say. Before she knew it, she was pressed back against the closed door, in the darkness, letting the shadow of his hands caress her neck.

"I can feel it," he continued, his breath growing heavier. "Pulsing, racing, rising."

Her eyes asked the question that her unsteady voice couldn't form into words. He seemed suddenly dangerous, but, still, Roselyn was unable to feel the fear her common sense was trying to push to the surface.

"Blood." He whispered the answer in her ear. "Don't you feel it? Any touch, any sensation is magnified infinitely where it gathers."

He pressed his hand gently against the skin of her throat. "Here."

He moved down to feel her breasts through the thin fabric of her dress. "Here." The last word was the quietest, his last destination the most secret. "Here."

Roselyn felt his fingers move her panties aside and touch the soft flesh between her thighs. This was crazy. Somewhere in the back of her mind, she knew it. But the part of her that gasped and moved against his skilled hand won the battle of wills. She grasped his shoulders and felt the sculpted muscles beneath his starched button-up as he pulled her closer to him, letting her feel the hard ridge of his cock against her thigh.

The simple sensation sent a flood of wet heat straight to the mound of flesh that Reggie was still caressing. He moaned and bit down on her neck. A sharp pain nearly broke her out of her reverie, but she was too lost in the pleasure that was building underneath of his fingers.

"Sorry," he said quietly, but she could tell he wasn't sorry at all. She was too lost to care. But his next words caught her attention.

"I'm just having a hard time deciding whether I should eat you or go inside of you."

Roselyn's eyes snapped open, and she stared into his hungry gaze.

"What...what do you mean?"

The shakiness of her voice was partly due to shock, and partly due to the ecstasy shooting through her quaking body. Reggie stopped, a smile touching his lips while he waited for Roselyn to calm down.

"Let's go to the bed."

She looked at him, confused, but his smooth voice once again put her at ease.

"It's okay. Michael is sleeping elsewhere."

She followed him reluctantly, the last shreds of her sense battling with the animalistic desire that rose inside of her.

"But what you said..."

"Joking." He waved his hand dismissively. "Besides, I already ate."

His look was reassuring, and he put his arm around her shoulders as he led her to Michael's bed.

"Where is Michael?"

"On the couch."

"But I didn't see—"

He cut her off with a kiss, caressing her lips slowly, sensually with his own. He was the most giving lover she'd ever been with. She'd barely laid a hand on him, and he seemed perfectly content with touching her, feeling her, following the blood as it rushed erratically through her system. It was strange. But she couldn't complain. He nipped her lower lip, drawing a drop of blood from the sensitive flesh of her gums. She barely noticed. He'd moved himself over her, hiking up her dress to rub himself against her through their clothing.

However, the rough treatment of her lip seemed to throw Reggie into a frenzy. He sucked her lower lip as hard as he could, irritating the wound. At the same time, she heard the sound of his zipper, and he ripped her panties down her thighs before pushing himself deep inside of her. Apparently the time for leisure was over. She moaned into his mouth as the hot, silky shaft moved in and out of her, seeming to find the sweet spot inside of her with miraculous ease. She was in a daze of ecstasy, unable to hold back any reaction, clutching at any part of her lover that she could find. Sounds she didn't know she could make hitched in her throat as more enthusiastic ones tried to break free.

His teeth raked the skin of her throat, shoulders, and chest— never breaking the skin, as if he was resisting the temptation. It seemed to excite him further, and his hand gripped her ass, crushing her hips against his, giving her clit constant contact with the flesh of his abdomen. It was too much for Roselyn to take. She dug her fingernails into his back as she felt the waves building, her defenses weakening, until with one powerful shudder, the impending rapture flooded her senses, and she cried out his name. He panted in her ear, and she felt him convulse against her, sliding himself in and out of her, riding out the orgasm and letting her do the same.

Roselyn couldn't move. All of her energy had been consumed in the throes of passion. She could barely comprehend the fact that she had just had amazing, unprotected sex with a perfect stranger. Reggie stood and zipped up his pants, then checked his hair in the mirror on Michael's dresser. He straightened his glasses and turned to look at Roselyn, who was still lying in a daze on the bed. A small smile touched his lips, and the glare from a light somewhere outside of the window made it so she couldn't see his eyes behind the lenses. It gave him an eerie look, and Roselyn finally found the strength to push herself up onto her elbows and speak to him.

"I...I'm not on birth control."

His smile widened, giving his now-visible eyes a knowing look.

"Don't worry. No offspring can come of this."

Then he grabbed his jacket from a chair in the nearest corner and walked to the doorway.

"It's been a pleasure, Roselyn."

He turned, but she sat up and called out to him.

"Wait! I thought you were staying here?"

He turned for a moment, smiled a gleaming white smile, and disappeared into the darkened house. She heard the front door shut quietly, and the sound seemed to bring her back to her senses. She stepped onto the floor and straightened her dress, then fumbled for the light switch. An embarrassed flush rose to her cheeks, even though no one was around to see it. As the light came on, her eyes were drawn to the floor. A trail of red footprints marked a path from the other side of the bed to the door and continued until she could no longer see them.

The blood drained from her face. She knew what it was in an instant. She knew why Reggie had left so suddenly and where Michael was. Roselyn sat down quickly on the edge of the bed. Her mind was unable to form a coherent thought as her body crawled slowly to the other side of the bed. There he was—what was left of him—lying by the dresser that Reggie had so casually stood in front of. The body was mangled beyond recognition. Some bones seemed to be picked clean, the one eye that was still in its socket was open wide, and Michael's intestines had been pulled from his body.

Murder, cannibalism—these things didn't happen here. They couldn't. And she didn't sleep with murderers and cannibals on the bed next to the dead body of the man she loved. Bile rose in Roselyn's throat, battling with the fear that was constricting it. What had she done?

Roselyn made her decision quickly. She crawled back to the other side of the bed and stood, avoiding the bloody footprints. Then, she checked her hair in the connected bathroom mirror, and headed for the front door. Although she lived in walking distance, she hailed a cab, knowing that Reggie was perfectly capable of jumping out from the shadows and killing her.

When she was home, she stripped off her clothes and climbed under the covers, keeping the light on. It took her a long time to get to sleep, and by the time she woke up the next morning, she'd convinced herself it had all been a dream—a dream that resulted in Roselyn losing the desire to ever call Michael again.

HADES ON ICE
By Kimberly Bennett

**Fish stories are always more interesting
when alcohol is involved.**

Kimberly Bennett was born in Warren, Ohio and has been a lifelong resident of Northeast Ohio. She Graduated from Kent State University with a degree in Computer Technology. She is a recently published independent author whose main goal is to provide readers of fiction a thrilling and memorable experience when they pick up one of her books and begin to read. For more information, visit her website at www.kimberly-bennett.com.

"Oh, Brian," Cara softly moaned in Brian's ear. Cara pushed her hips upwards to meet Brian's as he plunged his shaft deep within her. Cara's legs wrapped tighter around Brian's waist as he increased his rhythm. Her nails dug into Brian's back as she arched hers, signaling that she was close to climax. Brian watched as Cara's plump, bare breasts bounced up and down as he pumped her faster. Beads of perspiration formed on his back and ran in rivulets down his spine and disappeared beneath the flat sheet that clung to his buttocks.

A horn blared outside the bedroom window, startling Cara and Brian, while announcing Jack's arrival. Out of breath and annoyed at the interruption, Brian reluctantly rolled his eyes, pulled the sheet aside and rolled off of Cara and onto the mattress. Lying on his back, Brian tried to calm his breathing and his nerves. He knew he had better get moving because any second his brother would burst through the door and drag him away. Jack was an impatient fellow with a compulsion to run his life by a schedule of his design. Right now, Brian was throwing off Jack's brotherly fishing getaway schedule with his midnight delight.

The horn blared again, this time the next-door neighbor's dog began to bark furiously at the intrusion. Cara cringed and rolled towards Brian and gently nuzzled his arm with her breasts, as she moved dangerously close. The close proximity of Cara and the pressure of her bare breasts on Brian's arm did nothing to detract from his current state of arousal and unsatisfied need.

The horn blared a third time, making the neighbor's dog bark much more loudly. The distracting sound reverberated through Brian and Cara's one bedroom bungalow, causing the windows to rattle. "What the..." Brian's exclamation remained unspoken as Cara softly placed an index finger on his lips to silence his profanity.

"Shhhhh," Cara whispered in Brian's ear and leaned closer into him. "You better hurry up before Jack comes in here to get you." Cara placed a tender kiss upon Brian's lips and rolled away from him so he could get up and get a move on.

Brian sighed heavily and sat upright in bed. He swung his legs over the side of the bed and planted his feet on the carpet. Brian rubbed tiredness from his eyes, yawned and bent to pick up his jeans that lay haphazardly thrown in a pile on the floor. Brian hopped off the bed and pulled his jeans on in one swift movement. He zipped his pants and buttoned his button and bent a second time to retrieve his thermal shirt that had been lying next to his jeans, in an equally haphazard fashion. Brian pulled his shirt over his head and smoothed it out. Brian sat back down on the bed and reached for his work boots that he had kicked under his bed, before his intimate encounter with Cara had begun. Retrieving his socks from each boot, Brian straightened and shook out his socks and pulled them on his feet and then quickly put his boots on. Fully clothed, Brian rose from the bed, reached down and playfully slapped Cara's naked behind.

"You better be careful," Cara called after Brian, as he grabbed his coat and gear, before dashing out the door. "We'll finish what we started when you get back," Cara said with an impish grin.

"I'm holding you to it!" Brian exclaimed, as he gave her his signature smoldering look of desire. Cara giggled and then Brian was gone.

Brian dashed from the bedroom, briefly stopping to grab his fishing gear, jacket and case of beer. He raced out the door and slammed it behind him. Brian hurriedly strode around Jack's pick-up truck, opened the passenger door and threw his gear and beer in the back, pulled his coat on and got in.

"Damn, brother!" Jack exclaimed while scrunching up his nose. "You stink like sex and sweat," he informed his little brother, unashamedly.

"Thanks, man," Brian replied. "I hope you like the stench because you're gonna smell it all weekend." Brian leaned back in the seat as Jack revved his engine, took off down the drive and turned onto the street.

The night clung to its inky black canvass as morning was on the verge of peaking over the horizon. Jack's first mission was to get him and Brian to the fishing site before sunrise. His second agenda was to cut the fishing hole, while Brian unloaded their gear. Third, was that they would remove the fishing shanty from the trailer, that bobbed happily behind them at the present, and position the shanty over the hole. Jack's fourth and final agenda was to sit back and fish the weekend away while drinking beer with his little brother.

The drive to their ice fishing spot was relatively dull. Jack put the hammer down so they could reach their destination before sunrise and Brian took a much-needed nap. Brian briefly woke up once when Jack stopped for gas, to relieve himself behind the gas station building, and then it was back on the road again. They made good time because of Jack's lead foot, with some time to spare. Jack pulled slowly down the frozen dirt road to their secret ice fishing spot. Jack had found the spot at the end of their fishing season last year by making a wrong turn on their way home. It was a remote area that was down a very rarely traveled, frozen over, dirt road and it was secluded by dense foliage.

Jack's truck bounced down the icy road as they made their way to their final destination. "There it is!" Jack exclaimed as the area came into view. The snow and ice on the ground made it difficult to spot. It was hard to discern between the ground and the body of water, but they managed.

Jack and Brian arrived at their destination an hour before sunrise, which gave them just enough time to set up. Jack slowed to a stop while parking the truck facing the lake. He cut the engine but made sure he left the lights on, so they could see. Jack and Brian clambered out of the truck and began their work. As Jack grabbed the chainsaw out of the bed of the truck, he immediately fired it up to test it. The loud growling sound of the chainsaw echoed over the frozen lake and back. Jack shut down the chainsaw and walked out onto the ice. He selected a spot on the ice a few yards from where he had parked and started the chainsaw again. The power tool came to life successfully a second time. Jack carefully cut a hole three feet in diameter through the thick ice. Fine chips of ice and droplets of freezing cold water spat up into the air and covered Jack from head to toe.

Meanwhile, Brian unloaded the gear and brought it out to their new fishing hole. Brian slipped and slid the whole way, while Jack looked up from time to time to watch his brother's comical trek. Jack finished the hole by the time Brian had brought all their gear to their spot on the ice, including an unusual wooden box that was locked. Brian had discovered the box in the bed of the truck as he was unloading their gear.

Jack shut the chainsaw down and slid his way across the ice and to the truck with Brian so they could unload the fishing shanty from the trailer. When they reached the truck and trailer, Jack set his chainsaw down in the bed of the truck and brushed off all the flecks of ice that he could. Brian walked around the trailer untying the shanty and coughing, because of the wind chill, into his sleeve as he went.

"Man, it's cold!" Jack exclaimed, as he zipped his zipper higher on his jacket. Brian nodded in agreement and finished untying the shanty. The men then climbed onto the trailer and scooted the shanty off and watched as it dropped to the snowy ground with a dull thump. Satisfied with their progress so far, they then pushed and pulled the shanty to the ice and across to their freshly cut fishing hole.

The fishing shanty was a decent sized box of wood that measured eight feet high by ten feet wide by ten feet long. Jack and Brian positioned the shanty over the hole and began to bring their gear inside it. First, the men brought in the cots and sleeping bags for extreme weather. Next, was the fishing gear and last, was the booze. Brian made it a point to retrieve the first beer from his case and pop the tab. He guzzled the beer down like a college kid and then tossed the empty bottle to the side.

Both men set up their cots and rolled out their sleeping bags on top. Jack then proceeded to leave the shanty to shut the lights off on his truck. As he was gone, Brian searched around for their camp lights before Jack cut his truck lights. Smiling at his discovery, Brian retrieved the lights from a duffel bag and turned both of them on and strategically placed them by their cots. Brian turned around towards the fishing hole when he heard movement in the water.

"What in the world?" Brian asked out loud. As he turned around, something white and silky, like wet hair, slid into the water and made tiny ripples on the surface. Just then, Jack entered the shanty.

"What did you say?" Jack asked Brian.

"Nothing," he shrugged his shoulders and replied. "It's just my imagination working overtime."

Both men sat down on their respective cots, positioned opposite each other at the hole. They both then made quick work of preparing their fishing gear. Jack finished preparing his items first and as he dropped his line in the hole, he noticed the sun began to pop up over the horizon through a porthole on his side of the shanty. Brian wasn't far behind and followed suit by dropping his line in the water a few moments later.

Jack and Brian each opened a bottle of beer and sat back enjoying each other's company. The beginning of their day was dull and without any movement below the surface of the water, but after four hours of drinking beer and talking, there was a hard tug at Jack's line. Jack quickly set to work to bring his catch in. He wound his reel in some, but not too much, and when his prize became visible through the fishing hole he really reeled the catch in. Excitement on Jack's face was the real prize, but he was oblivious. Jack was whooping and hollering with joy as he reeled his catch up through the hole and placed it into a bucket of water nearby and plopped back down on his cot completely satisfied. Brain sat and watched his brother gloat from his accomplishment and threw back another beer.

"Hey, what's in that wooden box?" Brian asked his brother. The box had been mixed in with their gear and Brian had been curious about it since setting his eyes upon it.

Jack smiled an ornery smile, "It's something special that I wanted to share with you." Jack propped his fishing rod against the shanty wall and pulled the box from underneath his cot. He retrieved a key from his front pocket and unlocked the lock. Once the lock was undone, Jack lifted the lid, reached in and grabbed a bottle of scotch. Jack pulled the bottle out and tossed it to his brother.

Brian's eyes grew wide with anticipation at the gem of liquor he now held. Brian licked his lips as he undid the cap and took a sniff of the contents. "Wow, that's gonna pack some punch!" Brian smiled in appreciation and took a swig of the liquor; he then scrunched up his nose and squeezed his eyelids shut. Brian let the liquid scorch a path past his lips and mouth, down his throat and into his belly. "Damn, that was good!"

Jack smiled at his brother as Brian passed him the bottle for his turn. Jack closed his eyelids and threw back a swallow quickly and enjoyed the taste as it traveled a path to his nether regions. "Mmmmmmmm," was all Jack managed to get out.

After a few hours of drinking and laughing about old times, the scotch bottle had been emptied and Brian gave up on fishing and fell back on his cot to sleep off the alcohol. Through his buzzed up haze, Brian figured that dusk was on its way and they would have plenty of time to fish tomorrow. Jack quickly followed suit with his brother and within a few minutes they both were sacked out.

As the men slept fitfully, a creature slithered out of the hole and made her way over to Jack's cot. She noticed that he was fast asleep and a sinister grin spread across her lips. She turned her head to observe Brian and ascertained from his open-mouthed snoring and the empty scotch bottle dropped on the ice, that he was incapacitated for the time being. She crawled onto the cot and positioned herself over Jack's groin. She made fast work of undoing his pants and gently pulling out his shaft. She then began to slowly and methodically lick the tip of his head and swirl her tongue around his shaft. Jack shivered and moaned with pleasure in his sleep. The creature paused and smiled again as she took up massaging Jack's, now erect, penis. Jack pushed his hips upwards towards the creature's lips. She paused again and this time she opened her mouth wide and bared her sharp, dagger-like teeth. She then bit down on Jack's sensitive member with enough force to shear his pride and joy clean off. Jack's eyelids flew open and he screamed out in pain, waking Brian from his alcohol-induced nap.

Blood spurted from Jack's wound and he wasn't sure what to do to staunch the flow of it. In his panic, he grabbed a small towel that was lying nearby and tightly wrapped it around the end of his penis. His face went ashen as the blood continued to flow. Jack looked up at the creature and watched his blood drip from her lips as she spit the tip of his shaft out of her mouth and onto the icy floor. Jack nearly passed out from shock, still clutching his groin he managed to kick the she-devil off of his body. The creature fell to the floor but quickly regained composure and clawed her way back on top of Jack. She lunged at Jack and raised her talon like claws. She used one claw to pin Jack down and with the other claw she used to slash Jack's throat open. Jack didn't let go of his wounded member but clung to it as he bled out from both wounds. Satisfied with her actions, the creature smiled at Jack's lifeless form and began licking her claw-like fingers.

Before the siren could finish licking Jack's blood from her claws, Brian came up and grabbed her firmly from behind. He wrapped an arm around her chest and pulled her close to him while grabbing a hand full of white hair with his free hand. Her skin was cool and wet and she was hard to hold but Brian managed in his adrenalized state. She fought hard while clawing at Brian. She managed to open up gashes on his forearm but he ignored her struggle. Brian dragged the creature from his brother's dead body and threw her to the floor and watched as her head hit hard on the ice; a black colored liquid began to ooze from her fresh head wound. Stunned from the landing, the siren was dazed long enough for Brian to be back on top of her. He rolled her over onto her belly and sat on her back while grabbing a handful of white hair for a second time. He reached into a nearby tackle box and retrieved a filet knife.

"Eat this, bitch!" Brian exclaimed as he rammed the knife up through her neck and into her skull, piercing her brain and causing instant death. The evil siren didn't have a chance to scream out her agony. The creature's head slumped forward and Brian released her hair and let her drop to the ice. Brian got off the creature and stood up on unsteady legs. He slowly took in the horrific scene that had unfolded in an instant. Jack and the siren's blood were splattered all over the shanty. A large pool of blood had formed around Jack's cot and flowed into a tiny stream to the hole and into the water. Brian dropped his filet knife on the icy floor and put his head in his hands and wept. An overwhelming wave of disbelief and grief gripped his being.

It took several minutes for Brian to regain some composure and when he was prepared, he raised his head from his hands. Brian wiped tears from his eyes and took a good look at Jack's attacker. Brian knelt down near the creature's lifeless form. He noticed that she was a slender, pale skinned siren with a long tail of a fish. Her tail had flowing fins near the end of it and it was covered in a brilliant shade of blue iridescent scales. Brian reached down and rolled her over. He scanned her face and noticed that she had delicate, almost angelic features but when he peeled back her blood-encrusted lips, he sucked in a breath as he exposed sharp, dagger-like teeth.

Brian stood up from the unusual corpse and glanced at his brother's unmoving form. Brian took in Jack's pale complexion and vacant gaze, while sorrow gripped him again. The grief that struck Brian was almost unbearable but he managed to open the door to the shanty and leave his brother's body behind for the authorities to take care of.

Once outside, Brian sighed deeply. He wasn't sure how he was going to explain to anyone what happened but he knew he couldn't stay there a moment longer. Brian began his slippery trek to his brother's truck while reaching in his pocket for his cell phone to call the police and then to call Cara.

HIS OWN WORST ENEMY
By Laird Long

Can sibling rivalry be explained through science?

Laird Long pounds out fiction in all genres. Big guy, sense of humor. Writing credits include: **Blue Murder Magazine, Plots With Guns, Hardboiled, Thriller UK, Shred of Evidence, Bullet, Albedo One, Baen's Universe, Ennea (9), The Dark Krypt, Another Real, Eternal Night, Robot, Sniplits,** *and stories in the anthologies* **Amazing Heroes, The Mammoth Book of New Comic Fantasy, The Mammoth Book of Jacobean Whodunits,** *and* **The Mammoth Book of Perfect Crimes and Impossible Mysteries.**

Malcolm Turner was fully eleven years old when his brother, Ethan, was born. Unexpectedly.

The Turners were both in their late-forties, and after the difficult birth of their first son, Arthur, and Millicent had been told it would be impossible to have another child. But miracles happen, and that's exactly what mother and father considered young Ethan.

Whereas Malcolm was dark-haired and dark-eyed, dour and distant; Ethan was fair-haired, with sparkling blue eyes and a personality to match. He was an impetuous child, playful and physical, quick to smile and laugh, delighting his loving parents.

And where once the Turner household had been shrouded in dusty quietude, only the occasional rustle of news or book paper, an infrequent comment, to disturb the silence, now the home fairly bubbled with happy outbursts and endless activities, mother and father and son.

Malcolm became even more reclusive. He seldom left his room – crammed full of books and experimental apparatus – except to go to school. A tall, thin, frail teenager, he possessed a sharp mind and equally sharp tongue (when he used it), and had no friends. As an only child used to his parents' full attention, he'd been dismayed by the birth of his brother, and he shared in none of the celebrations of the boy's remarkable growth.

"Come out and play catch with me!"

Malcolm glared at Ethan standing in the doorway of his bedroom. "Can't you read, imp!?" He pointed at the 'Keep Out' sign posted on the door, then turned his attention back to the test tubes and coiled copper tubing on his workbench.

"It's the first day of spring!" Ethan chirped, glancing curiously around the room. "What are you always working on in here, anyway?"

"An antidote for unwanted brothers," Malcolm growled.

He slid off his stool and slammed the door in Ethan's face.

Ethan excelled in school, achieving grades even better than his brother's before him, with seemingly little effort. He excelled at sports, as well, a robust youngster who could run fast, jump high, and throw far; a natural athlete. His charisma and accomplishments drew friends, lots of them. His parents were rightfully proud of their son, and lavished him with gifts on his tenth birthday.

Malcolm didn't attend the boisterous party. He was studying for his final exams at the college library. He had a job lined up in the university chemistry department upon graduation.

"You should've been there, Malcolm. It was great!" Ethan enthused to his brother that night, when the pair briefly met in the second floor hallway of their home.

"Birthday parties are for little kids," Malcolm glowered.

Ethan flashed his bright, white, winning smile. "What did you wish for, by the way, when you blew out the candles on your 21st birthday cake?"

Malcolm stared at Ethan. Then stated coldly, "I don't need wishes. I have science."

The young man, who appeared much older with his stooped shoulders and shuffling gait, toiled long hours at the university lab, during the week and on weekends. While Ethan flew through high school, class president at every grade level, valedictorian upon graduation.

"Well, my boy," Arthur beamed at his son. "What do you intend on taking at the university, when you aren't playing football, that is?"

Ethan had been awarded a full scholarship to a major college in the east. "Well, old man," he cheerfully mimicked his father, "I believe that I will major in law, with a minor in political studies and girls. Providing the coach doesn't bench me, of course."

They laughed, Arthur slapping the strapping young man on his broad back. Millicent clutched Ethan's strong arm and gazed up at her son, tears glittering in her eyes.

Ethan walked over to Malcolm standing off by himself, grabbed up his brother's cold, clammy hand and vigorously shook it. "You're welcome to come out east and visit me anytime you want, Malcolm. The lab facilities are top-notch, you know."

Malcolm jerked his hand away. "My experiments are going very well, I'll have you know. And I don't care much for football."

Ethan smiled. "I guess you won't be seeing me off in the morning, then?"

Malcolm sneered, "No, I'll be at work." He turned to climb the

149

stairs to his bedroom. Then he stopped, looked back at his brother, a bitter smile stretching his gaunt face. "Sleep well, fair prince."

Ethan's troubles began as soon as he arrived for his first term. He crashed his car – a present from his parents – on the highway into the college town. He'd been speeding, swerving back and forth on the road, for some reason even he couldn't fully explain. He wasn't injured, but still he missed his first football practice, and was found drinking in one of the pubs that dotted the perimeter of the sprawling campus.

He was apologetic, vowing to never repeat the uncharacteristic mistakes.

But he did, repeatedly.

And whereas before he couldn't seem to stop himself from getting good grades, now he seemingly couldn't prevent himself from failing. He attended only every third class or so, and in that class he slept, as a result of staying out too late the night before.

He was soon cut from the football team, and expelled from the university.

"Don't worry, son," Arthur consoled him. "I've spoken to Mr. Granger, the plant manager, and he said he'd love to have you working there. He was chairman of the school board when you were in high school, remember?"

Ethan took the job at the plant and moved into an apartment. But he continued to make bad choices, doing the wrong thing. He was caught drinking on the job, then caught with a prostitute in a darkened alley later that same night. He couldn't explain it to his disconsolate parents, except to apologize profusely, again, as he had for all of his other self-destructive transgressions.

He descended from drinking into drugs, from the night shift to unemployment. His parents and old friends hardly recognized him anymore. Once muscular and self-assured, he was now emaciated and paranoid. Once gregarious and good-hearted, he was now sullen and mean-spirited. He had given up trying to resolve the raging conflict inside himself. But it was still tearing him apart.

"Can't you help your brother!?" Arthur appealed to Malcolm one night in despair. "It has to be some sort of chemical imbalance, some kind of psychological-"

"Mother never should have had him – at such an advanced age – in the first place," Malcolm cut the man off, his cold, dark eyes gleaming madly.

Arthur and Millicent drew back, shocked at the deadly bitterness.

The caretaker of the crumbling downtown hotel found Ethan's body when he came to collect the overdue rent. It was hanging from a hot water pipe in the bathroom.

No note was found. None was necessary. Everybody in town knew the cause of death; they'd witnessed the brutal decline firsthand.

An autopsy was scheduled for the following morning.

Malcolm stuck the suction cup to the basement window, circled the glasscutter around, pulled the cut-out piece of glass back. He took a last look around. The night was silent, dark. He reached in through the hole and unlocked the window.

He found his brother's corpse in the middle drawer of the cooling unit. Grinning grimly, Malcolm affixed the band with the embedded light to his head and removed the circular bone saw from the small black bag he'd brought with him. Then he slipped a painter's mask over his nose and mouth, a pair of plastic goggles over his eyes, to shield himself from the putrefying smoke and any stray bone shards.

He switched on the saw, cut into his brother's skull.

Ethan's skullcap was just ready to be removed, when the lights suddenly flicked on.

"I thought I heard something down here," Deputy Jonas stated. He looked from the startled man to the laid-out corpse with its skull cut open, and revulsion twisted his homely features.

Malcolm hesitated only a moment. Then he dropped the bone saw clattering to the floor and tugged at the loosened skullcap, ignoring the deputy's shouted orders to stop.

It took a blow to his own skull, from Jonas' nightstick, to halt the desecration. Then it took two more officers to drag Malcolm away from his brother's body and up the stairs of the morgue.

"You idiots!" he raved. "Don't you see!? It was me! I made him do it! I was his own worst enemy!"

He twisted his head around, staring wildly back at his brother and screaming triumphantly, "I created the imp of the perverse!"

Something stirred in Ethan's dead, damaged brain. A tiny creature crawled out from a cavity, through the slit in the skullcap and down the tormented face of the corpse.

The creature that had been inserted into Ethan's head the night before the gifted young man had left for university.

WRITER'S BLOCK
By Ryan J. McBriar

An author finds his muse (or vice versa).

Ryan J. McBriar was born in 1980, in Pittsburgh, Pennsylvania. He is a graduate of La Roche College and is currently a high school English teacher in Corry, PA. McBriar holds a BA in both English Language and Literature and English Education. When he's not teaching, McBriar enjoys spending time with his wife, also a teacher, as well as film, books, music, writing, and gaming.

He had been sitting in front of the monitor for hours. His elbows were planted painfully on the cheap, wooden desk, hands mashing his forehead into a collection of frustrated wrinkles. Jacob glanced, moving only his eyes, to the window set in his bedroom wall. Through the curtains he could see the solemn darkness of the night beginning to creep over everything. *He'll be here soon enough,* Jacob thought harshly. *If I don't have more pages, it's over.*

He pushed himself back from the computer desk, wheels of his chair struggling to push across carpet. Jake had been meaning to get one of those plastic surfaces so the chair would roll smoothly.

Ah, it's not worth it now.

Jacob Mallory lived alone. He made just enough money to rent the row house, although working two jobs to attain this feat had sapped his creative juices in the last several months. Jacob's real profession was writing.

He had had nominal success, a few short stories in a few notable publications, but that was the extent of it. He had been working on his first novel when the block in his mind came like the final blow of the guillotine: swift and unforgiving. There was no getting around it; the block was very persuasive. This had been the first real case of writer's block Jacob had ever experienced; he was fresh out of college, and it was to be expected. But when he couldn't write for three months straight, he began to question his own merit.

That is until you *came into my life,* he thought callously, but not without a hint of appreciation, and paced toward the window. He parted the curtains with his supple hands and breathed a sigh that cleared his restive head.

The sky was lighter than he had first suspected. It was still magenta-hued across several rooftops. He could see the willows planted in front of his home, spewing forth from the cement, looking strangely alien in the strip of sidewalk devoid of other natural life. They were swaying rather violently. The wind had picked up. His room was chilled slightly, the autumn air dying to get inside. He kept the house cool, preferring to dress warmly rather than swelter under high heating bills.

It's still early. I've got plenty of time. Time to see her.

She would have to see him, have to understand. Maybe he would tell her everything.

Jacob turned on the overhead light in his bedroom, allowing the room to be illuminated by more than just the blank computer screen. In the fresh light, Jake's eyes were drawn to a box containing the nearly completed manuscript.

He picked up his cell phone hesitantly.

She'll think I'm crazy, she'll hang up on me, and she'll call the police.

He dialed Rose Phillips's number anyway.

It rang twice, and then went to voicemail, finally beeping in his ear.

"Hi Rose. It's me," he said, stuttering into the receiver. "It's Jake. I need to see you. I know I haven't called, but I've been going through some weird stuff," he paused, wincing at the sound of what he was saying. "Look, I really need to see you. Tonight. You know where. I'll explain everything. Please, I'll be there until ten."

He ended the call.

Jacob Mallory was in trouble, and he needed to tell someone, in case he couldn't finish writing at least three new pages by midnight. He pictured Rose, sitting in her recliner, reading peacefully, wrapped in her favorite quilt, listening suspiciously as the guy she had been dating for the last eighteen months babbled away on her voicemail. Jake was sure by now that she was getting up, pacing, listening to the message again, thinking things over.

She would come, he was sure of it. That's why he was in love with her. She would come; she would give him a chance.

Jacob slid into his lightest jacket and grabbed his car keys from the wooden hook-rack.

***

The diner was nearly empty of other customers when Jacob slid into a booth near the back by a window. The lone waitress in the Venice Café was flitting between the two or three occupied tables like a pollen-collecting insect. She finally made her way to his table, reluctantly, as if reading something on his face that she didn't like.

"All by yourself tonight, hon?"

Jacob smiled up at her. He had been hunched forward, chin resting in his folded arms, lost in his own thoughts. "Not for long, I hope," he said convincingly, and the waitress seemed to immediately relax.

"Can I get you something while you wait?"

"Yes." He squinted, searching for her nametag. "Barb, yes you can. I'll have a coffee and water, hold the water."

She giggled and walked away.

He sighed heavily, and slumped back against the cushioned seat. Jacob's eyes darted every few moments toward the entryway, each time expecting to see her ushered in by the chill autumn air. He pictured Rose's beautiful brown hair, pulled up hastily and falling into her face, tickling her nose. She would sigh impatiently, smiling as she brushed it out of her eyes.

And suddenly he realized that he must look like shit. He hadn't even showered that morning, or the morning before that. The days had been hectic the last week, and his appearance was surely an indicator.

He moved hastily toward the restroom as Barb arrived with his mug of coffee.

"Be right back," he muttered.

***

Rose entered the Venice Cafe just as Jacob was stepping into the men's room. The place was desolate but warm and more inviting than the autumn night she had just escaped. The in-rushing wind as the cafe door fell shut made Rose's brown, shoulder-length hair kick-up and swirl around her face. She brushed it aside, pulling a few tresses from the corners of her mouth, and adjusted her glasses.

Rose scanned the diner quickly. The booths lining the kitchen were empty save one, which was occupied by an elderly man alone with his newspaper. He glanced up and smiled at her, and she smiled back courteously. She didn't see Jacob anywhere in the diner.

Rose Phillips was at the end of her rope and about to just lop it off at the knot. *He's not coming, and you're a fool,* she thought to herself, and not for the first time. She had come here with one purpose in mind. Rose tapped the plastic shopping bag at her side. The bag was full of CDs, movies, old magazines, and a few typed manuscripts. It was everything (at least all she could scrounge up in the last thirty minutes) of Jacob's that had been scattered around various corners of her home.

She stood in the doorway unsure how to proceed. She had received his call while working at her computer. Rose had scowled at the buzzing cell and made her decision almost immediately. She loved Jacob Mallory, but things had gotten too weird.

A portly Asian man brushed passed her coming from the restroom, looking pallid.

"Stevey must be off tonight," she said to herself wryly, glancing toward the kitchen area.

A voice startled her.

"Single coffee, table six. He's been waiting for ya'. He's in the restroom."

She turned and the young waitress was skirting past her with several filled plates. Rose found the table with the abandoned mug of coffee and slid in across from it.

She lifted the bag containing Jacob's accouterments onto the table in front of her, pushing it as close as she could to the cup.

After a few moments, she ordered a glass of water with lemon and then slid the bag off and onto the booth next to her. She stripped off her light jacket and covered the bag with it. She wouldn't stay long. She wanted to be locked up and snuggling safely in her bed by eleven. She didn't feel safe being out at night, whether the local serial madman was inactive or not. She would give him an hour, and then it was "So long, Sweetheart."

***

The Venice's bathroom was surprisingly immaculate.

Jacob stood in front of the mirror, deciding at once that he should not have come here.

"Even if she does come, I can't involve her. It's too dangerous, he could easily come after her next," he spoke loudly to himself.

"And you," he said to his own reflection, "You my friend have seen better days."

Jacob's hair hung in dark, wavy clumps, long enough to be held back behind his ears. A few jagged spikes fell forward, crossing against his forehead. A stubbly five o'clock shadow had mutated into a full-fledged face mask, sporadic and unkempt, moustache and beard trying and failing to connect in several places. His blue eyes, still youthful and spry, peeked out from behind the tangle of hair, but there were heavy black-and-blue bags underscoring each. Those eyes looked as if they had aged ten years in the last week.

Jacob felt the sudden urge to throw his fist into the mirror, shattering his own dirty visage, but he stopped short. Instead, he turned the faucet on and began dousing his face with cold water, hunching over the sink.

"It's been worth it," he said reluctantly, and then repeated it. "It's been worth it!" This time with more force and certainty, a certainty that at once made him uneasy.

The door to the single stall in the men's room opened suddenly, and Jacob jumped and spun around, startled.

A squat Asian man was adjusting his pants, eyeing Jacob suspiciously and moving in hurried little steps. The man scurried out of the bathroom without washing his hands. Jacob shook his head with a hollow chuckle.

There were no paper towels in the dispenser above the sink, so Jacob moved into the stall to pull out some tissue paper and dry his face off. Next to the toilet Jake noticed the front page of the current *Allegheny Tribune*. One of the headlines stuck out to him immediately, and he grabbed the newspaper the Asian man must have been reading.

The headline said, in big black lettering:

The Pennsylvania Prowler Inactive Whole Week:
Sudden Change in Killer's Pattern Baffles Authorities.

"Jesus," he said, his voice coming out in a ragged, choking gasp.

His eyes scanned the article, forgetting momentarily he was supposed to be waiting for someone, someone he may have already missed in the café.

He read:

Fear has gripped townships all over Western Pennsylvania for the past six weeks as a series of bizarre murders haunts their streets.

Audrey Dupree, Stanley Norville, Dave Springer, John Peterson. These people and ten others were found dead in their own homes, in their very own bedrooms, with no evidence of forced entry. Every three days a new victim was found, slain in the same fashion, almost ritualistically mutilated with no apparent motive.

"He seems to move sporadically," Chief of Police Derrick McCall said, responding to attempts at predicting where the killer may strike next. "One victim could be 100 miles north of the subsequent murder. Dupree, for instance, was found in Erie. The next victim, Springer, was discovered three days later in Allison Park."

The newest development also has the police scratching their heads.

"He's just stopped," McCall said. "We haven't had another reported murder that fits his MO in almost ten days now."

Does this mean that Western PA residents can begin leaving their windows open at night and breathe a collective sigh of relief? McCall urges not.

"The perpetrator of these horrible crimes is still at large," McCall said. "Execute extreme caution in your nightly behaviors until we can close this case for good."

Local residents have their own theories about what has

happened to the "Prowler."

"I think he's dead," Brad Raymond, a local retailer, said. "Took his own life on account of his actions. And that's the way it should be."

Another local resident, New Castle's Jamie Montani, said, "I'll bet it's found something to keep itself busy for awhile, a distraction. I don't think of it in human terms anymore, not this monster. But I don't think we've heard the last of it."

Jacob didn't finish the article. He swallowed hard; his throat was dry. He thought of his coffee, which turned to thoughts of Rose, and he panicked. *I missed her, dammit, she'll think I stood her up again*

He folded the paper, haphazardly shoving it into his coat pocket.

Jacob checked his watch grimly as he pushed open the men's room door. It was almost half past nine. Full darkness had settled comfortably outside the diner. *If she's not here--* he thought, but didn't have a chance to finish his own ultimatum.

He spied Rose from where he stood, sitting at his booth, the back of her head bobbing impatiently as she thrummed her fingers on the table. She sat alone with his untouched cup of coffee.

Jacob absently tried to straighten his hair, knowing full well it wouldn't improve his overall appearance, and made his way back to the booth. He felt nervous, and he wasn't sure why. It was that queasy, nauseated anxiety that came to schoolboys trying to kiss their first date on her front stoop, sure all the while that her father was glaring at them from inside. *This is the same Rose I fell in love with,* he thought, *the same Rose I made love to, for Christ's sake. Something sure is different, Jake, and it's not her.*

***

Rose couldn't hide her visual shock at Jacob's appearance as he took a seat across from her. Jacob winced a little at her expression, ducking his head and forcing a thin smile.

Neither of them spoke for a full minute.

Finally, Rose. "Jake, what happened, are you in trouble? Jesus."

"A lot's happened, Rose. I'm writing again."

She paused cautiously. "That's good, right? Have you been going to work?"

"Sometimes. Sometimes I don't make it. I have some time off coming to me."

She sipped her water through tight lips, mentally reprimanding herself for almost falling into what she perceived as a sympathy trap. "I've called, you know, almost everyday for the last week, and I get nothing. You're telling me you've been home and just ignoring me?"

Jacob shifted uncomfortably. This wasn't going as he had planned it. Rose noticed he was checking his watch every few minutes, almost manically, between gulps of coffee.

"Have other plans, Jake?" she said, sounding more accusing than she had intended. Nonetheless, her right hand shifted from her sweating glass to the jacket beside her and the bag underneath it.

"I've been writing, but it's been bad. Not normal, I mean."

Rose looked away, shaking her head and biting her lip in annoyance. "Come on, Jake. You've always been your own worst critic." She looked back at her boyfriend. Ex-boyfriend? She wasn't sure. "Remember the fantasy novel you tried to write in college? You told me every line looked like the bastard child of Tolkien and Piers Anthony, and that nothing you ever wrote was original, and that you were going to go into real-estate."

This got a smile out of Jacob, but it quickly faded. Barb strolled back over and filled up his mug. He began drinking it again, black.

"Not 'bad' as in style or craft, Rose," he said earnestly. "I mean bad due to the inspiration. Shit, I shouldn't even be trying to explain this to you. You'll just think I've cracked...another struggling writer gone off the deep end."

Both of Rose's hands were on the table. She thought in passing that Jacob was on drugs, but she knew better. Rose had seen something in his eyes; they were scared, haunted, terrified even.

Jacob continued in a low, measured tone. "He comes to me at night. I write to stay alive," he said and glanced nervously at his watch then out the window into the canvas of darkness.

"Who? Why? I don't understand."

Jacob put a hand up to silence her gently. He said, "Hear me out, then judge me as you will when all's said, but I have to make this quick. He'll be waiting if I don't get home soon."

Rose sat back and listened in rapt perplexity as Jacob spoke:

"I hadn't written anything in so long I was beginning to think that I had forgotten how. Everything was stop-and-go for months; write a paragraph, trash it, start over. You remember, of course. I was edgy with you. I was edgy with everyone. I was unhappy and something had to change, but I didn't know how to affect it. I couldn't get a handle on jumpstarting my own brain.

"Night after night I would sit and pull my hair out. A few times I almost threw my monitor and keyboard out the window. Then one evening I started thinking. Thinking about the murders and the Prowler. The mystery of it always intrigued me, and I've always been a touch on the morbid side to begin with, so I started thinking about the victims. I started to imagine I *was* one of the victims, or all of the victims, and I started to picture what images they could have seen before they died. What their synapses could have captured, imprinted on their brains, before they were tortured and disemboweled.

"Yeah, disgusting, I know. But it worked.

"That night I was on fire. I could have gone straight on 'til morning, and then a few more damn hours out of spite. Around midnight, though, I got the strangest feeling that I couldn't shake. The house was locked up. I could hear through the walls that Miss MacDonald had turned her TV off for the night, and on the other side, John Dillington had quit screaming at the dog long enough to lull himself to sleep.

"I kept writing about the murders in detail, about what happened to those people. And suddenly I realized what the feeling was that

162

was nagging at the back of my subconscious. It was the feeling of someone reading over my shoulder, breathing faintly just beside my ear and following word for word what I was typing. I stopped and sat up straight, not wanting to turn around, but feeling foolish all the same, like when you're a kid and scared to pass by a dark alley even though you know nothing from your imagination could possibly be lurking there.

"Then I heard the voice.

"'Don't stop,' it said, 'keep writing.'

"My computer screen went dark, conserving power like it always does after I've been idle, and in that second of blackness I saw the reflection. Towering behind me so tall I must have been blind or stupid not to sense it before, this dark shape was hunched forward, one eye reflected by the moonlight spilling in from my open window. I touched the keyboard quickly and the image was gone, but not before I could discern great hulking appendages, and shapes that looked like...looked like fucking wings. I knew it was still there, and its breathing became huffy, like it was growing impatient.

"I started typing and didn't stop for two hours, didn't dare look behind me or focus too long on the scattered reflections on my monitor. By the time I did turn around, it was gone. He was gone. The window was shut; I hadn't heard a thing. I collapsed in relief. It was short-lived.

"That was almost two weeks ago. The thing's been back every night since."

Jacob sat back and took a deep, painful breath. His throat was sore and dry, but he was out of coffee. Rose gently placed her palm on the side of her half-empty glass of water and pushed it toward him. He drank greedily, finishing it off.

Rose realized that things couldn't get much worse. Jacob Mallory, the man that she loved, was sitting across from her sounding like an escaped mental patient. She corrected herself. *His story sounds crazy, but his voice doesn't.*

Jacob was squinting uneasily into the glass she had given him, now only full of ice. He looked like he was expecting the bomb to drop any moment.

She extended a hand that covered his.

"How long do you have?" she asked quietly.

He looked into her eyes, unable to conceal his brazen gratitude. "You believe me?"

"Until you're proven wrong and I'm proven a fool, yes."

Jacob looked at his watch reluctantly. "He comes at midnight, usually like clockwork, no matter how well I lock up my sliding window or barricade it."

Rose's eyebrows creased. "Why do you call it 'he'?"

Jacob fidgeted uncomfortably. "We talk sometimes. He's obviously male. He's told me his name, but I can't pronounce it, Drah-ka-tzar or something. I don't know anything about him, where he's come from, why he's here. I just know that he didn't kill me because of my story, and the murders have stopped." He laughed vapidly. "I single-handedly stopped the Prowler. Shouldn't I get a medal or something?"

Rose wasn't laughing. "What do you think will happen if you stop writing?"

***

Things were so complicated.

Jacob wanted to sound noble; he wanted to say that he was writing to stop a vicious killer from continuing his handiwork. But the truth was, as Jacob had come to accept, that he hadn't written like this before in his entire life. He suppressed this thought and went with his first inclination.

"Whether he kills me or not, one thing's for sure. The murders will start again. I think, hell, wherever he's come from things had gotten dull, boring, vacuous. So he struck out, came here, to our," he paused, struggling for what he was trying to say, "our plane of existence. Goddamn, it sounds like we're stuck in a re-run of *The*

Ray Bradbury Theater. What I did entertained him in a way that arbitrarily hunting victims couldn't. It turned what he did into an art. I think where he comes from he's some kind scholar. 'The written word is the choicest of relics,' Thoreau said, and I think he appreciates that on some level."

"Christ, it sounds like you admire it."

"Don't be silly, Rose. I'm just scared. I can't live like this for much longer. I wanted to tell you, in case I don't make it. I had to tell you."

Rose gripped his hand with more force. "Stay with me tonight."

"Rose, I can't, he'll find me, I'm sure of it, he..."

"Jake, I live on the other side of town. If it finds you, it won't be right away. At least break the cycle. Maybe it will just leave for good."

"Yeah, and then the killings will start again. If it's not me, then someone else. A lot of others, in fact, I'm sure of it. Do you want to be responsible for that?"

***

Rose looked at her watch. It was five past eleven. "You're running out of time," she said. "I can't let you go back to your house tonight, Jake. Please, stay with me. I love-- You can't keep this up much longer."

His refusal to give in made her nervous. She got the feeling there was something else going on with her boyfriend than he was allowing her to see. His eyes were darting from her, to the table, to the window frenetically, as if he were itching to leave her, itching to run home and meet whatever had been visiting him the last two weeks.

Slowly, to Rose's relief, Jacob began to nod.

"You're right," he said. His teeth were clenched. He continued absently, "I'll stay with you tonight. We'll sort things out in the morning." He looked exhausted all of a sudden, and Rose thought fleetingly that she might have to carry him to her car.

They paid the check, leaving a few dollars for tip, and left the diner. Jacob made it outside without Rose's assistance. Rose watched as he collapsed into her beat-up *Hyundai*, crumpling into a ball and falling almost immediately into a fitful sleep. He slept as Rose pulled away from the diner, onto Route 8, and across the Fleming Bridge that took her into the city.

During the drive, Jacob's sleepy mumblings made Rose more uncomfortable.

"We'll be famous," he said suddenly. She looked over quickly, surprised, but the passing streetlights indicated his eyes were still locked tightly shut. "I'm not the murderer, he's done the dirty stuff. I'm just the recorder."

Jacob remained silent after that.

Rose parked against the curb and the slight bump roused him. She felt fear leading her dazed boyfriend up the long stairwell to her apartment, fear that was knotting her stomach into weighty clumps. Not fear of the outside. In fact, she thought she might feel safer out there tonight. The kind of blind terror she was feeling now was directed at the man she had invited to stay with her to keep *him* safe. But who would keep *her* safe?

Pushing these thoughts away, she unlocked her front door and guided Jacob inside.

She locked the door and turned around, but Jacob was facing her, eyes suddenly bright and vibrant. He smiled at her from behind hanging chunks of matted hair, his brows creased inward, his eyes trained on hers. Rose felt the desire to run from her own home build like the gases in a bottle of Coke shaken up before being twisted open.

"Thank you for this," Jacob said, still smiling that unnerving smile. "We'll go back to my house in the morning. I love you." He leaned in without warning to kiss her.

Rose couldn't explain to herself why she shied away from his touch, but she did and he caught her only on the left cheek. The feel of his dry lips and rough, unkempt beard sent a chill all the way down to her toes.

"Good night," she said shortly.

Jacob was asleep on her bed in minutes.

Rose couldn't sleep.

She alternated sitting in front of her computer, unable to add anything of import to her paper, and pacing to the front window of her apartment, which looked down on Butler Street, still active at this late hour.

The worst is over, she thought to herself, but it gave her little respite.

***

The next morning at ten Rose was driving back over the Fleming Bridge, back onto Route 8, and toward Penn Heights. Jacob sat in the passenger seat the exact opposite of the man she had conversed with the night before.

The graveness was gone, magically dissipated over night. His lethargy and sullen earnestness had vanished and left in its place what could only be called bouncy exuberance.

"Damn, Rosie, I haven't slept like that in weeks. My head's clear, my body is energized, damn I'm hungry, are you hungry? Do you want to stop for breakfast? No, no, better not, not now, let's just go to my place first. That's what we have to do, get to my place. Then we can eat and talk."

Rose thought about drugs again, the logical, easy answer, but it treaded no water with the current situation. The man didn't drink or smoke; in fact she was almost sure he had never been drunk in his life. Someone doesn't go from being anti-alcohol to undercover coke-addict in a span of two weeks. Maybe addiction wasn't the word she was looking for. Maybe there wasn't a physical substance Jacob had latched onto, but a mode of living, a kind of habit, an *obsession*.

"Oh no!" Jacob said, ripping her out of her own deliberation as she parked in front of his row house.

She followed his bulging eyes up to the bedroom window that hung directly over the front door on the second floor. The brisk fall wind had sucked the curtains from inside out of the casement, which was missing both glass and screen, and was now whipping them in an aberrant frenzy.

"Jake, wait!" she called, but he was already out of the car, passenger door hanging open, leaping up the six steps to his porch. He disappeared through the front door.

Rose felt sick. She didn't want to go after him, but she found herself pulling her hair back, fastening it with a rubber band, and pushing the driver's door open. She took her keys from the ignition and fingered the small canister of mace that hung amongst them without being aware of it. She had procured it when the murders had started.

She hoped it worked as she mounted the cement steps slowly, feeling an almost palpable dread coming from the open wooden door that lead into Jacob's house. She pictured the inside of the house before she actually got there; small living room, crammed with a television and too much furniture, stairway and chipped white banister leading to the second level.

She jumped when the door of the house to her left creaked open. It was Mrs. MacDonald, one of Jacob's elderly neighbors. Rose noticed she was wearing a pink nightgown that she held tightly clasped at her generous waist.

"Everything okay over there?" MacDonald asked warily.

"Y-yes," Rose said. "Jake's just a little under the weather, that's all."

"Must've had a fitful night last night," MacDonald said. "Some time 'round midnight sounded like he was throwing a tantrum, bangin' and breakin' stuff. Must have really been feelin' out of it."

Rose swallowed with some difficulty. She managed to nod, which placated the older woman, who slipped back inside her own home.

Entering Jacob's house, Rose didn't know what to expect. The Prowler? Not likely. She was almost certain that it was gone long before they arrived that morning, if it had ever been there at all. She gripped the mace canister tightly.

The living room was well lit from the morning sunshine. She noticed a fine coating of dust had settled on almost all the wooden furniture. Rose turned to close the heavy wooden door, and as the clasp clicked into place, she heard Jacob crying out from upstairs.

"Gone!"

She sprinted into motion; her fear was momentarily dispersed by the sound of horror in his voice.

"Gone," he called out again, softer this time, as Rose reached the top of the stairs and stepped into the doorframe of Jacob's bedroom.

It looked like a tornado had landed and been localized in that one room. The bed's mattress had been overturned, nearly removed from the box springs; plates of long-ago eaten food were scattered across the floor; books and magazines, some of them shredded, surrounded the man crumpled on his knees amongst the disaster area.

Jacob was kneeling with his back to the doorway, his head in his hands, shaking with convulsive sobs.

"It's all gone," he repeated.

Rose noticed with a jolt to what Jacob was referring. The oak computer desk on the north wall was empty. The monitor, hard drive, printer, were all gone. Some wiring and cables remained. It looked as if the hardware had been ripped right from the wall. All that was left was the keyboard and a few scraps of blank paper.

She stayed quiet, unsure how to react. Jacob reacted for her.

"He took everything. Backups, memory, the goddamn manuscripts. Hundreds of pages, gone." His voice was quavering with hysteria.

"Jake, I..."

But he turned with blinding speed to face her. His cheeks were wet, but his eyes were no longer manufacturing tears, instead they had contorted with rage.

"You bitch!" he said and lunged, arms flying out, hands twisted into hungry claws. His eyes were empty, bottomless pits.

Rose was so startled that she couldn't react in time. Jacob fell upon her, hands attaining their goal: her throat. He squeezed harshly and Rose dropped her keys, which landed silently on the carpet as Jacob pulled her roughly into the room. She took in one long gasp of air before his fingers wrapped around her windpipe.

"This was chance," Jake growled. "*He* was my chance to create something special, to achieve greatness."

He had her sprawled out on the bed, pushing with all his strength, and she could feel the exposed layer of springs dig into her back. Rose kicked wildly, beating at his arms with her hands, scratching at what flesh she could find. Her struggling was futile.

"I never wanted to stay with you last night, and now it's all ruined," he spat, almost unintelligibly. "You should have listened to me, Rose. I know what's best, I always have."

Rose blinked rapidly, her vision becoming clouded, dark, filled with blotchy, putrid-colored masses. She would lose consciousness soon. She couldn't scream. Her arms searched the bed wildly for anything, anything that could help her. In her breathless panic, the silhouette Jacob was casting on the wall seemed to expand, filled out with shadowy wings that enveloped the whole room.

Then her searching fingers found something near the edge of the bed: a plate, full of half-eaten pizza. Porcelain. Thick. Heavy.

She used her remaining strength to swing her right arm upward, toward Jacob's face. The plate shattered with a sickening thud, and she could suddenly breathe again.

Rose's chest was on fire as she drew in precious oxygen. Jacob had collapsed to the floor, cradling his head. Dark blood seeped through his fingers. She shook her head, trying to clear her vision. She saw Jacob getting up, blood pouring down his face like rain.

Rose heaved herself off the bed, lunging forward, toward the doorjamb. Her hands found the fallen keys, and she fumbled with the canister of mace as Jacob fell on her from behind. He gripped her legs and began dragging her back into the room. His voice had lost all coherence, now erupting in animalistic growls and moans.

She was on her stomach when Jacob let go. She had released the safety on the canister. She could see from the corner of her eye that Jacob was lifting something over his head. She turned herself onto her back and kicked up, hard, into his crotch.

He let out a cry of agony and dropped the heavy wooden desk chair at his side. He had meant to crush her skull with it. The mindless thing that had been Rose Phillips's boyfriend bent forward in anguished pain, and Rose brought the mace up into his face.

The spray not only soaked his eyes, but also seeped into the open wounds on his skull and face. Jacob howled in renewed pain, and Rose rolled back and dug a kicking heel into his chin.

Rose had never been physically impressive in terms of strength, but there was enough power in her last burst of defense to send Jacob stumbling backward toward the open window. The wind from outside suddenly flooded into the room, sending the curtains back in as Jacob's knees struck the windowpane, and then sucking them back out almost in unison with Jacob's flailing body, soaked in his blood.

Rose didn't hear him hit the ground, but in fifteen minutes she heard the sirens out front.

She was still sitting on the floor of Jacob Mallory's empty bedroom. The cops would be rushing in soon, she was sure, with dozens of questions. She would tell them as much of the truth as she could.

***

In the next few days the Prowler's murder spree remained at a standstill, although Rose noted a rumor was circulating that an unknown foreign author was soon to publish a book about the unsolved case. The work was said to contain incredible detail about the killings.

She had no interest in that particular read.

EVERY

By Charlie Kirby

Even doctors are in awe at the miracle of birth.

Charlie Kirby has been writing off and on for over forty years, mostly in the field of technical theatre and fiction. Born in Vermont, Charlie moved west to pursue an education. Charlie has been married for thirty-two years and currently resides in Stockton CA. When not travelling, Charlie works for a local community theatre as an office manager/resident designer and dabbles with the culinary arts.

Willis Hutchinson huddled over his glass of scotch and stared off into the rain-blackened night. He sighed and took a deep slug of the liquor.

"Willis? Willis, I need you!" His wife's voice cut into his reverie, a glass shard through silk, and he hated her all the more for it.

Damn, couldn't she give him a little peace?

"NOW, Willis!"

"I'm coming, you freaking cow." He rose wearily and reached for a nearby tray, which held various items. He paused in the hall, frowning at his reflection in the mirror. He looked eighty, not thirty-seven. Had she aged him that much that quickly?

Abruptly, a flurry of activity exploded in front of him and he jumped back, tripping. He just managed to catch himself in time to avoid a painful, if not deadly, plunge down the stairs. The tray clattered to the floor and he winced at the noise.

"You clumsy oaf! You practically scared me out of my skin."

"Good luck with that," he muttered. She'd need a map and a Sherpa for that task. He glared around for his adversary. The culprit, an apricot-colored poodle, growled menacingly at him and made a great show of its teeth. The light from the bedroom made its handmade-jeweled collar sparkle and gleam. "Spare me, you little scum or I'll boot in those teeth down your throat." He pulled a foot back and the poodle retreated enough to let him into the room.

He gathered the tray back up and replaced the items on it. Plastic containers of vegetables, bottles of vitamins and dietary supplements, all would be overlooked as his blushing bride made a headlong lunge for the packages of cookies and potato chips.

His wife sat in bed, propped up by pillows, the bluish glare of the television doing nothing for her overall pasty complexion. *Lord, what a sight she was,* he thought to himself, his mind only barely able to remember her as anything else besides the current swelling mass of flesh.

When he met her, it had been at a cocktail party. Her sleek, lithe figure caught his eye and before he knew it, they were sharing a table and sipping wine. How he had paid for that moment of distraction. He'd never thought much about her eating habits, never wondered how she maintained such a lovely figure. It was the classic bait and switch. Once she had his ring on her finger, the jig was up.

He was a gifted surgeon. He already had his own practice, fledgling though it was, and all the support of his colleagues on a variety of projects. All he needed was a wife by his side and, in time, Mikki became just that. She dazzled his friends and his family. She was perfect, supportive, demure, and ready to take her place by her husband's side as his partner and life mate.

He set the tray down, close to her side of the bed and watched the pudgy hand snake out for the junk food and carefully avoid the healthier alternatives.

How did I ever have sex with that? Aloud he said, "Mikki, you shouldn't eat any more of that garbage. Your obstetrician said—"

"Who the hell cares what he says?" She protested and stuffed a handful of potato chips into her mouth, the crumbs trickling from between her fingers. She paused to pat her distended stomach. "After all, I'm eating for two."

You're eating enough for ten. The kid's going to be born with a Big Mac in his hand and a premature case of pimples if you don't lay off the junk food. "I know you are hungry, but you need to consider what your present diet is doing to the baby."

"Now, Willis, you know that junk food isn't all that bad for you. Get out of the way, HG wants to come up and give his mommy kisses." The poodle climbed up the small step unit - he was far too old to jump up any longer - onto the bed and walked up to the woman's side, eyeing Willis with a mixture of fear and hatred. "Were you picking on Mommy's poor HG again? He's so abused." She made a clucking noise and the dog sprawled out in an obscene fashion so that she could rub his stomach.

"Damn near tripped over him coming up the stairs. He's ferocious, Mikki. We've got to get rid of him before the baby comes. He'll rip her throat out. Besides, the dog's nearly dead anyway. One good whiff of him should prove that."

"HG? Never! He's Mommy's baby, he's Mommy's precious angel. He's too full of love to hurt anything." She cradled him and the dog whined, its brown eyes filling with affection for the woman. Then its head turned and Willis could see the contempt the dog had for him.

"Right." Willis reached for an empty box and barely eluded the razor sharp teeth as the poodle lunged himself at the man. "Love, huh? That's your idea of love?"

"Isn't that cute? He's so jealous. He's never had to share me before. If it comes down to it, I'll give the baby up first before HG. After all, he was here first." She lavished kisses upon the grizzled snout, kisses that had once been reserved for her husband.

"You're joking." His voice was stunned.

"I'm not. Willis, I'm serious. I've been thinking about this a lot. If the baby can't get along with HG, out it goes. There are plenty of adoption agencies that would love to have it."

"IT is a child, our child." Willis's thoughts spun and he barely managed to stagger from the room.

"IT is secondary to Mommy's good boy," she called after him. "Did HG have a good time with his groomer today, your toes look so yummy sweet!"

And she'd do it too, Hutchinson knew it. She had divorced her first husband on account of that damned dog, although Willis hadn't known that before the ceremony. She'd give his baby away because of it too, just for that damned dog.

He remembered how thrilled he was when he heard the news of her pregnancy. From the time he was a little boy, he'd longed to be a father. Even sitting on his mother's knee he would ask her if he'd be a good daddy when he grew up. In fact, he suspected it was why he'd gone into medicine, the need to nurture and care for others. Still, he'd always wanted to have kids, lots of them. Being an only child and a late one at that had made him a loner, turning to books as playmates. He wanted a houseful of kids, but Mikki and that dog apparently didn't agree.

Sex with Mikki had become increasingly difficult. After the honeymoon, she'd started pulling away from him. It didn't help that that little monster was always right at her side. To even get a crack at sex, he had to lock HG in the garage. She didn't like it and he wasn't terribly happy with it either. As for HG, he just grew more and more aggressive towards him and more loving towards Mikki.

Before their wedding, sex had been fun, even explosive. Mikki had been a wild cat in bed. It wasn't until they'd come home from Acapulco and the dog had met him at the door, with a snarl, that Willis realized their twosome was a threesome.

The funny part was that Willis loved dogs and they loved him. It only proved that whatever HG was, he wasn't a dog. A demon, a monster, Willis didn't know, but he did know the dog's sole aim in life was to make the new interloper as uncomfortable as possible.

Then Mikki finally dropped the bombshell and told him she couldn't conceive, but only after the ink dried. Entrapment, he decided finally. She was a woman on the make for a husband and she'd caught him, hook, line and sinker. After that, she'd reverted back to her real self.

Willis had turned the tables on her though. He'd found her birth control pills and switched them out. No one was more shocked than she at the announcement. Shocked and furious because she knew she'd been found out and didn't have any recourse. He told everyone immediately and engaged his former roommate from university as her doctor.

He looked around the living room of the small rented cabin and sighed. What could he do to prevent this? A divorce? No, the judge usually awarded the children to the maternal parent. Besides, she'd have everything he'd worked so hard for. Murder? His job was healing, not killing and the thought of taking a life, even Mikki's, repelled him. Then what?

Willis had rented this place for a month, a sort of last hurrah before the baby came. He'd thought if he could just get her alone, and appeal to her motherly instincts, it would be fine. Until she waddled up to the car with HG in his custom made, hand crafted carrying case, then he knew it was game point in her favor. She was making sure Willis never touched her again.

Abandonment? Of course, he'd wait until after the baby was born. He could freeze all his assets and keep her...

A sharp tear of pain whipped his thoughts around and he cried out. HG stood there, grinning at him, blood, his blood on HG's muzzle. And all Willis could see was a child, his child, ripped to shreds with HG standing over the lifeless body.

Willis grimaced in pain as he forced the already soaked pants leg back from the wound. HG growled menacingly at him and Willis grabbed a poker and shook it at him.

"Willis? What's wrong? Is HG alright?"

"The little bastard ripped my leg open."

"Oh, thank goodness, he's not hurt. I don't blame him really. You probably haven't fed him yet, have you? If I could get up, Mommy would take care of her baby herself."

You cow, he wanted to scream. Instead, he uttered one short word, "Bitch" as he reached for a hypodermic to inject a local into his wounded leg.

The idea came to him then in a whirlwind as he was closing up the last inch of the bite. It sickened him, but it was a way out and when you came down to it, strangely appropriate.

Limping, Willis walked to the kitchen and took out a can of 'Canine Delight' from the shelf. He opened it awkwardly and shook the contents into a monogrammed dish. Glancing around to see if the dog had yet made an appearance, he carefully sprinkled the sleeping powder onto the meat by-products and mixed it up.

"HG, supper is served." He retreated from the room, entering only again when he was sure that the dog was ravenously gulping down the food. He shared at least one trait with his owner.

Softly he crept into their bedroom, carrying his bag with him.

"Willis, what are you doing?" Mikki watched him curiously as he swabbed her arm.

"Vitamins, Mikki. If you'd eat properly, I wouldn't need to do this."

"No lectures, Willis. I really don't care to hear any of them. Besides, what do I care what the kid is like? He or she is going to be someone else's problem, not mine."

"Then you've made up your mind."

"Yes and I will call the hospital in the morning and notify them of it. I won't have HG traumatized anymore. He still hates me for bringing you home."

"Of course, Mikki, anything you say, my sweet angel. Now rest." He stepped back and waited for her breathing to slow as she dropped into a deep sleep.

Willis Hutchinson wiped his hands on a kitchen towel and smiled contentedly to himself. Caesareans weren't a specialty of his, but he'd not done too badly at all. She'd heal with only a trace of the operation.

She stirred weakly as he was getting his coat from the closet.

"Willis, what happened? I don't..." she dropped a hand to her bulging abdomen and winced. "I don't feel very well. My stomach hurts."

"Must have been the shot, Mikki. Iron shots will do that. Some people react differently to them. Just rest and you'll feel better.

"Where's HG? He always makes me feel better. I can't sleep without my puppy. Where's my baby?"

Willis patted her tummy carefully. He thought of the poodle, now resting right where it belonged, and smiled widely. "HG is right where he belongs, my love. He's asleep, but I'm sure he'll let you know when he wakes up." *Well, providing it doesn't suffocate first.*

He pulled on his coat and hurried out, pausing to pick up the small bundle of life nestled in a temporary bed in HG's basket. He kissed his baby girl's forehead tenderly and opened the door, shielding her from the rain and night air.

He still had enough dynamite left over from that stump blasting job & take out the only bridge between the cabin and the main road. With that gone, it could be weeks before anyone would be able to get to the cabin. By then it would be far too late.

It was then that he heard his wife's scream and realized that HG must be awake and trying frantically to dig his way out. He smiled and held his daughter close to him. "After all, Mikki, every dog must have his day, dear." And he stepped out into the night.

CITY OF THE DEAD
By Clare de Lune

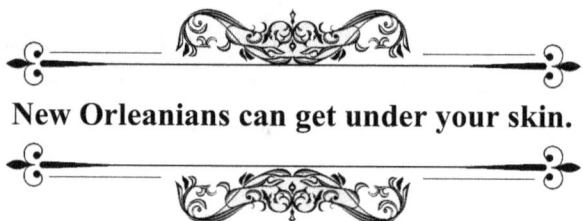

New Orleanians can get under your skin.

Clare de Lune was born and raised in South Louisiana. She studied at Louisiana State University and has a background as a librarian, journalist, web site guru, model and actress.

*Clare began writing as soon as she could hold a pen; her first short story was published at age 11 in an anthology of children's poetry and short stories titled **Ascending**. Clare's stories have also appeared in **The Horror Library**, **CRASH! Magazine** and on various erotica web sites. Several of her horror and science fiction stories have been made into film shorts, which have appeared on Santa Cruz's public access television show **Whirlpool**.*

Clare has lived in the San Francisco Bay Area, Austin and Los Angeles. She now lives and writes in the New Orleans area and enjoys the company of several rescued pets.

    Fingers traced exit wounds, turned a dark, rosy hue from the sluggish scarring of time. The only thing that was left to do was wait and hope the day would break and she would find her way out of this gruesome maze.

The little hatchback whipped around the crescent curve of I-10, forcing Holly to lean into the console. She looked out of Isaiah's driver's side window. The sky was scattered with dark, menacing clouds, pregnant with rain. She'd noticed the rise in humidity as soon as she stepped out of the New Orleans Airport, and her throat and nose seemed pinched.

Holly leaned into Izzy and he reached up absently to stroke her hair. On either side of the interstate, grey and white mausoleums jutted up into a blue-black twilight sky. A little city of the dead.

There were stories of coffins popping up out of graves during floods and heavy rains, then slowly cruising through the streets, corpses stiff and their caskets aged like old Cadillacs.

But that was if they were lucky. Those coffins usually swelled and burst, bloated with water, and out popped the corpse. Sometimes. Often, the toxic sludge of liquefied remains held the corpse to the bottom of the casket like super glue.

She had heard of something like that before. An old woman in the L.A. area befriended a homeless woman. The vagrant passed away in the passenger seat and the woman, who thought she'd surely be to blame, left her silent passenger in the car for nearly a month. When authorities removed the body, part of the seat cushion came with her before she was discovered on a routine traffic stop. The vagrant oozed generous amounts of thick, vicious matter and even had a few insects take residence in various orifices. Especially maggots. Funny how the lowest forms of life get right to work on the highest to send the body right back into the earth.

Holly bit her lip. She didn't like it here. At least in Los Angeles, they're courteous enough to give the dead a ride. Here, coffins in mausoleums are rudely pushed to the back to make room for the new 'arrivals.' And murder stories abounded. She only came in from Los Angeles when Izzy played bigger shows here. Tipitina's. The Howlin' Wolf. Honestly, she wished he'd get the fuck out of here and make a name for himself in California. Anything would be better than this.

Soon, they exited and crept all the way down into the Quarter, whipped down Decatur (Izzy promised they'd go to Fiorella's, then maybe Molly's later), then up Dumaine to the apartment.

They walked and talked and argued about him coming to L.A. or her moving down to New Orleans. Despite not being able to budge him, it was nice seeing him again and roaming the Quarter when it was cool, windy and overcast.

They ate dinner in near silence, so back at the apartment, they did what they always resorted to: they fucked.

It was kind of nice with the rain pouring in the background, lightening ripping through the sky like a white hot scar, thunder rattling Izzy's mismatched dishes. Soon, Izzy dozed and she lay back on the cool sheets, slick with sex-sweat and full of thoughts.

She started calling him Izzy instead of Isaiah right after they'd met, after Hurricane Katrina. She didn't like 'Isaiah' and his stupid prophetic message. 'The land will be completely laid to waste and totally plundered.' Remembering it, she scoffed. *Hadn't that shit already happened?* Katrina turned New Orleans into a giant cesspool, and Izzy came to stay with Holly's brother, Keith, an old band mate. That's how she met him, and it didn't take them long to fall in love and fuck.

Of course, Izzy went back to the cesspool, the only thing he'd ever known. And Holly called and cried, called and cried, until they worked out this miserable sort of long distance thing.

She twisted over to her side, propped her head up in her hand and gazed at him. He was completely still, and she had to stare to make sure he was breathing. An old lantern, hanging from the intricate iron lattice outside, provided little light through the old French doors. The faded amber glow crept in, providing just enough light to see shadows and outlines. She could see more detail in his face now that her eyes had adjusted to the light.

She heard the strange sound before she saw the thing. It was a low rattle, then a vague hiss. A black, sleek shadow scurried across Izzy's alabaster face, then disappeared into the shadowy contours of his dark hair.

She gasped, leaned over and looked for the thing.

No. Not possible. Had that really happened?

She didn't even want to think of what kinds of critters emerged when it rained like this. All kinds of things would be looking for shelter and warmth. She drew the crisp sheets around her, tried to forget about what she thought she saw. As she did, she reached down and scratched her thigh and felt something.

Fucking mosquitoes. They were relentless little things, she thought as she scratched the swollen bump right above her knee. *Must have gotten in from the French doors.* As she scratched harder, her eyes widened.

The bite was moving right beneath her fingernails.

She lurched out of bed and switched on the bedside lamp. There it was, wriggling under her skin, slowly making its way up her leg. As the thing travelled under her flesh, it left a raging red path behind it and the skin swelled.

For a moment, she was too freaked out to move; she finally whirled around to wake Izzy.

As she shook him, he felt stiff, and those familiar hisses seemed to be all around her now. Somehow, the rain was also much more amplified. The French doors must have opened. She absent-mindedly rushed to shut them and was met with another surge of bright lighting.

A crackle, then a loud electrical pop. The power was out, and now the fetid creature in her leg squirmed on up the highways of braided nerves. She screamed and cupped her hand over the squirming, disgusting thing, tried to stop it in its tracks, but it persevered. It moved and wriggled beneath her sweaty palm.

Another pulse of lightning showcased the tiny strings of bruises the thing had left behind, a violet ribbon of agony. As the worm-like abomination neared her hip, a tortuous burning filled her groin.

She raced to the phone on the nightstand, tripped on the edge of the rug, and careened across the room. She toppled the nightstand and fumbled with the phone.

No service.

Of course.

On the bed, Izzy seemed to be swaying to some phantom beat. With the infrequent lightning flashes as her only source of light, she saw scaly, glossy black bodies racing in and out of his mouth, nose and ears. He was also nearly covered with squirming white worms that had totally obliterated his once handsome facial features.

Holly darted into the kitchen, the pain searing up and down her leg like a rocket. The thing was carving into her skin and she pinned it under her thumb, trying to crush it. As she pushed, she could feel it boring further into her flesh, consuming pulpy nerves and tissue.

The thing was consuming her, and another flash of faint light told her there were more, multiplying like an infestation.

She yanked open a drawer, fumbled with the contents, and withdrew a small, yet sharp carving knife. It whispered metallically as it sliced the air.

Without hesitation, she planted the tip into her flesh, piercing the skin, and a dot of crimson welled up in its place. The tip of the blade bore into the little worm, and for a moment, the pain stopped. She stabbed where she could feel the foul little creatures squirming and writhing, hoping to eradicate them all with the sharp tip of the blade.

But within seconds, a new pain reared its agonizing, raw head. This time, Holly cried out, clutched her hands to her ears and screamed.

She could hear the insatiable chewing in her ears, could feel the slippery-scaly texture of some millipede-like creature ravaging her facial features as it ventured along with each tearing bite.

The rain and gushing water outside seemed to be a relief from the blossoming humidity of earlier, and now it seemed to be a welcoming, cooling sanctuary from the hot anguish of the creatures inside her. She was drawn outside, hoping somehow that the rain would wash it all away.

She ran and screamed, clawing at her face, hoping someone, anyone, would hear.

With mud caked around her feet, she sloshed through the lengths of growing, mucky puddles until she tumbled to the sodden earth.

There she sat, tracing the little exit wounds where the worms took residence inside her, hoping the storm would stop, that light would break.

Strangely, the gnawing stopped and it was quiet.

Or at least she thought it was. The pain began at the base of her neck; it bloomed all around, driving through her skull like a screwdriver.

In some raw, exotic insight, she knew.

As her screaming brain was finally descended upon, light did finally break, revealing the wet used husks of the bodies from the little city of the dead.

WANT
By Meself John

Contribution received anonymously near a bench at the Wheeling Civic Center. This is being published with the understanding that the author will not attempt any further contact with the editors or publisher.

God wanted for women to suffer,
For they are unearthly beings.
God made them to be help mates,
For this should be.
But these women are not.
For unto these women nothing is good.
The sun did not shine
The buds did not bloom;
For they are of Satan.
They shall pay with a gift of pain of birth.
For they should suffer this at least:
Nine times as painful as the burn of the sun.
For sunlight will not shine;
For their fornications are not manly.
They should suffer not this?
They are unwilling uncaring *selfish bitches*.
They suck one another.
They shall pay for their ways!
I will see to this,
Because they are willful tramps
Who will suffer pain.

My mother did it more to my father,
For this she shall pay first.
And her name is Brenda:
A strong and caring soul.
All children of god will pay.
He is the biggest lie,
For I prayed and nothing came right!!!!!!!!
My father died of horrid, horrendous suffering,
Which came from this *slitch*.
All will pay,
For none are without sin.
Including her.
May her every day upon this earth be hell.
And her sister is a class act too.
So, I fucked up.
I had both of them up the ass.
And they liked it,
Like they like all things men do.
Sherry will be mine though,
For she was the best.
No screaming or anything.
For this I will change them all.
For the death of them will occur time and time again forever.
I can and I will.
I promise with all of my cum, shit and everything.
Because that tramp exists,
I will make her every day a humiliation forever.
For Sherry is the love of her life.
Ten is one.
No, twenty is still pussy.
Cuntie *slitch*!
Slitches all of them!
She will pay with tail;
Just like mother,
Who was born without love of life.
For there was none…
Because I exist.

SCI-FI & FANTASY

ALIEN APOCALYPSE

By Zmortis

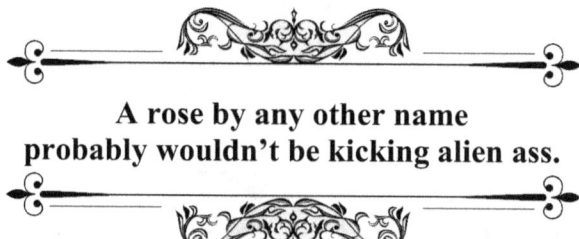

**A rose by any other name
probably wouldn't be kicking alien ass.**

*The blogger/fan fic writer **Zmortis** is occasionally known for his pedantic yet polite debate style in several Internet forums. His "anti-troll" stance of stubborn yet unflappable debate is also documented in several sites. His opinions on politics, religion, and "human rights" are generally considered abrasive, and certainly not of the politically correct variety. The story **Alien Apocalypse** in **The Big Book of Bizarro** is the first time Zmortis has seen print under the banner of Burning Bulb Publishing.*

Time: 08:37 hours zulu.
Date: October 13, 2218.
Location: Earth Station R-26 in high orbit.

The man in the dark green crisply pressed uniform stepped through the sliding metal doorway to stand before the durasteel desk with the synthoid secretary sitting behind it. The synthoid secretary made a soft "whiring" noise for a moment as its smooth plastic head with the glowing glass globes, where eyes should be, oriented in his direction.

The synthoid secretary spoke softly, "Greetings Major Aarron. Brigadier General Proxler is expecting your arrival. I am informing him of your presence now. Please be seated."

Just as Major Aarron began to sit in the chair along the wall the doorway to the inner office opened. Standing there was a trim fit older man wearing a crisp dark navy colored uniform with a shiny star on each shoulder.

General Proxler shouted in his best impression of an irate drill instructor, "You stupid worthless piece of shit!"

Major Aarron quickly stood at attention and saluted the General.

General Proxler reflexively returned the salute and then looked at the Major's stiff expression, "Sorry Major. I was talking to this useless low-bidder piece of garbage I was saddled with instead of a working human."

General Proxler shouted at the synthoid secretary, "I told you to send the Major into my office."

The synthoid secretary focused its globes on Major Aarron, "General Proxler will see you now. Please enter his office."

Major Aarron followed the retreating back of General Proxler back to his desk and stood at attention as the General took his seat. The door behind the Major slid closed with a soft hiss.

General Proxler spoke, "Report Major. How is Project Rose coming? We're in desperate need of some positive news. They even authorized the fifth from lowest bid on this one. Confidentially speaking it was only seven down from the top bid. I hope this impresses upon you how serious the brass and politicos are about supporting this particular initiative."

Major Aarron took off his hat and had a slight grin, "We've almost completed the project sir. We're only fifteen percent over budget. We're actually under schedule projections by three percent."

General Proxler nodded, "Are those the reported numbers, or the real ones?"

Major Aarron replied, "The actual numbers sir. We've only fudged the reports to show on time and 20% over budget. There should be plenty left over for an upgraded synthoid secretary model for you sir."

General Proxler gave a broad grin, "Very impressive Major Aarron. So this is what it is like to not be required to use the lowest bidder. Is the prognosis for a working product good?"

Major Aarron smiled, "The prototype is already up to eighty percent of expected efficiency. It only remains to iron out the last few details before we are ready for the first full open field test."

General Proxler leaned back in his chair, "Do you think it's ready for Metros Sector?"

Major Aarron raised an eyebrow, "Are you thinking the Gama Libra Alpha colony?"

General Proxler nodded, "That colony has been completely overrun with the facebuggers. If we can take it back, then there is a chance for success everywhere else."

Time: 17:26 hours zulu Earth Standard Time.
Date: February 26, 2221.
Location: in orbit over Gama Libra Alpha world six, human colony New Pleasance, aboard the UNSF cruiser Dykion.

The ship Captain stood next to the scientist wearing the Mesa Mons Multi-Conglomerate logo lab coat. They were peering into a view portal into a chamber sealed with a vault style door. The scientist looked beside the portal at a glowing status panel.

The Captain spoke, "Are you sure Project Rose will be ready to launch soon?"

The scientist nodded, "The recovery from deep hibernation is proceeding per our estimations. This model of biomechanical can withstand the rigors of long sleep much better than a typical human."

The Captain looked around cautiously to make sure no one else was nearby before peering back into the chamber, "The rumors are that human genetic material was used in its construction."

The scientist replied, "The accords prevent us from using genetic material from living human donors. This project was run above board according to all of the standards for genetic bio engineering."

The Captain looked over at the scientist, "Come on. It looks too human to not be based on human DNA. Where did you guys get the stuff without violating any regulations?"

The scientist looked around himself, "Completely off the record?"

The Captain nodded, "As long as it works, I really don't care how it was done. I'll not put anything in my reports."

The scientist gave a little grin, "I don't know this for sure, but the company scuttlebutt is that we needed DNA with a specific personality profile. I'm told we found a couple of graves of Twentieth Century era actresses who fit the profiles required, and liberated the necessary DNA. That's how we came up with the name Project Rose. They coincidentally both had the same first name."

The Captain looked back inside, "Fascinating. You avoided the accords by using dead tissue then. So Mesa Mons used tissue from people long dead with no living immediate relatives to object to a bit of grave robbery."

The scientist smiled, "The proper court orders were filed to open up the graves for forensic examination. It may just be that not all the material made it back into the graves afterwards. It is too bad we couldn't get the first choice of material. That subject would have been near perfect, but I suppose then the name Project Rose wouldn't have fit so well."

The Captain looked over at the chamber again, "For actresses they certainly weren't very attractive source material. The result is somewhat repulsive."

The scientist nodded, "Repulsive to you and I as a safety measure to prevent us from being accidentally harmed by her. I'm told the lab tests showed the facebuggers were not so discriminating, and suffered greatly because of it. If you think she is repulsive now, you should see what she will look like in six months after she regains the weight lost in hibernation."

The Captain grinned, "When can we be ready to commence the testing?"

The scientist checked the reading, "Project Rose should be readjusted to operating condition within the week, and prepared for drop pod insertion shortly afterward."

The Captain nodded, "Very good. The sooner we can show a successful deployment, the better it will be for us. It seriously creeps me out to even be orbiting a planet infested with facebuggers."

Time: 01:11 hours New Pleasance colony standard time.
Date: March 8, 2221 Earth calendar.
Location: near San Fragino City on Gama Libra Alpha world six New Pleasance colony.

A bright streak crossed the dark sky, watched by the compound eyes of a house cat sized bluish chitinous being. The creature only had four legs so it didn't actually classify by Earth standards as a true bug. However its appearance and notable behavioral trait certainly didn't lend itself to any more apt description than facebugger.

Facebuggers were the scourge of the outer colony worlds. They were deceptively clever for a species that didn't use tools. They seemingly understood the purpose of most human weapon systems, and instinctively avoided contact with any humans who carried them. They preferred to catch lone humans asleep or unaware, and then mount their faces to implant the human with their already fertilized eggs. They had a rather long appendage nicknamed their "fifth leg" for this purpose.

The "fifth leg" of a facebugger was tough and resilient, making it difficult to cut like most of their exoskeleton. Biting was usually a futile effort when a facebugger mounted a victim to fill them with their foul "spunk." Most colonists wore helmets to avoid the preferred method of assault, but the facebuggers would actually seek any available orifice if a mouth was not accessible.

The facebugger watching the glowing streak across the sky issued a call, "Sweeeeet."

Several other facebuggers crawled out from their nests among the arid landscape. A rising chorus joined the first facebugger, "Sweeeeeeeeeeet."

Suddenly the noise stopped, and a rolling wave of facebuggers began scuttling across the dusty ground toward the impact point for the drop pod. The loud bang of its supersonic passage rumbled through the sky, and its retro rockets fired to slow its rapid descent. The facebuggers began their inexorable hunt for fresh prey.

Time: 05:42 hours New Pleasance colony standard time.
Date: March 8, 2221 Earth calendar.
Location: drop pod landing spot near San Fragino City on Gama Libra Alpha world six New Pleasance colony.

The radio on the drop pod crackled with a frantic voice blaring from the wire mesh of the speaker grill, "I repeat you are in a quarantine zone. The facebugger migration is in effect. You are too far out to send immediate rescue. Stay in your escape craft until a patrol can reach your location. Do not attempt to journey to the city on your own. Please respond if you are receiving our message."

Rose looked at the grill through her heavy goggles. A black leather hood was stretched over her head with long fiber spikes forming a crest along the ridge. A wire grill covered her mouth. No facebugger was making its way with its fifth member through that or getting a good grip on her head around those spikes.

Rose's frame was lean and wiry. Her body was lightly attired with little modesty. Expandable nylamesh stockings were on her legs, heavy leather platform boots on her feet, and a spiked brassier covered her small breasts. Of particular note, she wore a set of heat resistant lyrion crotch-less panties leaving little to the imagination for anyone viewing her from that angle.

The long sleep had left Rose somewhat weak, and ravenously hungry. The man on the ship had promised her lobster, and by her creator she knew how to cook a mean lobster. Rose drooled slightly as she watched the monitor screen showing the first arrival of her promised dinner.

Rose mashed the large yellow button on the emergency com, "Take all the time you need boys. I'm going to cook myself some dinner first."

Rose then jerked the handle on the release level for the drop pod hatch. The explosive bolts threw the hatch clear of the pod. Rose stepped clear of the hatchway and met the first onrushing facebugger with a punch. The facebugger's tough exoskeleton protected it from serious damage, but it scrambled on its back for a moment.

Rose tread across the prone facebugger, but failed to damage it. She seemed confused a moment then peered down at her frame.

Rose shook her head, "Too light. I'm much too light. Like the creator said I need to feed."

Rose was knocked into the dusty ground on her hands and knees by a face bugger leaping down from the drop pod. It had instinctively avoided her sharp pointy head and breasts to attempt mounting her from behind. It skillfully guided its "fifth leg" into her vagina causing a rough grunt of satisfaction to come from Rose.

Rose gleefully called out, "I got you now you fucker! I'm going to get me some lobster tonight."

Rose squeezed her vaginal muscles like they had taught her. The pudenda dentata engaged, gripping the "fifth leg," and subsequently severing it. A gout of clear ichor oozed from Rose's vagina.

The facebugger squealed like a stuck pig and tried to frantically pull free. Rose engaged the mechanism hidden in the front of her bikini panties and a rain of hot sparks shot forward onto the ground. Her eyes narrowed a bit as she squeezed the massive amount of methane gas trapped in her intestines out from her rippling sphincter in a blooming blast of flaming furnace flatulence.

As the facebugger behind her went up in flames, Rose triumphantly cried out to the other facebuggers, "Can you smell what I'm cooking!?"

The chitinous exoskeleton of the facebugger behind her turned from a deep bluish color to a bright red. Rose grabbed the dead facebugger with her heat resistant gloves, and began impaling it upon the spikes affixed to her brassier until she managed to crack its shell open. She then pulled out chunks of the white meat inside.

Rose tipped her head back and began pushing the pieces of facebugger meat past the metal grill of her facemask. She moaned and murmured in pleasure as the nearby facebuggers who had witnessed the event fled from her presence.

Rose finished the last of the scraps inside the shell and smiled, "The creator is generous. There are lots of delicious lobsters here for me. Thank the creator."

Time: 12:22 hours zulu.
Date: November 11, 2224.
Location: Earth Station R-26 in high orbit.

The man in the dark green crisply pressed uniform stepped through the sliding metal doorway to stand before the mahogany desk with the android secretary sitting behind it. The android secretary leaned seductively forward with her striking green eyes and looked in his direction.

The android secretary spoke in sweetly seductive tones, "Hello Colonel Aarron. Lieutenant General Proxler is expecting your arrival. Please head on in to his office."

Colonel Aarron stepped through the doorway to see a pleased looking Lieutenant General Proxler wearing his new third star on his shoulder as proudly as Colonel Aarron wore his new birds on his lapels. They grinned at each other as Colonel Aarron saluted and General Proxler responded in kind.

General Proxler sat back down behind his mahogany desk, "Report Colonel."

Colonel Aarron replied, "Project Rose number 58 has been deployed at infested colony world Fantasia IV. As per our other deployments, Rose 58 had begun the counter facebugger operations. There has been a minor unanticipated hitch however."

General Proxler ran his hand across his sleek desk surface a moment before asking, "What problem is this? Is this Rose not fully conditioned, or are these facebuggers adapting in some way to counter our measures?"

Colonel Aarron shook his head, "No the program itself appears to be running according to the usual planned parameters. Drop the Rose project in the heaviest infested area, have it devastate the majority of the local facebugger population, and put her on a deep sleep ship to the next hotspot, which allows her to lose all that weight she gains in project performance."

General Proxler raised an eyebrow, "Are the facebuggers learning to avoid Rose then?"

Colonel Aarron nodded, "That has always been a side effect, but a planned one of course. They still avoid all humans after witnessing Rose at work on their kind. The facebugger's innate aversion to weaponry still hasn't genetically grasped that the project Roses are the only humans with these capabilities. The remaining facebuggers generally die out in a generation or two without a place to implant their eggs. No, the issue is the environmentalist movement sir."

General Proxler's brows knit together, "The environmentalist movement is causing problems?"

Colonel Aaron nodded again, "Yes sir. It seems they are studying the population density numbers of the facebugger incursions. They are claiming that before too long the facebuggers will become extinct if nothing is done to preserve their numbers."

General Proxler put his hand to his chin for a moment, "Easy enough to fix then I guess. Put out an announcement under the emergency powers act. Let it be known that any environmentalist who wants to preserve the facebugger population can sign up to volunteer for a new project Rose free colony on Sigma Mylon Ceta."

Colonel Aarron smiled, "Wasn't that the first colony sector to be overrun by the facebuggers and wiped out?"

General Proxler smiled, "Of course it was. That colony also had nothing in the way of developable resources worth mentioning either, so the failure of that colony had more to do with introducing the facebugger plague to every other colony planet than any other significant problem. The world is still technically habitable in any case. The only question is whether you like getting facefucked, and having to pass facebugger larva through your intestines every few days. If these environmentalists like the facebuggers so much, then they can volunteer to support their remaining population."

Colonel Aarron nodded, "That sounds like a good plan sir."

General Proxler stood, "Thank you Colonel. By the way good work on the project, and congratulations on your promotion."

Colonel Aarron smiled, "You too as well sir. It's amazing what can be done when you don't have to use the lowest bidder isn't it?"

General Proxler shook his head, "Don't get too used to it. That was a once in a career event. Make the most of the success you got from it."

Colonel Aarron nodded, "Very good Lieutenant General Proxler. Permission to be dismissed sir?"

General Proxler and Colonel Aaron saluted each other as General Proxler spoke, "Carry on Colonel."

Time: 09:54 hours New Pleasance colony standard time.
Date: March 8, 2235 Earth calendar.
Location: San Fragino City on Gama Libra Alpha world six New Pleasance colony.

The man looked at the obese leather clad spiky headed nightmare strutting through town looking through dumpsters in a vain attempt to locate any hiding facebuggers. She turned her cow-like eyes toward the colonist and ambled over in his direction.

The man spoke, "Look honey, you've ate the last of them already I'm telling you. No facebuggers have been seen in these parts for over two years now. You'll have to move out toward another colony to find more of them."

Rose had tears dripping down from her eyes, "They aren't coming to pick me up. They said all the buggers here run faster than I can anymore. It isn't my fault they're so delicious. The creators said I could have all I could eat. I'm still hungry."

The man shook his head, "Poor girl. They've really done a number on you with their conditioning haven't they? Look, maybe you can get a job doing something else. You can survive on different food can't you?"

Rose looked hopefully up at the man, "Do you have some steaks? I like steaks too. That's what the creators fed me in the training."

The man shrugged, "Sure we got plenty of good meat now that the facebuggers aren't hanging around buggering all the livestock anymore. Would you like a job at the videocast station? I hear they are looking for a talk show host. You'd fit in fine with those artsy types I think."

Rose looked up, "You really think so?"

The man nodded, "Freaks and misfits seem to be right up their alley. You should do great there. Let me make some calls. If I get you the job I'll only take a thirty percent cut as your agent. Then I'll buy you as many steaks as you like."

Rose smiled, "I can cook them myself."

The man winced, "I'm sure you can sweetheart. I'm sure you can. Maybe we'll get you a cooking show."

SAVED

By Thomas Fuchs

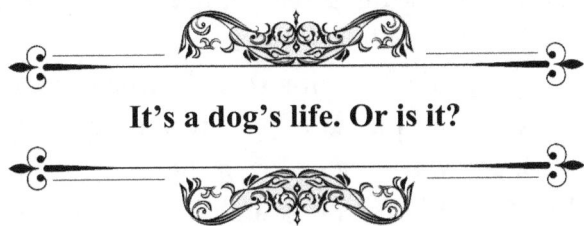

It's a dog's life. Or is it?

Thomas Fuchs has spent much of his career writing television documentaries and some print non-fiction. Over the past few years, he has been enjoying the freedom of imagination and invention afforded by the writing of fiction. He can be reached at fuchsfoxxx@cs.com.

He had done so many cruel things in his life, compulsively, unable to control himself even as he knew that in lashing out he was only making things worse for himself. A wife pushed away, a child who detested him with good reason, jobs lost, a year in prison for pointless violence. And all the time hating himself. He wasn't a monster. Not really. So when he opened his front door and found the beagle pup sitting there, he looked around for an owner, gave it a bowl of water, and later that afternoon walked the neighborhood looking for "Lost Dog" signs. That night, he fed the pup some scraps.

He worked at home, buying and selling on-line, and as he worked that evening, he was struck by how the pup settled so comfortably into its new home. Home? He corrected himself – not home, temporary surroundings.

The next day, he made up a few "Dog Found" flyers and taped them to lampposts and trees as he made his way to the market, where he bought dog food. A few days later, he started calling the dog by a name, "Bugsy" as in "Bugsy the Beagle."

He'd never had a pet before – never been completely and solely responsible for any living thing before, had never had such control, such responsibility. If he failed at this…

He took Bugsy with him almost everywhere he went. On his little sloop, his weekend pleasure boat, when the weather suddenly kicked up and Bugsy was knocked from his feet by the pitch of the boat and still looked at him with complete trust, he grabbed his dog and held him tight. Then, when the weather calmed, he held Bugsy over the side and let go.

The water was so cold that the strength was instantly drained from his legs. He was completely helpless, but he could see, see clearly the look on his face back on the boat, twisted in agony, a groan of loss and horror and self-loathing.

And then the numbing cold gave way to warmth. He could still see himself in the boat and he wanted to shout out, "You are forgiven, forgiven, forgiven."

PEARL

By Scott Emerson

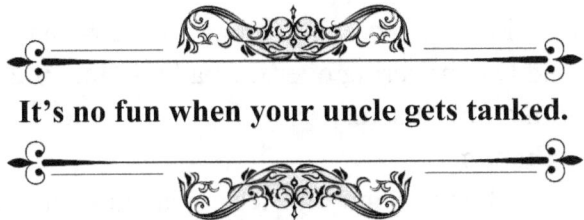

It's no fun when your uncle gets tanked.

Scott Emerson comes with everything shown here. (Mega Drunken Zombie playset sold separately). Perhaps best known for his blog 365 Days of the Dead, Scott's stories have appeared in Weird Tales' "One Minute" video series, Everyday Weirdness, Flashshot, and the undead e-anthology Putrid Poems and Sickening Sketches. Look sharp and you'll catch him in Greg Lamberson's film Slime City Massacre. He lives in Pennsylvania.

The creature I'd found in the garage looked like a pale gray melon streaked with unfamiliar colors. It had scuttled from beneath Dad's jigsaw on a cluster of short knobby legs, staring up at me with eye after eye.

I stared back, the box of Dad's porno mags I'd been searching for momentarily forgotten. Ever since that day the sky had cracked I was discovering things like this around the house. I immediately found something to poke it with.

Just as I started having some real fun, watching as the melon-thing tripped on the first few of its eyes I'd uncorked, Dad called me from inside.

"Zeke! Come quick!"

I dropped the stick and ran to see what was wrong. Only once had Dad sounded so urgent: that time a pterodactyl with a woman's face flew from a rift in the sky and carried off Pap-Pap.

***

The commotion was coming from the upstairs bathroom. I rushed in to find Dad hovering over the bathtub, looking frightened.

"What's going on?" I said.

"It's your Grandma."

Grandma was lying in the tub, legs splayed over the sides. Her housecoat had been torn open, revealing her sagging, mottled breasts and hideously distended abdomen. She flailed her arms, frothing the rising water.

"Is Grandma going into labor again?" I asked.

"Not now, Zeke," Dad said. "You head down to the kitchen, we're gonna need--"

Grandma cut him off with a shriek. Her hands clenched in response to the pain, hard enough that her fingernails dug tracks into the tub's fiberglass surface. The mound of her belly undulated as another contraction hit and Grandma's vulva hiccupped, disgorging a cloud of black ink. A glistening pink lump shot from between her thighs into the sullied water.

Dad bent and scooped it out. The lump was a squid-looking thing--roughly a foot long with a single vein-choked eye at its center. Its beak snapped at the air as the squid's tentacles wrapped around Dad's hand and suckled.

"Well I'll be," he said and started to cry. He'd always wanted a brother.

***

Grandma, I'm surprised to say, really took to her squid. She kept it in a 55-gallon fish tank by her bed, feeding it chunks of bread and canned tuna. She named it Pearl. When I mentioned it didn't really look like a Pearl, Grandma shushed me. She gave birth to it, she could name it Pearl if she wanted.

I liked Pearl. Often when Grandma was downstairs watching TV I'd sit on her bed and gaze into his big, veiny eyeball. My favorite pastime was poking him until he got mad and shot ink at me. It was fun, at least until I had to change his water before Dr. Oz was over.

When Pearl was a week old I was hunched beside his tank, wondering if Grandma would notice if I pried his eye out, when a thought entered my head. One I hadn't thought myself.

The decrepit one, the thought said. *She angers me.*

"Pearl? Are you thinking inside my head?"

Silence, you imbecile. That wretched crone from whose loins I emerged, she is a dim, despicable creature unworthy of anything but a slow demise.

"You want to kill Grandma? Why?"

I deserve better than this execrable existence, eating the substandard morsels she casts. I'm the first-born descendant of Brakahakathulubee, Squid Lord of the Eighth Realm. His bloodlust surges through my veins.

"So . . . what are you going to do?"

At the appropriate time, when that dried-out husk least suspects it, I shall call forth my tentacled brethren. And my first official act as ruler of this pitiful world will be to leap from this cheap glass prison and chew that bitch's face off.

"Did you tell her?"

Of course. But as my only method of communication is telepathy, she merely thinks she's senile.

I stepped toward the tank, reaching for the heavy brass paperweight on Grandma's nightstand.

Don't be foolish, biped. You too shall tremble at the might of Brakahakathulubee.

Nodding, I backed off. How was I going to tell Grandma her pet squid had just ordered her death?

Oh, and one more thing, you sick little degenerate: poke me one more time, and I'll see to it the Slaves of Cephalodom bite your prick off.

＊＊＊

Pearl meant what he said about killing Grandma, but when I tried to warm her she refused to believe me. She loved that stupid squid and would stop me if I attempted to hurt it. I had to do something, but what?

Nighttime, I knew, would be the best time to act.

Once everyone was asleep I crept down the hallway to Grandma's bedroom. Her snoring covered the noise as the door creaked open. By her bed, Pearl floated in his tank, also sleeping.

I tiptoed to the tank without much of a plan. If that squid could read my mind, I'd have a better chance of getting the drop on Pearl by winging it. Bending over the tank I reached into the oily water, wondering exactly how you strangled a squid.

Gingerly my hands curled around Pearl's body, just below his eye, feeling the gentle rhythm of his breathing. Slowly I started to squeeze, gradually increasing the pressure. Pearl's pulse thrummed against my skin, but the squid never stirred. I pressed my thumbs into his center, hard. Tiny bubbles gurgled from his beak. I allowed myself to grin; killing Pearl would be easier than I thought.

Then Grandma rolled onto her side and farted.

Pearl's eye flicked open.

Foolish human! You shall pay for this hubris with your life!

In a shimmering pink flash Pearl squirted from my grip and flung himself from the tank, tentacles thrashing. He collided into my face and before I could react he wrapped himself around my skull,

206

smothering me with slimy flesh. His beak clamped onto my bottom lip, drawing blood.

Struggling, I tried pulling him loose, but his suction cups were fastened tight to my skin and he wriggled too much to grab hold. Breathing quickly became difficult.

With a war cry muffled by writhing squidmeat, I lunged face-first into Pearl's tank. Glass exploded and warm, reeking water gushed over my head. Pearl remained in place.

Grabbing a wedge of broken glass, I jammed it as hard as I could into that stupid eye of his. Pearl screamed twice: once from his beak and once inside my head.

No, you Shogthirrup-damned fool! Look what you've done!

With another shard I sliced at the tentacles clinging to my head. It was difficult, the edge barely shaving the surface of his thick, squirming flesh, but Pearl's injuries had weakened him. He soon lost his grip, plopping to the floor.

I was free, able to breathe again.

From the ruined tank I plucked a jagged spear-shaped piece of the frame. Ignoring Pearl's frantic pleas in my brain I plunged it into the mass of tentacles while twisting the glass in his eye. Pearl thrashed, spurting ink. Spurting a lot of blood.

Spare me, human, I beg you! I can make you a god, worshipped by sea creatures in twelve dimensions!

Pearl writhed as I ran the length of frame through his body. His eye throbbed, bulged in its socket, until it was nudged free by the frame's pointed tip. The liberated orb rolled beneath Grandma's bed.

You may think you've conquered us. Pearl's voice grew faint inside my head. *But the vengeance of Brakahakathulubee is legendary. We found one channel into this wretched world, we'll find another. And you will know the true meaning of suffering.*

The last drop of ink oozed from Pearl's body and he was still.

***

Grandma was pissed when she found out what I'd done to Pearl. I tried telling her it was self-defense, offering my shredded lip as evidence, but she wouldn't listen. Oh well. She forgets things pretty easily and who knows, maybe next time she'll give birth to something friendlier.

As for me, I knew Pearl's dying threat was more than a melodramatic send-off. For many sleepless nights I'd lain wondering when his time to exact revenge would come.

Tonight I've stopped wondering.

The pain first appeared as a slight cramping somewhere within my intestine, quickly intensifying as it spread throughout my abdomen. In a matter of seconds it felt as if my belly was too small to contain the sensation, for the pain began branching toward my crotch.

Just now I put a palm below my navel, where the swelling is worst, and felt something, a lot of somethings . . . wriggling. Unbearable pressure builds in my groin until a single bead of black ink drips from my urethra.

The vengeance of Brakahakathulubee is legendary, and I think my suffering has just begun.

WORMS

By George R. Galuschak

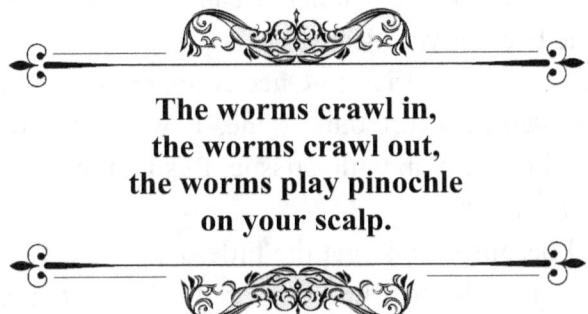

**The worms crawl in,
the worms crawl out,
the worms play pinochle
on your scalp.**

*George Galuschak is a graduate of Viable Paradise. His short fiction has appeared in **Strange Horizons**, **PodCastle** and the **Apexology: Science Fiction and Fantasy** anthology. He is currently writing a novel, just like every other author on earth.*

Things the worms don't like - 1) alcohol; 2) tobacco; 3) porn.

When I'm in charge I do all three.

Watch *Taboo XXIII* one hand on my malt liquor the other on my cock cigarette in my mouth ashtray overflowing pizza boxes everywhere Tracy in the other room crying because I'm messing up the carpet.

I'm not always in charge, though. The worms drill deep. My brain riddled with holes. They leave the parts that make me walk and talk and sleep and eat because I'm no good dead.

For some reason they left me, too, but I'm not always there.

***

At the video store.

Gun in my pocket.

I'm at the video store, gun in my pocket.

Dark shades covering my eyes. I can't stand light, but my nose. I can smell if you're sick. I can smell if you're having your period. I can smell what you ate for dinner. I can smell a six-hour ago fart, clinging to the back of your jeans.

Not here for porn. I drive to Queens for porn, and it's worth it – watching the worms spurt out of me, a wet mass of angel hair spaghetti. Wiping them up with a tissue, flushing the toilet, and that's when I think I can win.

It's stupid because I only get the little ones – the swaying hair on the roof of my mouth; the blind ones that infest my crap; the ones I puke out, reeking of cigarette smoke and bad booze.

The big ones don't come out.

***

At work.

Yesterday.

"Bad night?" Max asks. We sit in his office, lights dimmed, boards nailed across the windows.

"Yeah." My head hurts because I drank eight beers the night before. The morning sun woke me, curled up in Tracy's flowerbed, a blanket tucked neatly over my shoulders, puke and fat sticky worms crusted all over my shirt.

"Your brain makes a certain chemical, because it's different." Max pours himself a cup of sludgy coffee. "Not a lot different, just a little. We can't stand the taste, so you're not processed. Not all the way."

"What can I do?" I ask him.

"I don't know." Max shrugs and sips coffee. "If I knew what to do I'd do it."

Max is a friend of mine. When he's not working on the worm's Vision Statement (World Conquest by 2015) he tries to help me out. It's not Max's fault he's the King Worm. It's not his fault I spit into the office coffeepot. The worms incubated there, swimming round and round like tadpoles in a pond, and infected everyone in the office.

***

Tracy.

Love making.

Making love to Tracy.

The lights on. We want to see each other.

The worms squirming out of my cock. into her.

She, saying: "Henry, I feel funny."

The last time I saw her alive.

***

"Why read a book when you can scan a magazine?" Max asks. "Why scan a magazine when you can watch TV?"

"How should I know?" I mutter.

"I'm asking you because I don't know." Max sighs. "You read books."

"Not anymore," I tell him, which is true. When I'm not in charge, it's like I'm asleep, and when I wake something's changed. My books, gone; a TV set in the bedroom, turned to *Dancing with the Stars*; a magazine rack installed above the toilet paper holder, stuffed full of *Reader's Digest* and *Sports Illustrated* and *Time* magazine.

Max looks at me. "You can learn twenty ways to jump-start your sex life, or how to run a marathon, or J-Lo's fitness regime. What more do you want?"

"How should I know?" I shrug, annoyed that I'm repeating myself.

"That's what you want." Max makes a tent with his fingers. "People, you know. We hired a market research firm, and that's what they told us. People want TV; they want food full of grease and fat and salt; they want to live in houses that take thirty years to pay off; they want big unsafe cars that guzzle gas; they want sex 3.7 times a week…"

"Where do you get the .7?" I'm getting interested in spite of myself.

Max nods, wisely. "Spontaneous sex."

***

At the video store.

People, rushing back and forth.

Gathering moVies.

A fat guy brushes pAst me, towards a kiD shelving boXes.

I'm Getting tired. gOing to Sleep. Something i neEd to do. First.

"I'm looking for a movie." The fat guY SAys. "Don't know the name. It's about this female cop whose partner gets killed."

"Does she go undercover?" THE kId'S NamETag sayS rODNEY. "At a strip club, maybe?"

"Yeah." The fAt guY nods. He's A regulAr woRM cONdoMInium. "You know the movie?"

"*Fatal Embrace.* Action-Adventure." RoDney TurNs. to m.e. "Can I help you, sir?"

"Yes, thank you." i TakE tHe Gun from My pocKet aNd Blow His bRaiNs out.

***

Tracy: wHy WoN'T yOu TaLk To mE? wHy Won'T yOu MaKe Love tO Me?

Me: bEcaUse You Are A woRm.

Tracy: i'm LoNelY. I'M sCaReD.

Me: i'M SoRRy, TrACy, But yOu Are a worM.

Tracy: I love you. dOn'T yOu BelievE me?

Me: ***

Tracy: I Am PrEgnAnT, hEnrY. wE arE GoINg tO havE a bAbY.

Me: Oh my God.

***

RoDnEy hiTs the Floor. I see hIs brains, Spraying out, looking like peTRified coral, swarming with whiTe maggots, and when the Adrenaline hits, it wakes me up.

"Holy shit." The fat guy gapes at me. He says it louder. "Holy shit."

"Shit's not holy," I say, and shoot him five times in the belly. His gut splits open and a tar black worm thick as a bicycle tire spills onto the carpet. It thrashes about, watery egg eyes rolling, sucker mouth full of snapping teeth, wheeling and thrashing, tearing at the pieces of gut and worm dripping all over like snot, gnashing it's own tail, feeding, feeding, feeding.

"Oh God," the fat guy moans. His ribcage seethes with worms of all colors, like gummi bears. A pair of banana-green worms rip at his heart. I put another clip into the gun and shoot him in the head. He grunts and goes down.

"Excuse me," a woman brushes past me. "Can I get some help here?"

"I'm the manager." A man wearing glasses steps over Rodney's body. "Sorry. We're a bit short right now."

"I'm looking for a movie," she tells him and then I jam the gun into her ear and pull the trigger. She buckles, worms and slime running down her legs, and topples on top of the fat guy.

"Do you need anything?" The manager asks. I point and shoot. His glasses explode, and then his head.

***

"Tracy's unhappy," Max tells me.

I shrug: "She's a worm."

"She doesn't know that." Max sighs. "None of them know. We're not cruel. All we're doing is obeying our biological imperatives: to feed and to reproduce."

I shudder: "She's pregnant."

"We know, Henry. We thought having a baby might make you happy. So we didn't eat the fetus."

"Will it be normal?" I ask.

"The secret of your species is that you're pack animals," Max pretends he doesn't hear me. "You band together because you want security. You spend your lives collecting safety objects to ward off the fear. Fear is your species' greatest enemy."

"What's yours?" Like I don't know.

Max shrugs. "Light."

***

I'm on my knees, dead bodies everywhere.

My gun is empty.

The floor twists with blood and entrails and snapping worms. People walk in and out, around me, stepping over the bodies, gathering movies to take to the register, making faces when they get blood on their shoes.

"You alright, Henry?" Max stands in front of me, his hands in his pockets. He looks at the bodies. "Stupid question. Sorry."

"Why don't you just die?" I throw the gun at him; miss.

"Why would we want to do that? We hit one sextillion last month." Max pats my shoulder. Tsks. "We'll have to garnish your wages, though."

I moan: "Why?"

"Well, you made a real mess." Max looks pained. "They'll need to shampoo the carpet, probably."

"No." I feel the tears, gathering, but I won't cry. "All this. Why did it happen?"

"Oh, well…" Max shrugs. "Someone undercooked a pork chop, that's all."

"It's not fair," I bawl.

"I don't know anything about fair." Max grimaces; nobody likes a whiner. "Life happens, know what I mean?"

"Henry?" It's Tracy. She weaves her way through the bodies, towards me. She's wearing black bicycle shorts and a Tweety bird t-shirt. "Max told me there was an accident. Are you alright?"

"Leave me alone," I groan, and the tears spurt out of me. Tracy jams my head against her belly and strokes my hair. I can smell the home-baked lasagna on her fingers.

"Get a good night's sleep." Max slaps me on the back, suddenly all manly. "And I'll see you at the office tomorrow morning."

"Please, honey." Tracy puts her hand under my chin, pulls my head up. "Come home. Come home with me."

Her eyes are green. They haven't changed.

I go with her.

IN COCOON, I AM EMBRYO

By Kenzie Mathews

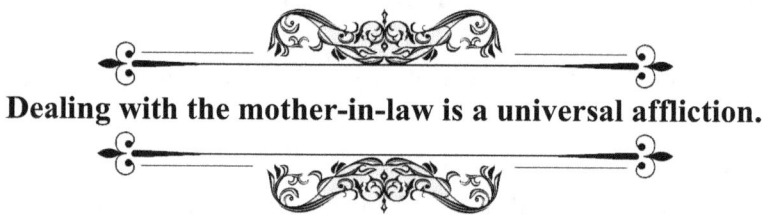

Dealing with the mother-in-law is a universal affliction.

*Kenzie Mathews lives in rural Alaska. When not writing, she paints landscapes and spoils her dogs rotten. Kenzie writes erotica, science fiction, gothic fairytales and dark fantasy. Her erotica stories have appeared in **Lesbian Lust**, **Lesbian Cops**, **Rumpledsilksheets: Lesbian Fairy Tales**, and **Best Lesbian Erotica: 2011**.*

Of this story, Kenzie says, "There's a lot of my childhood in this. My family vacations were haunted houses, graveyards, old natural history museums, and forgotten murder sites."

I had just turned thirteen when the barber-cutters came for my hair. The barber-cutters were tiny round women, their flesh tightly wound in white bandages. They wore black leather aprons over white shirts and black breeches. They made beautiful chiming music with their silver scissors. Their voices rang out over the sound of their glistening shears. I looked at Mother, biting my lower lip, fretful.

But, this is our way. We follow the traditions of our House.

I sat on a stool in the large empty ballroom. Pearl-knotted strings connected me to the mold-scarred walls of the ballroom, to the age-yellow peeling ceiling and to the slashed wood floor. I kept scruffing my bare feet on the pitted floor until I got one of my big toes to bleed. The barber-cutters flung my hair, the strands swirling in the air like pale sea foam.

It felt like a little something in a whole lot of numb.

Mother danced around me in a crushed red velvet dress from centuries ago with a gold tattered shawl tied across her breasts. A million mirrors reflected her. In reflection, Mother was whole and young. In true form, Mother was close to bursting.

Cut from me, the long white braids hung from the ceiling, and the walls, tracing circular patterns on the floor. I closed my eyes, humming so not to cry and drew lines in the air. I was trying to memorize the symbols.

I will forget the meaning of the words tomorrow.

In the long ballroom the early sunlight slithered slinked in to spread like veins to warp the wood. Red traces here, gold there, then shades of violet and silver as the light streamed through the colored window glass. The gods approved. They let in the sun.

I am a garden weeded.

"Now," Mother said, "Now, you will have a wig once your body rots and your true hair falls out."

I was happy for her, for she was so happy. I had started my menses just that morning. Crimson lines crisscrossing darkly the soft white sheets of our large bed.

I am mapping the inner country.

I felt sick then and later, looking in the winding mirrors that line the walls of the long gilt ballroom, watching Mother whirl in dance, I bled through my linens and through my thin shift. The blood pooled underneath the stool, gathering on the white drop cloth. It was just a little bit. Not like oceans. Not like Mother. Not even enough to worry about really. Hardly any at all.

I jumped off of the stool. In the curving mirrors, I stared back at the wavering reflection of a thin bald girl in wonder.

I stood there, frozen. The barber-cutters snowflake-fluttered all around me, collecting my hair from the floor. Some used ladders to take down my hair. They were gathering the fruit for later. I forgot to ask for my stained drop cloth. What I made.

They took it away, the barber-cutters. To make my wig. To press a lock in a Memory book for later. I don't know. It is something, Mother says. The physical remains. It proves existence. It's important because we all forget so easily the forms we are, the ones we have been, the ways we will be tomorrow.

I was a doll when Mother bathed me hours after. I was a doll as she placed food in my mouth. I am pale and thin and empty. I have bled right through and onto the drop cloth and now my limbs, they are the wax. Now, my limbs, they are the glass.

I should fear the sun more often.

I should stay in rooms where the strings will attach me and hold me safe.

I came alive that night when she held me in her arms to whisper, "When you sacrifice everything, you have everything to gain."

I have a wall-sized easel set up in the green glass hothouse. I have a cool breeze from the ocean that comes streaming through the cracks in the glass. I have dead and dying greenery plants in shattered pottery. I have pale white flowers living off the remains. Only the poison flowers thrive this close to the ocean, this far from the greening lands. Only the poison resides here, near a house set adrift on the wide Seanassey Cliffs.

That copper scent filling the hothouse is the ocean. The bitter dusty taste of it will remain in the mouth for days. And nights. It crawls to bury under the tongue. Food and drink will make the taste live again, live all over anew. It coats that which is devoured.

I can always taste the full depth of cells. The memory of writhing tissue.

I once wrote in a painting before I covered it up with more paint so that no one would know except for me: That which thrives, survives. That is my very favorite painting.

I will paint forever, sleeping now and then on the soft damp loveseat, covered in thick woven blankets. It is always moist here but I can bathe whenever I like. I have a porcelain claw-foot tub in the hothouse just for that. I keep my extra linen wraps in the big carved trunk by the loveseat. I am allowed to wrap myself tightly in corseted bandages as long as I don't tie them too tightly. Some youth are so vain, they bind themselves until they are cut in two.

I cannot swim in the ocean, however. It is forbidden. It is taboo. We fall apart without structure, Mother says. That is one law to keep us safe.

I am checked often by our doctor to make sure I do not have a fever or chill. Sometimes the doctor takes blood while I paint. I can paint with either hand. I am clever that way.

When he takes my blood, it goes through the tiny wires into a thin glass tube cylinder. He shakes it, taps it, and holds it to the light. My blood is a deep purple with small shimmery gold lights. Sometimes, if he stays to talk to Mother, my little blood cylinders gain a smoke, a blackening that swirls the lights.

I paint the ocean at evening tide. I paint the poison flowers and differing perspectives of our house. Our house always looked choked in the white flowers. A throat swallowed in diamonds. Our house pushes back at the ocean. My painted house is black with red veined vines and the full blush of white. My painted ocean is black with blue swirls and silvery flakes.

The secret of the abyss is this: I could be drowning not so much to surrender as to self devour. I think I have painted that in. I think I have it somewhere.

When I paint people, their faces blur and glide and the bones seem to liquidify within the flesh. Sometimes their limbs are replaced with wings and wire. Sometimes they shift into other animals like the fossils left in Memory books. Usually, they are very hungry. It is something about the charred holes of their eyes, the loose hold of their jaws.

Mother makes dolls. They open up at the chest. Inside she puts bits of the flesh that she keeps in the large glass containers in the walk-in pantry of the kitchen. She uses large tongs. She does not trust the formaldehyde. She does not trust the rupture of flesh, the keeping of wax. She does not like to put her belief in the science of others.

There are hearts floating in the thick yellowing liquid of the glass containers. To take a piece, she uses a special wooden chopping board and her largest butcher knife.

As a little girl, I would sit on a large stool drinking straight from the cooking pot, watching her and marveling that such a large knife could slice delicate teacake size portions of heart. These bits of heart belong to the children who did not survive. They are my brothers and sisters. Other parts are kept in the walk-in walk-about pantry in the walls of shelves in glass.

Whenever I dance around the kitchen, I leave the pantry door open. I dance for my brothers and sisters. It is a good thing. It is a giving thing. They like it. The eyes always follow. Sometimes their tiny hands wave within the formaldehyde like sea-grass in the ocean, like the tongues of the mermaids from the Memory books.

I am not allowed to tap on the glass.

Mother's dolls are collectibles. They are extremely expensive. I am not allowed to speak with the customers but I can spy on them with Mr. Gaines. The customers, they come to trade. All of their flying ships work. They are very careful and suspicious, customers. They are very delicate, customers. Fragile.

Mother knows Mr. Gaines and I watch. She simply asks that we do not giggle.

We sit in a big comfortable armchair in the secret passageway of a crawlspace within the parlor walls. I sit on Mr. Gaines' lap. My legs entangle his. I like to wrap my legs around him. He likes to stroke me where I split open. Where I gape open mouthed, in my burial places.

Mother feels I should know the business and the conduction of money but I should not have to dirty my hands until after I have been married a few times. I am expected to take over then. When I have matured. When I have developed fully.

I am sixteen when I get my first suitor. I meet him in the violet parlor. The flowers here are white in the morning and brown by evening. There is the hint of fingerprints on the petals. There is the crush in the stems that speaks of murder. That milky comfortable smell of baby's breath does not reside within the flowers. That scent can be traced to the dust within the fabric of the violet walls.

Our lives in arrangement of flowers. Our lives in the patterns of cracks.

If I close my eyes and trace the symbols left in the air, I might remember the words.

Mr. Gaines watches. I can sense his giggling. I wondered then, if Mother watched also, sitting on his lap and holding Mr. Gaines' big hands as I would have. I wondered then, as I have so many times before, if his big hands also stroked her burial places.

I don't know what I am supposed to do with my suitor so when he talks, I just smile and nod. I don't understand one word he is saying. I think he is foreign. I think he is alien. I don't think he is male. He is not of a house. He is from the stars. He came in a ship. It is broken. Then, he walked right up to our house. Our house. He chose our house. He chose me. I can choose him. I choose him.

I am only a doll when I lay down. I am only a doll sometimes. I am something other than the rest of the time.

When he is done talking, he takes off my blouse. I stare at the wall.

I am looking for the peepholes in the walls. I don't know why. No one can see them from out here in the parlor. The secret passageway of a crawl space is completely hidden. But, I imagined, anyway, that I could see Mother and Mr. Gaines. I try reading their thoughts. It is faint at first because the male is doing things to my neck and it is hard to concentrate. Then, I hear Mother and Mr. Gaines thinking.

Mr. Gaines is thinking about flashing lights. This makes me giggle. Mother is not thinking of anything at all. This makes me sad.

My suitor pushes his cold damp hands past my shift bodice. He pinches my nipples. I fall deeper into the couch. I am drowning in feathers. I have rough pearls clenched in my teeth. They are biting into my lip. I have the roar of the ocean in my ears, it is saying something to hurt the wide Seanassey Cliffs. To break them open.

My suitor climbs on top of me. He fumbles with my skirts, then with his breeches.

He is puzzled by my bandages, by my white wraps. I have only bound myself up to my waist. It is not time to bind further than that yet. He really is a foreigner. I open my mouth to explain and I can hear Mother thinking. She is thinking: Shhhhh.

I giggle instead to keep him.

I sing, "I am in cocoon. I am embryo."

That which distracts, lives to splinter another day. I will paint this. I will paint these words with the lace bones and feathered wings of birds from the Memory books. I will then press into the paint the insect bodies and shells from the Memory books.

He is cold all the way through. From shaft to stern. He is space without stars.

He is happiest just before I pierce him from within. He is happiest just before I take a nip. He draws back, startled. He looks at me.

I smile up at him. I am happy for him. Mother is thinking in blues. Mr. Gaines is thinking in flickers of lines and folded space.

My suitor looks around, warned suddenly and listening. There is nothing in the room for him to see. There is nothing for him to sense. There is no danger here.

My suitor comes back in to me to drink. Sweat breaks his brow. The locks of his long brown hair has a thick texture that when taken in my mouth spears the pearls.

And, we are married.

We move into the little carved stone garden house behind Mother's house. The writhing stone of the little house jets out into space and cuts into the skies, into the folding oceans that spread out into far reaching distance. It has two rooms. One for sitting and eating. One for bedding. The carvings follow the stone inside. Inside, they are cut into the stone so that the walls withdraw into crevices. Fingers must go in seeking to find.

I don't have to cook, but I do try to make the foods he likes. I don't have to clean, but I do try. He teaches me what his words mean. His language is beyond repetitive. His language is limited and awful. He has a foul scent like something heavy and clotting.

I rub his clothes in the poison of the flowers to change his scent. I soak his clothes in the tide of the black ocean to bring him into our being. I drag his clothes behind me on the rocks as I climb the Seanassey Cliffs. Nothing clings to him. He smells just like he did when he first got here. I cannot save him at all from himself.

He is too different from us. He hates the pale green dust that covers everything. He hates the white flowers with their blue and violet veins, with their cloying scents. Like death coming, he says. He hates the black ocean that breaks below. Like a million voices singing off-key, he says. He hates the wideness of the Seanassey Cliffs. Empty, forlorn and going nowhere. He cannot abide the stillness.

He says it is fading here. Everything is shifting themes of water.

He keeps his little ship in sight of our little carved stone garden house. He says he is making repairs. He says one day he is going to take me away from all of this. He says I would like the deeper oceans of the skies.

He says the stars come in the spinning walls of the ship like lights that pierce the skin. He says the stars are the missing parts of who we are. What we have drifted away from. I have no idea what that means. I think he is a liar.

That which is important and real is kept in Memory books. My husband does not keep Memory books. My husband keeps everything locked in his head. How can he trust himself if it is all kept in his head? Doesn't he realize the falsity of that? My husband thrives on illusion.

Mostly, I paint, walking the short distance from the little stone house to the green glass hothouse. My husband's name is Mr. Jesse and he sleeps a lot and goes out walking at night. There is nowhere for him to go. We all keep to ourselves here. We all keep to our houses.

I am not the only one wrapped. I am not the only one held in glass.

Mostly he screams at his little ship.

Then, he goes back to working on it. He says soon we are leaving. He is dedicated. To his little ship, to me, to leaving. He has a computer on board that reconstructs little ship skin out of the soft thick air. Together, my husband and his computer are rebirthing the little ship.

When he comes home, as the sun is rising, he stumbles into bed, fully dressed. If I fight him in my sleep, he remains persistent in his wooing. If I continue to resist, he eventually gives up and pouts, his back shrugging off my hands. Then, he will not speak to me, will not look at me for days. If I am open to him, and I do learn to be so, he will slip himself in, cold and damp and push at me until he is warmed again. He kisses wetly, sucking at me, with his hands clamped onto the back of my neck.

I cannot find words in his language to tell him. I would like to wrap him. I would like to stop the bloom. Sometimes the most precious moment is the stillness before.

I would not like it so much if it did not make me feel needed.

I like being necessary. I like it when he is necessary, too.

And I only take a little. Here and there. Now and again. He notices it less and less. My husband is starting to grow used to me. I am becoming the only familiar constant. Sometimes I really like him. He has this thing he does with his tongue.

I told him, "I am not going anywhere, this is my home."

He said, "Yes, but it is not my home. And you are mine. You will come with me when I go."

I said, "What is there for me?"

He said, "Me," and laughed.

I persisted, "What is it that the stars could give me that I do not have now?"

He grew serious, staring down hard into me. That is what the narrowing of his eyes means. He is thinking. He is considering me.

He said, quietly, "They give you back the parts of yourself that have been lost. They make you whole."

Now, when I paint, my paintings are dark, all the forms hazy and blurred as if seen through a lace veil. I am concerned that my husband is not lying.

I am worried I am becoming alien. I think I have been contaminated. I think I have been consumed.

I think I do not mind his horrible smell so much anymore. I think I even like his fleshy heaviness. He is something that keeps to its form as much as it can. He is something that resists and struggles. He does not taste so much like the copper scent of ocean as he does of a tangy musky salt well spiced.

When he is working on his ship sometimes, I feel very alone. I feel like something is missing. Like I am starving.

I feel then, like I am the wax of childhood. I am limbs waiting to be filled.

"Are you happy?" Mother asked me as she sat on my loveseat in the pale green hothouse. She shivered slightly. It is changing outside. It is growing colder. The hint of snowflakes that summons sleep. Quiet here, underneath. Slow stirring that promises. Just an ember, just a breath. Just a folded wrap. Every year, the ocean draws near. Every year the skies yawn broader and deepen.

My husband is crawling in and out of his little ship. He is very busy. He is very driven. Seen through the pale green of the hothouse, he bleeds at the edges of himself. He looks like a thinning shadow collapsing.

"Oh, yes," I answered and I stabbed my canvas. It is a flood of color, it is spotted and nothing blends. Up close, my painting is a mess but from far away, it is a vibrant scream. At my feet, water gathers. I have overflowed my claw-footed tub. I cannot remember if I have taken a bath. I cannot remember the last time I did. I am flooding the stone floor of the hothouse.

"But, I miss you and Mr. Gaines," I added, slowly.

Mother rose from the loveseat and came to me. I peer down sideways, listening. Brown vines and white flowers filled to bursting, made thick from the water, cling to her ankles. The perfume chokes the air.

"Look," she said, holding out her hands to me.

I look down and find her hands full of her long gold hair. Mother puts the hair into my hands. My hands are paint smeared. The hair tangles there, clumps of black, red, violet, and blue meshing into the gold strands.

"I am rotting already," Mother sighed. "And you are still so young."

Then, she walks out of the hothouse. I take the handful of hair and sweep it into my painting. It clots there, heavy and unmovable. I stab the canvas with the sharp end of my brush until there is a hole. I shred and rip at the hole until it forms a crater.

My eyes leak. I brush the wetness away with the back of my hand.

There is something that is filling me, surging through me. It doesn't belong to me, with me. It is foreign. It is learned. I have adapted it to me. My husband does this sometimes. He has given me this. He says it means we have touched. He says it means we are translating. He says it means we can understand each other. We care to. We want to.

Then, through the hole in my canvas, I can see the calm green glass of the hothouse walls. I am looking inward, seeing without.

I am comforted.

I am feeling calm and still. The wetness dries.

And the ocean screams up into the Seanassey Cliffs. A crack forms in the green glass of the hothouse walls as seen through my little crater hole.

Mother is dying. And it is all my fault. I was raised better than this.

I go back to the little carved stone house and wait at the stone table where I set the meals my husband likes to eat. My husband watched me cross the yard from the hothouse to our house but he hasn't stopped working on his little ship. He is still working on his ship and here I am, telling him to come see me. It is right there in my head.

I pick at my bodice. I am leaking through my bandages. I am staining my dress. I am tearing on the outside. I pull the bodice away and look down. It is crusted black in places, in the creases of my wraps. Mother is dying and here I am ripening. Nearly bursting.

I really should pay more attention. I am always thinking of myself.

I am not alone. I am belonging to a house. There are others to think about.

I am not a little doll anymore, watching from the secret crevices of the crawl spaces. I am not sitting on Mr. Gaines' lap with his large hands in my burial places. I am a married woman. I have a husband. I am going to have to sew that up. I am still young enough. I am not Mother's age.

My husband still doesn't come.

They are slow where he comes from, I think.

Finally, I called out to him, "Mr. Jesse."

He still doesn't come.

So, I said, "Mr. Jesse, Mother is dying."

Now he comes. He stands there in the doorway, watching me.

"My computer has the medical intelligence for analyzing most viruses," he said. He wipes his hands on his breeches. "I know you all are superstitious when it comes to technology....but, I would like to help."

I am quiet still, staring at him. I am trying to understand him.

"We are not like you," I said finally. "Your computer cannot help Mother."

"I know I know," my husband said, shaking his head, "I am blocked here no matter what I do. I keep trying to fit in and you all make damn sure I know I will always be an outsider."

My husband comes up to me very quickly. He slams one hand on the table. He lowers his face closely into mine. I am still. I do not know what his kind do. I do not know what this means.

"We are not so different," he said through his teeth. "We are not. You will see. I think I have finished all the repairs."

My husband squats down until he is looking up at me with my thighs caught between his hands. I make a motion with my hands. I am not conscious of it. I let it come on through. It feels strange. I put my hands on his face until I am cradling his head. He smiles, nuzzles his mouth into one of my hands.

He said softly, gently, then, "I will drag your mother on board if I have to and prove it to you all. We are not incompatible species. Then, you and me, we are leaving this place. I can show you real civilization. A real life....not like this...."

"Mr. Jesse, Mother is dying," I said slowly.

My husband stares at me. Then, he nods. "You cannot leave the house until the elder...of course. I am sorry, I have been blind. It is very traditional here."

He takes my hands into his. I smile at him, nodding. I am very happy for him.

I push him away gently and I rise from the wooden bench. I take off my jacket and unlace my shift. I step out of my skirt. My husband stares, frozen.

"You are hurt," he murmured. His hand motions at my bandages. The leaking has spread to blacken the white bandages.

"Yes," I said, softly, coming to him.

I brush his hands away and press up into him. He is slow to respond. They are truly slow where he comes from.

Then, I find his tongue and he is glad for it. I latch onto his tongue and go into him gently. He tries to draw away. He thinks I am using my teeth. My tiny little sharp edged teeth. But, when the scent comes through me, through the seedling tendrils in my mouth and into his, when the poison releases, he relaxes. It has a calming effect.

I only took a little from him. Here and there. What I return now is based on his own DNA. He can translate it. The poison I give him is part of him.

I look into his eyes to watch his pupils dilate. His eyes are gray.

Before my husband, I did not have that word, gray. We do not have that color in our house. I do not know of any house that does. Gray. It is amazing. I asked him once: Where you come from, are many things like this? Yes, he said, many things. You will see many things you can't even imagine.

When his eyes are fully dilated, I know that it is safe. I want to hurt him as little as possible. It is strange. I did not know that we could come to care for our husbands like this. Mother leaves parts out.

That which varies from instinct is lost in translation. I must remember to paint those words. I would like to leave something for someone. I may even not paint over the words.

His shaft grows hard so I have to take that in, too, finally. He hisses and bends backwards, away from me, breaking the kiss. I rock gently to release. He is very heavy. With his legs numb, he cannot hold up either of us. We nearly fall. His mouth keeps trying to form his words. It would take me too long to figure them out. I cannot understand him. His words are just sounds.

The gray of his eyes leak clear. I cannot stop looking into them. In his language, this means something to me. I almost can remember it. There are emotions for the words. It is like another life. It is like something I dreamed while in cocoon. When I was just an embryo, an infant. Wings wrapped in cotton wisp.

My husband shudders. I let him go. He falls heavily onto the floor. He is choking on his tongue. His numb pierced tongue. The more he struggles, the more he resists, the faster the poison works through him. The round curves of his cells mutate. Follow the laws of poison. Dance the protein strings. The birth of little spinning hooks.

It is like looking through lace. But, it is my fingers. I am holding them up before my face and peering through them. I am.

My face is wet, too, like his for some reason and I need my fingers to wipe it dry.

I will not remember this later. I cannot retain the knowledge. It seems, though, a waste. The wetness is just so unnecessary.

I can only put physical things in the Memory books.

My husband twitches on the floor. The poison is rendering him. My fluids are preparing him. Husbands cannot be taken in their natural state, they have to be prepped. They have to be molded. I have been a good wife. In some houses, the husbands scream.

I call to Mother. In our way.

In the little yard that separates the house from the stone house, Mother loses the back part of her scalp. The tear runs from her head in strips and pulls down some of the skins of her back as it falls. She is nearly nude, dress-less. Only the decaying fraying white wraps remain. One breast flops past her stomach, the flesh barely keeping within the bandages. She nearly stumbles. Her bones are weak with holes.

Just past Mother, Mr. Gaines stands in the hothouse watching. He is grinning. He is the loveliest shade of green. In the ever weakening sunlight, Mr. Gaines glows brightly.

The sound of his whirling chittering teeth comes through the glass faintly. If he were to stand in the hothouse doorway, the scent of him would flood the yard. The smell of sweet tinged copper as it mingles with sharp herbal overtones and the sharp underneath nesting of rot.

The males of our house. They smell divine but they are impotent.

On the floor, my husband has rolled to his side in an effort to lie on his belly. He starts vomiting up his insides. It is uncontrollable. A sound escapes me that is foreign.

And, driven on by the smell of that vomiting, of a breeding ground made fertile, Mother comes, humming vibrantly.

Panting at the doorway then, Mother rests, leaning against the stone. There is a blackness at the corner of her mouth. A mucus thick liquid. It is part of the enzymes she needs to break down my husband. The blackness runs down her legs as well, from deep within her burial place.

Mother pushes herself forward and falls. She has to crawl to get on top of my husband. He shudders beneath her but he is past caring. When he is beneath her, she nearly shreds him trying to turn him over onto his back.

Her burial place mouth takes in his soft member. Her face mouth delivers the kiss.

Mother rocks. Mother takes. Mother gives.

One kiss inflicts pure material, undiluted. One kiss swallows the cross-bred adaptation. Husbands filter.

When her black kiss becomes the sticky clear tinged with blood, Mother will be pregnant again. It murders her that so few of us survive. It makes Mother very sad.

Her sadness is always screaming in my ears. No child should ever hear their Mother cry. It is an act of violence.

Mother starts grunting and thrusting. I walk out of the little stone house.

Mr. Gaines is throwing himself against the green glass of the hothouse wildly, nearly breaking it. Already lines have spread from that crack the ocean gave it earlier. I look away from him.

There is a sudden silence in my head. A stillness. I have an inheritance.

My husband has left behind a working ship that flies. My husband has left behind a working computer with maps to the stars, to other planets. To other husbands.

THE ONLY ONE TO SAVE
By Derek Tabor

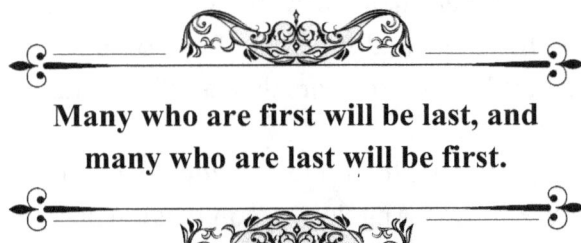

**Many who are first will be last, and
many who are last will be first.**

*Derek Tabor is a graduate of the University of Massachusetts at
Boston, having majored in English and Nursing. He spends his time
between computers and children, writing stories in the brief
interludes between, while building state of the art machines obsolete
as soon as they leave his fingertips.*

Broken silence awoke Jim from his slumber on the warm
rooftop. He rolled over under his blanket as the sand beneath him
scratched at his skin through his worn jeans and t-shirt. Pulling the
old Indian blanket over his head to shield him from the sunlight it
had occurred to him he had slept almost all day. The sun was setting
along his artificial horizon, the sky a cloudless blue and the air was
cleaner than he had ever seen.

It took him a moment to identify the sound, which was familiar
but odd. It was higher pitched and he didn't know why. Pulling the
blanket off his head he looked up and then surrendered to the idea he
had to stand up. The sand that had blown across the concrete over

the last few weeks had formed a drift Jim had made camp on, a place he had called 'concrete beach.' Strewn with debris, Jim had made his home here when people started coming up to the roof of the parking structure.

Jim stood up in his tattered state, rubbing the sleep out of his eyes and squinting in the sunlight. Looking around he found his sunglasses and canteen. Taking a swig of lukewarm water he recapped the canteen and put his sunglasses on. Standing nearly six feet tall, Jim had been an impressive man in his time, but ten years of homelessness had taken their toll. His weathered face, the lines and creases around his eyes, and the loose flesh on once muscular arms spoke more about the last ten years than anything Jim could say. But no one asked.

Looking over the wall of the rooftop level of a twelve story parking structure in Los Angeles he could see what was making the sound he heard. Most jet airliners fly like limousines, true and level, and it is rare to see one in a dive or a 'corkscrew,' like a world war two fighter crashing into the countryside. Watching the massive 525-seat Airbus 380 spiraling in from altitude would be unnerving for almost anyone who saw it. Jim stood stone still as the superjumbo jet spiraled in a couple of miles away. The four turbines were screaming as the amount of air being forced into their intakes exceeded the throttle setting they had been set for. The final impact took out a quarter mile area of residential housing. The fireball was minimal since the aircraft had simply ran out of fuel.

"Well, there goes Qantas' perfect flight record." Jim remarked. He knew there was no one alive onboard. Another moonlight flight. Most simply flew high overhead to crash in the mountains or eastern desert, but some went on out to sea. Jim stood and watched to see which way the fire was going to go. Most of the area had burned last week so there was little left, but it was still a small concern. Fire drove Jim here six months before. After the fire died out this garage was the tallest building left standing. There wasn't a thing taller than three feet in the Los Angeles area for nearly five miles around the garage. That's when the "Happy/Smiley" people started to come out.

Having convinced himself of his safety Jim decided it was time to eat. Opening the back of the truck he pulled out a camp stove and a can of spaghetti. He could have set himself up at the best hotel in LA but decided to camp out on the parking garage near the airport instead. This wasn't a defensive measure. There were no sandbags, firing positions or weapons. All he had was his small bedroll and blanket, a truck full of food and water, and his bible. And for the last three weeks he had been alone.

The smell of spaghetti filled the air. For six months Jim had performed this ritual and every single night people had come to his garage. He provided them with food and shelter, preached a little and helped them find a place to sleep. Every night the numbers became fewer. Every day he would find more bodies in the morning. They all had smiles on their faces as if they had drifted off to blissful contentment during the night. Then last month the numbers dropped off dramatically. For three weeks no one had come. Jim stood there stirring his pot of canned spaghetti, adding oregano liberally. He had found some onions and had started cutting them up and putting them in. After half an hour he filled a small bowl and went over to the wall to watch the sunset. And wait.

The fire of the jet had almost gone out. The smoke drifted south, away from his camp on the roof, yet he could still smell the burnt aircraft.

"We did it to ourselves." He said aloud.

"I know."

Jim turned around startled, spilling his spaghetti. Behind him stood a man in a white pullover and white pants. The sandals on his feet looked older than dirt. His long brown hair had been pulled back, his beard and mustache were neatly trimmed, but most strikingly was how clean he was. This did not look like someone who had just walked through LA to get a meal. He also looked familiar in some way.

"Relax. I'm not here to hurt you. I smelled your food."

"Would you like some? I have enough for everyone here." Waving his arm to show the vast nothingness. Jim felt safe and what bothered him was how he hadn't really felt threatened before. He had survived. He could be here for decades undisturbed. He had more to fear from his own mind than anyone he saw, yet he felt 'safe.'

The man looked out across the same skyline Jim had just been pondering. "No, thank you. I am sure the food is wonderful but I just don't have an appetite right now." Seeing the fire from the crashed jet he shook his head. "Yes, you did this to yourselves."

"Yeah." Jim followed the man's gaze. "Started with the drugs the terrorists put into the water supplies of troops in Afghanistan. Made them want to sit down and smell the flowers instead of manning their posts. Then some bright assed chem student figured out what they had done and started marketing it. Soon everyone was enjoying the bliss, smiles on their faces, no worries. It was so popular we ended up selling it back to the terrorists who had used it on us. We were all hooked. No side effects! Everyone just kept on smiling; even when people started dying. Death wasn't even a problem for them."

"Hmmm. The chemical used quietly eats away at the protective myelin sheath of the nerve fibers until the nerve itself is exposed but protected by the new chemical, which slowly dissolves the nerve tissue. Each and every brain cell. The chemicals released by dying nerve cells are used to create more of the chemical and the process accelerates rapidly. Eventually the entire system is erased and the person dies within ten minutes to four hours. Except for those who didn't use the drug."

Jim was watching the man speak as someone writing the story himself. "And since those on the drug put it in the water supply..."

"Everyone got some. Except you."

"And you, too. My name's Jim." Jim's expression was hard. "You seem to know a great deal about what's going on? What's your name?"

The man shook Jim's hand. "You know my name. I know you are James Martin Rothman, named after your mother's brother and your father's grandfather. You were a preacher at the Trinity Congregational Church thirty-five miles southeast of here. Of late you have been the pastor of "Concrete Beach" in Los Angeles. You are known unto me."

Jim stood dumbfounded. Dropping to his knees he simply couldn't make his mind work fast enough to comprehend what he was seeing. Maybe it had finally happened, he had snapped, all the bodies and cremations had finally gotten to him.

"Jim. Stand up." Jesus took him by the arms and helped him to his feet. Jim stood but was soon looking for the wall to lean on. "Relax. This isn't a mental breakdown."

"What else would you call it?" finally finding his voice.

Shaking his head a little, looking around at the last remnants of human civilization, "Looks like the end of the world to me."

"Jesus, you have a sense of humor."

"I know."

"I'm......I'm sorry. I didn't mean that the way it sounded and ..uh. damn. Screwed up again." Jim was flustered. "Here I am taking your name in vain and you're standing in front of me." Jim looked down. "I'm sorry."

"Saying sorry is a sign of weakness. Try asking for forgiveness, it is a sign of strength of spirit. It's harder because it leaves you feeling exposed but it's better because you choose to be vulnerable before your Lord."

Once again falling to his knees, "Please forgive me."

"You are already forgiven. So get up. It is hard to talk with you this way."

"Talk with me?" Jim stood but was looking away toward the sea. "There isn't much I can say for myself. Intellectually I understand what is going on. This must be judgment day. My faith hasn't been exemplary and as a Christian I see myself as a complete failure."

"Really?" Jesus paused. "You have had your moments, but no, you are not a complete failure." Jesus heard the plane before he saw it clearly. A few moments later Jim saw it too. Coming in over the eastern hills it looked like a model airplane until the brain processed what it was seeing, a 767 flying five miles off, less than one hundred feet off the ground before crashing into South Central. It was the silence. Another aircraft out of fuel and on a flat glide path. It took almost a minute for the sound to reach them. Jesus stood there, radiating despair. Jim could see the tears on his face.

"I'm pretty sure everyone on that plane was dead before it hit." Jim spoke softly. "Been no one up here for days so I am pretty sure there was none on the ground either."

"I know there wasn't anyone on that plane. They were all dead four hours ago. It seems so sad how people chose to board a plane and fly in a vain attempt to be closer to God, as if the altitude would make up for what they had done." Jesus turned away. "But I am not here about them today. It appears you have run out of parishioners."

Jim looked down. "I failed them. They felt so good they believed they were invincible, that nothing mattered." Jim looked around. "And now they're dead. Only you know how many were saved. I'm not sure I want to though. People started showing up. I didn't know any of them. I fed them, gave them a place to sleep and tried to talk some sense into them. They would smile as they walked off the roof." Jim paused. "It just didn't make any sense and they wouldn't stop."

"It's been hard on you. You feel you have lost your faith. It started with your affair ten years ago. Regardless of the justifications you may have felt at the time it was still wrong."

Jim was about to say something and immediately realized he wasn't going to be able to spin this with Jesus. "Yeah. I thought I needed something. Jesse just didn't seem to love me anymore. I was a meal ticket and she enjoyed the prestige of being a Pastor's wife, except for the wife part." Jim looked down at what now seemed very inviting pavement. He had struggled with thoughts of suicide after the affair broke and the very public divorce. Jesse turned him into a villain of the worst kind. "I thought I had found a way out. It just took me further out than I planned." Jim let out a deep sigh. "This is how far out things have gotten."

"You're right, you know." Jesus replied.

"About what? Which part?"

"She was having an affair too. You knew it but never looked into it. Vengeance was not in your heart. You could have destroyed her easily, torn her case to shreds, but that isn't your way. You took the blame and punishment and kept moving. You actually have brought more people to me since your homelessness than anytime before that."

Jim stood silent as he felt a small pit of anger build. "You planned this? You deliberately let me suffer all these years?" Jim's tears and anger, the conflict within his heart raged as his mind tried to find a handle on the chaos it caused in his head. He didn't believe in predestination and he knew he was supposed to do God's work but he couldn't wrap his head around the idea God would put troubles in his path.

"No, I am not what you would call a Calvinist. The reality is you made a choice. Every decision you make, whether to do the right or wrong thing, determines what happens. Like I said earlier, you did this to yourselves. All of it. From your affair, to the development of jet engines, you did it. Whether mankind would ever make it to Mars was not my concern. What matters is my relationship with you if you ever went there. 'Judgment Day' wasn't something I was going to do to you but something that would signify to God you were done. I came here to save people. Millions have killed themselves, condemning themselves in the process. Millions more laid down and died, unaware of what was killing them. Some never knew they were dying." Jim could see how Jesus was affected by this. "They did this to themselves. I sent people out into this world, gave them a calling to preach the gospel, and no one cared."

Jesus sat down and rested on a curbstone. The tears streamed from his eyes. "So many souls lost. I sent every possible chance to them and they rejected me for something much less."

Jim kneeled before Christ. "What can I do? Where do you want me to go?" Jim reached out to Jesus, as if he could do anything to relieve the pain of so many lost souls. "I am sure I can be useful somewhere else. There must be other pockets of people who need preaching to."

Jesus looked up. "Don't give up on me." Jim's puzzled face made Jesus chuckle.

"What's so funny."

"You really don't understand, do you."

Jim leaned back a little. "No."

"You're the last soul to be saved." Jesus stood and took his hand. "I have returned to collect the faithful souls here on earth. You are the only one left." Jesus stood and helped Jim to his feet. "Follow me. Let's go home."

SCOTOMIZATION
By D. Harlan Wilson

From the secret files of J. Edgar Hoover...

*D. Harlan Wilson is an award-winning novelist, short story writer, literary critic, and English professor. His most recent works include two novels, **Peckinpah: An Ultraviolent Romance** and **Blankety Blank: A Memoir of Vulgaria**, and a book of cultural theory, **Technologized Desire: Selfhood & the Body in Postcapitalist Science Fiction**.*

*Hundreds of his stories and essays have appeared in magazines, journals and anthologies throughout the world in several languages, and he is the editor-in-chief of **The Dream People**, a journal of irreal texts. Visit Wilson online at **www.dharlanwilson.com** and **dharlanwilson.blogspot.com**.*

To form a mental blind spot . . .

I had been part of the Kennedys' inner circle for so long I could barely remember the finer details of my indoctrination, with the exception of the hazing ceremony during which I was ordered to stand naked in the library of the Aquinnah Estate and hold a hot tamale between my teeth as the Kennedys shouted obscenities and laughed at my anthropomorphic shortcomings. Whenever my lips faltered and grazed the tamale, they burst aflame . . .

Daylight.

Enemies fired from the Incurable Coast—heat missiles carved a black frown in the sky. We had to usher the Kennedys across the ocean. I dressed in an adrenalized fury, opting for a clip-on tie. The lady of the manor pleaded with me to don the Real Thing and presented to me her upturned ass on a hand-painted Victorian platter. I reluctantly turned her down. I knew I would regret it. But there was no time.

Jack and Lee were in the guesthouse rolling and smoking cigarettes. The place smelled like shit; they had just skinned a llama and draped the hide over a chaise to dry. The underparts of the animal had been dissected and primed for All Out Praxis. Nobody in the family wasted anything. "The sky is frowning," I reminded them. "We need to get underwater."

Lee salvaged whatever accruals of tobacco could be stuffed into a shirt and he and Jack shoved their arms into powerful frock coats that seemed to move of their own volition. I ushered them outside, the stigma indelible of mushroom clouds leaping onto the horizon like bullfrogs. Already the vines had begun to shrivel. Soon the plasma would turn to rust.

"Mind the guardrail," said Betty as we fell into the chute and stepped aboard a submarine.

The roots of Martha's Vineyard hung in the water like withered udders . . . I placed my hand against the glass wall of the aquarium. Warm to the touch. The air was thick and infinitely green . . . The captain tripped and fell into the control panel. Sparks leapt from unmanned wires and he caught fire. Eddie tackled the captain with a horse blanket, put out the flames and accidently suffocated him.

There was a ceremony on the fly bridge and the Kennedys threw a collective fit. I respected the upheaval, eyes fixed on clasped hands. If the munity occurs before the ship sets sail, technically there can be no mutiny.

Anatomy of a submarine: conning tower, sleeping quarters, boiler room, trim and ballast tanks, nuclear reactor, ballistic missile repository, Cold War wine cellar, snorkel, anechoic plating . . .

Perception as a red hatchet.

Fidel wanted to drive. He had put on the captain's frayed, smoldering hat to ensure that nobody argued with him. Nikolai punched him. Fidel punched him back. They clutched one another by the lapels of their suits and threw one another from side to side and then they crashed through a decayed floor panel and fell out of sight. Jackie salvaged the hat and slipped behind the helm . . . Octopi and squid covered the nose of the sub. She shook them off, violently, yanking on the controls. Her forearm inflated with color and I traced the cephalic vein from wrist to crook with my fingernail . . .

. . . determined saboteur. The impromptu dialogue quickly evolved into another ceremony imbricating all of the major players. Accusations and accidental blowups produced corresponding plyboard-partitioned tristes. Procedural disputes coiled into jurisdictional wranglings. I tripped over the rhetorical morass like a wounded calf. Eventually I paid for it. The catalyst, claimed Bobby: my Gaelic upper lip – "interminably long and menacing."

Dry land and rancorous indictments.

Internal Affairs briskly took me aside. They unplugged the Zapruder camera in the interrogation room and pushed me into a chair by the shoulders. "Why don't you like me," was Teddy's opening line.

I said, "I don't know. I think it has something to do with that shiteating grin etched into your puss." The grin folded together like curtains. I shrugged. "I've got nothing to say."

"All right," said Teddy. "You can go then."

I got up to leave.

"Sit the fuck down asshole!"

The others looked on as Teddy sat across the table from me and tilted his head. "I have to speak to you immediately," he said. He stood and exited the room. Eddie came in and said he was serving as Assistant to the District Attorney in Joey's absence. A waiter served zweibacks from a misshapen porcelain plate that threatened to topple off of his palm. We observed a luminescent battle grid. Blips raced up and down the fractal lines. Eddie took me by the shirt and said, "I'm trying to communicate with you. This is a *communiqué*. What's wrong with you?"

"Nothing. I'm just a glacier monkey like everybody else."

I kept talking until somebody acquiesced, expressing interest in my belief system. It was John, Jr. Once I had him on my side everybody else fell into rank. I received a formal letter of apology and forgiveness at a ceremony presided over by a Kennedy without a Name (KwN). We drank a lot of brandy and then the family doctor performed mock electroshock therapy on me, easing me onto a rollaway bed, placing a leather bit in my mouth, and producing a series of wet alveopalatal shocking sounds.

Marilyn wheeled me up to the honeymoon suite.

I awoke in the early morning. John was sitting on the end of the bed in his favorite gray suit, elbows on knees, swishing the last drops of a scotch in the basin of a rocks glass. The shoulder-to-shoulder articulation of his back preoccupied me.

I sat up in bed and the covers fell into my lap.

"I don't like crowds, is the thing," noted John in his signature accent. "I have social anxiety. But nobody will prescribe me medication. That's why I drink so much. And the drinking makes me talk funny. I don't know what to do." He reached behind him and laid a hand on Marilyn's exposed ankle. She didn't wake up. I suspected she might have passed away in her sleep.

The last thing I remembered was the smell of coffee, the sound of the percolator. The angled silhouette of a man set against a tall bay window.

FALSE IDOLS

By Sean Martin

An old-school writer finally gets wired.

*Sean Elliot Martin has always enjoyed the dark, disturbing, and mysterious aspects of the world, sharing his unusual interests with others through a number of artistic and scholarly projects. **H.P. Lovecraft and the Modernist Grotesque (2008)**, based on his Ph.D. Dissertation, develops a new perspective on the literary and philosophical contributions of Lovecraft, and his academic projects and university classes ("Literature, Film, and Fear," "Gods and Monsters," "Identifying and Analyzing Propaganda") explore the role of the fear impulse in diverse cultural expressions.*

After residing in various cities throughout the United States, Martin settled in Pittsburgh, where he earns his living as a university instructor, martial arts instructor, freelance writer, and wood carver. He also enjoys Medieval and Renaissance events, traveling to mysterious places (Egyptian pyramids, Mayan ruins), community service, and any creative project that deals with the macabre or the bizarre.

[The following document is transcribed from a legal pad found on the floor of the apartment of Thomas Tobias of Wheeling, WV. It was collected as part of a missing persons investigation that has not yet been solved.]

Got to loosen up. My writing will continue to suck (or not exist) if I keep falling victim to what Jon calls "paralysis through analysis." That's why I am here.

OK. Get out of the car as soon as you capture these initial impressions of the place. It's just as Doreen described it. I didn't even know a factory could be so huge. The small trees that have grown up around it seem to cling to it like potential drowning victims clinging to the sides of a giant ship with a hull they can't climb. That was kind of cool. Maybe I can polish that simile up and use it in something later. I think this exercise of writing down every little thing that pops into my head really helps. I'll keep going with it.

From here I can't tell if the ugly brownish color covering the factory is rust, dirt, or something else. Most of the tiny pane windows are broken, probably by some of the little bastards I teach at my day job. Probably the quiet ones like Mark and Jessie, maybe even Denise for all I know. God this thing is big. I can see why Doreen didn't want to go inside. Depending on the layout, you could easily get lost, and even more easily get really badly hurt. Who the hell knows how much jagged metal and broken glass are all over a place like that? Then again, I am insane. And I'm desperate. Got to shake off this creeping decay of the self that I feel for no real identifiable reason.

I am here to write about Emily, to make her real. I have had this character in my head for almost 15 years, this girl who combines innocence, passion, raw anger, and tragedy in a teenager who seems so real that I sometimes think that maybe I knew her somewhere long ago. A past life? Maybe I was her. I know everything about her except her story. I know her personality, her fears, her desires, even how she would react in any situation, but I just can't decide how to write her life. Perhaps she took her father his lunch to this factory each day. Perhaps she grew up to work at this factory. Perhaps she was killed in this factory. I just don't know where to take it.

I've never seen a building so haunted as this. I don't know if I believe in ghosts in the traditional sense, but if ghosts are old, intense, repeated memories, then this place is chock-full of them. I wonder just how many men, maybe women also, spent their ENTIRE LIVES in this place, twenty, thirty, HELL – FORTY YEARS MAYBE – working here every day only to be forced into retirement or laid off. I heard they made pipes here. That sounds like it could be dangerous. How many were impaled on a copper pipe for a nice bathroom or maybe crushed to death by one of those big sons-of-bitches that they use for oil? Is that stupid? Probably. I don't even know what kind of pipe they made. Just trying to get into the mood. This is the first time I have ever felt that Mother Nature was cooperating with me by giving me a crappy day! It is not raining, but it's like the sky is in agony trying to hold it in. The sky is like an old lady riding down the highway whose husband, suffering from dementia, forgets that she told him 739 times that she has to pee or she will die, and he misses the rest stop. The sky is doing the "pee-pee dance" like a little kid whose bladder and inner plumbing have not yet fully developed enough to hold it in for long.

Well, I suppose that, considering the pee-pee-dance sky, I should either go home or go into this creepy-ass place and at least hang out in the doorway for a while and get some good ideas. Hanging out in the rain is no fun, and going home is not an option right now.

It is totally different in here than expected – well, not TOTALLY, but it is very open and very cleaned-out. They took EVERYTHING: all the equipment, all the raw materials, all the desks and benches, or whatever else they used. I don't know what is missing exactly. All I know is that there is really nothing here in this main area, which is the size of the biggest double airplane hanger I have even seen in the movies, like the kind they use to store those giant military troop transport planes. What I didn't expect is that weird things seem to be missing, like switch plates and socket plates, light fixtures, door knobs. Someone REALLY cleaned this place out. It's a good thing I got out here this week, because they are scheduled to tear the whole damn thing down very soon and build something over it – not sure what. Streaks of light from the broken, dark-glass windows illuminate the dust in the air, making a weird effect of dusty light beams shooting from the cathedral-like walls across to the floor on the opposite side. I can picture this place in some post-apocalyptic movie where some kind of leather-clad mutants join in gladiatorial combat here, surrounded by howling throngs. This would make a great night club, if it were not already so far gone. I don't think you could salvage the place at this point. It closed about 20 years ago, and it was probably falling apart before that. Shit – I should have brought a hard hat, now that I think about it.

I guess I should probably look around and get a feel for the whole place before I settle in for a long writing session. Of course, I had the presence of mind to bring one of those mega-wang, indestructible flashlights that shine forever, and a smaller backup version of the big one.

OK. The bathroom was not quite as disgusting as I had feared, but it was really stripped down. The toilets, the fixtures, everything gone. I just wizzed in a hole in the floor, but that was no different than places I have traveled abroad.

This office is not stripped so bare as the other places. I figure the company probably went out of business and decided to scrap all the metal and porcelain to help cover their costs. This may have been one place where they didn't trash everything, especially if some manager who was supervising the process oversaw the final operations from here. We have a dust-covered desk and a chair, even a coat hanger. The drawers of the desk are open. Let's see – a few old pens, unused ledger books, some personnel files... an envelope of HOLY SHIT! Money!!!!! I am surprised no one took it. It's not a fortune, but it has to be... $120!! Screw it. I'm taking this. Emily – what a sweet girl! Did you bring me here to lead me to this money? I wonder why the person who owned this left it behind. Maybe he expected to come back and get it later, and something happened. I say he. Maybe it was a woman, but I would imagine that this business is pretty patriarchal. Wow!! I can't believe the luck!!

Now that I shine my light on the desk, something kind of odd comes up. Some things may have been taken from here recently. There are spots in the dust showing that things were removed. I am guessing that one was a lamp of some kind, because of the shape of the base and the position on the desk. I have no idea what the other may have been. Here is something else that's odd – I have here a day planner with the cheap little calculator missing. Judging by the dust patterns, it seems like it was handled recently too. It's fun to play detective. Now why the hell would they take a lamp and a cheap calculator and not an envelope full of cash? Who cares?! The money is mine now, and man can I use it. Junior High teachers don't make a hell of a lot.

I am tempted to take the money and go, but I want to see what else is around here.... More cash? Other valuable stuff? A psycho-killer? I could see it going either way, maybe more than two ways. This could be the stuff of sweet dreams or nightmares. I squint my eyes just a bit and I can see girls in beautiful dresses dancing wildly to fast, driving beats while their boyfriends drink beer and look on with a combination of lust and genuine pride. I squint my eyes just a bit more and I can see a dark and grimy figure slinking into this place with something large and limp over his shoulder. The moonlight through the broken windows glints briefly off of a metal object in his hand, and I hear the faint trickling sound that leads my eyes to the trail of dark fluid dripping behind him as he moves toward…

THE BOILER ROOM

This room is really weird too. I guess it was some kind of boiler room or engineering room. There are places and fixtures where large machines used to be, but they are away from the main factory floor, behind a large steel door that used to have a sign on it, probably saying

"Keep Out

Authorized Personnel

Only"

Those signs crack me up. The sign seems to depend on the spacing to take the place of punctuation, but it literally says to keep out the authorized personnel, implying that anyone except authorized people can go right in. I always bring that up in my English classes. Punctuation is important for clarity. The switch plates and socket plates are removed here also, leaving behind the exposed electrical outlets for all kinds of plugs. Some of them look like the big, industrial electrical plugs used for clothes driers and heavy machinery. Everything is covered in something beyond dust – a kind of grime that is so thick that I can't even identify the nature of most of the debris on the floor – just bumps and shapes of hidden debris.

------------ What the hell is this????

There is a hole busted into the wall – broken roughly into the cinder block. The sockets on this wall actually have plugs in them, attached to heavy extension cords that go through the hole in the wall. There shouldn't be anything left here. The extension cords don't have much dust on them at all, and certainly no grime like the rest of the room. Maybe these were put here by the people preparing to tear down the place. The breaker box has been disturbed recently, and it looks like all of the breakers are turned on. I would have thought that they would have shut the electricity off to this place, but maybe they re-wired it and turned it back on to assist the demolition crew to get the preparations together. I didn't even think to try to flick any light switches on. Hell, there were no bulbs in the lights anyway. Let's see if there may be one down here.

There we go! One bulb in the whole place, but it does work! Now I am curious as hell. If I were not technically trespassing, I would call around to ask questions about what the hell they are up to, but I can't very well say – "I went into that factory with all of the 'Danger: Do Not Enter' signs to do some creative writing exercises, rifled through everything, and came up with some questions for you out of my own stupid curiosity." Plus, what would be the fun in that? Conjecture is so much more entertaining than truth.

So we have newer extension cords going through a big-ass, rough hole in the wall of an abandoned, dilapidated factory that no one has supposedly entered in years. Maybe I should switch over to writing mystery novels. Those sell really well if they are even semi-decent. Well, I guess I should grow some balls and look through this hole in the wall. Emily, would you stay behind and wait for me, or are you the adventurous type who would go right in with me? Of course I know the answer.

It doesn't look like much – a dirty little crawlspace full of rubble and with the extension cords going downward through a hole in the floor. I'll crawl through and see what I can…

GOD IT HURTS!!!!!!!!!!!!! The fucking floor gave way and I fell through into some kind of a fucking tunnel!! God My Ankle! I've twisted it before, but never this bad. I've been lying here for a while. I don't know how long. I never wear watches. They never seem to work for me for long. The batteries always go dead in a few weeks and the watch never works again. That's it think about something else – watches, school, cleaning the apartment, porn, anything but the pain. Keep writing writing writing and the pain will go away. Stretch out the leg and foot, move them around. Nothing broken, just one hell of a painful twist, probably sprained all to hell and back. I found the big flashlight using the small flashlight, thank God. The weight of the big one pulled it out of my pocket when I fell. My satchel was sealed up so I did not spill anything out of it. How the hell am I going to get out of here? Looking around with the light now. The fall was bigger than I thought – at least fifteen feet, and I couldn't make that even if I hadn't hurt myself. AAHH!!! This sucks!!! Alright. Deep breaths. There's a ladder lying right over there, I think, maybe about eight feet.

Broken. That ladder isn't going to do me any good at all. Damn it! Well, I guess I will rest up and then go down the tunnel. Maybe there is a way out. I can hear my students and my family chastising me already. I am the only person on the planet who doesn't own a cell phone. They tease me about it all the time, and I have to admit now that they are right. This is one of those times when it would probably come in REALLY handy, provided that I could get a signal in a place like this. Probably no signal. God this sucks. Painful.

I never thought I would be writing something like this. I actually hope I'm going crazy from the pain and stress. The tunnel snaked around this way and that. Maybe it's an old sewer tunnel, or maybe it goes to some supply source that used to connect up with the factory. Who knows? I didn't get to check out the whole place. I limped along until I heard noises up ahead. I called out over and over but no one seemed to hear me. The noises were cacophonous, a mixture of electrical tools, several TV's or radios, human-like grunting and jabbering. I thought maybe it was the demolition crew setting up some other part of the factory for destruction. The factory is so huge, I figured that maybe their cars or trucks were parked on the other side, so I didn't see them coming in. That would have been nice. Assistance to a doctor and a slap on the wrist for trespassing. AAHH!! My ankle still kills, especially when I move it certain ways. I almost forget I hurt it and then I do something stupid and bang it or strain it. But it looks like I have bigger things to worry about.

The noises I heard are coming from this room I just entered. It's so well lit that my own light didn't attract their attention, and so noisy that they didn't hear me yelling. Once I got close enough to see them, I knew something wasn't right, so I turned off the light and snuck in the shadows. The room actually stretches out below the tunnel I've been traveling, my tunnel entering the room at a slope. I was able to slip behind a large pile of junk just inside the room. With some minor shifting, I have been able to make myself a fairly comfortable space back here where I can see the whole place. Although it's loud, I'm not taking chances. I have got to bite down and bear this pain. It has to go away sometime. Oh shit! What a dumbass! I forgot that I have a small bottle of Tylenol in my bag for those caffeine headaches. I wish I had taken that right away, but better late than never.

Alright – how do I describe these things? I don't know if I'm just being stupid being afraid of them, but they are definitely not normal. I say things. I am sure they are people, of a sort. I don't know. They look like they could have been normal people at one point. There are about thirty or forty of them, enough that if they are hostile, I am totally screwed, even though they look incredibly unhealthy. They are flabby, slow, and their skin is sickly, pale, ashen. Did they get trapped down here too? Is this the demolition party? Have they been stuck here? Is it a group of homeless people, like the Mole People of New York? They are dirty and their clothes are old and torn. That could mean anything. They are grossly obese and move strangely, and I can't recognize their speech. I'm not a weightist, and I am no GQ model myself, but they are not just overweight. You can be big and healthy. Their fat looks wrong, sickly. I'll take a closer look. Something tells me not to approach them. I almost feel bad that I am acting so weird. Maybe they need my help as much as I need theirs. They just don't seem right. Maybe I've seen too many horror movies and documentaries on cults. I will observe for a while longer. Not like I can go much of anyplace right away anyhow. Well, I wanted something to write about. I think this qualifies.

OK – There is no fucking way I'm going to talk to these creatures. They are not just flabby and weird-moving. At a closer look I saw that they are into some kind of sick self-mutilation. Their skin is filled with wires, piercing through and hung with gadgets, battery packs, devices. At first I thought these items were just hanging from their clothes. How could they do that to themselves? Why? The pain! The disfigurement! My God! What are they? They mill about this chamber, maybe 100 by 100 feet across, sometimes going down the other tunnels that extend from this main room. I have been here probably at least a few hours now, and I have seen a group of four go down one tunnel and come back with nothing. They are like apes. They point, grunt, jabber, and pantomime, but they don't seem to speak a language that I have ever heard of. I have seen them eat, which they do sporadically and very frequently. Strewn about the chamber in piles are all kinds of pre-packaged foods and drinks. They basically eat what I would call vending machine food and sodas. No wonder they look so unhealthy. It is so much to take in. I can't get my head around all this, and I am so tired. I hope to God they don't come this way and look behind this pile of desks and debris. I just can't keep my eyes open.

It was all real. I just woke up on the top platform about ten feet above a huge chamber filled with the strangest sight I have ever seen. I feel physically better than I did yesterday, more awake, and my ankle is not as painful, but it is in no shape to run or try to fight off these things, no matter how slow and flabby they are. Emily. Sweetie, I am so glad you found me. I need you more than ever. I looked for you but did not see you. You must have run up ahead to get help after I fell. Smart girl. I know I can always depend on you. You have more guts than I have. That's one of the reasons I want to tell the story of your life. We just have to stay here and be quiet for a while. Between the two of us, we will figure this out and get back home. Look at it as an adventure!

Time to look around again and see exactly what we are dealing with. They seem to spend most of their time screwing with these old electronics. They are obsessed with electrical devices. In fact, the place is like a shrine to everything that carries a current. Four decades of gadgets are horded in here. Now that I look more closely at the surroundings, I see that they have extension cords going down all of the tunnels, several in each. These are plugged into scores of different devices with power strips, powering lights, stereos, TV's, computers, video games, fans, kitchen equipment, heaters. Fans and heaters run simultaneously, TV's glow with static, some getting faint signals. The radios still blare with noise of different songs of different genres, mixed with talk radio from five or so different shows. The zombie-like things each seem to have different personalities, if you can call them that. Some are industrious, sifting through debris, yelling out like triumphant beasts when they find another battery to throw into one of the large piles. Another industrious one is sorting through the batteries and trying to fit them into various devices. He does not seem to have any concept of battery size upon looking at them. It's all trial and error. He can't seem to tell that he may as well not even attempt to make AA batteries work in something that requires C batteries. He tries every battery in every device, sometimes using the right battery but putting it in the wrong way and still getting no action from the shaver, flashlight, vibrator, walkie-talkie, toy robot, or whatever the hell else he is playing with from another big pile. You would think that he would be the mentally retarded, low-on-the-totem-pole guy, but he seems to get some respect. Others bring him candy bars and soda, and show glee, followed by deference when he gets something to work. Then it goes to the Big Cheese, a female who sits in a special section that is less cluttered. She is titanic, and is constantly being fed by those who seek her favor. She sits on a large, plush, ragged chair and plays stacks of old video games, switching from one system to another at her whim. When the battery tester gets something working, he takes it to her, and she determines who keeps it, assigning ownership to whomever has been catering to her lately. I guess she is the Alpha Female. Jesus! I feel like Jane Goodall watching the damned gorillas!!! By far, she has the most random electrical shit hanging off of her. She looks like a living junk pile. Once I re-positioned myself to see where the working toys were being taken, and I caught a glimpse of her, I almost yelled out loud in surprise. How can they handle the pain? How do they not get infections? Why don't they bleed more? Some of them walk around dripping just a few drops blood from fresh implants, having recently twisted wire through their arms or cheeks, even cutting their necks and threading cables through to let gadgets hang off of them like ornaments. I have no problem with body modification. Half of my students have piercings, but this is different, although there's a weird kind of logic to their actions, I am sure of it. It is some kind of a strange status issue. Sometimes the Alpha Female points to a large pile in the center of the room and Battery Tester goes and attaches the device to the others in the pile, not just stacking it, but connecting it with wire or cord. He seems to show a kind of reverence when he does this, and they seem to be pretty good items that they attach to this pile, which rises probably ten or twelve feet into the air. I wonder if this is some kind of religious offering. It seems to include food as well. One of them unwrapped a candy bar and climbed carefully to the top of the pile, leaving it carefully in a hole in the junk. I cannot believe I am seeing all of this. When I get out of here, I don't know whether to call the authorities or just let them go. I guess they are not hurting anyone but themselves. I need to eat something and think about what I am going to do. Thank God I brought some stuff along. It has to be the next day now. No one will miss me yet, but I need to get the fuck out of here by tomorrow morning.

OH GOD!!! This is too much. Please get me out of here!!! If they catch me, I know they'll kill us, or maybe worse. What are we going to do? They went down a different tunnel and they came back with a guy. He couldn't have been more than twenty years old. Five of them carried him with a bag over his head, squirming and screaming. They took the bag off and forced him to kneel before the giant pile in the middle of the room. They forced him to look upward to the top of the pile, tilting his head roughly, and they barked in their language, barely audible above the din of radios. They held candy bars, packaged crackers, sodas, and all manner of electronics in front of him as though offering bribes to do something, but I had no idea what. I don't think he knew either. I couldn't hear his words, but I could see that he kept thrashing his head, straining in their grasp, and screaming at them.

Then they went to the next step. It was horrible. No movie, no book, no dream, could prepare you for seeing something like this for real. They took wire and forced it into his flesh. They ripped his clothes pulled him to the floor, and began to pierce his body all over with blades and wires, wrapping electrical cords, coaxial cables, stereo wire, through his skin. Now I could hear him just fine as he screamed and screamed and thrashed. Then I heard it. The howl that came from the pile itself. The pile at the center of the room was alive! It howled and trembled – a triumphant, jubilant, beastial howl like nothing I had ever heard before. Within minutes, the poor kid was bleeding all over the place. The thing at the center of the room – did it want the kid for a sacrifice or as a new member? Or something I could not even imagine? I wanted more than anything to help that kid. Forgive me, Oh God, I am SO SORRY. I am injured, and even on my best day I couldn't have helped against so many. And I have Emily to think of. She needs my help, and she is just a young girl. I have to be strong for her. I have never wanted anything more than I wanted to help that guy... except getting Emily out of here so she can grow up safely and happily. That is one thing I want more than anything.

They dragged the bleeding kid to the space where the Alpha Female stays (I think I know where the Alpha Male is now) and acted like nothing was wrong with him. They held him up as they cheered and patted him on the back and head as though he just passed some initiation, and they sat him down on the chair next to the Alpha Female and handed him a video game controller. His head lolled and his hands fell limp, dropping the controller. They handed him another and turned on another machine, popping in a different type of game. He dropped that one too. The kid was probably in shock, maybe even dying from the fear, trauma, and blood loss. His neck was really bloody. Maybe they nicked a major vein or artery. They kept shoving food in his mouth and handing him the controller for new games until their constant fumbling around left too few hands to prop him up and he fell face-first in the middle of the floor. They poked, nudged, and pulled at him, but no response came. Then the wailing started. God, it was terrible, wasn't it, Emily? I was keeping my hand over her eyes for most of this. Even a girl as tough as Emily should never have to see such things. But when they knew the guy was dead and the wailing started, I ran out of hands. I couldn't cover her ears as well. She did, though, and she couldn't help but cry out a little. I did too. The Pile reverberated with a thunderous howl and screens all over this hellish cavern blinked on and off several times. Before I could stop myself, I yelled, "You're the ones who killed him, you dumb bastards! What are you crying about?!" They didn't hear. They took the victim to the Great Pile, the Alpha Male, and smeared blood all over the pile. They then took two of the better pieces of working electronics that they had sewn onto the kid, a functioning walkman and a keychain flashlight, and attached them to the Great Pile. The body was taken down a tunnel by three of them, and they returned without it.

Alright. I have to get my head together. What can I do to focus? I can't believe I am writing this, but we may die here. If I don't pull myself together, we probably will die here – nearly forty years old, no family, a mediocre career. I have three Master's Degrees and I can't figure out how to get away from a pack of mentally challenged gadget worshippers.

I could give up because of this, get all depressed and go ask these things to make me one of them, or another sacrifice. Or I can figure a way out of this, go back to my home, and completely reinvent my life. I will make up for lost time and correct every mistake I have ever made. That's it. I will volunteer more, do more with the kids. Emily will meet all of my students, and she can live with me. I will adopt her. I sometimes forget why I do my job in the first place. I am too young to give up. I have to think about Emily and my students. What will they think if I just disappear? What if their compliments are not just ass-kissing? What if I really am their role model, at least for some? OK.

There are six tunnels total, including the one I came down. That leaves five possible exits. I have to cross enemy territory to get to any of those other tunnels. I would make a mad dash, put the pain out of my head and run for it, if I only knew which was the right tunnel. These things love light and there is never a time when all of them are asleep. They are constantly just listening, watching, and playing with their crap they have accumulated. There is no way to get through undetected. At least we have sound cover. It is always so damn loud. I guess that helps.

259

You have an idea Emily? That's… No, I don't think I can! Can you?! Isn't there another way? Give me some time to think.

I wish I could come up with something else, but you are right. It's the only way to be sure we can get out. We have to join them for a while. We have to pass as members. They are too dumb to keep track of their own members that closely, and they seem to want new members anyway. We can give them the smaller flashlight as an offering, and hide the big one to help get out. OK. Now we have to disguise ourselves. Rip the clothes, and get enough stuff to put through the skin. God this is going to hurt! I have the Tylenol and I did bring a bit of booze – some gin in the flask that Bernadette bought for me. I thought it might help to get the creative juices flowing, but I didn't think it would be anesthetic for self-mutilation. Oh Christ I can't believe this is happening!

I thought the ankle was bad. FUCK!!!!!!! I've gotten drunk, taken Tylenol, and this still hurts like hell. We even cheated as much as possible, trying to weave through our clothes instead of flesh. Doing that to Emily was the worst. How could I hurt her like that? She is everything to me. She is my reason for living. How could God make me hurt her to save her? The fact that she was so strong, not protesting, not crying out once, makes me feel even worse, and makes me love her even more. Our wounds are much shallower than that poor guy they brought down. I know from my students and their cutting addictions and piercings a few things about what parts of the body handle that kind of thing the best, but a pair of earrings is not going to get us past these guys. We had to mess ourselves up pretty badly. I am going to have to face the fact that these scars will probably be permanent, and the pain feels like nothing else. Writing really helps me to control it, but it is time to put the notebooks away and join the throng. I have been trying to figure out as much as I can about their communication and mannerisms. Time to put that community theatre acting to the test. We are ready, I think.

I LEFT HER!!!! OH GOD HOW COULD I DO IT???!!!!!! I WAS SO SCARED. She sacrificed herself for me and she must still be down there. I have to calm down and create a plan to save her.

What happened?

Got to figure out what to do next. Play it back in my head -

The brood accepted us openly. We placed the lit flashlight on the altar and stared up to the top of the Great Pile as we bowed. I could see its eyes through the clutter, staring down at us in demonic, frenzied glee at its new disciples. We blended for some time, splitting up enough not to seem suspicious, but not enough to let her out of my sight. We took three trips into the unknown tunnels. The first was down the Tunnel of the Dead, where they took that poor kid. There seemed to be no set pattern to their rituals. They just did whatever popped into their heads. Some followed and some did not. I saw a pack gathering to go down a tunnel. Hoping there was a way out, we joined, only to find a sealed room with corpses everywhere in various states of decay. The group stood for several minutes, chanting random noises, and then returned. The second trip went from cement tunnel to a sealed room, to a rough-cut dirt tunnel that snaked around for probably a mile. On this excursion, we found where they get much of their crap. It appeared as though we were underground by a landfill. The tunnel ended in a widened room with a wall of sloping, shifting trash on the opposite side. We sifted through it for hours looking for anything useful, and found a few things. We could see no opening to escape through, so we continued to play along.

The third trip ended with a hole into the sub-basement of what turned out to be a giant storage facility. We were in another real building now, at least a mile away. It was a giant warehouse where endless shelves of huge cardboard boxes reached to the ceiling, requiring a forklift to get. We shuffled around to a section that contained boxes of the very foods I had seen them eating. I realized just how hungry I was, and tore into several packets. Emily did the same, but less barbarically. Then I saw it. An open door leading to a stairwell. My mind went blank and I ran. I ran on my hurt ankle, full bore, sometimes feeling my ankle flop to the side, landing on the side of my foot, hearing and feeling further tearing of the connective tissue, but I kept running. I looked back to see my fellow scavengers running after me, holding out candy bars, as if to tempt me back to their fold. Their facial expressions and vocalizations seemed more plaintive than angry, as though they were afraid for me rather than enraged by my desertion. As I entered the stairwell, Emily was close behind. Although I had started running first, her superior health and youth made her catch up quickly. As we all entered the stairwell, I stumbled and fell. This time a "Pop" accompanied the pain. I looked back, expecting to see them closing on me, but Emily reached into my bag and produced the flashlight, probably the biggest one they had ever seen. She held it up to them and addressed them in their own language. They fell to their knees as she turned it on and began to sing. Somehow she was singing in their language and her whole demeanor changed. The wires in her flesh seemed to come alive and glow and move and her radiance filled the room as she held them transfixed. I heard her thoughts saying "Go! Go now! This is not your place!" so I limped up the stairs, down a hall, down another, and out into the sunshine of a Monday morning.

I have to go back to get her. She is my angel, my daughter, my mother, my goddess, my queen, my redeemer, my lover, my............ I need her. I need her now. I am home now and I have pulled the wires out, shed my sacrificial blood again for the salvation of my soul and the return of my holy angel and I will rent a car and go back there and take my rope and lower it and she will be waiting for me in that tunnel with the broken ladder and she will forgive me for leaving and for piercing her flesh and she will live here with me forever and she will stay right here where it is safe and I will bring her all the things she needs and wants right here and I will offer them up to my goddess and she will beam down on me as I pile all the things that will bring her pleasure high to the sky and I will bring all the children here to talk to her and worship her and be her friends and follow her wisdm forver

[The writing at this point becomes illegible and continues for several pages.]

I'M GOING TO THE MOON
By Christy Leigh Stewart

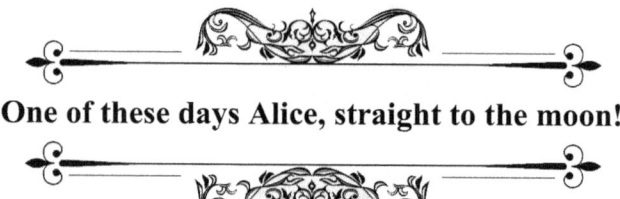

One of these days Alice, straight to the moon!

*In her own words: "My name is **Christy Leigh Stewart** and I am one of the bottom feeders of the art community; the independent/self-published author. I hope you enjoy the following story and any of my other work you might come across, but my real goal is to encourage anyone and everyone to publish a book, no matter how bad or ridiculous their work. I hope the publishing industry gets flooded with mediocre work and people finally have to find good work on their own instead of just checking the label like some stereotypical teenie bopper buying shoes.*

"In ten years I hope to not be dead in a ditch, but I also hope someone from Random House is eating shit and having to negotiate a book deal with some kid who self-published the crap s/he had scrawled on their school notebook."

I'm going to the moon and I'm going to meet God.

If God isn't on the moon, I'll try to find him when I have more time.

It's late now, almost midnight, so my family is asleep. No one hears me get out of bed, not even my little sister. She's got great hearing too because she has cat ears. She wanted them for Christmas and my parents got them for her.

I wanted to feel joy again but they got me indignant outrage.

I played with it a little but got bored pretty quickly. My sister borrowed it when a boy she liked called her names and broke the outrage. I wasn't mad, I just felt indignant.

The moon is far away but tonight it's full so it's hanging lower. I still need a way to get up there and it'll take me awhile. It's above my roof. Above my neighbors' trees. Above the incessant scratching noise I hear when I close my eyes.

I've figured out how to build a ladder though; so far it isn't very tall but it'll grow. It's made out of bones from those new mice that can regenerate now that scientists have sliced their genes with lizards. I got one from my father's work. He's a scientist. He's never cried. He flips through Googled image searches of burn victims while he touches himself. The bones will grow into new rungs of the ladder as long as I feed them cheese. I have as much as I can carry but there will be more on the moon.

I'm pretty high now and I can't see my house. I can't see the city. I can't see my future. I passed it by about five rungs ago and it told me to be careful who I trust with my heart and that I should start using my left hand more often.

I'm at the moon now. There is a little girl here and she is holding something close to her body.

"Hello," I say to her and she smiles at me. "What are you doing?"

"I want to go to Earth," she tells me. "So I'm gathering the dreams of children and holding them tightly. Soon enough they will get heavy and I'll fall with them. Do you want to come with me? I'm going to meet God."

I don't want to go back just yet and I'm having too much fun to meet God, so I tell her yes but secretly hope for the world to end and as it does, I grab her arm and we both float to Mars.

DIETHYLAMIDE

By Michael C. Thompson

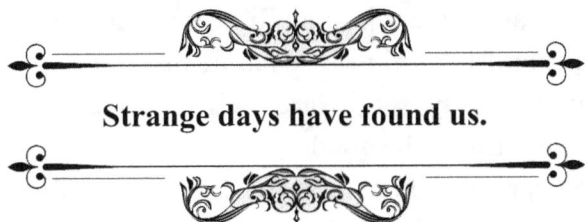

Strange days have found us.

Michael C. Thompson has been previously published in the November 2010 "Gothic" issue of Collective Fallout, which featured Bulletproof Faces. This story will also be re-printed in an upcoming Static Movement anthology. On 5/22/11, Michael's flash science fiction piece entitled Bubbles was featured on the front page of Weirdyear.com, and on 6/6/11 he was the featured artist on Weeklyartist.com.

Michael's short-fiction piece entitled Dimorph was published in the June 2011 e-zine, Deadman's Tome. His short science-fiction piece Aldo will be published in the Summer Edition of Icarus' Magazine.

Eight of Michael's poems have been recently selected by Static Movement for publication in an upcoming print anthology of dark poetry.

"1. Drip."

"Philosophy is useless. Only entertainment has value. If one is going to waste his time, he might as well enjoy it."

Drip.

The EGO on the monitor elucidates with absolute authority, a spiritual attribute of his explained greatly by two immediately preceding self-proclamations; a) that the speaker is a nihilist, in foremost sentiment, and that b) he is an entertainer in post. These *abstractions* float inside his aura like innocent bolts of counter-charged reiki amidst the fluorescence of his electric personality. A contradiction, yet fully self-aware, self-realized, a symptom of a viral negative too true to be good.

The curtains melt around him, the Technicolor flickers and for a second I see the static unreality of television blinking before my heavily dilated pupils. I witness the lie behind his own eyes, choking out his abused and defiant shame for the last time, finally murdering it. This crusaders' existence is revealed to me in a flash of lightning, a popping illumination above my head, showering hot sparks to the ground below. Nihilism is but a devil's advocacy to him - his true nature is evident in his fanciful perversions. He is an **Entertainer**, with a capital **E**. Foremost, an archetype. And he knows it better than anyone.

Drip.

The first few <u>LSD</u> blotters are kicking in.

Took four more a half hour ago... supposed to wait... they may have arrived ahead of schedule. Blur into my pain like paint splatters and I know it immediately:

Drip. Drip.

Puts me up to six blots of Apollonian blood, needle-fire *ambrosia* rocking up my veins, shooting a novel mania behind my shimmering eyes like fire in a furnace, like the eyes of **Ifrit**. I heard it, the sound God makes when the bubble pops, when man transcends his boundaries and finally eats from the perpetually rotting fruit of knowledge.

When the drugs start working.

This is the instant;

SUCCESS.

SUCCESS is when the world becomes animated *lysergy*, when matter becomes magick and magick becomes power; when energy can be snatched from the paint of a wall, or the tie of a preacher, and made to weave fresh stars anew, waiting to be possessed of identities.

The eyes of the **Entertainer** pierce through me, I can see the galaxies in his irises spinning, blue, green, purple, circling a dissolute **Ouroboros**, a singularity, shifting hue with the magnetic contrast of the television screen as they try to escape the sucking graviton. The hallucinogenic mirage poisons my consciousness... evolves it...

Ambrosia, nectar of the gods, as rotten as spoilt fat, as nourishing as the milk of Mother Mary.

"*Philosophy itself has no end, no answer, no purpose save the dissolution of human understanding by promoting worldviews which attempt to boil reality down into a simple formula, one which can be easily understood and thus controlled.*"

Black blinking, an intelligence broadcasting from behind his komodo retinas, telling the true lie.

"*The truth is that there is no control.*"

The galaxies spin faster, crunch into the abyss, popping out of the wavelength like dying sparks.

"*Only chaos reigns. Only **discord**. All attempts to control order will inevitably be thwarted, because order is a vain construct, a* *particle amidst acid needlessly suffering to prevent its own demise. Entropy is the God of this world. And only entropy."*

Entropy.

Acid.

It's like the **Entertainer** is talking to me. The **rabbit hole** widens, and so does the Stygian black pool at the bottom of it. I watch it as my mind falls, I know what it is, a lake of bottomless diethylamide, and me, I'll be the particle, dissolving…

The **Entertainer** stares on, as if waiting for me to pay him mind. The moment is frozen. His brown hair waves in slow-motion like stalks in a field, likely caught in the artificial gale of studio fans, and the moment of dread creeps in my skin, goose-bumps erupt on my arms, my legs. My balls draw up in my body, needing protection from the blossoming drug-cold, the LSD washes over me with a great wave, dragging me out to Sea/to see.

Only the **Entertainer** exists. He preaches the awful truth, the euphoric lie, opposed only in perspectives, constructed of the same rotten reflection.

"When deprived of entertainment, a man may resort to its intellectually bankrupt counterpart; philosophy. It is through misery that religion and ideology have been created, constructs which fail to escape the natural rule of entropy. Who can say what sort of history a world of satisfied, artistic men and women might have created?"

Trip

WHO?

WHAT?

WHEN?

WHERE?

WHY?

?

Questions. Riding the question mark down on a wave of liquid dream, the **Entertainer's** face hangs overhead like that of a deity, a static emanation speaking through the aethers, writing himself into my trip with the pen of the rebellious creator Lucifer. I sense the workings of fate amidst this *lysergic* arcadia. I hear the **Entertainer** in my own soul, vibrating chills with each intonation of this televised kin-spirit's dissolvent social virus.

|Saint Michael, where are you?|

"Every empire that has ever existed has fallen, every institution, no order ever reigns supreme save for the order of nature alone, by its very definition a state of chaos. It is only by the hubris of man, a symptom of philosophy, *that such material disease erupts in the first place."*

Disease. Entropy. Natural attachments to philosophy… parasitic, or endemic?

The **Entertainer** continues: *"What lasts? There are but two constants throughout the span of recorded human existence; two mortal enemies; GOD, and its challenger. Both spirits emanate from the same source, the inescapable symptom of intelligence: EGO,"* he reveals. The black holes in his eyes grow larger, the irises swell outward into the vacancy of purgatory beyond but a moment fore' their devouring.

Do I see the devil in those orbs?

*"EGO is what man refers to when he speaks of GOD, for EGO is but the **philosopher's** stone so long dreamt of - possessing the power to create slow self-destruction. It is EGO's symptom, GOD, that leads man to create order. But EGO has two aspects, two emanations in constant flux during the play of human shadows."*

I fall down the O in EGO and land somewhere in "*I am.*" That's the name of THE LORD. I expect it to echo through the syrupy <u>diethylamide</u>.

Nothing.

Back in reality for a merciful moment. Staring at the <u>entertainment</u> box, the digital picture show has gone as black as the bottom of a deep pit. I drive like a demon from station to station, the remote control my vehicle, and disappointment abounds. All channels are creepily vacant of energy, news, advertisement; my living room grows cancerous in the dysphonic vacuum. Only blank onyx glass presently maintains its existence amongst sociable atoms, my other-dimensional doppelganger peering outward through the modern wizard's ball that is my television screen, a dark reflection. On the chrome palate, my face, captured in its simple design.

Entertaining me in an electric coma.

Though the screen is black, the voice of the **Entertainer** remains.

"GOD remains constant,"

ART

"And ART."

My reflected face stares back at me through the magicked mirror, I scry with intensity, swimming through pools of Thetan laughter and the corpses of drowned Narcisses. The image looks like a modern-day Caravaggio. I zoom out, de-focus, the world is lit stardust for a moment, quarks reflecting lights, beaming ultra-violet hallucinations into my optic receptors. My mind goes epileptic and I am suddenly drowning in a lake of cold, cracked television screen.

"ART as a concept stands in direct opposition to GOD," says the nihilist. *"ART is the celebration of chaos, of disorder."*

I see the arabesque **Grendel** at the bottom of the TV lake, glaring up at me with ink-stone eyes, his gills sucking up the liquid LSD like nutrients. Black sand kicks up, catching in his scales. The **beast**. The only **beast**, the archetype, the spirit before me as I trip on drips. The man in my mirror, twisted, made naked, shown for what he is.

Drip.

"Philosophy is the propaganda of order," says the **Entertainer**. *"Entertainment, however, a sewer of dreams; and from each discarded lucidity can still sew inspiration to dissolve, from each reflection there is an opportunity to break free of the bondage which captivates us to worship order for a false sense of security, of sanity in a world of abstractions."*

Grendel reaches up for me, the pitiful substitute for Beowulf, I choke on the liquid dream. In reality, worlds away, I choke on air.

A smile breaks out on the face of the **Entertainer** God in my mind, a grin, confusing me on an almost primal level.

"So for the love of GOD!" he shouts, *"Be entertained!"*

Grendel is he, and I, the monster parted like light through a crystal, separate yet the same. The realms are as black as the holes in his eyes.

I'm afraid.

Reality flashes for a moment. Still sitting in front of the blank TV. Lights are out. How long has it been?

(Drip.)

Another wave crests, a tidal quicksand grabs me and pulls me out to drown. I see it now. The nihilist is right.

*The **devil** is an **Entertainer**.*

"2. Poison."

The air smells like machine oil, but I inhale it anyway, let the grease dust cling static to the burst capillaries in my expanded lungs. Breathing the world in, getting high on the fumes of nature. The sidewalk brightens in front of me as the beam of a car lights upon it, painting it with effulgence, reminding me of…

Lysergic animation…

A voice, shrieking. I turn to face it and remember where I am; in existence, a pinpoint of focus, cursed to walk the world amidst the hysteria.

But public. **Still in public**. Under the influence of highly restricted…

"Once you a dope fiend, they never trust you!" shouts the ragged lunatic, trench coat blowing out behind him in the breeze, the source of the wretched, vacuous shrieking, creating a satellite of my attention in spite of my drug-induced displacement. The character throws his hands in the air, almost comically, but it appears as though his desire is to threaten. I can't even hallucinate his target, but its likely he's already doing that.

"Give me a fair fuckin' shot!" he commands the world, his fists still shaking comically, arthritically in the air, blaspheming against his caste. I can see the steam of red aether rising off of his fists, repelled by gravity into the bruised, purpling pre-dark sky.

He looks directly at me. I can see the **snake** in his eyes, eating its own tail.

"What about you?" he interrogates.

I say nothing. He is a drawing, a sketch, charcoal lines blinking him in and out of my present distortion. He expects nothing.

"You motherfucker," he mumbles resignedly, cursing me to fuck my own mother.

Drip.

A heartbeat, reverberating throughout the kingdom of my own consciousness. Echoing, haunting even upon its initial creation. A flash of light, a cue card, a marker snaps.

The scene shifts. The world is as black as the bottom of **Grendel's** lake.

Ink <u>diethylamide</u>. Still feel like I'm floating, sinking, caught in a paradox like a man in the jaws of a shark. It devours me whole, and inside of its atoms I feel the world twisting, drowning me. I'm caught in a whirlpool, letters everywhere, I try to grasp onto one but they're all heading in the same direction: down, into a sea of letters.

A

A

L

S

D

T

h

en

words.

I see it now. Tattooed tree flesh, scarred, bloody with black ink. In the chaos, a natural formation. A phrase:

"Then I will swear beauty herself is black,

and all they foul that thy complexion lack."

Are the words part of a story? The numbers make themselves visible.

1.

3.

2.

<u>Sonnet</u>.

I close the warm flesh of the book, more gold letters leave scars through the leather. Then a name, I recognize it.

Shakespeare.

I gaze around the library. No one minds me. It is as though I am invisible. I look back down, a lucid moment commencing. I cling to the shore of sanity, the <u>diethylamide</u> ocean of quicksand yanking at my heels. My fingers dig into the dirt, clutching at sane order, back into the skin of **Shakespeare**. It bruises, calluses, bleeds, rots. I drop his corpse onto the mutilated corpse of a table tree. Other dead philosophers lay beside the **Bard**, rotting and stinking with toxic vanity, necrotizing until their foulness is dissolved to sterility.

On the way to the exit, I spot **Friedrich Nietzche**. He gazes at me vacantly, a soulless meme, unreal.

Drip.

Lysergic waves crest again, nearly yanking me back into the crawling chaos, the ocean of ideas and ambitions, of wasted nightmares, rotten fruits. Still I manage to hang onto reality, if only by a fingernail.

<u>*Lucid. Stay lucid.*</u>

Should have stayed home. But the *lysergy* speaks to fate; the animation penned about me reminds me that I had no choice but to come here. Lines drawn into confines, no escape from the track…

"<u>*You*</u>," says **Nietzche**, rudely interrupting my paranoiac possession.

I gape at him. Am I dreaming? I ignore the manifestation, looking at the other patrons of the library. They move about like insects, whispering, chittering, conspiracy to scavenge the dead cells of the defenseless, snacking on the corpse of **Shakespeare**. Strangely, all female. All cockroaches. Pale imitations of human beings, disguised with cheap Xerox.

Drip.

The chaos finally pulls me under, I drown in artificiality, thirteen letters, I choke on this sentence, but swallow it whole, gagging at its absurdity. And then I am stranded upon the ocean, entangled in a reef of vanities. A cloud of words bursts overhead, drenching me, I try not laugh at the absurdity of it all.

"*I know why it is man alone who laughs*;" says **Nietzche**, as if on cue, a symbol simply waiting for his place on stage. "*He alone suffers so deeply that he had to invent laughter.*"

More <u>philosophy</u>. The <u>enemy</u>. The true distortion. A jagged paradox, the nihilists ascending the throne of order to respect.

Nietzche, another hack, another rotting **Shakespeare**, another-

Mark Twain by the exit. I stand up, walk like an LSD-fueled machine to the door, twitching junkily, still ignored. **Twain** brushes past, but I put on my Ray Ban, my screen between the world and I.

Drip.

Losing grip again. Peaking.

Out of the eye of the storm now.

I see **William S. Burroughs** in the parking lot, being devoured by a skittering pack of whispering cockroach women. I walk by, head down, low-key.

Listen to what they're talking about, chewing on withered junkie jerky.

Philosophy.

"3. Sugar."

Porno-Christ judges me with cold wooden eyes, crucified high above his **Catholic** captors. He's trapped inside of a sculpture, an idol, sexuality, mortification. He hangs low, weary of gravity's bondage and suffering for the sins of science. A chiseled masterpiece, the face of an androgynous angel save the mahogany beard, an ancient Roman ward against faggotry.

Words spring from the dry earth of my mind like oil, blasting into the air, making connections. The suffering Christ, sexualized, glorified, beatified - torture transmuted to salvation. Circuits alight, connections paint into visible eye's mind.

Letters:

B

D

S

M

Words: <u>Bondage</u>. <u>Discipline</u>. <u>Sadism</u>. <u>Masochism</u>. All evocations of the naughty idol.

Times New Roman thoughts, a ticker-tape of ingredients, letters, vowels, concepts, spurting like death from the wounded top-soil of my frontal lobe. Oil - ink floods it again.

Not ink.

<u>Diethylamide</u>.

Breathing it in now, feeling the slow death of reason. Order spins away from me as the maw of **the beast**, of **Satan**, of **Grendel**, gnashes away at even the peace of silence. My mind is devouring itself, a Jungian **Ouroboros**. One side of me cannibalizes the other, then plans to starve to death.

I look up, painting the world with insight since the memory of it was first dissolved in the acid pool a few short moments ago. A steeple hangs high above the puppet messiah, sewn together with fabrics of sugar and poly-cotton blend, effortlessly intertwining the realm of dissolvent lunacy with stoic sanity. So easily the myth made truth, even the puppet savior strung up above knows that he has been forsaken. The image trapped within the glass, a ghost in the machine, is **Mary**, the Mother of GOD. As if in Hell, she stares down eternally at the suffering and sexual degradation of her only son, the fuck puppet **Porno-Christ**.

My eyes notice a new distraction upon the graven image. On his torn mahogany flesh rests a crown of sculpted wooden filth, anointing the mannequin lord as royalty over those who desire to eat his very skin, and drink his life's blood, and piss and shit all over the very spirit that his fiction was meant to inspire. With their ignorance, they flog him each day, praying upward to nothing, wasting their energies on a useless dream, while the inanimate tree rot suffers high above. Their prayers lash at him like razor wire, tearing open the wounds from which they greedily suck, all the while feeling righteous.

"*Son?*" a voice asks me, a voice of the voice of God. It echoes, vibrates throughout the cold singularity that has poisoned every atom of the church. "*Would you like to pray?*"

"*Yes,*" I say, waiting, wondering what will happen. Lost in the LSD.

Drip.

The priest grabs my shoulder, bows his head, I realize he's a preying mantis. He chirps his insectile recitation, judging me all the while. An <u>Act of Contrition</u>. For me, the sinner.

"**Merciful Father**, *I am guilty of <u>sin</u>. I confess my <u>sins</u> before you and I am sorry for them. Your promises are just; therefore I trust that you will forgive me my <u>sins</u> and cleanse me from every stain of <u>sin</u>. **Jesus** himself is the proposition for my <u>sins</u> and those of the whole world. I put my hope in his atonement. May my <u>sins</u> be forgiven through his name, and in his blood may my soul be made clean. Amen.*"

One word on repeat in my head:

Sin sin sin sin sin sin

I turn to look at him. I want to laugh at his clothing, his rituals, desire to bathe in the blood of his supposed savior, but I can't laugh because he's staring directly into my dilated eyes, into his own enlarged reflection, bounced back to his cognition by twin lakes of pupil singularity. He knows I'm **dripping**. <u>Tripping</u>.

I gaze around, shaking the chaos from me like an animal flings water. I'm still soaked. The preyers are mantises, rubbing their claws together, waiting to fuck and cannibalize or be cannibalized. All the praying, all the preparation, all for a swift and brutal end.

<u>Philosophy</u>: The mask some would have these lost ones wear. But I see <u>Entertainment</u>. I see the **Porno-Christ** hanging high in the rafters like the phantom of the opera, I see a Crayola Virgin god-bearer trapped in magicked crystal above her inanimate still-born maso-**Christ**. I see people in funny hats, drinking blood, eating flesh, devouring their living selves until nothing is left, not even a scale or a snake-skin. Closing the circle. Dying. Not really understanding why.

Hypnotized by <u>Entertainment</u>. Worshiping their very devil.

"What are you reading?" the priest asks to me, honestly curious. It snaps me from my drug-trance, my pupils constrict, the priest catches it. Tossed ashore onto sanity cove by the merciless ocean gods of Discordia, I run away from the waters, back toward reality, <u>lucidity</u>, logic, and yes, the dreaded Order. I know I will not make it, the tide will sweep me back out again. But I run harder, faster, my eyes on the prize. Escape from the trip.

I finally look down at his book, my schizoid thoughts feeling too uninspired to dissolve me. I expect to find a Bible, picked up from a pew. The world swims around me as I stare at it, wondering where it came from, why it's here with me - why I'm here, why I would ever set foot in a **Catholic** Church on <u>LSD</u>.

Or a library.

Drip.

Lucidity is slipping. Autonomy flakes as a sickle strikes in the blank abstraction that exists just outside of the confines of the idea.

I open it to the last page, a book-mark falls out. A torn and folded curse from the book of Deuteronomy. I pay it no mind, but the mantises look immediately putrefied and ready to swallow me whole. Their preying palms rub together in synchronicity, the dry friction becomes a part of me forever.

The letters on the page jumble as my spirit rises, the world is juicy once more, tasting as cherry as the virgin Mary. They form a face. A young boy, an angel, a fiction, a truth - **Mark Twain's** inner child. Bitter, broken, outraged, and old. The angel says to me aloud, speaking through me, telling his name, speaking the words of the mysterious stranger.

"*It is true, that which I have revealed to you;*

there is no God, no universe, no human race,

no earthly life, no heaven, no hell.

It is all a dream -

a grotesque and foolish dream.

Nothing exists but you.

And you are but a thought -

a vagrant thought

a useless thought

a homeless thought

wandering forlorn

among the empty eternities!"

Twain must have slipped it to me as I was walking out the library, a phantom narcissist, before dissolving back into the chaos like so much static.

Empty eternities glitter across my mind, scanning space, dimension, until finally they are caught in the super-massive black pupils of the **Entertainer**. I hear the atoms popping light-years away. In the center of the inner circle, cloaked amidst penumbra, a clenching abyss, lined with jagged incisors, bloody gums, the mouth of my beast **Grendel**, the **Entertainer**, the **devil**. It gapes, reeking, polluting the air with decay beyond the most putrid natural entropy.

Dante saw this. I shall be less fortune.

The face of the monster bites out toward me, gnashing and gashing, whispering, soothing, hypnotizing...

"A nightmare. You're having a nightmare..."

Fade to black...

Open my eyes. Looking up. **Porno-Christ** looks well-endowed. Naughty. I see the grin of Loki on his face, the golden apple of Eris tucked into his crown, the euphoric secret of Lucifer locked away behind his eyes, Jesus Christ, the self-proclaimed Morning Star like a shining light amidst the dark, naked church rafters. A maso-**Christ**, the big secret; the crucifixion his penultimate masturbatory act. His seed spilled to the ground through the hole in his side, fertilized the dirt, and out of it grew absurdity.

Chaos.

Entertainment.

The **Grendel**-Priest speaks again, to someone else this time. An angel in white, though I see two **devils** on his shoulder, one smarter than its opposition. He doesn't notice me.

The domination of gravity ensues, my body lifts into the air like **Christ** out of his tomb, and I make a quiet suggestion to his suffering wooden arbiter as we leave the border of the joke;

"For God's sake, be entertained."

Porno-Christ doesn't laugh. He only stares jealously as I leave behind this upright absurdity, and the doors of the church close behind me, cutting off the hateful glare of Mother Mary. I cross myself absently.

The angels carry me to the ambulance and take me away. I can even hear what they're talking about.

Entertainment.

THEIR QUIET, BOOKISH LIFE

By Chadwick H. Saxelid

They always said she was the quiet type.

Chadwick H. Saxelid left his low paying job as an administrative assistant for the even lower paying career of full time writer. He currently lives a somewhat quiet and reasonably bookish life in the San Francisco Bay Area, with his wife and son. He can be kept track of by visiting www.chadwickhsaxelid.typepad.com.

Rebecca's box arrived.

Mark unpacked her and got her freshened up and situated in the living room before he went back upstairs to his home office. It was hard to concentrate there, knowing that she was downstairs, waiting for him. But he had a deadline looming and had to get a set number of pages finished that day in order to meet it.

It was dark by the time he finished. He shut his computer down and arranged his notes and papers for the next day's work.

A cold winter rain had rolled in off of the ocean and it tapped at the window beside him. During the summer he would open the window, so he could hear the rhythmic pulse of the ocean as it crashed against the nearby bluffs. He could hear the crash of the waves through the window, but the sounds of the wind and of the rain were louder.

Mark turned off the lights and went downstairs. He paused for a moment at the living room doorway to watch Rebecca. She sat in his favorite reading chair, the one beside the fireplace. There was no fire, so he had draped a quilt over her legs.

He smiled. He loved how her raven black hair glistened in the soft glow of the reading lamp beside her.

Mark slipped into the kitchen and made a cup of tea. He placed it and a small plate of cookies on a serving tray and carried it into the living room. He set the tray down on the coffee table.

"So, how are you doing?"

"Good."

Mark motioned at the book he had placed in Rebecca's hands. It was an anthology of short stories that contained his very first professional sale. "Do you like the book?"

"I like it very much. Your story is the best, by far."

Mark smiled. "Thank you, it means a lot to me that you like it." He sat down on the sofa that faced both the fireplace and the reading chair. "I always read before I have my dinner. It relaxes my mind and it gets me out of my own work and into somebody else's." He shrugged. "If it's good reading, that is."

"That is fine. I am not ready to finish reading just yet, either."

"Great."

Mark took a sip of his tea. The chill and damp evening weather put him in the mood for a ghost story. But first, he needed to light a fire. Just to complete the mood.

He put a Duraflame log in the fireplace and lit it with a match and waited for it to catch. When it caught, Mark returned to the couch and looked through his piles of literary magazines and genre anthologies to find a suitable ghost story to read.

He picked *Bulgrummo's Hell,* by Russell Kirk.

While he read there was no sound save for the quiet crackling of the fire, the soft moan of the wind and the tapping of the rain on the window hidden behind the drawn curtains. Every now and then he would pause and sip at his tea or pop a cookie into his mouth. When he finished the story he closed the book and put it back on the coffee table. He swallowed the last of his tea, which had gone cold, stood up and smiled down at Rebecca.

"I think that I should start making my dinner."

"Don't let me keep you, please."

Mark carried his tea setting back into the kitchen. He heated a bag of frozen teriyaki chicken and then a bag of frozen broccoli in the microwave while he cleaned and put away the tea setting and set the kitchen table for dinner.

He lit two tapered candles that he had purchased for the occasion and went to get Rebecca. He took the book that he had given her to hold while he read and set it back on the coffee table. He removed the quilt that he had draped over her lap and carried her to the kitchen and sat her at the table. He motioned at the candles.

"Do you like it?"

"Yes, very much."

"Good." Mark smiled. He gave her cheek a kiss that lingered on her cool latex skin. Then he draped a napkin across her lap and sat down and ate his dinner.

"I have so looked forward to this."

"So have I."

"Really?"

"Yes."

"Good." Mark stared at Rebecca. "That is good."

He finished his dinner, cleaned up and put away the dishes and the leftovers. He would have the leftovers for lunch tomorrow, during his afternoon break.

He froze. He had not told her of his daily work schedule and when he would spend time with her.

Mark turned to Rebecca. "Just so you'll know, I work eight hours a day, every day. Four hours in the morning, then four hours in the late afternoon, or evening. Some times I take a long lunch and some times I don't. It depends on whatever project that I am working on. The one I have now is rather involved."

"That's okay."

"I just don't want you to become bored."

"I won't, not with you to entertain me later."

Mark blushed and wiped away the nervous sweat that he felt prick at his forehead. "I, um, am going to get dressed for the evening. I have a nightgown for you to wear."

"Thank you."

He carried her upstairs to his bedroom and sat her on the edge of the bed. Mark undressed, but he kept Rebecca's back to him as he did so, and put on a pair of pajamas and a bathrobe.

Then he showed her the nightgown that he had gotten for her.

"Do you like it?"

"Yes, very much. Thank you."

Mark removed Rebecca's clothes and slid her into the nightgown. He carried her back downstairs and into the living room. He set her down on the sofa, so she could sit next to him.

"I have some old time radio recordings that I like to listen to on nights like this."

"That sounds wonderful."

Mark got his laptop out of his office and set it on the coffee table. He played an episode of the *CBS Radio Mystery Theater* and held one of Rebecca's hands in his own while he listened to the program and watched the fire burn in the fireplace.

It was perfect.

When the episode ended he played an episode of *The Whistler*. When that one ended he just sat in the silence and watched the fire die and held Rebecca's hand gently in his own.

Outside the wind moaned. The rain tapped at the window.

"I guess it's getting late."

"Yes. Yes, it is."

"That would mean…"

"Yes. Yes, it would…"

Their first evening together had gone by much faster than Mark had thought it would.

"I don't know…"

"Are you nervous?"

"A little." Mark studied Rebecca's lovely profile. "Well, more than a little, actually."

"Don't be. This is why I am here. This is why you…"

"I know. I know." Mark ever so slightly tightened his gentle grip on Rebecca's hand. "But that isn't…"

"What?" The doubt and worry was evident in the question.

Mark shifted on the sofa, so he could face Rebecca's profile.

"It's just so very hard. I feel so alone."

"I know you do."

"I have been trying to get out more, but I am so busy with my work and people are just so difficult to get to know."

Mark released Rebecca's hand so he could brush some of her raven black hair back behind the cup of an ear.

"I just need someone around, that's all. Someone quiet."

"But you aren't going to leave me down here alone, in the dark, are you?"

"No, I won't. Never."

Mark carried Rebecca back upstairs, up to bed.

Trying to find a comfortable position in which to sleep with her turned out to be far more difficult than he had thought it would be. He sighed with frustration.

"This is so very awkward for me."

"It doesn't have to be."

"I know, but it just is."

Mark covered his face with his hands. Why had he done this?

"You don't like me. You spent all that time and money choosing me and now you don't even like me."

Mark took Rebecca back into his arms. He kissed her cheek. "But I do like you." He kissed her cheek again, this time closer to the suggestively parted lips of her mouth. "I really do. Let me show you."

He slipped his hand beneath her nightgown and caressed her soft and smooth latex skin and explored the contours of her beautiful body. He nuzzled her neck. Her skin had a slight fruity odor that was not at all unpleasant. He kissed more of her, working down her neck to her shoulder, then down further, to her chest and breasts. He suckled the stiff bud of a latex nipple.

"That's better."

It was better.

Mark removed her nightgown and his pajamas. He then applied the recommended amount of lubricant that the manufacturer had suggested he should use.

He mounted her.

"So much better."

He entered her.

"*Oh...*"

Afterward he cleaned her of his mess and snuggled with her. He drifted between sleep and wakefulness. Intense joy kept him from falling asleep, but he did not mind. He was no longer alone in his small, book choked home. Now he had someone that would always be there for him.

He smiled as he pictured their life together, their quiet, bookish life.

Mark began to drift off to sleep and he began to dream of her as he had seen her in his mind, sitting and waiting for him in the chair beside the fireplace. Soft music was playing on the laptop sitting on the coffee table while she read.

Rebecca sensed his presence and looked up from the book that she had been reading. A warm, loving smile spread across her beautiful face.

"Hi honey," she said.

GLORIANA

By Angela Caperton

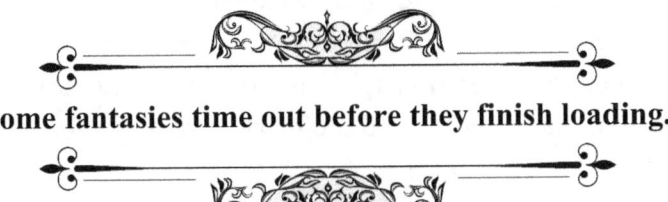

Some fantasies time out before they finish loading.

Award winning author **Angela Caperton** *writes eclectic erotica that challenges genre conventions. Her stories have been published in numerous anthologies from* **Black Lace, Cleis, Circlet, Coming Together**, *and others. Her latest work is a novella,* **Playing God**, *from eXtasy. Her eclectic short story collection* **Darkness and Delight**, *and her acclaimed erotic science fiction novel* Man's World, *were published in 2010. She is currently working on a novel called* **Kink of the Month Club** *and on editing her 2010-2011 blog serial,* **Woman of His Dreams**, *for publication. Catch up with Angela on her blog:* **blog.angelacaperton.com**.

Gloriana, fallen princess of the Old Forest elves, stepped naked and dripping from the pool of rebirth. Her guardian and chaste lover Aelborn awaited her on the shore wearing his distinctive white cloak. They embraced and kissed, a token of passion and suppressed desire, born of the vow between them.

"I have a confession to make," Gloriana said. "Strayhorn of the Dead Forest has courted me and wishes me to be his mate."

291

A shadow passed across Aelborn's noble features. Gloriana saw sorrow in his eyes and ached with him.

"I cannot hold you," Aelborn said. "But if you go to him, be wary, for his tribe is our sworn foe."

Fading sunlight painted her ivory skin the hue of red plums as she dressed, wishing that Aelborn would take her in his arms and make her whole, but of course he turned away and vanished into the haze at the end of Gloriana's vision. The love between them could not be consummated, no matter how much she desired it. He had been very clear about that when they exchanged the Vow of Eternity.

She sighed, weary and forlorn. Fine. She would visit Strayhorn and see what he offered her, either diversion or adventure. She whispered her magic words and the world turned white.

(Loading)

When the Phantasy world appeared again in fine resolution, the Dead Forest loomed about her, its trees sharp, black scratches against the perpetual gloom of its sky.

Gloriana stood in the center of a clearing. Teddy didn't know if Strayhorn's player used a voice app or not, so she tapped /t and typed, "I'm here" in florid scarlet letters.

"BRT," came the red reply.

Soon the forest darkness birthed Strayhorn, his ebon majesty emerging from the shadows.

In a corner of Teddy's screen, in a box directly over Gloriana's lovely, robed form, Instant Messenger chirped and its window opened. A message from Daddy appeared there.

"Dinner's on the stove when you want it, honey," Daddy's message read. Teddy smiled, and sent him an X in reply.

Dinner could wait. Teddy wanted action.

She tapped the keys to make Gloriana pirouette as she burned in the heat of Strayhorn's virtual gaze. The Ebon Elf's face seemed carved of obsidian, inhumanly beautiful and cruel. Teddy knew the ancient rivalry between her kingdom and his and they both knew the penalty for breaking it, but she did not care. She opened herself to him.

"Bow down before me, elf of the Old Forest," Strayhorn said and she knelt with fluid grace, submissive before him.

He touched her.

Teddy imagined his touch and she burned where she saw his fingers stroking her. Images spun in her head, composed of fantasies she had read and those born in her own dreams. Orgies of perfect beings, shaven elf bodies, a cock the length of her forearm wielded by a rough lover. Her pussy began to pulse. She was so horny.

She stood and embraced him.

Strayhorn kissed her throat and ran his hand down her back, taking liberties she delighted in granting him.

She arched her neck, gasping, weak in her knees, sagging against him.

Strayhorn gathered her robe in his hands and his strong hands cupped her bare bottom. She imagined his fingers playing in the cleft, teasing her asshole then finding the wet slit of her pussy. With a violent motion, he tore her robe away, and forced her to her knees again, opening his own armor, then casting it aside. The smooth, 24-bit color, graphic body had no cock, but she imagined one, long and thick and perfectly formed. Strayhorn grinned like a devil. With urgent heat, the lord of the Ebon Elves of the Dead Forest ravished Gloriana's nude splendor with his merciless hands.

/I stroke your breast, she read, invisible passion across the sea of electrons. /I am hard for you.

"Take me," she typed then /I touch your cock, shy at first, then more boldly.

He placed his hand against her cunt. /I put a finger inside you.

/I am wet for you.

/I stroke your pussy lips and find your clit.

/I let you. "Do what thou wilt with me, dark lord."

Teddy hiked up her skirt and touched herself through the thin satin of her panties, imagining the Ebon Elf's hand there, rough, demanding, skilled fingers exploiting her folds, teasing her clit mercilessly. She took a moment to shed her thong and then, as they typed, she began to probe and rub more earnestly.

/I lower you to the ground.

She tapped keys and, on the screen, Gloriana spread herself upon the forest floor, open to the dark lord, eager to take him into her. She thought wistfully of Aelborn, her true love, always with her, ever apart. Would he condemn her for this? She was so lonely sometimes. Surely he would forgive her wicked desires.

/I fuck you, in ur cunt

Teddy's legs shivered as she began to feel the approaching orgasm.

"Oh my lord, I am open to you. Do anything to me. I have no strength to resist."

/I fuck you in ur ass.

How about a little more class? Teddy thought, but she let the fantasy ride on, stroking herself closer and closer. The images on the screen, the beautiful naked elves, the dark romantic forest, were nothing compared to the images in her mind or the real desire in her heart. Somewhere some guy – probably a guy – was almost certainly holding his cock and jacking off to the fantasy they shared. She loved that she could be a part of that.

It was almost like real fucking, she thought, but so much nicer and safer.

She began to pant, afire with the need to come, to be one with this remote, unknowable stranger, then a message box appeared, and scarlet words, fresh typed, bled onto Teddy's screen, spoiling the picture, ruining the moment.

"O Teddy, u r a slut."

Her stomach lurched and it took all her strength not to close the window and break the connection, though she knew it would do her no good. He knew her name. He knew her name!

"It's me, you cunt. Trey. U R my Cyber Slut now.

"Cum on CS play with me."

(Logging out)

***

Daddy made franks and beans at least once a week. Sometimes he ordered pizza and sometimes he cooked tough steaks and soggy carrots. Sometimes he and Teddy ate together, but Daddy always seemed eager to get away, back to his own online world of contracts, travel plans, and bargaining. When his work took him away, she cooked for herself and they stayed in close touch through their computers, almost as close as when he was home.

Tonight, Teddy picked at the beans. The franks looked like dicks and she wanted no part of them. Would she ever want a part of franks or dicks again?

"So this little shitheel insulted you, honey?" Daddy asked her.

"I was so embarrassed," she sniffed, tears threatening to fall again. She could not meet her father's eyes. "I just want to die. I don't know how I can go to school tomorrow or ever. He'll tell everyone."

"Don't worry, honey," Daddy said as he hugged her. "Everything will be all right."

***

She walked into the high school the next day and it was as bad as she thought it would be. Trey followed her in the hallway, making kissing sounds and humping the air. All the kids played Phantasy, so they understood him when he told them how she had let him cyber fuck her – how he had even cyber ass-fucked her. Everyone laughed at her and she had to stop looking at the incoming texts on her phone. Sometime before lunch, someone drew a crude Ebon Elf with an enormous cock on her locker.

Teddy couldn't bring herself to play Phantasy for almost a week. She and Daddy ate together most nights and he asked her about school, but nothing about Trey or what he'd done. He didn't ask about her adventures in the Old Forest or the Faraway Lands, nothing about anything that mattered.

Then, on Friday, she logged back in and the game was the same as always and she found it easy to avoid the real life people she knew who played Phantasy. Most of her subjects and peers didn't go to her school and didn't know Trey, either as himself or as Strayhorn. The world of pixel forests and castles was enormous and she found places to go where no one knew her, stayed out of the chat channels, often brooded alone atop a secret golden tower that Aelborn had built for her long ago.

Sometimes she went out into the forest and slaughtered goblins or hunted unicorns for their pelts, but mostly she stared into the virtual distance, lonely and alone.

On Saturday eve, Aelborn appeared beside her in the tower, radiant and sublime in his ermine robes. She had never seen anyone more handsome than the golden-skinned elf.

"The swine will die," Aelborn promised her. "My clan will hunt him until the end of time. He will have no peace." He embraced her and they shared a chaste kiss, though Teddy imagined how he would taste, how strong the circle of his arms must be.

He held her as the virtual suns set, producing a shimmering rainbow across the imaginary sky, and for the first time in a week, Teddy felt whole and happy.

***

Although Teddy returned to the world of Phantasy, she stayed away from Facebook and Twitter and didn't look at her phone. On Monday, she blended into the halls and lockers of school, her long week of infamy behind her, and no one said much to her until after lunch, when Jilian Bentley and her ginger-topped friend caught Teddy alone in the hall and pinned her between them.

"I bet you're glad he's dead," Jilian accused.

"Sure," Teddy agreed. "Whatever you say," and she pushed past the redhead's outstretched arm.

"Stupid fucking geek," Jilian spat at her. "Stupid fucking games."

Teddy blinked. What was she talking about? "Who's dead?" she asked.

"Trey, you bitch."

Teddy's belly clinched and her cheeks burned as if slapped, but, to her acidic glee, the blow felt good. Tears stung the back of her eyes.

"What happened?" she asked, needing to know, wanting all the details of her enemy's demise.

"Jesus fuck, you really don't know, do you? Trey died playing that stupid fucking game. They think he choked on something, or maybe OD'd."

Jilian's friend chimed in, wickedly joyous. "Like maybe he put rubber bands on his dick and a rope around his neck and was jerking off kinda choked," she giggled. "You know about that stuff, don't you CS?"

"I'm sorry," Teddy managed, letting the barb slide off her back. Tears crept over her lashes and down her cheeks. "I'm so sorry."

This time they let her walk away, respecting her tears, ritual mourning for the Ebon Elf, the false lord of the Dead Forest, gone forever.

***

Gloriana visited the Dead Forest, alone in the stark immensity of endless, silent night. The lord of this dark land lay dead and the shadows beneath the tangled limbs seemed thin. His extinguished will no longer held dominion here.

The Dead Forest was truly dying, its black branch etchings faint as pencil lines against the bruised sky. She returned to her own kingdom, the Old Forest (loading), and spun in a slow circle, watching for her champion, smiling broadly when he appeared, her pussy slicking as the distance closed.

Golden Aelborn of the holy white cloak, her protector and her lover. He showed her his long, curving sword, its blade dripping red.

"It is done," he said to her. "Strayhorn is dead. He will not insult you again."

Gloriana pressed herself against Aelborn, knowing her mentor guarded her against slander and lies. He guarded her against everything.

Aelborn held Gloriana, his hand brushing her ass before he corrected his stance to circle her waist chastely.

"Don't worry, honey," he said. "Everything will be all right."

BLEEDIN' HEARTS
By Salvatore Buttaci

Do all roads lead to Rome or an American coin?

The 2007 recipient of the $500 Cyber-wit Poetry Award, **Salvatore Buttaci** *has been a published author since 1957. His poems, stories, articles, and letters have appeared in The New York Times, The Writer, Cats Magazine, Christian Science Monitor, Chicken Soup for the Soul: Celebrating Brothers and Sisters, A Cup of Comfort for Fathers, and many other publications.*

He has conducted countless writing workshops, and as an activist for Sicilian-American pride, Buttaci has lectured widely on "Growing up Sicilian." His book, **A Family of Sicilian***, is available at Lulu.com.*

His new chapbooks: **Boy on a Swing** *is available from Big Table Publishing, and* **What I Learned from the Spaniard** *from Middle Island Press.*

Both his collection of 164 short-fiction stories, **Flashing My Shorts***, and his follow-up collection,* **200 Shorts (All Things That Matter Press)***, can be purchased at Amazon.com. Buttaci lives with his wife Sharon in West Virginia.*

Grandpa did not take his secret with him. Instead, he left it with me, on this side of the grave. I would've kept it forever, along with the golden coin he pressed into my hand the night he passed, but the coin was a bicentennial commemorative of Barack Obama, dated 2208.

"Ave et atque valle," he said. Hail and farewell. My Latin-loving Grandpa's last words.

The time it took to lift the coin from my outstretched palm and read it, the old man exhaled his goodbye breath and never heard me blurt out, "What the freaking hell..."

The coin should not have shocked me, not after Grandpa related two days before a story so damn incredible that I thought, maybe the old man's mind, once sharp as cut mosaic, now in the end was shattering into tiny colorless shards of glass. Later at his bedside, I remembered crying uncontrollably, both for my loss and for this two-day-old revelation my loss had dropped on me in parting.

My eyes darted from the open-eyed Travis Scott, lying there wreathed by a pillow nearly as white as his pallid face, to the golden stern-faced Barack Obama eventually dead as well, commemorated in a world more than 200 years in the future. It was too surreal, a scene to which only a Salvador Dali could do justice: a morose painting symmetrically divided in light and dark grays between the now and the later, and on both sides, split down the center, a man with a coin and eyes full of tears.

Do you know how difficult it is to keep your mouth shut when every nerve in your body is waving its tail and screaming at you to "Tell them! Tell them! Tell them!"?

It changed my life. How else to explain it? If there had been any doubts about the secret or the coin, with the passing years they faded away. I lived in a kind of dream haze. I questioned my own identity. I watched the woman I loved draw a last straw and hop a train out of town. I took a pink slip from the senior partner of a prestigious law firm that had been grooming me for better things. I felt whatever pieces I still called "me" torn apart when my two sons walked out of my life.

Why hadn't the old man ditched the Obama gold piece when he was well enough to dig a deep hole somewhere and bury it forever? Why couldn't he have entertained the likelihood that secret keeping of this magnitude would have been for me an unbearable ordeal?

He was Grandpa, the man who had suddenly appeared in my life when I was ten, shortly after both my parents died from the Cat Virus of '23. I never heard mention of him before that day. He took me into his home in Wilmington, sent me to the best schools and from each one I consistently failed to prove myself worthy of his investment. I was no great Scott, no pillar of Wilmington society, yet despite his disappointment, he loved me. That I wrote stories and poems did not diminish that love. I was blessed.

Two days before he passed, I sat doing The Herald crossword puzzle. Oddly enough, I was jotting down "arcane," the six-letter word for "mysterious," when he touched my arm and said, "Try to stay with me on this. What I'm about to tell you is not so easy to digest." I put aside the puzzle and my pen and nodded.

"I'm not who you think I am, Howard." So began Grandpa's last confession, perhaps too smooth a spiritual leap into Paradise. I don't know. Maybe the weight he carried was so heavy he couldn't die until he crawled from beneath it. The same weight he then loaded on me.

Grandpa had died on a Wednesday. He told his story on the Monday before when he seemed fit enough to live at least another ten years. Somehow I felt he had convinced himself he had lived long enough at 82 and yet could not die until he turned over my inheritance, not his money, his home, his land, but his secret and that coin.

"The 'Bleedin' Hearts' were rebels totally against capital punishment. They did not believe in the old Hebrew law that demanded 'an eye for an eye, a tooth for a tooth'."

" 'Bleedin' Hearts' are nothing new, Grandpa."

301

He looked at me, long and hard, then shook his head.

"Listen to me. I'm not talking about politicians today, you understand? The 'Bleedin' Hearts' grew out of a different time when prisons were shut down, converted into pleasure palaces, and all murderers and thieves alike, were taken from their cells and executed."

"Old Mother Russia?"

Grandpa stood up and gripped the back of his wooden chair. He paused a long while, and then said, "No, not old Russia." Then he got quiet again until I was just about to ask, "Where?" when he whispered, "New America."

I laughed. The two of us had spent delightful hours tearing apart American politicians. Neither Democrats nor Republicans nor even Conservatives. Grandpa and I shared a common ground: we hated everything and everyone that smelled even vaguely like the stench of politics.

"New America," I said. It was a question, but I accented 'new' and let my voice drop as I waited for him to explain.

He was pacing the kitchen like an expectant father, looking down at his polished black loafers as if expecting to see his wrinkled face reflecting back up to him. At the sink he tightened the dripping tap. He parted the window curtain, gave a hurried glance outside, then let the curtain fall shut again.

I went back to my crossword puzzle. A seven-letter word for--

"In the future," Grandpa said finally. "Another America."

"You been there?" I said. Levity couldn't hurt. Maybe a good laugh could snap him out of it, whatever "it" was.

"Forget it, Howard."

Grandpa put on his winter coat.

"Where you going?"

"Get some night air."

"Sit down, Grandpa. You're not leaving me hanging. You started something. Finish it. A new America. Not this one. Go on."

Grandpa removed his coat and draped it behind an empty chair. He sat down again, inhaled deeply and sighed. "How do I convince you?" he asked. "It's not a story. It's the damn truth. It happened." He paused. "Okay, it will happen."

"So they called themselves the 'Bleedin' Hearts'?"

"That's what others called them. They called themselves 'The People's Party,' but they were really scientists who had found cures for cancer, AIDS, deadly viruses, and they fought the Pharmacrats who tried to suppress those cures. 'Bogus sugar tablets' the government drug panel labeled them while at the same time Americans continued paying for the panel's green placebo pills. Nobody gave the scientists much credit. Most pegged them for crazies.

I thought to myself, I got to write this one! I had managed to sell a short story for 100 bucks to Not of This World Magazine. This one of Grandpa's could earn me another 100. All I had to do was egg Grandpa on, let him ramble away, then later go peck at the keyboard and write "Bleedin' Hearts." Maybe I'd split the money with him. Or take him out to the Appian Way Italian Restaurant for lasagna and red wine.

"When does all this take place?"

He folded his arms across his chest, the traditional body language of one intent in protecting himself from danger or at least from deprecating laughter. Then, with a straight face, devoid of subterfuge, he replied, "About 200 years from now."

I rubbed my hands together. "All right, for my next question..." I rubbed my hands again like a street-corner hawker, even rolled up my shirt sleeves, and sang the four bars of a drum roll, "DA TA DA DA!" Then slowly and loudly asked, "HOW - DO - YOU - KNOW - THIS?"

He continued with his story. "I mention the 'Bleedin' Hearts' were scientists?" I nodded. "They cured the ills of the world?" Again I nodded. "But what I did not yet tell you is, these scientists who had worked in their labs in search of cures had also stumbled upon a

303

discovery that for a long time had been every scientist's dream. Einstein came up with the formula that said it was possible, but not until these scientists put their heads together did that theory become practical."

"Time travel?"

Grandpa nodded.

"You got to be kidding me!"

My grandfather lit up his pipe, his face glowing like an evil mask. A puff of aromatic tobacco blend clouded his bald head, an incongruous halo, and he said, "Not kidding at all, Howard. Time travel and you can bet they kept it under wraps. If it leaked out, they'd not only be 'Bleedin' Hearts' but bleeding everything else. Remember what I said, in New America executions were as common as London rain. No, they kept it quiet. Only seven of them in the main, they swore an oath of secrecy because they knew damn well if one of them revealed the TiMachine Bubble, all seven of them-- maybe their thousands of followers as well--would hang."

My story was writing itself. Or I should say, Grandpa was. An easy 100 bucks. I didn't know the old man had it in him. Writing genes he passed on to me. It made sense to let him go on, so I asked him, "They try out the machine?"

Grandpa puffed away. "They did."

"It work?"

Now my grandfather tamped out the smoking tobacco into the ashtray, tapping against the glass until the pipe bowl was empty and cool enough to return the pipe to his shirt pocket. I waited patiently.

"It worked," he said. "So well they devised a plan to use it to rescue people from execution."

"How the hell could they do--"

"Do you know anything about time travel, Howard?"

"What's to know? You move from now to before or later."

Grandpa smiled.

"What else is there to know?"

"Nothing can be changed," he said. "Not one little insect can be stepped on. Not one simple event can a traveler mess with when he visits the past or the future."

I remembered a sci-fi short story whose main character travels to the past and unknowingly murders his own great-grandfather! Needless to say, he never returns to his own time because he had never been born.

"Nothing can be changed. The 'Bleedin' Hearts' understood that."

"So they escaped into the future and everybody lived happily ever after."

"Not quite, Howard. They were on a mission, remember?"

"Wait a second. How could they time travel and not change anything?"

"Ever read about parallel worlds in your comic-book days?"

"Sure."

"Thank God for that! Then you know what happened when they traveled into the past. Either they changed nothing or they changed something."

I let my eyebrows meet in a dark arch. "If they changed nothing, no problem, right?"

Grandpa smiled.

"But if they changed something, the future of that time would also change, right?"

Again Grandpa smiled. "The 'Bleedin' Hearts' went back into the past and rescued murderers from the gallows. They temported them in the TiMachine Bubble to, not New America, but Old America where they could live out their lives atoning for their crimes. Humble lives maybe, but at least they would live."

It wasn't so clear to me. "If they rescued murderers from the gallows, wouldn't that past time be changed?"

Now Grandpa had the look of the teacher who finally wangles out of a slow student a light bulb-moment of wisdom. "Exactly!" he said. "The past was changed. Each time the 'Bleedin' Hearts' went back to save still another murderer destined to swing from a rope or fry in a chair or gag on gas, the past was changed."

"How…"

"Parallel worlds, Howard."

I was mentally scratching my head. How does this story end?

The kitchen got quiet except for occasional groans from the fridge and that drip from the faucet no amount of tap tightening could silence. We sat there, grandfather and grandson. Travis Scott and Howard Scott, discussing parallel worlds, bleeding-heart politicians, and time machines. I'd never heard the old man talk as much in all my years living under his roof.

Then I remembered how he had started this sci-fi tale in the first place. Hadn't he said, "I'm not who you think I am"? That meant what? The old man wasn't the quiet unimposing gentleman who sat in his Lazy-boy® rocker, passing his time smoking a pipe while watching old films of the '30's? He was a man bursting with tales to tell? A man with an imagination wild as my own?

"Who the hell are you, Grandpa?" I asked, half laughing. "You're full of surprises. What brought all this on?"

"The 'Bleedin' Hearts' traveled back in time," Grandpa continued. "First, while in their own 2200's, they'd read the history books, searching for tyrants who never got the chance to repent. Mass murderers, heads of state, evil men--all condemned to die for their crimes. The 'Bleedin' Hearts' swore to rescue and deliver them to another world, far from the world their rescue had changed."

"How did they return to the 2200's? Wasn't that world also changed?"

"Good question!" Grandpa said, fidgeting again with his pipe, stuffing it with tobacco, setting a match to it while he puffed it to life. "The TiMachine Bubble's destination was anytime the 'Bleedin' Hearts' chose, but their home-base departure point somehow remained intact. I suspect, or at least how it was explained to me, only the time points they traveled to were compromised.

Somehow that changed world got unhinged, splintered away from the same time path that preceded the 2200's of New America."

Grandpa could tell it in my face. I didn't understand one crap iota. Still, one niggling thought kept knocking around in my head.

"Picture the universe with its trillions and trillions of worlds," said Grandpa. "Many are parallel Earths. From them, like threads from a ball of yarn, spin out new worlds, especially when time is tampered with by travelers who--"

"Grandpa, you said 'At least how it was explained to me.' What does that mean? Who explained it to you? For God's sake, this is a freaking story I plan to write, but it's sci fi. If somebody explained it to you, you're having some weird dreams, Grandpa. Or there's something in that pipe you're smoking."

"How well do you know about the Rubicon?" Grandpa asked and I thought, Okay, another off-the-wall tangent leading nowhere. I was seriously worried now, questioning my grandfather's mental state and finding it severely wanting.

"You mean, as in, Caesar crossed the Rubicon?" I would humor him and hope to God he'd snap out of it or laugh and say how he had me going. We'd share a brew, watch the sun drop down, and we'd call it a night.

"The man's name was Roy Vasquez, one of the TiMachine pilots. A man with unshakable belief in his mission to save the condemned."

"So 'Bleedin' Heart' Roy explained this story to you? In a dream? A vision?"

"It was the Ides of March. The 15th. The 44th year before the birth of Christ. Vasquez traveled back to Rome."

"Roy parked the Bubble on the Senate floor?"

Ignoring me, he said, "Vasquez traveled back to save Julius the Caesar."

I laughed. "He got there too late, Grandpa. Brutus, Cassius, and a handful of knife-happy Senators put Caesar down. We all know

'Veni, Vidi, Vinci' got assassinated because he forgot to beware the Ides of March."

Grandpa shook his head. "In another world, a spin-off of that Ancient Rome, Caesar was not murdered at all."

"But he was murdered!"

"He appeared to be murdered. Vasquez, within a warp of time, paralyzed the Senate, lifted Caesar's body, and temported him to moments before the stabbings. Then he decided on a time and place where Caesar could be delivered, safe and sound, to spend the remaining years of his life far from politics, ambition, greed, and murder."

"And where the hell is Julius now?"

"Vasquez brought him to Delaware."

"Our Delaware or Delaware of some parallel world?"

"Ours."

Now my head was spinning. Was I dreaming? Did I have a story here or would the white-frocked boys come soon, scoop me into a giant net and cart me off to a rubber room?

"I've made up for my sins, Howard. I did not disappoint the 'Bleedin' Hearts' who saved me. And I have loved you, Howard, all these years as if you were my own." He reached across the table and lay his hand on top of mine.

Two days later Grandpa pressed that gold coin into that same hand.

THE IMAGE OF THE LORD
By Jon Judy

See no evil, hear no evil, and speak no evil.

Jon Judy teaches communication studies courses at a large community college in northeast Ohio. He first discovered the power of the written word as a small child when his mother hit him on the head with a rolled up newspaper. He has been a burger flipper, a sales clerk, a job trainer to the mentally retarded, a writing tutor, a pizza delivery guy, and a movie theater usher. He has published one piece of film criticism, several comic books, and now the short story appearing in this anthology. He has therefore decided he is now a film critic and writer. He likes masculine pronouns and simple sentences. He likes long walks on the fire and cuddling up next to a beach.

The Moor was on his knees, naked to the waist, his sweaty body glistening in the oppressive Gibraltar sun. Dania had to strain to hear his words, a confession made in excellent Spanish: "For some weeks I have been stealing from the tributes intended for the Holy Roman Empire and the Kingdom of Spain."

Dania glanced surreptitiously at Junipero beside her and noted that the unctuous old priest was smiling slightly at this show. Unable to return her eyes to the humbled Moor, she scanned the small crowd of slaves and priests that encircled them and then the tower of the Moorish Castle. She followed it with her gaze until she reached its top, high above the island, and thought what an impressive sight it was, how much more impressive it must have been a thousand years before, in the eighth century, when it was first built. Standing in the right spot, leaning in the right way, one could blot out the sun with the top of the tower. She did just this, pretending she was creating an eclipse, then shifting her feet so that the sun reappeared, then shifting back to eclipse.

Eclipse. Sun. Eclipse. Sun.

And all this time the trial carried on.

"Ah, Yasir," Junipero sneered. "You could be in chains bound for the New World right now. Or baking in the desert with your heathen brothers. But for the mercy and kindness of sweet Spain. Are you not ashamed?"

The Moor lifted his head slightly, as though it were a great effort, and smiled sadly as he answered the priest: "Yes, of course I am ashamed, for I have sinned against my Lord. How could I? Am I not made in His image?"

Junipero struck Yasir savagely and suddenly, his wrinkled face contorted into a menacing grimace. The sound echoed off the walls of the small courtyard which was the scene of this farce. "Blasphemy, you pig. You were most certainly not made in the image of the Lord." Junipero smiled at his entourage. "Although Lucifer was an angel, so I suppose there is some darkness among the divine." His sycophants laughed, nudged each other, repeated this bon mot. Dania clenched her fists and eclipsed the sun. Junipero turned back to the Moor. "Your image is nothing like our Lord's."

And then Junipero turned his sneer to Dania, who met his glance with unreadable passivity. "There, *sister*," he spat this word, shat this word, leered and sneered this word. "There is the source of your missing tributes." Junipero snatched the chain that extended from Yasir's neck to his wrists and yanked it up, jerking the helpless slave forward and lifting his arms up so that Dania could see they ended in stumps where his hands once had been. "He has confessed to his crime and has been dealt with."

Dania regarded Yasir for a long moment as the small coterie of clergy leaned forward and Junipero's sneer melted into a blankness. Dania considered the slave's arms, extended there, stretching skyward, chiseled and massive from his years of labor, mutilated now by an act that took seconds. Finally Dania answered the priest. "Perhaps. But I must continue my investigation. It is my duty to my Church and State."

Junipero looked for the smallest fraction of a second as though he had been slapped, then turned to the small, twisted figure beside him, a tiny, misshapen young man in a plain brown robe, a hood pulled up to conceal most of his face. "Unchain him."

As the boy set about releasing the Moor, Junipero smiled at Dania. "Of course. You are our welcome guest for as long as you like. I'm sure you do excellent, thorough work. Why else would the Cardinal send a woman on such an important task? Go," he said to Yasir. "Sin no more."

Dania shot Junipero a look that could have killed him if he had bothered to look at her. Instead he had already turned to walk away, strolling through the courtyard garden. "The Cardinal trusts me because I've earned his trust."

"Yes," Junipero said. "I am certain you have worked very hard under his Holiness." He said "worked" and "Holiness" the same way he had earlier spat out "sister."

"I'm not sure I like your tone, Junipero," she said through bared teeth.

"And I'm sure I don't know what you mean," he smiled innocently.

As they came to the main courtyard before the central gate, the malformed little man gimping along behind them, Dania was suddenly distracted from her anger by a disquieting sight. In a way, it was more disturbing than the poor, butchered Moor. Four priests groaned and strained as they dragged a massive, hairy form from inside the castle out into the courtyard. As they came closer, Dania saw that the naked thing had arms and legs and even a face that was vaguely man-like, but it was massive, larger than any man she had ever seen, and covered in thick brown fur.

It was dead, and its contorted face said that it had not died easily. "What is – ?"

"Ah," Junipero said, a genuine smile on his face for once. "Ah, yes. One of my hobbies. But an important one. This is a gorilla. I have these beasts shipped in from the jungles of Africa." The priests gratefully paused in their efforts, panting and doubled over, as Junipero gestured for them to stop. "Notice how remarkably man-like they are. I have learned much about our similar anatomy from my work with them." He turned away and the priests grudgingly resumed their work. Dania gradually pulled her gaze away. "Come. Let me show you."

Junipero led her through the castle gate, down a long hall of doors, through one of them, down a winding, narrow, torch-lit, stairway. The fire threw weird shadows on the subterranean scene, a dance of shapes and blobs that was Dania's only distraction from the lingering vision of those dead eyes. They came to the end of the stairs and to a large, wooden door. Junipero took a ring of keys from under his robe, unlocked the door, and stepped through, gesturing for Dania to follow.

"Unfortunately, I have but one of the beasts left," he said as she entered the room. Her face became as stony as the walls of the chamber, a chamber which was filled with objects for which Dania had no name. Well, she had no name for all but one of them. She had read of iron maidens, and an object matching her readings stood in one corner. In the middle of the chamber was a large table with straps in the four corners. The straps were connected to what looked like a winch. Dania imagined victims were strapped to the table and then the winch was turned, stretching them out like they were being drawn and quartered. Whips and chains and knives and things she could only assume were surgical implements hung from the two sidewalls of the chamber.

But there – there against the far wall, just opposite the door – was the thing from which Dania could not look away. It was a cell – metal bars from the floor to the ceiling. The floor was strewn with hay and feces and puddles of urine and blood. And there, its arms stretched out and chained to the wall, slumped in a sitting position, was another gorilla. This one was alive, albeit barely, and as they entered the chamber it raised its head slowly – very slowly – as though it were a great effort – and then sighed, hung its head again, resigned to its fate.

"There. My last one. Ah well. I have learned much from them about the limits of the body, about the possibilities for… torture, for lack of a better word." They both stared at the creature, Junipero wistfully and Dania otherwise. "Should the Church ever let the Inquisition return to its former… efficiency… oh, the souls I could bring to Christ." A moment or two more, then he shrugged and turned away.

Dania was frozen in viewing the creature when a shrill cry pierced the air, a loud squawk that had evolved to cut through the forbidding density of mile after mile of jungle, to be heard over the competing cries and roars of monkeys and gorillas and lions and cheetahs.

"Oh!" she jumped, to Junipero's amusement, turning to the noise. It had come from a darkened corner in the room, something she had overlooked upon first entering the chamber, distracted as she was by the creature. A bird, one Dania recognized as a parrot, squatted on a perch. It appeared in the shadows of its dimmed corner to be grey, but Dania could not be sure of that. She was, however, sure of what she heard next. The bird looked at her suspiciously, stretched to its full height, a foot or so, and spread its wings as it shouted, "Saith the Lord: I shall not pity!"

Junipero beamed, which made the room seem even darker. "Yes, Solomon. Thank you. Ah, Pedro." Dania turned to look at the person entering the room, the misshapen, deformed servant who had followed them in the courtyard. Now that she had an excuse to look at him, she took him in completely. The boy was 15 or so, a small, slight boy, no more than five feet in height. He had a hunchback and one of his legs was significantly shorter than the other so that he walked with a pronounced limp. His face was twisted upwards, his nose turned up like a pig's, his eyes set far back in a sloping forehead. The effect was the sense that the lad was always glancing upward, as though he wanted to look straight up but was resisting the urge. Underneath all of this there was a strong resemblance to Junipero. It was as though someone had taken the priest, shrunk him, and then took a hammer to his face. Dania silently asked for forgiveness and felt a little shame when she pictured such an assault and found it a pleasant thought.

"Poor Pedro," Junipero smiled, placing an arm around the boy. He was a good foot taller than the child. The boy took his place under the priest's arm with slumped resignation, like an obedient dog submitting to a ritual it regularly endures. "My late sister's boy," the smiling Junipero went on. "His father is a mystery. His mother was the victim of some beastly male and took his identity to her grave. And someone, sometime, removed poor Pedro's tongue, apparently to keep him from telling what he knew. Ah well. If thy tongue offend thee."

"Well, Pedro," he said walking away from the boy. "I take it you have our guest's lodgings prepared for her? Please, Sister Dania, if you will be so kind as to excuse me." He picked a sharp, knife-like instrument from off the winched table and considered it with a hint of a smile. The gorilla hung its head a little lower. "I've been distracted from my work long enough."

"So then you... you have a key to this room?" Dania stammered as she watched Pedro unlocking a door in a torch-lit hallway. She

314

caught herself and added, as he pushed the door open, "To all the rooms? You have a key to all of the rooms?"

Pedro returned a ring of keys to its place on his belt as he gestured for Dania to enter the room past him. She followed his wave into a large, plain, high-ceilinged room, furnished with a simple bed, a changing table, and a full-length mirror. She turned then to dismiss the boy, and jumped when she saw that he was somehow, silently, immediately behind her, holding out a candelabra for her to take.

"Th - thank you," she managed to spit out, and then he was suddenly and silently gone and she was alone. Dania set the candelabra on the dressing table and walked to the large, open window, as though to put behind her the eerie sight of the candle flames cavorting amongst the shadows of the room. From there she looked up to the sky above the castle, a sky that was black from the massive clouds that eclipsed the moon. From this high window, she could almost believe that the winding stairway she and the boy had ascended led not to a high floor in the castle tower but instead to the foot of the throne of the Lord himself. She took a moment to breathe in his divine presence and, thus comforted and steeled, she looked down to the ground so far below.

She strained to make sense of the sight below her, dozens of priests moving very slowly about a vast, dark shape. And then the clouds moved and the full moon illuminated the scene with a brilliance approaching daylight, and little by little the shape became discernible, as did the smaller shapes around which the priests were gathered. She realized then that the smaller shapes were more dead gorillas and that the priests were struggling to move them into the larger shape, a mass grave of other apes in varying degrees of decomposition.

As horrifying as it was, she was unable to look away, and gradually the candles burned to smoking nubs, and the clouds eclipsed the moon once more, and all around her was darkness, and still the pile of dead things kept growing. And then Dania realized that the room had been brighter for some time – for how long she could not say. She turned to see Pedro holding a lit candelabra in one hand, the immense ring of keys in the other.

"Jesu!" she shrieked, her hands coming to her chest in a gesture that was a combination of shock and ready defensive posture. Long seconds ticked by as the frightened nun struggled to regain the ability to speak, and the mute lad watched on with an unchanging, blank stare. "What, what do you –" she finally stammered.

In response, Pedro gestured for her to follow as he turned away and started from the room. He paused at the doorway, turned to see that she had not followed, nodded his head in the direction of the hall, and then went out. Dania steeled and crossed herself and followed after, saying under her breath as she went "The Lord is my shepherd, I shall not want…"

Pedro led her down the ominous, darkened hallway, the flickering shadows cast by the candelabra once again their only companions. At the end of the hall, the boy pulled aside a tapestry and then pushed on a section of wall, revealing a concealed stairway. In the oppressive darkness and silence of the scene, it was easy for Dania to imagine that they were the castle's – and perhaps the world's – sole inhabitants, that the rest of mankind was extinct. Easy for her to imagine, or perhaps it would be more accurate to say that it was difficult for her not to imagine.

At the stairway's end they came to another hallway, and at the end of that another stairway, and at the end of that another hallway, and so on, until Dania had lost all sense of location and direction, and was actually becoming accustomed to her eerie surroundings. Finally one stairway ended in a heavy wooden door, which Pedro opened with one of the keys. Then he held the candelabra high and turned over his shoulder to look at Dania, whose expression was gradually evolving from surprised to confused to understanding.

It was a large room, a horde of gold and silver and precious stones that reflected the candles' flicker with a brilliance that was blinding compared to the darkness they had been navigating.

"Thank you, Pedro," she said as the boy closed the door. "You will be rewarded for your courage and honesty, and Juni –"

She did not finish the priest's name, for it was just then that he crept up behind her and drove the side of her head into the wall with one hand as he backhanded Pedro with the other. Dania howled with pain as she fell to her knees, and Junipero set to beating the boy's face in with the fallen candelabra. When the boy was no longer moving and the blood-splattered priest seized her by her hair, Dania cursed through gritted teeth as Junipero dragged her up the stairs.

Her screams and spits of rage were accompanied by his laughter and taunts. "I understand now why the Council should send a girl to do its work. Really, it's so simple. Who better than the spawn of Eve to follow her idle curiosity wherever it should lead?"

"It will lead you to the hangman's noose and from there to the gates of hell," she snarled, much to the priest's amusement.

Up stairways and down halls he dragged her until he pulled her into a torch-lit room – the torture chamber to which he had proudly led her before. The gorilla looked up sadly from its cell, the chain heavy on its neck, and Dania realized where they were.

"Oh, no, please no," she sputtered, amusing her captor.

"No need to beg," he laughed, beating her about the face until she was pliant and unable to resist. "You're going to get just what you want." He dumped her on the table and strapped her arms down. "You're going to get what all of you whores want. The same thing my sister wanted." He then climbed on the table, pushing his weight down to keep her unmoving as he reached under her robes. "The same thing she got."

And then Dania's line of sight was taken up almost entirely by the leering face of the priest just inches before hers. And beyond that was the ceiling of the cell. And then, just as she mercifully lost consciousness, Dania saw the ape, somehow freed from its cell, as it seized a horrified Junipero by the hair and pulled him from her.

And then Dania was climbing out of the pit of her unconsciousness, her face throbbing and swollen but her arms unbound. She looked about the room. The gorilla was closing the cell door behind it, and it then returned to its chains where it replaced the manacles around its neck and mournfully slumped to the floor. And then Dania noticed what was *not* there; the priest was nowhere to be seen.

"Where –" she began to no one in particular, when the ape, as though in response, as though it understood, raised a weakened hand and pointed to – to what? Dania followed the gesture with her gaze and saw the night sky through the window. With difficulty she stood and made her way across the room, then looked out the window.

She saw nothing – nothing in particular anyway. The forest far below that surrounded the castle, the black that was the sea on the line of the horizon, the moon and stars –

And it was then, as she turned her eyes toward the heavens, that she learned what had become of Junipero.

And the Council learned what became of Junipero too when, weeks later, Dania reported the strange events of her visit to Gibraltar. The dozen old men – men who ruled half the world from their secret chambers and their towering pulpits – listened to her tale. They glared down at the woman who had served them so well so many times, who now stoically awaited their judgment. Finally, the High Cardinal spoke.

"Sister Dania, the Council recognizes all that your Church and your country owe you. And that is the only reason you are not being excommunicated for this heresy. But should we ever hear that you have repeated this…" – and here he sneered – "…story… to anyone, you will find our patience has reached an end."

She nodded once, then turned from that chamber for what would be the last time.

Dania never told anyone else what she saw when she looked up out of the window of Junipero's torture chamber, but many decades later, after the last of the Council had died, and her hands were so twisted and arthritic that she could barely hold the quill, she scrawled her story by candlelight, but for whom she wrote it, who would see it, she could not say.

And what she had seen that night was this: Junipero, ascending into the night sky, a chain around his neck. The chain was joined to shackles around his wrists. Those wrists ended in fresh, bloody stumps.

An angel seized the chain and howled with something like laughter. Beside them, on the cloud on which they ascended, stood Dania's Lord. She knew him from the stigmata marking his hands and side.

And that angel looked for all the world like a chimpanzee. And her Lord too seemed to be so much less than what Dania would call a man, but which she now knew was actually so much more. She knew then that Junipero had been right, that the Moor was not made in the image of the Lord.

She knew that none of us are.

PUNCH AND JESUS

By Anonymous Christian

If your right-hand man offends you...

*In his own words: "Who in the hell is the **Anonymous Christian**? Well it's me and it's multitudes of others who don't wear their religion on their proverbial sleeves and don't make a spectacle of themselves in public with loud prayers or boisterous protests for righteous causes... Oh, and I also wrote one of the best treatises on modern Christianity, entitled, **The Anonymous Witness**."*

Like most Iraqi youth, Youseff loved candy, but hated American troops. He was impartial about puppet shows.

Word had circulated amongst the street children near the infidels' Green Zone that a puppet show was planned for that morning near the main entrance of the compound and twelve-year-old Youseff knew what that meant: free candy.

The only problem was that Youseff's father had forbid him from attending any American-organized events near the Green Zone. Youseff's father was not home that morning, however, and twelve-year-old Youseff knew what that meant: free candy.

Youseff's bedroom was on the first floor of his family's home, which made it convenient for him to sneak out the window whenever he deemed it necessary to avoid the distrustful glares and lengthy interrogations of other family members within the house.

On that particular morning, Youseff was a bit late in climbing out of his window and had to run a half-kilometer toward the site of the scheduled puppet show. As he approached the street that led toward the gates of the Green Zone, Youseff could see about a dozen or so other children sitting in front of a makeshift puppet theater. He hoped that he had not missed out on the obligatory candy dispersal, but knew that such distributions usually occurred at the end of the events – sort of as a reward for enduring the Americans' propaganda.

Closing in on the gathering, Youseff could see a couple of hand puppets moving around inside a window that was crudely cut out from a wooden booth. Jogging along, Youseff was able to see that there was a puppet that looked like the prophet Jesus and it appeared to be using a club to pummel another puppet dressed in traditional desert garb. Youseff could hear the children laughing hysterically at the violent antics of the puppets.

But then Youseff slid to a sudden stop, kicking up stones and dust from the street, as soon as he saw one child rise to his feet at the back of the group of children. A feeling of dread came over Youseff as he noticed that the boy rising up had an unusually large backpack strapped across his shoulders. Still about a half a block away from his original destination, something inside Youseff told him to quickly turn around and run in the opposite direction, but his reaction was too slow and he heard an immense explosion as soon as he twisted his head and torso away from the puppet show. Youseff felt a sharp pain in his ears just before being knocked to the ground by the force of the explosion.

Youseff later regained consciousness amid a cloud of dust that burned his eyes and a steady hum of muffled screams that rang inside his ears. He rolled over on his back, quickly feeling for his arms and legs and other appendages, in order to make sure they were all intact.

With great care, he slowly rose to his feet and began stumbling toward the area where the puppet show had taken place. As the smoke and dust in the air began to dissipate, he rubbed his swollen eyes and was able to witness the scene of many panicked parents who were desperately seeking – or already mourning – their dead children. Soldiers were also running through the area, demanding that the scene be secured and yelling into their radios about sending in medics.

Youseff walked through the chaos in a daze, questioning himself whether he was in a dream. For some unknown reason, he was drawn toward the wall of the Green Zone where the puppet booth once stood. Was it candy he was still seeking? He asked himself that question, even though he did not feel like eating anything at that particular moment.

Then he saw it. It was lying in the grass against the wall, peeking out from under some wooden remnants of the puppet booth. It was the Jesus puppet. Certainly no one would care if he picked up this curiosity and snuck it back to his room, he thought.

Youseff leaned down and tried to pick up the hand puppet, but soon realized it was stuck under the wood plank. He then glanced around to make sure he hadn't attracted any attention before leaning back down and tugging on the puppet with more strength. The puppet broke loose from under the wood, but Youseff quickly dropped it when he saw that there was still a human arm attached to the toy.

Youseff gasped at the gruesome find and watched as the heavy-laden hand puppet hit the ground with a disturbing thud. The impact with the ground actually caused the puppet to separate from the dismembered arm, while Youseff just stood by and stared at the gory spectacle. Did he still want the puppet or should he just run home and forget about it?

Without thinking it through, he reached down and snatched the puppet. He then began running from the scene and quickly picked up speed when he heard a soldier yell, "Hey, kid, did you just take something?!"

Grasping the puppet by its plastic head, he desperately raced through the streets toward his home, afraid to turn around to see if he was being pursued. He climbed through his window so quickly that he fell onto the floor of his bedroom, and then just laid there trying to catch his breath.

Eventually, he got up from the floor, took a quick look outside for soldiers, and then made his way over to his bed. Sitting on the corner of the bed, he carefully put the puppet over his right hand, slipping his thumb and little finger into the arm sleeves of the toy. He joylessly played with the puppet, almost thinking he was obligated to do so after having taken the risk of running off with it.

He looked at the ragged puppet and mumbled to himself, "That was stupid, Youseff, why did you do that? Why did you take something you don't even need? What if father finds out? What if mother finds it hidden in your room? You are stupid, Youseff, stupid, stupid, stupid."

"Calm down, Youseff," called a mysterious voice from within the room.

Startled by the voice, Youseff quickly hid his puppet hand behind his back. With a shaky tone, Youseff asked, "Who was that? Is there someone in my room?"

"It's me, Youseff, bring your hand back around."

Scared and trembling, Youseff brought his right hand back in front of him and looked down at the puppet.

"There's no need to be frightened, Youseff."

Youseff was looking directly at the puppet when he heard those words. Was he imagining it all, perhaps hallucinating from the trauma of the explosion, or was the puppet actually communicating with him in his native language? Not caring about the answer to those questions, Youseff tried tearing the puppet off his hand so that he could dispose of it. But it wouldn't come off.

Youseff tried again and again to pull the puppet from his hand, but it felt as if it had become molded to his flesh. "Come off, come off, please come off…" Youseff cried as he continued to tug on the toy.

"Youseff, if your right hand offends you, cut it off," the voice said.

"What?" asked Youseff, speaking directly to the puppet.

"If your right hand offends you, cut it off," the voice repeated.

"No," answered Youseff. "I am not going to cut my hand off."

"Then you are my disciple from now on," explained the puppet.

"I cannot be the disciple of a puppet!" responded Youseff raising his voice. "Do you know what my father will do if he catches me with you?"

"But yet you cannot deny me either, Youseff."

A sudden knock at the door made Youseff jump to his feet and twist his right arm behind his back. His older brother cracked the door open and poked his head inside. "Who are you talking to in here, Youseff? Have you invited company to our home without consulting father?"

"No," answered Youseff, "I was just practicing my verses. No one is here as you can see."

"Fine," his brother said with a quizzical look, "Mother has made us a meal of rice and eggplant, so please join us at the table."

"I will be there shortly," pleaded Youseff.

As soon as the door was closed, Youseff brought the puppet back around to face him. "What do I do now? I cannot go to the table with you attached to my hand."

"Then we must leave here," the puppet answered. "We have much to prepare for."

Seeing no other choice, Youseff climbed back out his window and solemnly walked away from his home with his right hand tucked under his shirt.

In the central mosque, Youseff's father was speaking with a cleric about the tragedy near the Green Zone and the rumor that the Americans had orchestrated the attack in order to blame terrorists. The mosque was quite busy at that time with people walking back and forth throughout the building. The cleric scanned the crowd of people and then interrupted a comment being made by Youseff's father. "Is that not your youngest son?" asked the cleric.

Youseff's father turned to see young Youseff walking through the prayer room toward the elevated minbar platform. The cleric commented, "It looks as though he is holding something underneath his shirt."

"Youseff!" his father yelled, trying to overcome the collective conversations taking place inside the building. "Youseff, what are you doing here?!"

Youseff ignored his father's voice, if he even heard it at all. Youseff just continued to march through the prayer room, directly toward the platform, purposely not looking at anyone to his left or right, but keeping his puppet-covered hand hidden under his shirt.

When he reached the speakers' minbar, Youseff turned to face everyone gathered in the room. He caught a glimpse of his father approaching the platform, but quickly looked away to avoid eye contact. "May I have your attention?!" Youseff announced as loudly as he could.

"Please may I have your attention?!" he repeated, but this time he brought his right hand out from under his shirt and raised it in the air. "I am here to proclaim the second coming of the Lord Jesus Christ!"

Youseff's father came to a dead halt in his approach and his face took on a shocked expression of disbelief that the young man at the minbar was his son. The man dropped to his knees and covered his face in shame.

Youseff expected an angry response from the men within the mosque, but was surprised by their stunned silence. Youseff looked up at the puppet in order to draw everyone's attention to it.

"Consider me the White War Horse who bears the burden of the Faithful and True," Youseff proclaimed, manipulating his fingers to make the puppet's arms move feverishly. "In righteousness he will judge and make war!"

Seconds later, Youseff reached under his shirt with his left hand in order to pull a metal wire, which instantly detonated explosives within the backpack that he was wearing. The entire mosque was violently rocked and collapsed in on itself. Debris rained down upon the city as stunned crowds watched the demolition in horror. One child noticed a plastic and cloth object fall at his feet...

JUMPERS

By Michael Bracken

A lesson in not jumping to conclusions.

*Even though he is the author of several books—including the young adult romance **Just in Time for Love** and the hardboiled private eye novel **All White Girls**—Michael Bracken** is better known as the author of almost 900 short stories published in **Ellery Queen's Mystery Magazine, Espionage, Fantastic, Flesh & Blood: Guilty as Sin, Hot Blood: Strange Bedfellows, Midnight, Mike Shayne Mystery Magazine, Out of the Gutter, Specters in Coal Dust, Weirdbook**, and many other anthologies and magazines.*

*Additionally, Bracken has edited five crime fiction anthologies, including the three-volume **Fedora** series.*

*Learn more at **www.CrimeFictionWriter.com** and **CrimeFictionWriter.blogspot.com**.*

Three weeks after moving into the corner office, Milton Williams saw his first jumper. Milton was contemplating revisions to a memo he had drafted that morning and was staring out at the city when the jumper flashed past. He leapt from his chair, knocking it over in his haste, and rushed to the window. By pressing his cheek against the glass he could see the sidewalk below.

He saw nothing but the usual mid-afternoon hustle and bustle of people going about their day. No gawking crowd gathered around a body because there was no body.

Milton blinked, shook his head, and stepped away from the window, thinking that he had, perhaps, mistaken a bird for a man—a dark-haired bird wearing a two-piece blue pinstripe suit, red tie, and black wingtips.

He returned his chair to an upright position and settled into it.

His administrative assistant—ten years younger than Milton, blonde and slender—rapped twice on the open door and stepped into his office. "Everything okay?"

"Why?"

"I heard an unusual sound, like something had fallen."

"My chair," he explained. "I knocked it over."

She examined him for a moment. "Can I get you anything? Coffee? Tea? A soft drink?"

"No, thank you."

Emily crossed the room. The far edge of his desk indented her thighs as she leaned forward and touched her fingertips to his forehead. "You're pale as a ghost, Mr. Williams, and you're shaking. Are you certain there's nothing I can do for you?"

He ignored the breech of office etiquette and thanked his assistant for her concern. Employees did not touch one another for fear of yet another sexual harassment suit. "It's nothing. I'll be fine in a moment."

Emily slowly withdrew her hand. "If you don't mind, I'll check back with you in a few minutes."

"That would be fine."

Milton's assistant turned and he watched her exit. Then he returned his attention to the three-page memo spread across his desk.

By the end of the week he had forgotten all about the jumper. Friday evening he met Andrea for dinner and took her back to his apartment for a nightcap. The statuesque brunette left before dawn, as was her habit, and Milton found himself sitting on the balcony in nothing but his boxers, a scotch rocks in one hand and a cigar in the other, watching the sun rise over the city. Their relationship was one of convenience, born of mutual need after his divorce and her husband's debilitating coronary. Love did not enter the equation, nor did lust, and they both realized that one day they would move on to other, more fulfilling relationships.

Until then, they had their weekly assignations, and he had his corner office, something he had pursued so single-mindedly that his first and only wife had left him for a plumber, taking with her their home in the country, a new BMW, and much of their combined savings. Milton took a long drag on his cigar, followed it with a slug of scotch, and waited until the sun finally crested the horizon before stepping inside to shower and prepare for his early morning round of golf with three co-workers.

Milton saw the second jumper five weeks after the first. He was on the telephone with a buyer in Mombai, working a deal that would net his employer several hundred thousand dollars at the low end and as much as a quarter of a million at the high end, when a sandy-haired man in a charcoal gray suit, gray tie, and blood red oxfords sailed past his window. Startled, but not as much as he had been the first time, Milton continued his conversation after only a slight hesitation while he switched the phone to his other ear and pressed his cheek against the window.

As before, the people on the street below went about their business, unconcerned or unaware that a man had leapt to certain death from a floor above Milton's yet had never reached the pavement several dozen floors below.

He completed his conversation with the buyer in Mombai and replaced the handset in its cradle on the desk. Then he called his assistant into his office.

"Are any of the companies located on the upper floors experiencing economic problems?"

"We're in a recession, Mr. Williams," Emily said. "They all are."

"Any of them worse off than any others?"

"I suppose," she said.

"Ask around, especially about companies with offices directly above mine."

"Is there something specific you want to know?"

"Layoffs, terminations, that sort of thing."

"I'll see what I can find out."

Over dinner that Friday he told Andrea about the two jumpers he'd seen sail past his office window. She listened but seemed unconcerned that the men had never reached the ground. She suggested that perhaps Milton had been under a bit of stress, and then she commented on something he'd said earlier that evening about his conversation with the buyer in Mombai, comparing negotiations with foreigners to successfully grasping a greased pig.

After dinner, he suggested a nightcap at his apartment, a formality that had become a ritual in the two years they'd been seeing one another, but Andrea demurred, saying that she didn't feel well.

When Milton phoned her Wednesday to arrange dinner the following Friday, she claimed a prior engagement prevented her from dining with him that week. He didn't bother asking about the coming weeks because he knew from the sound of her voice that their tenuous relationship had ended.

He saw the third jumper the following afternoon. Dark blue suit, blue tie, black brogues and closer to his fifty years than the first two.

This one looked at Milton as he sailed past Milton's window. He looked at Milton and he smiled.

Startled, Milton knocked his coffee from his desk. Hot liquid splashed across his thigh, and he swore. Loudly.

Emily rushed into his office, saw the mess, and promptly beelined herself to the break room. She returned moments later, handed Milton three paper towels to soak up the coffee he'd spilled on himself while she used other paper towels to dry his desk and absorb the coffee puddle on the floor at his feet. When she finished, Emily retrieved his coffee mug and asked if he wanted it washed and refilled.

"In a moment," he said. Then he asked the status of her inquires about the companies on the upper floors.

"Nothing to report," she said. "Things are tight for most of them, but no layoffs or terminations—at least, none the other admin assistants are gossiping about."

He thought about that, wondering what had caused the men to jump, if they had jumped.

"Are you okay, Mr. Williams?" his assistant asked. She stood on his side of the desk, only inches from him, and he felt the heat radiating from her body. She touched him as she had the first time he had seen a jumper, only this time she covered his forehead with her palm as she might to check a child's temperature. "You're a bit pasty," she said, "and you feel warm. You certain you haven't caught the flu or something else that's going around?"

Milton gently removed his assistant's hand but hesitated before releasing her slender wrist from his grasp. "I don't think it's the flu."

Scotch rocks and an illegally procured Cuban cigar smoked on his balcony that evening helped Milton dismiss the three jumpers as little more than stress-induced hallucinations—and he'd certainly experienced stress since moving into the corner office. Although his wife had divorced him two years prior, news of his promotion had prompted her attorney to seek an upward adjustment in alimony payments. He'd been living on carryout since the divorce and carried an extra twenty pounds around his waist, weight that caused him so much difficulty on the golf course that he had begun using a cart. The sinking economy had depressed the value of his apartment below the balance remaining due on the mortgage, achieving his sales goals had proven elusive, and his only relationship, tenuous though it had been, had ended with a whimper and not a bang.

The buyer in Mombai became obstinate, insisting on changes to a contract Milton had thought complete, and Monday morning he had to explain to the vice president of his division why he had not sealed the deal. That afternoon Milton saw his fourth jumper, another dark-haired man in a pinstriped suit, a whimsical tie covered with tiny cartoon characters, and black wingtips.

The jumper didn't sail past. He floated, giving Milton time to examine the man. He saw the mustard stain on the jumper's tie, the scuffmark on the toe of his left shoe, the rough stubble of early five-o'clock shadow. The jumper's pale blue eyes twinkled and, like the third jumper, he smiled.

Milton slapped the window with the flat of his hand and cried out, "What do you want?"

"I'm sorry," Emily said.

Milton spun around at the sound of his assistant's voice. She had quietly stepped into his office while he stared at the fourth jumper.

Flustered, Emily said, "I didn't mean to disturbed you, Mr. Williams, I just—"

"Do you see that?" he demanded. He pointed at the window.

"See what?"

He glanced back. The jumper was gone. He pressed his cheek to the window and looked down. As before, the people on the street were oblivious to what was happening several dozen floors above them.

Milton returned his attention to his assistant. "There was a man," he said, "outside my window."

"That's impossible," Emily said.

Milton described the man. "Do you know him? Have you seen him before?"

She crossed the room, took his hand, and urged Milton back into his seat.

"He wasn't the first." He described the three previous jumpers.

Emily stood with her back to the window and patted Milton's hand, treating her boss like a doddering uncle.

"You've been working too hard," she suggested.

The fifth jumper appeared behind Emily. He didn't sail past or float past. He just appeared.

"There's another one," Milton said.

His assistant didn't look, didn't even turn her head.

The jumper outside the window was better dressed than the others, with a crisply pressed, tailored black suit over a white button-down shirt and red silk tie. His black patent leather shoes reflected the mid-afternoon sun. Milton's age, smooth shaven, and with only a hint of gray at his temples, he smiled and beckoned, urging Milton to join him.

Emily still had his hand, was still patting it, but Milton barely felt her ministrations.

He stood and stepped toward the window.

"Mr. Williams!" Emily shouted. "Mr. Williams, come back!"

Milton stepped through the glass and turned. His body slumped forward and slid from his office chair. Emily screamed and people rushed into his office.

When the jumper floating next to Milton disappeared, he fell several stories, passing the windows of other men in corner offices just like his, seen by some but not by others.

Milton never reached the pavement.

NUDE SUSHI WITH A TWIST

By Keith Dugger

Ask not what your country can do for you.

*Only lightly tethered to what others call reality, author **Keith Dugger** creates popular works of bizarro, dark, and sublime fiction that range from mildly creepy to twist-your-brain intense. Though one of his fictitious multiple personalities suffers multiple personality disorder, Keith remains intently devoted to his craft and frequently enjoys writing to the anti-melodic baying of his invisible dog.*

My name is Jimmy Tickles and I broke the world. It's not quite dead yet, but when it goes, I can say that I killed it. I killed Earth.

Law: Humans exist for consumption.

Survivors call me <Censored under directive of the Regulatory Control of Information, Title 42, Part 7, Chapter 11, Subpart B of the Amalgamated Rules for Public Disposition of Truth, amended by The Department of Censorship and Monitoring, Government of Earth>, the helpless bastards. I'm not kidding and today I ate my fill at the body buffet on the corner. The service is rarely wholesome and the food is mostly out of date, but they often serve delicacies other restaurants lack. The fried scalp is divine. I ate too much, and though there is nothing wrong with eating too much—it is advertised as all-you-can-eat—bits of skin, rubbery and marred by ink, get stuck between my teeth. Ink from regulator's tattoos.

I ate my fill and I'm not hungry any more. I tucked away a pinch of skin bits in my jowl for later.

"Have a hateful day," I snickered to the doorman. A tall thin man with a humped shoulder and a hairy wart on his left eyelid.

Holding the door he pointed randomly, "Hit the road, peckerhead."

My name is Jimmy Tickles, peckerhead, and I crave human flesh. The government mandated human trafficking to meet the demands for food and to cater to the passion of those like me. I eat people, we all do. But I prefer fresh meat.

Of course we all eat people now. There's an industry dedicated to the growth of human samples just for food. Virile males can get jobs at stud farms to keep the flow of fresh meat coming. Little pale animals fed chemical growth concoctions locked in cages never to see the gaslight. Milk-fed is the best if you can afford it. And I especially like rump steak. Rare.

My name is Jimmy Tickles, I crave human flesh and I'm a man-meat snob.

Law: Public displays of morality are punishable by death.

On the sidewalk outside the bistro, a businessman brushed against me by mistake.

"Good day, asshole," I said. As he walked away, I drew my government-issued pistol and I shot him not quite on center in the back of his head. "Fucker." A cleanup crew scuttled in behind me and scooped up the dead businessman. Tonight he'd provide food for seventy people; citizens who can't afford their own organic meat. Industrialized animals are expensive.

The planet is dead because of me. A lowly research physicist at university lazily working toward a useless degree. That was when I cobbled a truth. And that truth did not set us free.

Two naked teenagers fucked on the bench at the bus stop waiting for a fictitious bus that would never come. They were so intertwined it wasn't clear if they were male or female.

Darwin smoked crack.

No, that's not the truth, but it may as well be. When I published my truth, *The Irreverence of Human Existence: Life is Not Among Us,* the world was already rife with social inaction striking a disharmonious chord of social chaos. Destruction, war, pestilence, disease, death, murder, rape, politics, still an occasional pillage, and damn good drugs made sure to divide differing peoples and cultures into segments of what was supposed to be one world.

I published that paper over 30 years ago and it only took a decade for the meek to absorb and spread my truth like an information STD seeking to drive the world insane with crotch itch.

The world and its oppressive governments needed a truth. I discarded reality and invented a truth so vivid that just reading it caused the sky to fall, its weight squashing a thousand years of hope and belief.

Law: No living thing shall utter the truth.

The ash snow from the constant fires burning society around the world blocked the heat of the sun. It was dark and nothing of much use would grow. My nose was raw from the oxygen mask I wore to live. We all wore masks to live.

An explosion, the fifth or tenth or fiftieth today, rocked what was left of shattered windows of storefronts. Rows and rows of suicide shops, corpse vendors and cash-for-limb stores lined every road. Roads that were hardened arteries of times past, just more sidewalks for potential food now. No automotives had rumbled these streets in forever. Explosions were a more common scene.

My favorite restaurant was an invitation-only place on the north side. The chefs expertly carved a live animal tied neatly to a table. Nude sushi with a twist. Standing room only, guests gorged themselves on a still-warm body, heart still beating; the screams of eater and eaten mixed with the tribal beats of street drums just outside. Drum beats and heart beats. Med-techs tended the food, pumping the meal with fresh blood, monitoring vital signs. Warm to the last bite.

I still remember my last meal there, her soft eyes looking at me, silently prodding me to hurry. To get the invitation I had to donate a live sample to the restaurant. It was the price of exclusivity and I gave my family's only daughter. If I could have faked a tear, the salty liquid would have seasoned the warm meat as I swallowed it whole. She respected the process, she refused to beg for mercy, yet she looked up at me with a quiet protest against a governing rule meant to save a planet. She might have pleaded with me to hurry, but her tongue was the first to go. It was the best meal I'd ever squandered.

I sucked the gooey juice from a skin bit and imagined the satisfying tug of struggling livestock.

We all lived under the three-law system, laws that kept the hungry fed. The weak, the stupid and the ugly died, sometimes violently, to ensure the survival of the race. I helped write the first of the three laws. "No living thing shall utter the truth." I didn't really write it, but my ideas, truths and lies, were its catalyst. The details and summary, theorems and formulae, facts and *fiction* of my publication were used by governing bodies around the world to vet the first law. It was my truth they bastardized justifiably to protect the public. It was my truth that made truth illegal.

The truth is I made <Censored>. And for that I'm sorry. Or would be were it not illegal. Survivors call me <Censored>, the bastards, and the government censors my thoughts.

As I crossed the street, I grabbed an ugly woman's ass. Her mate, in a sharp motion, shoved a blade into my heart. The pain felt excruciatingly beautiful and I fell to the ground, mask twisted around my neck. I drew my government-issued pistol intending to kill him, and while I stared down that well-used barrel, I realized that death isn't the punishment. After twenty long years, in that single moment, I realized living is harder. My gun arm fell limp to the lonely echoes of drumbeats.

A cleanup crew scuttled in behind me and scooped me up. Tonight I would provide food for seventy people; citizens that can't afford their own organic meat. We are not sadistic animals, we just are. And industrialized humans are expensive.

TALKING HEADS
By Nicole E. Peffer

A lonely bartender learns the many facets of castration.

Nicole E. Peffer spent almost two decades being kicked from one newspaper to another before serving time at a metropolitan daily. It was not nearly as glamorous as she might have hoped. She left the newsroom for good in 2009, working for the U.S. Census Bureau and UPS while searching for a "regular" job. During this time, she returned to writing pure fiction (something newspapers print every day of the week, according to some people). She shares a small house in western Pennsylvania with her husband and an assortment of pets. This is her first foray into the bizarro fiction genre. She is currently writing a science-fiction/horror novel and collaborating with an artist for a web comic.

The Log Cabin used to be a tiny dump of a watering hole along Route 19 until a restaurant chain bought it and cleaned it up.

After extensive remodeling, it cleaned up mighty pretty. So did its clientele. No more scruffy patrons nursing whatever beer is on draught or liquor that burns its way down into the belly of all but the most hardened drinkers. The Cabin now caters to the upwardly mobile classes.

This became plainly apparent when driving past on Friday and Saturday nights. Instead of the usual row of pickup trucks with more primer than paint and a few beat up old muscle cars, rows of shiny luxury sedans and sport utility vehicles overflow the parking lot. You know, the ones you can fit an entire compact car in the back seat and still have room for a full-grown thoroughbred racehorse. Don't even bother trying to get a table on the weekend, when the antique hunters come out en force to sup at the "oh-so-quaint" rustic establishment.

The formerly sparse menu (strictly for those on a liquid diet of beer and hard liquor) has been replaced with high-end beers and fine wines. The Spartan décor has been embellished with rustic prints and rural mementos. Three mounted heads serve as the sentinels of the main dining room; a caribou (or reindeer, depending on which part of the world you hail from, although I prefer the former – the latter makes my inner child curl up into a fetal position to think one of Santa's sleigh team might be mounted on a wall in some Pennsylvania restaurant), a surly bison and a regal elk.

Al, the barkeeper, had been dating one of the waitresses, Sue, for eight years. Sue had been nagging him for seven of those years to marry her. He played deaf until one night she decided enough was enough. When he pulled up to their duplex, his clothes, his guns and his video collection of pirated porn were piled on the front lawn. At work, she refused to speak to him unless it was to fill a drink order. In the meantime, he had moved back in with his folks. He was beginning to think that hell might be a more pleasant place to call home. Sue was an amateur nag when compared to his mother.

Saturday was busier than usual. It was the weekend after Thanksgiving, when the cup of suburban sprawl runs over into Butler County. Everyone wanted Ye Olde Time experience of trekking out into the wilderness and hacking down their own Christmas tree. The next best thing was driving a half hour across the county line to one of the tree farms that do a brisk business this time of year, hopping on a tractor-drawn wagon, going out among the rows of blue spruce and Fraser fir and sawing one off its stump. And then O Tannenbaum was corded and tied to the SUV's luggage rack. Sometimes, more than one: one for the living room, one for the family room, and one for the mudroom. Pity the poor kid who has a tree allergy.

The Cabin's parking lot was filled with SUVs sporting pine toupees, and the dining room was filled with surly teens texting their friends under the table ("OMG ths iz so lame IM SO BORD"), overtired toddlers hopped up on cola and running around the dining room with demonic glee, and parents who had every intention of ordering a second glass of wine. Maybe even a third.

Al bumped into Sue when she was out back having a smoke. She shot him a baleful look as he lit one up to indulge his own nicotine fix. It was the wrong time to ask Sue if they could patch things up. She'd had her fill of snobby teenagers, pretentious, rude adults and lousy tips. These assholes could afford fancy cars, obscenely expensive houses and three effing Christmas trees, but they couldn't leave her a decent tip? And she knew why Al really wanted to reconcile. She had met his mother. Part of her felt a perverse sense of satisfaction that he had moved back home.

Sue didn't let him finish his fumbling apology. She stubbed her butt out against the side of a dumpster and flicked it into a butt-can. Then, she turned and walked away. Her silence was more eloquent than if she had stood there screaming at him, and left no room for discussion, debate or reprieve.

Al knew he was well and truly screwed.

After the last patron had left, the sleek surface of their carefully polished Mercedes-Benz reflecting the light of the full moon as it slunk off into the night, the tables were cleared, the dishes washed and put away and the floor swept. In pairs or by threes, the waitresses, hostess and busboys made their way out into the parking lot, shouting out their goodnights and see-you-tomorrows.

341

Paul, the manager closed out the drawer, smiling with satisfaction as he left for the night.

Al was too miserable to be impressed by the evening's business. All he knew is that his head ached from the boisterous Saturday night crowd, and he didn't look forward to going home. If he and Sue were still together, right about now he'd be rubbing her feet after a long night hauling trays back and forth between the kitchen and the dining room. Maybe she'd return the favor by rubbing something else for him. All he had to look forward to now was tiptoeing in without disturbing his mother, who was almost guaranteed to wake up, get out of bed in her curlers and fuzzy pink bathrobe and shout at him for waking her up and asking him when he was moving into his own place.

He sighed wistfully. Very quietly, he heard his sentiment echoed high in the rafters.

Slowly, Al stepped away from the register and peered into the main dining room. The three mounted heads stared back with sightless glass eyes. The docile-looking caribou appropriately hung at the north wall, his impressive rack spanning almost to the ceiling. To the east was his Midwestern cousin, a bison who must have been as surly in life as rendered by the taxidermist. The elk, which also boasted some impressive headgear, occupied the south wall.

Not for the first time, Al wondered if the Cabin was a host to spirit activity, like in the reality TV shows Sue liked to watch. He'd doze off, bored out of his mind, and she'd wake him up with an violent jab of her elbow into the side of his head because one of the ghost hunters had captured voices from beyond on their digital recorder. Those freaked her out every time. So much, in fact, that she would pop him one on the shoulder whenever he imitated the raspy, supernatural voices. Invariably, "Get out!" would turn into "Get ou—ch!" Sue could be a real buzz kill sometimes.

There had been claims before from staff that closed for the night. Mostly, they heard the sound of someone sneezing. During the holidays, no matter how much tape they used to keep jolly red, white-trimmed Santa caps on the mounted heads, they always ended up on the floor. Until Joanie, the one in charge of the decorating this year, had the brilliant idea of using a staple gun to keep them in place. Occasionally, a patron would exclaim that he or she swore they saw the buffalo wink at them. Al figured they had imbibed a little too enthusiastically.

After a quick look around, Al found that the dining room was quiet, and the three mounted heads weren't sneezing or winking. He was sure they were all quite dead, just skins molded over wooden forms. He decided that they looked a little dusty, and noticed strands of spider silk spanning the elk's antlers. With a sigh, Al turned down the lights and locked up for the night.

And then Al sat himself down at the bar and proceeded to get mind-numbingly drunk. He didn't bother with beer or wine; he went straight for the tequila. No lime. No salt. Just shot after shot until his head began to float and thoughts of Sue and his mother, both of them scowling at him with accusation and disappointment, began to fade. At some point, he lay down his head on the smooth surface of the bar, closed his eyes, and succumbed to the alcohol dulling his senses.

When the voices started, he thought maybe he had forgotten to turn off the TV that hung behind the bar. He tried to ignore them, keeping his eyes closed.

"Hey! Where's my ass?" Although the voice seemed muffed, the panic was unmistakable.

"Oh, shut up about your ass," came the brusque reply. "No one cares about your ass."

"It was attached before." The voice held the confusion expected from someone who had lost their wallet or their cell phone and was trying to remember where they last saw it, and then it became an angry shriek. "I want to know what those bastards did with my ass!"

"Really, must you go on about this *every* night?" a third voice, this one indignant, chimed in. "In case you hadn't noticed, neither of us have our asses, either."

Al lifted his head, eyes fuzzily focusing in on the main dining room, more or less fifteen feet away from him, and gaped stupidly.

From where he was mounted sixteen feet above the floor, the caribou tossed his head and snorted through dusty nostrils. He was staring, cross-eyed, up between his antlers at the Santa hat stapled to his skull. "But you don't understand: I had a great ass! And those bastards took it! I want to know where it is and what they intend to do with it!"

"Oh, would you please just shut up?" the elk pleaded in clipped tones, eyes visibly rolling toward the ceiling.

The caribou was grunting, jerking his head back and forth, trying to dislodge the cheap dollar-store hat from his head. His barrage of insults was punctuated with snorts of effort. "You probably had a nasty, flea-bitten ass while you still had it. They did you a favor when they lopped your head from the rest of you. You probably would have frightened customers with your big-ass hindquarters!"

"Y'wanna know what they did with your ass?" the buffalo rumbled, looking from the elk to the caribou with narrowed eyes. "A family of Eskimos probably ate it. Yup. Roasted it on a spit. What remains of your precious *tuchus* is probably still around...as frozen little Eskimo turds. Not that you're in any position to trot your ass – oh, pardon me – back up to Alaska to get them. Should I tell you what they probably did to your hide? Or how about your testic..."

The caribou's jaw snapped shut, the white tuft of the Santa cap swinging between his eyes widening with astonishment, and then narrowing with outrage. "Only you could be so vulgar, stupid midwesterner that you are! Your butt was probably turd-encrusted from the time you could slip in coyote shit!"

"Enough!" bellowed the elk. "I don't want to hear another word about anyone else's ass tonight, is that understood?"

The buffalo wiggled his small ears and blew a cloud of dust and dead mosquitoes from his snout. "Come over here and make me, Steroid Boy."

The caribou began to giggle as the elk's jaw gaped. "What exactly is that supposed to mean?"

"All you are is an overgrown white tail," the buffalo snorted.

The elk arched a brow, taking a condescending tone. "I'm much bigger than a white-tailed deer, or a mule deer, for that matter."

"Oh, sorry." The buffalo sounded anything but apologetic. "You probably had nuts the size of a prairie dog."

The caribou was laughing so hard now that no sound came out of his mouth; his eyes squeezed shut as he wheezed in a fit of amusement.

"Why don't you come over here and say that!" the elk snarled, cobwebs swinging from his rack as he tossed his head.

"Wish that I could," the buffalo drawled. "But, if I did have my ass, and everything else still attached, I would love to get out of here just to get away from you two. Between Rudolph over there whining about his missing ass and your snotty attitude..."

"And what about your preoccupation with balls?" the elk taunted.

Buffalo tried to shrug, realizing he couldn't; a stingy taxidermist had deprived him of his shoulders. "Don't you know what they do with buffalo testicles?"

The elk and the caribou shook their heads, mouths gaping like a kid's when they see their first road kill up close, amazed and yet repulsed and too fascinated to look away, eyes bright with morbid curiosity.

"They make the scrotum into drawstring purses to sell at those highway Indian trading posts. Then they fry the testicles in butter with onions and serve 'em up on a platter as Rocky Mountain Oysters. *Bon appetite.*"

The caribou was incredulous. "You've *got* to be joking! They actually...they actually *eat*...ugh!" he spat, and eyes squeezed shut as he shuddered with revulsion.

The elk, on the other hand, chuckled.

"And what is so funny about some drunken asshole eating my nuts with cayenne pepper sauce?" the buffalo growled.

The elk began to half-heartedly try to work the Santa cap between his antlers free, making the tufted end flip over with a gust of breath. "I was thinking how lucky we are."

"What?" the caribou snorted, incredulous.

"Ever hear of tiger penis soup?" the elk drawled.

After a moment of stunned silence, their chuckling became uproarious laughter.

It was at this point that Al stood up abruptly, knocking his barstool over with a crash.

The laughing ceased, and the talking heads slowly turned to look at him, wide eyed and gaping.

"Holy shit," the caribou said, as though he'd been the one to see a ghost or something else just as implausible.

"Am I losing my mind?" Al wondered aloud, standing on unsteady feet.

"Possibly," the elk answered, sarcastic. "It's more than likely you're just inebriated."

The buffalo chuckled. "Dumb shit. Go home. Sleep it off. You probably won't remember a damn thing."

"I've been drunk before," Al muttered, blinking and shaking his head, trying to clear the fuzziness. "On tequila. Never seen anything like this before."

"Well, I guess there's always a first time, isn't there?" the buffalo said, giving him an exaggerated wink.

The sound of laughter followed Al as he lit out of there like rabid raccoons were at his heels.

It was the last time Al ever drank. He's sure he hallucinated the whole thing. Pretty sure, anyway.

But even after he made up with Sue, whom he married a year later and who effectively emasculated him in every way, barring a sharp instrument and his most valued appendage (which, after six months of wedded bliss, became his right hand), he would never close the restaurant alone. And when he was in the main dining room, he felt like the eyes of three mounted heads followed him wherever he went.

Sometimes, he swore he heard chuckling. And there were times when he could have sworn he saw the buffalo wink at him.

But he always considered himself lucky.

At least, he surmised, he wasn't a tiger.

BOOM CLICK CLICK

By William Pauley III

When Russian Roulette and Nintendo accessories are involved, the outcome can't be good.

William Pauley III writes because he's too poor to make films. He is the author of Doom Magnetic!, The Brothers Crunk, and Demolition Ya-Ya - all of which are weirder than pickles on an ice cream sundae. He honestly believes that the '80s were the most important thing that's ever happened to the world and he anxiously awaits its return. He's the editor of The New Flesh magazine and BizarroCentral.com

For all things III, visit www.breaksaidsilence.com where he mostly babbles on about David Bowie and how underrated the Super Mario Bros movie is. It really is a great movie. Give it a second chance.

Divey Crunk wriggles his fingers through a spaghetti mess of wires, examining each of them closely before tossing them back into the chaos. His goggles are dark and fogged from the perspiration pouring down his forehead. He wipes the backhand of his glove along his hairline and again digs into the knot-ball of wires.

"Damnit, Divey, this is taking too long! I'm out, man! I'm facking out!" says a tall man with a thick Cockney accent.

"Shut your goddamn mouth, Reynold, and watch the door! I'm telling you, it won't take but a minute to solder. I just have to find the right facking wire first. If I have to…" His words trail off into undecipherable mumbles.

Reynold walks to the back door of the van, peeks out the window, and anxiously bobs up and down, as if he's holding back a river of piss.

"Do you mind? You're breaking my facking concentration!"

"I can't help it. This sneaking around business always gets me heart a thumping." Reynold tries to calm his nerves. He holds his breath. Unconsciously, he begins to swing his hips, doing his piss dance again. Divey slams his toolbox against the metal floor of the van and clutches his skull with both hands. The vein in the middle of his forehead is throbbing in anger.

"You know, I think I'm going to get a bit of fresh air. Yeah, that's what I need. It's getting a tad bit stuffy in 'ere." Divey doesn't move. "Yeah… so, ah, well… I guess I'll just beat on the side of the van if I see him coming, yeah?" Divey grumbles. Reynold nods and hops out of the van.

The concrete is wet and glistening like a blanket of diamonds underneath the ginger glow of the streetlamp. The van is sitting in an otherwise empty parking lot, outside of a minor league baseball stadium. The air is clean, fresh, as it always is after a good rain. He takes a deep breath and wipes his finger along the edge of the side glass window. The yellow paint of the van is beginning to chip away, revealing the original egg shell white color underneath. The words, 'BRACKFAS BURRITOS ¥99" are written in giant red lettering across the side panels and doors.

A flitter of light reflecting off of a small metal object lying on the ground catches the corner of his eye. He walks over to it and picks it up. It is a small round coin with Japanese lettering on either side.

"Ha, fancy that... a 500 yen piece! I guess it's me lucky day."
Reynold bites the coin and buries it in his front pocket.

"Whatchu got there?" a man's voice asks from the darkness,
deep and gravelly. Pete's voice. Reynold's nerves jump.

"Ah, heya there, Pete... I just found me a bloody 500 yen piece,
just lying 'ere on the pavement. Imagine that, huh?" There is a
nervous quiver in his voice. He slowly backs towards the van. Pete
steps out of the shadows, revealing three hundred and forty-nine
pounds of pure American meat tightly tucked into a pair of black
sweatpants and a red Members Only jacket, no shirt.

"Heh, yeah, imagine that..." Pete lights up a fag. "Go get your
brother, we'll have one last smoke together." Reynold nods his head
and jumps in the back of the van.

"Christ, Divey, put that shit away! Pete's outside!"

"Just in time, too..." Divey tosses a screwdriver in his toolbox.
He turns around quickly and aims an orange plastic gun directly at a
remote sensor installed in Reynold's right eye socket. The gun he is
holding is a 1984 model Nintendo Zapper.

"Have you lost your facking mind?!" Reynold says, cupping his
hands over the sensor.

"Relax, the gun is rigged to go off on the third pull of the trigger.
All we have to do is get Pete to go last."

"And you're sure you fixed the generator too, right?"

"Of course I fixed the generator, what kind of dumb-arse bloke
do you take me for?" Divey takes off his gloves, pulls a wooden pipe
out of his front shirt pocket, and smiles. "Let's smoke, brother."

Divey stuffs the plastic gun into the waistband of his jeans and
hops out onto the pavement.

"Hey there, Pete... no luck I see," Divey says as he lights his
pipe

"No... no luck." Pete takes a long draw from his fag and exhales
for what seems like an entire minute. Reynold hops out of the van,
his cigarette already lit.

"Well, you know what that means…" Divey removes the light gun from his beltline, "We zap for it."

"You know, I was thinking, we could always wait until the next town to do this. I mean, shit, we still have a couple days worth of rations. We may not have to do this at all."

"That's what you said in the last town. And the town before that. Things gotta change 'ere, Petey boy. We've gotta stay ahead of the game. Right now, we're eating up all of our profit - *literally*. We're supposed to *sell* our burritos, not eat them. And now with the shortage of meat, well… one of us just has to go." Divey pulls a long black chord out from the bottom of the gun and plugs it into an electric generator sitting on the pavement behind the van. "This is the only fair way to choose which one of us has to make that sacrifice."

"Okay, boss. You're right." Pete bites his upper lip. "But, if it's all the same to you, I'd like to go first." He takes one final draw from his cigarette before stomping it out with his boot. Reynold's mouth drops open. His cigarette burns a hole in his shirt as it falls to the ground.

"Wait, why should he get to be the one who chooses?" says Reynold, batting the ashes off of his shirt. "Yeah, you know, I think I want to be the one who goes first." He smiles smugly at Pete and puts another cigarette up to his lips, lighting the wrong end by mistake and inhaling a lungful of torched filter. He hunches over and begins to cough. "Shit, that was me last ciggy."

"Well, I'll tell ya what, princess," Pete says with a smirk, "Why don't you take out that shiny lil' 500 yen piece you got in your pocket and let's have us a good old-fashioned coin toss. Winner goes first, loser last, and boss here will go second. How's about it?"

Reynold looks over at Divey, but Divey shies his eyes away. "Sounds like a plan, Pete." Divey says. "But Reynold gets to call it. Fair?"

"Fair," Pete replies.

"Rey, coin please?"

Reynold digs into his pocket and hands the coin over to Divey. "You sure about this?" he whispers.

"It doesn't matter what I think, brother, it's up to fate. All of this is by chance, isn't it? Whether or not you win this facking coin toss, it doesn't necessarily mean you've lost the game. The gun could still go off on any of us at any moment." Divey winks. Reynold takes a deep breath and nods, trusting that his brother knows what he is doing. Divey places the coin on top of his fist. "Call it in the air."

He flips the coin.

"Heads."

The coin flickers under the streetlight and lands in Divey's palm. He balls his fist around it. An unpleasant stench fills the air - it smells like burnt tire rubber.

"For fack's sake, tell us what it is!" yells Reynold.

"Wait a second, what the hell is that smell?" says Divey.

The generator begins to crackle and smoke.

"Shit, Rey, you set the generator down in a facking rain puddle!" yells Divey.

"Well, where else was I supposed to have put it? *Everywhere* is a facking rain puddle!"

"Well now the generator isn't going to work properly, you dolt!"

Pete's eyes narrow like two coin-slots. "Are you both fucking putting me on? That generator has been broken for ages. You know that. That's the whole reason why we are using the fucking thing, because it's impossible to know when it will fire!" Pete yells.

Reynold and Divey exchange *'oh shit'* glances. Pete is getting suspicious. Oh shit, indeed.

"Wait a second, you two fucks are trying to set me up! The zapper has been rigged and that's why you don't want me to go first, right?!"

Reynold and Divey stare ahead blankly and slowly shake their heads 'no.'

"Right." Pete says. "Give me the gun." Divey hands the gun over to Pete, butt first.

"Fuck it. We're still doing this. But I'm going to go first." Pete holds the gun up to the remote sensor installed in his head – his is in his left temple. "You guys have t'wake up pretty early in the morning to outsm--" Pete pulls the trigger. His skull explodes and brain sludge erupts from the crater, spraying along the side wall of the van. His body falls limply to the ground.

"Holy shit! I thought you said the gun wouldn't go off until the third pull of the trigger!" Reynold yells.

"Fack, but yeah, that was when I thought the generator was working right! Shit! I wasn't expecting that!"

Reynold holds his hands over his mouth and takes a deep breath, both of them shaking.

After a moment of silence, Reynold speaks, "Shit. Why did it *have* to be Pete, Divey? Why not either of *us*?"

"I told you before, he is bigger than the two of us put together. The business could run nearly three times as long from the meat off of his bones than it would from either of ours."

"You know what I mean…"

"Oh shit, you're not going to get emotional on me, are you, Rey?"

"I just want to know. *Why Pete?* I mean, fack, we rigged the zapper to go off on him, it didn't work out the way we planned, but the bloody thing *still* went off on him. It's not just that the odds were stacked against him, no, he really had no facking chance."

"Fate."

Reynold wipes the sweat from his upper lip. "You know, I never believed any of that shit before today, but I think you're right, brother. Fate. Damn." Reynold bends down and removes a pack of fags from Pete's jacket pocket. He puts one up to his lips and lights it. "Do you think we have the power to change our fate?"

Divey unfolds his palm. The coin is facing heads up. "No, brother, we don't." He places the coin in Reynold's hands.

"But what if this is just some sort of *lucky* coin? What if it has nothing to do with fate… only luck?"

"You're asking questions that I can't answer, Rey," Divey says as he puts on a pair of canary yellow kitchen gloves.

Reynold holds the coin up to the light. The Japanese writing shimmers in a way that he hadn't noticed before – as if it possessed some sort of magic. He presses the coin up to his lips.

"Hey, once you're done snogging with that coin, you think you could give me a hand 'ere?" Divey begins hacking Pete's limbs off with an axe and tosses the bloody hunks of meat in the back of the van.

Reynold stuffs the coin in his pocket and ties a surgical mask around the bottom half of his face.

"I'll get the trash bags."

SUCCOR THE CHILD
By Mercy Loomis

A picture is worth a thousand unspoken words.

*Mercy Loomis graduated from college one class short of an accidental certificate in Folklore. She has a BA in Psychology, but don't hold that against her. Her favorite pastimes include road trips and studying ancient history. See what she's up to and find links to her other work at **www.mercyloomis.com**.*

The school carnival is a tradition older than I am, one that sweeps through my hometown each year with the same weighty inevitability of harvest-time. With no children of my own, I find myself attending more out of nostalgia than anything else. The halls of the elementary school are narrower than I remember, and children dart around me on their way from one activity to another, trailing glazed-eyed parents in their wake like embers from a sparkler.

The hallway walls are covered with art, each class showing off the young talent. I meander through the long corridors with no agenda save stopping outside my old classrooms and peering in at memories, listening to the chaos and looking at the pictures on the walls. The round yellow suns, the slash-of-blue skies, the m-shaped

355

birds are all sort of comforting; there'd been no computers in my classrooms as a child, and even television had been a rare treat. Those familiar symbols remind me that, then as now, children see the world with the same eyes.

As I move through the building the drawings become less symbolic, attempting greater realism. My interest wavers, but I'm nearly to the far doors and I might as well go out that way than try to swim back upstream to the main entrance. The sixth graders are the last stop. Their pictures are depressingly mundane; still-lifes and portraits and animals reproduced from books, and I'm walking quickly now, hardly bothering to glance at the walls when I see it from the corner of my eye, like movement.

I stop and go back.

It's a stark picture, almost vulgar in its contrasts compared to the colorful pieces on either side. It hangs crooked, off-center, as if it were taped up hastily. My eyes can't quite make sense of it, but it draws me as its more traditional neighbors do not, and after a brief hesitation I carefully peel it off the wall and hang it properly. Despite my care, some of the chalk rubs off on my fingers.

As I take a step back I see that it's not as monochrome as I first thought. Among the black and white and grey are smudges of color; a dark blue blending into black here, an underscoring of burnt umber there, creating a surprising feeling of depth. Sinuous lines rise out of the swirling background to writhe across the paper and beckon me closer. I oblige, one slow step at a time, until my nose is inches from the surface. There's something to this drawing that's not familiar, exactly, but I feel as if I should understand it, as if it's one of those 3D pictures that will at any moment snap into focus if I can just figure out how to see it right. And yet, it's not like that at all; these arcs and shades and highlights define something concrete, not some seemingly random explosion of colors. I'm giving myself a headache staring so hard, the edges of my vision going dark, black and grey and deep vibrant blue, until it feels as if those great sweeping lines are curling around me, about to envelope me and drag me into the picture and drown me in that roiling chaos…

"Weird, isn't it?"

I stumble back a step, lightheaded and dizzy, and turn toward the voice. A middle-aged woman is behind me. She has that worn, life-drained look all parents get after their children have been around long enough.

"It's…very different," I murmur, rubbing my powdery fingers together. I glance back at the drawing, but it's sullen and motionless.

"That's what comes of letting your kids watch too much TV," the woman sniffs, looking down her nose at the picture. "We'll be seeing that boy on the news in a few years, I have no doubt."

"Geez, Mom." A youngster I hadn't noticed rolls his eyes so hard I fancy I can hear them rub against his skull. He peeks around his mother and tugs at her arm. "Come on already."

I don't spend much time around children, but this one seems like he could be the right age. "Do you know the boy who drew this?" I ask her son.

The look he gives me drips with scorn. "I'm in *seventh* grade."

"Of course you are." The words cross my lips automatically. One grade and the next are two different worlds and nary the two shall meet. Even I remember that much.

"Daniel, don't talk to your elders that way," the woman whines, her voice inflaming my headache. I want them to just leave. I want to be alone with the drawing again. Except we aren't alone—people continue to walk around us, the parents shooting us dirty looks as they squeeze past, their squirming children hardly seeing us, their gazes fixed on whatever shiny thing farther down the hall they've set their hearts on.

Turning to me, the spineless matron continues her babbling. "Peggy—that's my Daniel's best friend's mom—she told me, on very good authority, mind, that this Tyler Leidowski," and here she waves dismissively at the drawing, "is in a *gang*."

She whispers this with a shudder, as if the word has some power to harm. I barely manage to not sneer. A town of seven thousand people in the middle of farmland, and this sixth grader is supposedly in a gang. I abruptly find myself excusing her son's behavior.

"I see." The words are little more than a growl. I try to moderate my tone, but my patience is nearly gone. I swear I can see the drawing shifting restlessly out of the corner of my eye, equally impatient. "A shame, I'm sure. But I don't want to keep you from…" I gesture on down the hall.

"Yeah, come *on*, Mom, the astronomy demo starts in a couple minutes."

"Yes, dear, that's right." But instead of heeding her son's tugging, she keeps nattering on at me. "A planetary alignment of some sort –"

"It's a *conjunction*, Mom, *geez!*"

"A conjunction, yes, I'm sure they're quite rare—"

"No, they happen all the time, but you won't buy me a telescope!" He's tugging at her arm so harshly I'm surprised he hasn't dislocated it yet.

"Stop interrupting, Daniel. You see, he's so excited about it, my clever boy, he's going to be a scientist…"

"Enjoy the demo." The inflection is much more along the line of "Go to Hell," harsher than I intended, and her eyebrows fly up in shock. I can see she has no intention of leaving while she has an audience, and is now probably going to lecture me on my manners. I force myself to turn and walk away, away from the drawing. I can feel it watching me as I retreat. It's hard to move, as if the air before me has turned into jelly and I have to push through it. My head pounds, the sound of my pulse filling my ears. I glance over my shoulder, but she's still there. Her mouth is moving but I can't hear her over my thundering heartbeat, and I have to keep walking.

A red-haired woman pokes her head out of one of the classrooms in front of me, probably attracted by the noise. She looks past me at the huffing matron. Her brow furrows. She looks at me. Her gaze pierces me, baleful and accusatory, as if she knows I don't belong here, not truly, that I am one of those weird childless people that parents tend to view as a separate species and possible threat. She waits in the doorway and watches me, and now I have no choice but to keep going right out the door at the end of the hall. The drawing pulls at me and the woman's scrutiny drives me, and I feel nauseous and dizzy when I finally emerge into the cool evening air.

I stumble coming down the steps, and can't help turning to look back. The red-haired woman stands on the other side of the glass door, expression stern and inscrutable. Daniel's mother is just behind, jaws flapping. I don't see the boy; maybe he's finally abandoned the silly bitch. I try to look casual as I put my back to them, but my feet are unsteady beneath me and I wobble from side to side as I walk away from the school. They probably think I'm drunk. I feel drunk, the bad end of drunk, where it's all throbbing head and sour stomach and the feeling that you're being smothered in cotton, except I haven't had a drink in two days, and all I can think about is the drawing. I'm walking away from the drawing before I've deciphered it, and this carnival is the only time I have any reason to be in the school, and those two harpies will be watching now, they'll know if I come back in the other entrance, they'll be watching to see if I come back so they can swoop down and peck me to death.

I clutch my head. I keep walking.

Somehow I manage to travel the half mile home. I let myself in and lock the door behind me. The house is dark, but the dark seems to breathe. Things seem to slither in the shadows, and the air is hot and close. I strip and crawl on top of the covers. The dark presses down on me, soothing my aching head. It's too much work to open the windows, and I'm half afraid doing so would let the dark out. I close my eyes.

The picture seems to be etched on the backs of my eyelids, but it's frustratingly incomplete. I try to recapture the sweep of the lines, the sense of movement, the burnt umber, the blue bruised shadows. The tips of my fingers throb, and I raise my hands to my face. The familiar scent of the chalk has an unexpected sour tang to it. My fingers brush against my face and leave a heavy trail of pigment behind that sinks into my skin. I shudder, dragging my fingers down my throat, feeling the colors seep into me, drawing myself into a twisted caricature. My breath comes hard. I'm breathing the colors, the chaos of the drawing's background swirling in my lungs. My fingers slide lower, dragging across my nipples and they tighten, my whole body tightens. Color pools around that puckered flesh, around those tiny, useless organs that were designed to nurture, and I feel the rightness of it, the primal instinct of parenthood, the gut knowledge of being needed. There is a humming in my ears, soft but strident, as if someone far away were shrieking. I can almost hear words in it. A word. A name.

I smile in the hot, pregnant darkness. Of course. It was a portrait.

The colors begin to heat, to burn. I gulp the stifling air, but it's no good. I must get out. The memory is just a shadow. I have to look on that portrait now that I know it is one. I have to look into that...*face* is not the right word...the hum is a knife in my ears and I'm on my feet in my bedroom. The red numbers on the digital clock sear my eyes. 2am. Somehow minutes have turned into hours.

The school should be empty.

I dart through my silent house and out the door, leaving it open.

I'm still naked, but the colors in my skin hide me as I scamper softly through yards, taking the most direct route. I know the doors will all be locked, but once I reach the school tendrils of color lead me to an open window. I start to make my way to the sixth grade wing, but the air hardens against me. I stop. Blue like an icy moon's halo shudders in streamers down the hall, and I follow its lead eagerly.

The doors of the large multi-purpose room are open, and I stride in with my head held high. A dozen townsfolk shrouded in robes of black and grey fix their eyes unwaveringly on me, but I care only for the easel at the end of the room. I can't quite see the portrait, but I feel it tugging at me. A short, robed figure stands before the easel, adjusting the angle, fussing with the lighting. Behind me, I hear the heavy wooden doors thud shut.

The figure turns to face me. He is a child with eyes that seem to run and melt and reform. They don't of course, just as the only colors on my skin are the red welts of scratches, but I still see the mark of his station just as I see my own. I stand before the artist, the prophet, the one that Daniel's mother named as Tyler Leidowski.

Not a gang; a cult, comes the irrelevant thought, and then the prophet speaks to me in a high, childish voice.

"You come freely."

"I do." Saying it loosens something inside me, exhilaration and abandon and an all-consuming sense of purpose. The prophet has called the faithful and I have answered.

"The Child is hungry." Tyler's words echo, reverberating in my ears, shivering across my skin.

"All will be One when the Child comes of age," a dozen voices chant from behind me.

My nipples prick and throb. "I am here to feed the Child."

"The Child will unite us in Eternity," the voices reply.

The Child's followers close in. Hands touch me, guiding me forward. Tyler steps aside, and I fall to my knees before the drawing. The lines in their graceful arcs seem to tremble impatiently. My heart sings in my chest. It sings a name I don't know how to say.

My arms are bound behind my back, the ropes then tied to my ankles. I barely notice. The drawing is pulling me in again. The Child needs me. My whole chest burns and aches with anticipation.

"Only those who have never given are fit to feed the Child," Tyler intones.

"All I have ever been I give to the Child." The words fall from my lips with a life of their own. I can do nothing but stare. I can almost see it. Almost touch it.

The voices sigh with longing. "Blessed are those who nurture the Child."

I feel the prophet move behind me. There is a smell of hot metal.

"Call the Child," the prophet commands, and something burns into my back.

I scream, and the name bursts from my lips. It is a sound born of incoherence, of chaos. I realize that it's a name that cannot be spoken by human tongue on purpose—not correctly, not with the proper inflection—and I am grateful to the prophet.

I scream the name, and the portrait moves.

The roiling confusion pulls me in, wraps around me, the colors drawing me deeper, and as I watch the lines begin to grow firm, to take more definite shape, I realize that this was but a child's scrawling of the Child, the round yellow sun and m-shaped birds of portraiture. My eyes bleed but I dare not blink, and I hear myself laughing, high, screeching laughs, and those long, sinuous shapes reach out to me. They touch my nipples first, sucking down, hard, and rip the flesh from my chest.

I shriek the name again, and distantly I hear the voices moan in rapture. The name is a gift that I give them, they who cannot speak it. I give it freely, but all else is for the Child.

My flesh nourishes the Child, becomes one with it. Greedy as all children are it snatches at me, faster and faster, feasting on muscle and sinew, organ and bone, mouthful by dripping mouthful until no scrap is left and at last it swallows awareness, swallows my screaming.

Sated, the Child sleeps.

We sing to the Child. We, for I am not alone; others have given themselves before me. We sing and wait for the Child to come of age, and unite all life in Eternity.

SHE WHO CLEANS: A DUNG STICKER'S SHITTY TALE

By A.D. Spencer

**Here is the church and here is the steeple –
open the door and see all the people.**

A.D. Spencer resides in northern Alabama, where the month of August inspires tales of Hell and the woodlands make fine horror muses. Though she holds a degree in English, she credits her true education to a teenage love affair with the supernatural. Her works have appeared in anthologies from Pill Hill Press, Horror Bound Magazine, Whortleberry Press, and Twisted Library Press.

Some years back, before a third of the country's population had been chewed up and shat out by a flesh-craving, forty-foot mutant with digestive problems, Paulette wouldn't have been caught dead cleaning someone else's toilet. She'd been the pretty girl in high school, a walking stereo-type with natural waves of brunette hair and a smooth manicure a dozen Korean parlors would have a hard time replicating. Obtaining a husband, preferably from a good family, had been her life goal. She'd even picked him out by her sixteenth birthday. 'Course, things did have a way of changing.

Life was funny like that: twenty years older and standing six yards from a steaming pile of fecal matter taller than her partner's Pentecostal poof, Paulette was simply happy to have a paying job. Times were hard, after all, and they weren't getting any better so long as there was a killing machine stomping across the land.

The community known as Littleville consisted of a few fill-ups, a few churches, and a few tacky saloons. But it was atop the crumbled remains of the police station that Runt had chosen to relieve himself. Paulette parked the truck far from the crushed blacktop that had once been a parking lot and pulled the trash-sticker from the bed. It was modified and of her own design, a larger version of what roadside cleanup crews used to use back when they still existed. The sticker's sharp, metal shaft tapped the barrel of neutralizing agent with a loud ring.

Ginger whistled at the flattened trees in the distance.

"Looks like old Runt took a nap over there," Ginger said, straightening her long denim skirt. The hem brushed her once white sneakers. "Probably left behind more than one pile if he stayed the night."

"Want me to radio in for a second team?" Paulette asked, a smirk on her face.

Ginger raised a brow. They were paid by the cleanup, not the time it took to do the job. And Ginger's Timmy was laid up in bed after losing both arms during Runt's pissing contest with the Coast Guard last year, so she needed every penny she could scrape together. As far as who signed the check, both women assumed it came down from Uncle Sam, but their job wasn't what one considered "on the books," and no one was going to call HR about too many hours on the field.

"Didn't think so," Paulette said.

"What you think we'll be doing after he reaches Florida, Paulie? Once the army gets him trapped."

Paulette shot the other woman a glance. "Draw unemployment?"

Ginger chuckled. "I'm gonna miss Disney World."

"I'm gonna miss my paycheck."

Common knowledge: Runt left behind his own fair share of messes, but not even the media acknowledged the role of the Dung Stickers. The news preferred to focus on the men in uniform, the scientists, the politicians--people with a *plan,* the current incarnation of which included trapping the beast on the Peninsula. And promptly slaughtering him, if that was actually possible.

Paulette didn't particularly look forward to putting together a new résumé.

"Looks like the leftovers are stirring." Ginger nodded at the excrement, tapping the cross against her chest. She picked up her own stick, holding the pointed end out in front of her. "Let's get this over with."

Something in the pile was twitching. The movement sent black-green muck sliding down to the pavement with a splat. Fingers, more bone than flesh, poked free, grabbing air as if they were trying to catch fireflies floating just out of grasp. Another wiggle, another wet splatter, and a face broke free. Its skin was ruddy from the stomach fluids, but there was enough of the corpse left to make out a bubble nose and black hair caught in its gaping mouth. Its jaw was hanging to one side, crushed, even as the muscle tried to lift it in a chewing motion. Paulette couldn't say for sure whether the break was made before or after the unfortunate had been swallowed whole. Defecation had a way of bending a body out of shape.

The dung doll, as the clean-up crews affectionately called the moving remains, cocked its head, as if it could hear the woman's thoughts. And found them *rude*. Paulette snorted, shook her head, and raised her sticker a few inches off the ground.

The broken jaw was a good thing. Meant this one wouldn't be much of a biter. There weren't enough antibiotics in the world to fix-up a dung doll bite.

A cheery gurgling sound spilled up over the corpse's loose, flapping tongue. *Hello there!* The corpse lifted its torso free from the pile with surprising strength and an air bubble popped. A spray of brown matter hit Paulette across the shins. The dung doll wiggled down the pile, leaving her lower half behind, strips of shredded intestines still stuck in the hot glob and slowing down her crab-like elbow walk.

"Shit," Paulette muttered. She reached up, dabbing vapor rub into her nostrils before she pulled up the cloth mask.

"Paulie, hun, you got a talent for stating the obvious," Ginger replied.

Ginger made no move to cover her nose. Anosmia, Paulette was pretty sure that was what it was called, whatever Ginger had wrong with her. She'd been in a car accident on her twenty-first birthday. Her head hit the pavement and she lost her sense of smell and gained religion with the Holiness bunch. Paulette spent most her working day jealous of Ginger's nose. Not so much of the church part, though--Paulette was too attached to her blue jeans and salon-owning dreams.

So, Ginger, with God's gift of a lacking nose, didn't smell the second dung doll approaching.

"One at your six," Paulette noted. It was slow moving, tired, and stumbled out from behind the only standing wall of the station, but the slap of its feet and the stench of its shit bath was announcement enough.

"I'll let you have that one, Paulie," Ginger said, not giving it a glance.

Paulette raised her stick and moved to the brick divider. The dung doll waiting for her was male and posed like an old school monster, arms raised, mouth agape. She gave it a good look-over. Paulette wasn't sure why, but the folks who sent her on new gigs required a report with each cleanup. Wanted to know what Runt's feces were lookin' like. As if his health somehow mattered.

Paulette couldn't tell if this doll had ever had a six-pack or a beer belly. He was missing his middle, only his intact spine keeping him moving. Paulette wasn't sure if he'd dug his way out of the pile they'd found or if Runt had defecated again nearby. The crap clinging to his wounds was bile yellow and slimy. Runt's meal hadn't agreed with him.

The corpse groaned, proud of the speed he was gaining.

The dung doll had one foot tangled up in an uprooted briar bush, and he was dragging a wooden cross and cell phone charger behind him. As pathetic as he appeared, Paulette thought he made up for it in effort alone. When he saw the woman was closer than ever, he tried to double his speed and tripped over his prizes.

Paulette kicked him across the forehead and took a step back, scanning the area. Clean-up usually involved multiple dung dolls, though, for the most part, the corpses were in bits and pieces, twitching and snapping but unable to do any real damage.

Littleville's first church was the only remaining structure, just across the roadway. Runt must have given it a side brush because its steeple leaned forward, held up by the caved rooftop. Must have been where the cross came from, *God slowin' down the sinners.* Paulette smirked, knowing her partner would get a chuckle out of the comment.

No more movement across the land though. No more dung dolls.

Paulette shrugged and pushed down on her stick. There was a slick pop when its thick needle slipped into the dung doll's brain stem. He went still, his fingertips curled against her ankle. Another yank, the metal tip pulled free.

A crack sounded and brought Paulette's gaze back to the church. She stared up at the towering steeple, her body stiff, waiting for it to fall. Because that sound had surely been the splintering of wood.

But the steeple was still, fixed and secure against the beams inside.

It took Paulette another second to feel the tremble beneath her feet. Not splintering wood then. Not a falling structure at all. The ground beneath her shook again. She recognized the rhythm of the movement. Footsteps. Big ones.

"Ginger!"

The other woman slid out from behind the wall, her skirt

flapping against cotton legs. "I know," she said, "I know, dangnabit. *I know!*"

Paulette grabbed Ginger by the arm, making sure she didn't slip on over the doll's cross. "I thought they said this area was clear?"

"Runt must have backtracked," Ginger reasoned, pulling the other woman along with her. The truck was a good twenty feet away, and her eyes were trained on the fat barrels laying across the bed. "We got time to neutralize this one."

"The hell we do." Paulette sucked in the words, her breath short. She let go of the other woman's elbow, slamming herself against the driver's side door. Slick fingers fumbled with the handle. "Get in the damned truck, Ginger."

"Gotta finish this job first, Paulie. We won't get paid unless we neutralize." Ginger's voice was focused. She was unrolling the hoses in the back, holding the double-ended nozzle against her arm pit. "It won't take a second. Will go faster if you help out."

Paulette's slipped behind the wheel. Half-turned to watch the other woman. "Get. In. The. Truck!" Paulette slapped her palm against the back window with each word.

Ginger's lips were set in a thin line, her brow low. She appeared at the side window, the red and green hoses wrapped over one shoulder like a coil of rope. "I'm getting Timmy's meds with this check. And I *need* a big one, Paulie. This might be the last for a while."

Paulette watched the woman lead the taped-together hoses around the side of the wall, kicking bricks in her hurry. It didn't take long, not at all. One spray from the red, followed by one spray from the green. Mixed together, they activated, becoming acidic and slowly eating the organic material. Including the corpse and the shit pile to which it was attached.

Paulette slammed her palms against steering wheel.

"*Fuck.*"

She was out the door before the oath had time to leave her mouth. Circling the truck, she twisted the knob on the first barrel, counted to seven, and moved to the second. She'd just hit "six" when the ground nearly pitched her skyward. Paulette gripped the side of the truck in a vice and turned to look over her shoulder. She didn't like what she saw.

Runt's forty feet consisted mostly of legs, and if he'd been born into the shape of a woman instead of a slimy freak of nature, he'd never have spent another night alone. His knees went backward, letting his body hang low against the remaining tree-line, and the massive limbs connected where his ass cheeks should have been. His anus was hidden by the tumor at his groin, a lumpy wart where his junk wasn't, but the most disturbing part of him, at least for Paulette, was the wet mouth at the center of his face. It was toothless but the jaw was strong as a gator's, so muscular that there didn't appear to be a neck on the beast at all. An assortment of arms spread out from his sides, some of them boneless, flaccid abortions, others strong and clawed, too many fingers to count.

"I hate scientists," Paulette whispered, because it was the first thing that ever came to mind when she saw the mutant. This was one foul-up she wasn't going to blame on God, that much she and Ginger agreed upon. Mankind made this monster, all in search of a solution for death.

And, the sad part was, they'd succeeded in what they set out to do, prove that a creature could have regenerative cells that could be harvested. Unfortunately, that kinda broke down to meaning the folks he munched on got shat out as mindless zombies.

By all rights, his makers hadn't planned for him to quadruple in size and escape. Maybe it made her a bad person, but Paulette hoped the incident put a damper on their research funds.

She nearly tripped over the dung doll's rugged cross running back to the station's ruins. As far away as Runt was, his giant legs could cross an acre in an instant, and he had his eyes set on live meat.

Ginger was still dragging the hoses with her in some last ditch effort to save the equipment. Her eyes were wide, more white to them than color. Her legs flapped against her skirt, running in air as she was lifted up by a single finger around her chest. The hoses dropped, and she waved for help, hands grasping nothingness like the dung doll she'd put down moments earlier. Paulette skidded to a stop, falling backward onto her elbows as she watched her partner flail far above. There wasn't time for a scream when Runt popped Ginger into his oversized sucker headfirst. A single white tennis shoe fell back to Earth, hitting Paulette across the leg.

It was enough to wake the woman from her stunned state.

Paulette scrambled up, her feet getting caught in the tangle of hoses. Without a second thought, she aimed and fired both chemicals at the closest of Runt's toes. It wasn't the recommended method, and she realized why when white-hot pain shot through the tips of her index and ring fingers.

So much for owning a nail salon.

Paulette didn't have time to let that sink in. Instead, she held the hoses steady until they'd unleashed their full seven seconds of load.

Runt howled, a thick choking sound that broke free around his latest meal. His foot lifted, away from the source, but he didn't step forward onto the little human who'd attacked him. The mutant stumbled back, flaccid arms waving at the sudden jerk. His legs hit the church and he collapsed onto it, falling onto his ass.

Paulette was tense, ready to make an ill-fated run for it when he regained himself. What she didn't expect was the widening of his gaze, such a mocking interpretation of Ginger's last moments. He howled again, a sob finishing the desperate whine as he lifted himself off the flattened house of worship. The sound turned into a whimper, and he limped sideways, the angle of his backwards legs strange, his upper body hunched forward in agony.

It didn't make a blame lick of sense. Paulette had seen the creature pile-drive through banks and stomp on school buildings. One tiny church shouldn't have made a difference.

The mutant didn't look at her, didn't seem to see anything but huge tears collecting in his own vicious gaze. And then, without another roar, his stumble became a gait toward the tree-line.

Paulette stared after him, her brow crawling up to meet her scalp when she saw Runt's behind. The tip of wood was fat and squared off, but she realized what it was immediately. The mutant had just put in his first steeple-shaped butt plug.

It send a smile to the woman's face. She huffed a breath of relief, knowing the mutant was headed south once again, as far as his damaged feet could take him. And, unfortunately for her career, old Runt wouldn't be able to make another corpse-filled deposit before reaching snow bird country.

"Guess you'll get to see Disney World again, Ginger," Paulette said, and began reloading the truck.

TIFFANY'S!! IT'S GET EVEN TIME!!

By George Kosana

A pistol is a guy's best friend.

George Kosana *starred as Sheriff McClelland in the horror classic* *The Night of the Living Dead*, *and delivered the famous ad-lib line, "They're dead! They're all messed up."*

He played an abortionist's front man in George Romero's follow-up movie, *The Affair*, *which was a romantic comedy. He continued his acting career with roles in* *The Booby Hatch*, *The Devil and Sam Silverstein*, *and three other independent films. Still active in the entertainment business, he delights his many fans when he appears at horror conventions for autograph signings throughout The United States.*

George is an accomplished writer as well as an actor. His original screenplay *We'll Try Again*, *won the Silver Award at the Houston International Film Festival. George's current project* *Madness, Times Three* *deals with three distinctly different psychological disorders. He is a welcome addition to this exciting anthology of short stories.*

The first time I robbed Tiffany's it was raining. I was fifteen. So were my buddies. Joe Farzilli, Walt Panlewski, Willy O'Shea, and me. I'm George Stalovich. Some crew. One Italian, one Polish, one Irish, and a Serbian. We grew up together, were in the same grade, the same school, and in the same boat. We were broke, and full of rage.

Our neighborhood, rundown and poor, offered us no way out. The only way we'd get anything was to take it. We all shared that sentiment, and were destined to self-destruct, only we didn't know it. We had our act together. We were ultra-hip and no one better get in our way. We hated school, cut classes at every opportunity, never did school work, failed most classes, and took care of those who complained.

When teachers brought us to the attention of the Principal, or Superintendent, we'd put a brick through their car windows, slash their tires, or use a flat file and destroy the paint job. The school never could prove it was us.

One instructor wouldn't back off. Mr. Smith, our English teacher, intended to catch us, and prove we were the vandals. He got a little too close once, so I set his car on fire, then joined the crowd that had gathered to watch it burn. A sick look swept over his face when the gas tank exploded. I thought that would discourage him. I was wrong.

More determined than ever, Mr. Smith documented our every move. He compiled written records, photographed us when we hung out, and was beginning to cramp our style. I told the crew to relax, I'd take care of it. I found out where he lived, studied him, and the area. Everyone put their trash out Tuesday evenings for the Wednesday pick-up.

Mr. Smith put his trash out after supper, usually around 7:00pm. I watched the weather reports and picked a Tuesday when there was no moonlight. I hid in the shadows and watched him approach. His back was to me as he opened his trashcan. I left him lying on the street in a pool of his own blood with a chimney brick nearby.

When Mr. Smith was well enough to return to the classroom he took his "evidence" to the School Board, and with the Superintendent, presented his case. All four of us were called before the board and suspended for thirty days. I really didn't care. Hanging out became routine, and pinochle a ritual. Walt and Joe came up with wild ideas about how to make money. Willy wants to rob neighborhood bookies, but that's argued against when reminded mob guys don't appreciate being held up, and they hit back big time.

After three idle days, and many get rich quick schemes that could never work, it hit me. "If you're gonna steal, steal once, steal big, and steal enough so you never have to steal again. Who has that kind of money?"

The four of us rack our brains searching for an answer to that question. Joe offers, "A business. It has to be a real money making business." Suddenly it was crystal clear. I spout out, "Tiffany's. It has to be Tiffany's."

All of us agree they are big money. We also agree to hit it. We take turns studying the store. We notice armed uniformed security guards show up first. They turn off store alarms and open the vault.

Ten minutes later employees arrive. They busy themselves by removing dust covers and cleaning glass counters. They disappear inside the vault, re-appear carrying trays of valuable gems, and arrange those in the display cases. Nine a.m. on the dot the doors open and the day's business begins. Armored cars make special deliveries at irregular hours several times a day.

We need a weapon so we visit the library and study how to make one. Across town in a hardware store, I take a twenty two caliber bullet out of my pocket, find a pipe it fits, and the store cuts four five inch pieces. They then thread one end of each piece and fit a reducing nut on each one.

A piece of wood is wired to the pipe and a nail with the point hammered flat makes the firing pin. The crude, but effective, single shot, homemade weapon works. We're ready.

Near closing time we cross the street, assemble at the entrance, pull ski masks over our faces, and as the leader, I am the first one through the door. "This is a stickup," echoes throughout the store before I realize I stand alone. My crew chickened out. My buddies never entered Tiffany's. Shocked and surprised I stop.

Security Guards, guns drawn, immediately surround me.

During the trial none of "the boys" are in the courtroom. The Judge sentences me to juvenile detention until I reach twenty-one. Since I carried a "gun" during the attempted robbery, there was no reduction of the sentence, and no possibility of parole.

Inside the facility I am labeled "fresh meat," beaten routinely, and sexually assaulted. With each episode my desire for revenge against my crew grows. It festers, until it blossoms into a full-blown rage. Suddenly the key to surviving my sentence becomes clear. Turn that rage. Use it against all inmates, regardless if they attack me or not, and bring that hatred against anyone in my way.

A shank, deeply imbedded into the kidney of my main offender, puts him in the cemetery and his two followers meet with similar fates. Authorities never prove it was me. A by-product of my attacks elevate me to the status of someone who holds his own. No one in the facility bothers me. In fact, they give me a very wide berth.

The sentence served, and released, my obsession for revenge against the former crew intensifies. The only one in the old neighborhood is Walt Panlewski. After some persuasion, he shows me where the other two live. Then he is "accidentally electrocuted" while attempting repairs to a circuit breaker.

Joe Farzilli spots me coming down the sidewalk. I notice him as he panics. He fumbles frantically with a jacket pocket. He attempts to pull out a loaded pistol. Panicked, he darts out into the street and runs head first into a large delivery truck. The force of the impact tears his hand and weapon free. It sails through the air and lands at my feet. People rush to help Joe. I pick up the gun. Witnesses cry, "He's dead!" I laugh.

"I didn't touch him. No way can they connect me to this one."
That leaves Willy O'Shea, and the big one.

Willy has morning coffee and a jelly donut at the same coffee
shop every morning before work. He cuts through the same alley to
save time, and he is jittery. When he's in the alley he hurries his
pace, and constantly looks over his shoulder to see if anyone
follows.

I wait at the far end of that alley, a loaded, cocked, pistol, rests in
my hand. Willy approaches. He turns his head for one last look
behind him. A bullet tears the back of his head apart, and I make a
quick getaway. That leaves the big one.

I stand across the street from my destination and check the pistol
– it's fully loaded. A light rain begins to fall. At the entrance, I pull
the weapon out of my belt, cock it, throw open the door, and shout,
"TIFFANY'S!! IT'S GET EVEN TIME!!"

COTTON MOUTH

By Christopher Danaher

Never put anything larger than your elbow in your ear.

*Christopher Danaher is an author whose work has been published in **Bare Bone**, **Doorways Magazine**, and **The Dream People**. He lives in Pittsburgh, Pennsylvania, with his wife, the sculptor Jessica Danaher.*

Harry Kovair shoved the tip of his little finger into his ear as far as it would go. He rooted around for a good ten seconds, only succeeding in making his outer ear sore.

When he had stopped digging, Harry examined his fingertip. He found only a few flakes of dried white wax – or a few loose skin cells – not the cotton ball that felt like it was jammed into his ear canal.

His head felt fuzzy. Harry tilted it to one side and tapped his fist against the side of his skull, the way he had seen swimmers do it when they had gotten water trapped in their ears, but that only made his head hurt.

Harry rolled out of bed, steadying himself against his bedroom wall. He was feeling dizzy.

"I must have stood up too fast," he thought as he made his way toward the bathroom.

Harry found himself leaning over the sink and staring into the bathroom mirror, trying to see into his own ear. He pulled the lobe forward and rolled his eyes all the way to one side to get a better look at the cotton ball, or skein of yarn, or whatever it was that was scratching against the inside of his head.

He was distracted by the sight of his own crooked smile, reflected back from the bathroom wall. Harry found himself wondering if he had gingivitis, like they mentioned in all the mouthwash commercials, or if he should be using a "whitening" brand of toothpaste.

"Teeth should be white," Harry thought; white, like the pet hair mashed and trodden into the burnt-orange carpet of the hallway outside his apartment unit. The maintenance staff vacuumed every Tuesday and Saturday, he knew, but they always missed something. There were always those hairs that were too small to see, or too woven into the carpet to pick up, and so they were left behind, to accumulate.

The maintenance staff wasn't the problem, though. Harry knew that, even if they were a bit careless and lacked a passion for detail. The culprit - as Harry would have told the world and the cops, if they would listen - was that toothy young woman in 38D, the neighbor girl with the boyish hair cut and the ever-present can of pepper spray clipped to the belt loop of her jeans.

More specifically, the real problem was her damned dog – a long-haired Afghan hound that shed like a... (What sheds too much?) *A long-haired Afghan hound.*

The toothy pet-lover, whom Harry liked to call Julia Roberts, although he had never actually spoken to her – neither the neighbor, nor the actress (although he had liked her work in the movie *Flatliners*) – liked to walk her dog in the park below his living room window. Harry knew this because he had seen the woman and her dog crossing the parking lot of his apartment complex, moving away with their backs toward his living room window above them, crossing the street, and climbing the small hill at the edge of the park.

At the top of the rise, "Julia" usually disregarded the city's leash law, unhooking the cord from her hairy Afghan, setting it free to run in manic circles then disappear over the crest of the hill and into the park.

God only knows what the shaggy mutt would do out there, running around, out of sight; probably picking up dirt, and bugs – and growing more hair. All of which would get deposited right outside of Harry's doorway in the usual manner.

After every walk in the park, the Afghan hound and its owner would return home, walking past Harry's door, from the elevators at the far end of the hall. Harry would never see them, but he would hear the jingle of the Afghan's dog tags as it walked. The noise would get louder as they got closer and closer to his apartment; usually climaxing with a furious rattle as the damned dog shook itself, like many dogs do to shake off water after they have taken a bath.

With Harry's luck, this dog probably had not had a bath in a long time. It was probably just shedding the dirt, and bugs – and hair – that it had collected during its illegal romp in the park; depositing them all in a neat little pile, right in front of Harry's door.

"It's probably a wad of that damned dog's fur stuck inside my head," Harry thought as he absent-mindedly jammed the tip of his index finger into his head, searching. His attention was focused on the small gap between the bottom of the front door to his apartment and the press-on tiles of his kitchen floor. The door opened directly out to the hallway.

"That's probably how *they* get in," Harry guessed.

Without thinking, he reached for the doorknob.

***

Harry had had the strangest dream. He had been falling through a long dark tunnel, a worm-hole that was lined with an ungodly pattern of acrylic orange carpet. His head had hit something hard.

In his dream, he had seen a sideways version of a bank of elevators, just like the ones at the end of his apartment building hallway. He had heard the distant jingle of metal on metal.

Eventually, a too-tall version of Julia Roberts had been looking down on him with an expression of genuine concern on her face. She had been pulling something out of her pocket in a hurry.

Harry had closed his eyes, sure that she had been reaching for the pepper spray. He had braced himself for the cold wet sting. Pressing his eyelids shut, he had waited.

No wet pepper juice had hit his face. Nothing had burned him. All he had felt was the dry sprinkle of something sandy as a too-big dog had shaken itself over him, depositing its payload of hair, and dirt (and bugs, he had been sure, even in his dream) onto the side of Harry's head.

In the distance, someone had been calling for help.

***

When Harry opened his eyes again, he had been in a hospital bed. He had tried to sit up, but his head had still hurt.

"A dream inside a dream," he thought, and decided to ride it out.

The old familiar itching had returned. Harry had instinctively jabbed his finger at it, only to find that someone had covered the tip of his finger with a clipped-on medical device that was too big to fit inside his ear (a pulse-ox-something-or-other, one of the dream nurses would later call it).

The scratchy irritation in his ear had been just as maddening as when he had felt it in his real-life apartment. He still couldn't reach it.

In the dream within a dream, Harry had looked around for help. He had noticed an uninterested-looking orderly sitting next to the side of his bed. The too-pale too-pudgy redhead had been balancing himself on a chair, rocking himself on the back two legs. The kid had been absent-mindedly turning the air-conditioning unit off and on as he drummed the fingers of his balancing hand against the window-side unit.

Harry had tried to get the orderly's attention, but the kid had seemed mesmerized by a television mounted to the wall, near the ceiling. He had been watching one of those Somebody Somewhere Has Got Some Kind of Talent (Or Something) shows. It had reminded Harry of The Gong Show – and of watching people in the park.

The act of the day on the dream-within-a-dream show had been an amateur magician who had pulled a string of colorful handkerchiefs from his "empty" shirtsleeve, like a string of Tibetan prayer flags. Although probably not a fan of Tantric iconography, or the enlightened mind, the redhead had loved the charade.

For a big finale, the magician had performed a color-changing handkerchief trick. The illusionist had waived a dark blue handkerchief in the air, holding it by one corner. His other hand had been open, to show that it was empty. He had clenched his empty hand into a ball, stuffing the blue cloth into the top of his fist, slowly pulling it back out of the bottom of his hand, and – *prest-o change-o* – the cloth was orange. The orderly had squealed.

Harry knew this trick. It was simple. He had seen it on some Spoil The Magic exposé. The cloth wasn't just a cloth; it was a square bag, blue on the outside, orange on the inside. There was a hole in one corner that allowed the magician turn the bag inside-out.

"Ta-Da," Harry had said, out loud.

The television-watching orderly who had thought that the patient was in some kind of a coma or something, and had never expected him to speak, had tried to stand up too fast, rocking the last two legs of his chair right off the floor. The pudgy dream kid and his seat had tumbled backward, knocking a plug out of the wall.

On The Gong Show substitute, a circus of wannabe pop stars had continued to belt out a clashing mixture of children's songs and Christian spirituals:

THE NECK BONE'S CONNECTED
TO THE SHOULDER BONE...
...WAY UP IN THE MIDDLE OF THE AIR

Harry had hoped that a hook was making its way onto the stage from behind a curtain.

Somewhere in the distance, an alarm was ringing.

***

"Hello, my name is Doctor Heart," the physician in charge had introduced himself. Harry had been sitting on the edge of a cold plastic examination table, which was covered by a too-thin sheet of paper that crinkled too-loudly whenever he moved, no matter how slightly. The paper was stretched across the table from a roll that looked as if it belonged on a kindergarten art easel.

"Doctor Heart," the man in the lab coat had been saying.

"Does this mean that I've had a heart attack," Harry had asked. He remembered hearing a rumor that "Paging Dr. Heart" was a sort of hospital code for "All hands on deck, someone is having a cardiac arrest."

The doctor had laughed.

He was a fairly tall man, sitting on a wheeled stool that had looked far too short to be comfortable for him. His knees had been folded at an awkward angle.

Dr. Heart had pushed his foot against Harry's table, rolling toward an ominous row of medical instruments that were lined up on a metal desk. He had reached for a lighted tube, pressing a plastic cover onto one end.

Dr. Heart had crab-walked his stool back toward Harry, waiving his magic wand as he went. He had roughly pressed one end of the tube against Harry's ear, and had squinted into the other.

"Um-hmm," the doctor had said. "Just as I thought."

Dr. Heart had calmly explained that a bundle of long white hairs had become lodged in Harry's inner ear, irritating his external auditory canal. The doctor had further explained that this blockage could be the source of Harry's recent problems with his balance, "and that nasty spill you took."

"Well, take it out then," Harry had said. The doctor had wrinkled his eyebrows and frowned.

"I'm afraid it's not that simple," he had said. Doctor Heart had explained that, after remaining untreated for so long, the bundle of hair had become "impacted," firmly anchored deep in Harry's inner ear, clogging the labyrinth of semicircular canals behind his eardrum. Harry had shrugged, wishing that he had a Q-Tip.

"Furthermore," the doctor had continued with his expert opinion, a colony of tiny parasites (damned dirty bugs, Harry had thought) were living in Harry's ear; attracted by the oil and dander attached to the foreign hair.

"Oh, Dear God," Harry had thought. "Get them out," he had shouted, a little too loudly for the doctor's liking.

"I'm afraid that it isn't that easy," Doctor Heart continued. "There is more." The colony of parasites had grown, unchecked, for some time. Maybe a month ago a Q-Tip would have worked, but now?

The tiny bastards had multiplied. They had filled Harry's middle ear, cramming against the ossicles, the tiny bones that let Harry hear the world around him. They were filling his Eustachian tube, which connected to his nasal passage. The bugs were pressing against his auditory nerve. They had taken over all of the empty nooks and crannies, and had been forced to look for new places to live.

Harry's eyes had been wide and unmoving as Doctor Heart had explained how the newest generations of parasites were already

383

moving into Harry's brain, swimming in his cerebrospinal fluid and heading toward the cortex. In the same practiced tone with which he had introduced himself, Doctor Heart explained to Harry how this would lead to vivid hallucinations, lucid dreams and, finally, to a complete break with reality.

The doctor had smiled as he carefully removed the used plastic cover from the tip of his scope, and had thrown it toward a "hazardous waste" container, which had been lined with an ominous-looking red plastic bag.

Harry had felt sick. He could feel something scratchy inside his ear as he had begun to slide forward.

"I'm not a fainter," he had thought as he had clumsily reached out, grasping for the edge of the exam table that had raced up past his head. Lying on the cold linoleum floor, next to Doctor Heart's too-big feet, with the walls of the doctor's office fading to black, Harry had pinched himself to wake up from this nightmare.

***

Harry was dizzy; from sitting up too fast, he guessed. His alarm clock had been ringing for God knows how long.

"Where's the fire?" he slurred. "It's not like someone's dying." He swatted at the snooze button, noticing that the mismatched sheets and pillowcases in his familiar apartment bedroom were soaked with sweat.

Harry rolled out of bed and noticed that he was sleeping in his boxers (of course), not a flimsy hospital gown.

"Back again," he thought as he walked to the bathroom. Splashing water on his face, he stared into the mirror, looking for evidence of a bump or a bruise. Not finding any, he smiled. He wondered if he had gingivitis or if, maybe, he should start using a "whitening" brand of toothpaste.

Harry's head felt fuzzy. As he made his way into the living room, he was surprised to see sunlight pouring through the windows. It was the middle of the day (lazy bones).

Harry stood next to his living room window, staring at the light coming through the blinds and, for the first time in (how long?), pushed it open. Sunshine and the muffled sounds of people playing in the park below flooded into his apartment.

Harry leaned out the window, feeling the wind on his face. He saw the Mister Happy ice-cream truck cruising outside of the park across the street. He saw a kite in the distance being tossed around by the breeze.

Harry saw Julia Roberts and her damned Afghan hound crossing the parking lot of his apartment complex, moving away with their backs toward him in the living room window above them; crossing the street, and climbing the small hill at the edge of the park. He was still leaning out of the window.

Something about that sight of his toothy neighbor caused Harry to unconsciously reach for his ear, like he had so many times before. Only, this time, he felt something.

Just the smallest piece of *something* was hooked under the tip of his fingernail.

"That damned lump of dog hair," he hoped.

Harry pulled, slowly, and felt something move. He pulled harder, as hard as he could.

Out of the corner of one eye, Harry saw a yellow square of cloth flapping in the breeze beside his head. The wind picked up, and the yellow square of cloth drifted farther away.

Now, Harry could see that the yellow square of cloth was attached to an orange one, which had not been there a moment ago. Harry could also see that his left foot was collapsing up into his shin.

In fact, as the yellow and orange squares floated still farther away – joined by a growing chain of green ones, and blue ones, and red ones – Harry's shin was drawn up into his knee. Then his whole left leg disappeared up into his hip. The toes of his right foot began to fold inward.

Harry's legless torso hovered in front of his living room window, enjoying the view. Children were playing in the park, and a colorful train of little cloth squares had sprouted from the side of his head, riding the breeze like semaphore flags on an old wooden battleship – or the "circus flag" pennants that were too-often strung up by too many used car salesmen, to advertise their lots.

A green one emerged. A purple one passed by, followed by another orange one. Harry's arms disappeared. His chest was slowly drawn into his strangely floating head. Someone was humming gospel music.

...WAY UP IN THE MIDDLE OF THE AIR

With a final *pop*, the last of the little cloth squares turned inside-out as the wind pulled it out of the window. It was a white one.

The strand of colorful flags was set free, floating above the world.

Down below, on the hill near the park, Julia Roberts shaded her eyes with the palm of her hand, squinting up into the sky, wondering which of the children had lost a kite.

Beside her, the long-haired Afghan hound didn't bother to look up. Jingling away, the damned dog dropped its haunches onto the dirty ground, dipped its head, and scratched its ear.

INBOX
By Brennon ThompSon

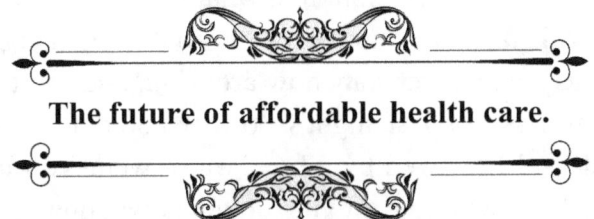

The future of affordable health care.

Brennon ThompSon lives in the Midwest United States, with his wife and cat. Here he spends most of his time thinking up new stories, some of which, he actually writes down. In addition to his many short stories, Brennon is currently working on two novels: One a Bizarro story, of alien invasion set against the backdrop of Reality TV, titled: **Brain Goo**. *The other is titled:* **Touched**, *it is a horror tale about an orderly who has a special touch when it comes to his patients. But in a matter of life and death he makes a mistake and all Hell breaks loose!*

"What the hell do you think you're doing with my arm?!"

"We're removing it sir." He said matter-of-factly.

"What the fuck for?!" Feeling it was my right to know.

"Have to sir."

"Have to?" I repeated, strangely calm.

"Yes sir. You see, we need to get all of you in that box over there."

"See? No!" It was then that I realized that I couldn't see. Well I could, but somehow my vision was all wrong. I didn't see any fucking box! And I said as such: "I don't see any fucking box!" Now less calm.

"Of course not sir. Your eyes have already been wrapped for shipment." I felt him reach across me.

I brought my hand up to my face, probing around like a gorilla with a new butt-plug. Feeling my fingers against the gauze wrappings, I knew that I was in the right place. Straining, I managed to push through the cheese cloth into what felt like the wet asshole of that same gorilla *after* the "not-now-new" butt-plug had been used in earnest. It was strange, yet somehow arousing, and I felt a heating in my loin, that was not last night's pork. I could feel the pressure. Then the release! Followed by a brief warm wetness, running down my skin. My hand was now moving down, down, down. It seemed to float away.

Stainless steel cold shocked all my scenes! "Fuck! Cold!" I protested.

"Yes. Yes. Sorry about that sir. We really should warm the trays."

"Trays? What trays?"

"The tray where your arm is sir."

"My arm? My fucking arm is right here!" I informed him. Lifting my arm, I extended my finger to show him my favorite one. "This is what I think of you!"

"I'm sorry sir. What? What are you trying to do?"

"I'm flipping you off motherfucker! Flying the bird, exposing the monkey, shining the torch, displaying the flag, hoisting the sail, picking you a parsnip!" I could tell from his voice that he was looking right at me, but I could only see black fuzziness. Then his head turned and I was face to face with his fuzzy face, facing me. I stared back feeling like I was gawking through a longishly long, deep, drawn out, elongated tunnel and he was at the other end of it. I couldn't make out any details, and his eyes never met mine. -*Wait! I didn't have eyes. Or did I?*- Instead, his eyes trailed to the left.

"Ah yes of course. Phantom Motor Manipulation and such a nice use of it."

"What in Christ's shit are you talking about?"

"Separation anxiety. It is a side effect of parts removal. The brain does not handle the cleavage or defection well and tries desperately to reconnect. No cause for alarm sir, it will soon fade."

"No cause for alarm?!" Just then everything faded to black.

"None sir."

"And why the hidey-hole-hell-fuck are you doing this?!" I was getting pissed!

"We have to fill the order sir."

"Order? What order?!"

"The order placed by..." He paused. "I am not at liberty to say sir. That information is confidential. Now if you will just be still while I remove your tongue."

"Not bloody likely! You're not gonaahh..."

"That's it sir." I felt the cold pinch of metal on my tongue. "We wouldn't want you to bite your tongue off during shipment, now would we? This will all be over soon."

The pulling on my tongue and the snip, to remove it from my mouth was painless. Then I tasted something like warm oatmeal, with a hint of cinnamon, *that* was less painless. I hate cinnamon!

"I hope that you like the taste of cinnamon sir. I love it myself. I find it helps to have a pleasing taste on your tongue." I could hear the smile in his tone, and it fucking annoyed me. He was pleased with himself! "Almost done sir. Only one last thing left to do."

The sudden high-pitched whine of the motor startled me, and made my ears hurt, but the biting of the rotating teeth into my skull did not. It was a strange and unnerving sensation, feeling my whole skull vibrate from the inside, while this thing chewed at me like a hungry rat from the outside, and not experiencing a bit of pain.

389

Worse still, was the long, slow, cut being made by the saw, all the way around my head and the shock of the cool antiseptic air creeping in, floating around the inside of my skull, before settling on my pink, confused, panic stricken brain.

With a loud crack, the top of my skull was peeled back like a lid, and I could feel the weight of it hanging there, hinged from a bit of tissue. A white light devoured the darkness, sending fiery, hot knives into my brain. The white quickly dulled to a blur, the blur to a shape, the shape to a face... the face of shock. A loud gasp followed, and when the face finally spoke I knew that voice in an instant!

"Oh my!" Waving his hand. "Quick everyone, you must see this." He was grinning now.

Many more heads appeared above me, each grinning and seeming more excited than the last. Taking turns, they all gawked at me. They mumbled and laughed, slapping each other on the back. I listened, but was finding it more and more difficult to concentrate. Everything was starting to feel hollow and slip away. The voices, sounding like whispers under water. I only managed to catch a word here or a phrase there of what they were saying. And what I did manage to decipher, wasn't making any sense.

"Incredible!"

"Fascinating."

"One in a Million."

"I don't believe it!"

"The third Eye."

A man in a black suit peered down at me and grinned. Standing up, he shook the hand of the dark haired man in the white coat, before walking away. The man smiled.

A pair of hands took hold of me (whatever *me* was left) and lifted me up. I could see his smiling face better now, it was broad and toothy. A face I will always remember. "You are very special sir. And because of you, I got a promotion." He nodded his head slightly. "Thank you sir."

Then I felt something like plastic being wrapped tightly around me.

"All finished. All we have to do now sir, is get you organized and you will be ready to go." His voice was distant and muffled, the warbling sounds from it, fighting to find my ears, the last sense left to me. But it too was fading, and in time, I knew it would be gone as well. I listened to the shuffle, thuds, buzzes, and pops, as things were moved and shifted this way and that.

Minutes passed and the sounds stopped. Either that, or I was now deaf. In a flash, the room spun around. In a daze, I could see it all. The room was white with tables of stainless steel gray, lined neatly in rows. On each table was a naked body. And each naked body had a person in a white coat (some of whom I recognized from earlier), attending to him or her. They were dissecting them and removing parts, like kids in science class!

The same smiling face eclipsed my view and then my vision was blocked out by an enormous hand. Next thing I knew, I was looking upwards and the smiling face was gone.

Above me, a large white sheet appeared. It grew larger as it got closer, until the oversized sheet was right against my eye. It was a piece of paper and I had no problem making out the gigantic words with my third eye. They read:

"HAVE A HEART? NEED A HAND? OTTO WILL KEEP AN
EYE OUT FOR YOU."

OTTO'S PARTS STORE
37 WINDY CITY BLVD.
CHICAGO, IL 60603

ATTENION RECIEPENT: Special item enclosed. Additional
charges will apply.

LOSING CONTROL
By R. Scott Steele

Oh, where oh where, can my baby be?

R. Scott Steele is a devoted husband and father of five boys. He is a Renaissance man, whose motto is "Nothing is impossible as long as you are willing to try." This attitude has helped him teach himself how to knit, become a computer programmer, and lose 150 pounds. (Not to mention surviving five boys). He also enjoys riding the bike trails and weekly role-playing games. He is currently working on editing three novels, and hopes to get them edited enough to publish by the time the Mayan calendar runs out. You can find him online at **rscottsteele.wordpress.com**, *or on Twitter as* **@RScottSteele**.

Lightning sparked across the sky, echoing thunder heralding the start of a spring thunderstorm. The sky opened up, sheets of rain washing over the pavement, turning the normally reliable surface slick and treacherous. Sarah slowed the car as she strained to see the road through the downpour.

She was already late. Her boss was sending her to a corporate retreat in the Florida Keys, but there had been another problem at work and she hadn't been able to leave Miami until almost midnight.

A flash of brilliance speared down, blinding her as it struck the small island that anchored the highway. The crash of thunder rocked her Mercedes as she blinked furiously to clear her vision. The noise pummeled her, a deep roar like a lion rudely woken from a nap.

She yelled back, yanking the wheel as a large blur appeared on the highway in front of her. The car spun off the highway and crashed down on the assaulted island. The nose of the car slammed into the wet sand, and the airbag exploded into Sarah.

She woke up slumped over the spent airbag, feeling like she had just been punched in the face. She fumbled at her seatbelt, numb fingers stabbing at the release button several times before it let her go. The door handle was just as uncooperative, but she eventually rolled out of the dead car and into the pouring rain.

She was drenched immediately, her expensive silk blouse and pencil skirt ruined. She crawled across the sand, vague fears about the car blowing up pushing her to get as far away from it as possible. She made it about twenty feet before collapsing, her body betraying her as tremors drained the strength from her bones.

The storm passed as quickly as it had arrived, and the roll of thunder faded as it moved to the north. She rolled over onto her back as the rain stopped.

The lightning was still burned into her retinas, and the last thought her addled brain managed before darkness claimed her was that the golden flash resembled a beautiful, bat-winged dragon.

***

Sarah woke to a soft caress on her forehead. She opened her eyes. A large man was kneeling in the sand next to her, humming a soft tune as he brushed her blonde hair off her face. He was handsome, with short, blond hair, a strong chin, and hypnotic blue eyes. His golden skin glowed with health, muscles rippling with controlled power as his caress moved down to stroke her cheek. His body shone in the moonlight, as if he was covered in glitter, or tiny scales. Sarah blushed when she realized he wasn't wearing any pants.

I must be dreaming, she thought, closing her eyes as his hands slid down her neck. His touch sent sparks of sensual excitement down to her stomach, making her moan with arousal. *I must have passed out from the accident. This can't be real.*

No man had ever made her feel like this before. The last guy she had slept with was so bad she wanted to give him an instruction manual. She had kicked him out and ended the night with the vibrator she used when she couldn't be bothered to find a man to satisfy her needs.

His fingers moved to the buttons on her soaked blouse. Her hands flew up, and her eyes opened wide. "What do you think you're doing?" Her attempt at sitting up was quickly aborted when her head threatened to explode. She lay back down and closed her eyes, her arms crossed over her chest.

He didn't say a word. He just went back to stroking her neck and humming his hypnotic song.

His attention was flattering, but there were lines you shouldn't cross with someone you just met. He had no right to take advantage of her, even if he was the hottest guy she had ever seen, and the brush of his fingers on her neck had the power to make her forget the world.

His hands massaged her neck, relaxing her body despite the fire growing in her belly. She was used to setting the rules and getting what she needed, and the more he touched her, the fewer reasons she had to stop him.

Screw it, she thought. His hands slipped under her collar across the top of her shoulders, and her own fingers started working on the buttons of her blouse, opening her body to the cool night air.

His tune grew louder, capturing her mind in a musical cage. Despite her implied invitation he didn't stray from the safe zone, and Sarah was going crazy with desire. She wanted to grab his hands and put them on her chest. She wanted him to cross the line, even if she had to drag him over it.

She rubbed her breasts, squeezing them until they ached. Her nipples hardened painfully and she arched her back, offering herself to him. His hands moved across the top of her chest, but stopped short, leaving her wanting. She popped the catch on the front of her lacy bra, opening herself to him, and his caress slowly circled in a maddening spiral over her skin. When he finally touched her swollen nubs it was like an electric shock through her body.

Damn, he's good. She slipped her hand down to the catch on the side of her skirt and raised her hips as she pushed the wet material down her legs, taking her panties along with it. The cool air on her damp skin sent a shiver up her spine even as she melted in anticipation. He stopped his maddening touch to help her, and soon her skirt landed with a splat on the damp sand and his hands returned to their work, starting with her toes and moving up her legs.

His touch on her thighs set her core on fire as he sang his strange tune. He was casting a spell over her. She was snared in a musical noose as she let him touch her intimately, possessively. She was trapped in this dream, or fantasy, or whatever it was. She had given him control, and could only wait for him to give her what she needed.

She parted her legs as his head lowered between them, his tongue zeroing in on her sweet spot. She squirmed in willing captivity and pinched her nipple, welcoming the distraction of the pain as she twined the fingers of her other hand through his hair.

She moaned, a wordless testimony of desire. *I can't take it any more.* She pulled him up by his hair, moaning again as the sweet torture stopped. But it was only for a moment. With a quick thrust he was inside her and her brain shut down.

The simple mechanics of the act didn't do justice to the feeling of his hard cock as he stroked in and out, in and out. Each thrust rocked her back into the wet sand, abrading her sensitive skin. But she didn't care. She was lost in sensation, trapped in a world of pleasure, captured by sex.

He pumped faster, driving her to heights of passion, until she couldn't take it any more. She cried out, an animal scream as the world exploded in ecstasy. Her body shook with her climax, and she barely noticed as he shuddered along with her. She wrapped her arms around his neck as his seed pumped deep into her womb.

And then it was over. Without warning, her mysterious lover vanished from her arms, dissolving away like fog over the sea. His brilliant blue eyes were the last to go, gazing deep into her own as he disappeared.

Her eyes closed. It wasn't real. A concussion-induced fantasy. She fell asleep, the hallucinatory tune dancing through her dreams.

***

She woke with a shiver. The moon still lit up the night, and the ocean breeze had chilled her wet clothes. Her head was still sore, but there were none of the pleasant aches of sex, no other footprints in the sand. Only her and the deserted highway. *It was just a dream.*

Three hours later she pulled up to the retreat in a rental car as the sun rose over the Gulf. She told everyone that she went off the road in the storm and tried to forget the rest. But she couldn't relax, and kept dreaming of her golden man and waking up on the verge of orgasm. By the end of the week she was ready to go back to work, just to distract her from the memories of her fantasy encounter.

She threw herself into her job, working late and driving her staff crazy. She had hand-picked her employees, and they had always done well, but now nothing they did satisfied her.

By the end of the month she felt bloated. She ate less and pushed her daily workouts until she dripped with sweat, but she couldn't shake the feeling. Her tailored clothes still fit, but she was convinced she was gaining weight, despite what the scale said. She bought a pregnancy test and it turned out negative, but she still wondered about her island fantasy.

Then she lost feeling in her toes. She ignored it, but it spread to her ankles, and then started on her hands. It took three tries to dial her doctor's number because she couldn't feel her fingers.

Her doctor scheduled an MRI, a CAT scan, even a spinal tap. They ran dozens of tests over the next couple of weeks. By the time they finished Sarah had lost most of the feeling in her arms and legs, but the doctors couldn't find anything wrong.

Her reflexes were fine. She could still move her limbs, but she couldn't feel them. It was like she was wearing a heavy coat, cutting her off from the outside world. And the pregnant feeling was worse. She felt confined in her own body, as if it was a size too small.

She had to take a medical leave of absence, but the enforced isolation was driving her crazy. She worried about losing her job, and kept calling her office trying to stay connected.

She also spent a lot of time on the Internet, searching for something that might tell her what was happening. Since the doctors didn't have an answer for her she was determined to find one on her own. But she couldn't find anything. There were a lot of things that could cause numbness, but none of them quite matched her symptoms.

The loss of feeling grew worse, spreading to her torso. Her hands and legs began to twitch spasmodically, until she wanted to tie them down. She started waking up in a different room from where she had gone to sleep, feeling like she had just interrupted something.

It was maddening. She was losing control. Her life had always been in order, and now it had turned to chaos.

***

One day she woke up in the kitchen, with an empty plate in front of her and the taste of peanut butter in her mouth. *Maybe I should call a psychiatrist*, she thought. *If there isn't anything wrong with my body then there must be something wrong with my head, right?*

"Wrong."

She was shocked. The voice was hers. The word came from her

mouth. But she hadn't said it.

"No, you didn't. It was me."

I've had a psychotic break, she thought. *I have a split personality and I'm going insane.*

"You're not insane." The voice mocked her with its comforting familiarity even as it tore her world apart.

Her mouth was talking without any contribution from her. Sarah felt like she was teetering on the edge of a razor thin line, about to fall into the abyss. *What the hell is going on here?* She wanted to speak, but her rebellious mouth wouldn't respond. At least, not for her.

"You are about to be a mother." Her voice was excited, like someone going to a party.

Sarah strained to speak, but nothing came out. She tried to cover her mouth with her hand, but nothing worked. She couldn't move a muscle.

But something else could. Her body walked to stand in front of the bathroom mirror. Sarah was faced with her own familiar image, but now it was alien. It had been stolen away from her.

Who are you? What do you want? Sarah was losing it, frantic as she struggled against whatever had hijacked her body.

"I am your daughter." Her face smiled, but the gentle expression looked like the grin of a psychopath to Sarah.

I don't understand. I haven't had sex with anyone!

"No one?" A memory came, unbidden, of a stormy night, with the waves pounding against the small island with the same rhythm as the radiant man thrusting into her.

"It wasn't a dream. My father's spirit left his seed inside you, and soon I will be born."

Sarah wanted to shut out the words. To put her hands over her ears to keep from hearing them. To scream at the top of her lungs to drown them out. But she couldn't do anything. She had lost control of her life, her body, her voice, even her mind. She couldn't even cry.

Sarah watched helplessly as her body calmly picked up her keys and climbed into the car. They drove south, taking the same route that Sarah had driven that fateful night. There was almost no traffic this late in the season, and they arrived at the tiny islet shortly after dark.

Sarah would never have been able to tell which of the little islands had been the one, but her daughter knew, and pulled off the road without hesitation. They got out of the car and walked down to the shore, stripping off their dress as they went.

They stood naked on the edge of the tiny beach. Sarah could no longer feel anything. She could only imagine the soft give of the sand under her feet, the stifling warmth of the moisture in the air, the tangy scent of the salt in the ocean breeze. She just felt dead.

No matter how hard she tried, she couldn't move a muscle. Her prison was her own body, and her jailer was no longer speaking to her. She was forced to stand there, helpless and alone, waiting in the dark.

Sarah tried desperately to regain control, mentally yelling useless threats, then reasoning with her captor, finally pleading desperately, promising anything in her power if it would release her. But her daughter ignored her, standing in silence and gazing out over the waves.

As the moon rose to a point directly overhead, the moment they had been waiting for arrived.

"It is time."

A wave of pain washed over Sarah. More intense than anything she had ever felt, it wracked her entire being with agony. It went beyond physical pain, excruciating torment that rivaled the tortures of hell, agonizing to her very soul.

Another blast of anguish smashed into her, and another, and another. She was being squeezed, crushed within her own body. Her world went black as she felt her mind being forced out of her own head, smashing her soul down into her chest. The pain pounded at her spirit, compressing her into a tight ball. The contractions came faster and faster, until she could take no more and cried soundlessly at heaven to make it stop.

And it did.

The pain was gone. Sarah was free.

She stumbled forward, as if she had been leaning against a door that had opened without warning. She cried out, exalting in the sound of her voice once again under her own control.

Her joy stopped short at a sound behind her. A cacophony of disturbing pops, like someone cracking their knuckles. She turned around, terrified. She didn't want to know what was happening, but was too afraid not to look.

A nude woman was standing on the edge of the shore, waves lapping at her feet. She was giving off a soft golden glow, and undergoing a terrifying metamorphosis.

Her arms stretched out, hands curving into talons, tips ending in razor-sharp claws. Her legs thickened and bent, the graceful limbs twisting into something powerful and feral. Her shoulders shrugged, a set of bat-like wings peeling free from her back with a wet tearing sound, shining as they stretched across the moonlit sky. Her face elongated, chin and nose jutting forward, teeth extending into fangs. Thick horns sprouted just above her ears, curving forward over her skull and ending in wicked points. And finally, gleaming golden scales sprouted all over her body, replacing the supple skin with cold, metallic armor.

Sarah screamed, but it was drowned out by the carnal roar from the beast the woman had become. The transformation was complete. The golden dragon looked down at her, fangs gleaming in a grotesque smile.

"Thank you mother," it said, in a voice reminiscent of Sarah's own. "This body will serve me well."

The manners her own mother had taught her came by reflex. "You're welcome," she said, voice trembling. Could her nightmare be over? "Can I go home now?" she asked with a glimmer of hope.

The dragon chuckled, a low sound punctuated by wisps of smoke leaking from its scaly lips. "I'm sorry. Don't you realize what has happened?"

The tender words were crushing. She looked down, wondering if she would have a chance if she tried to run. At first she didn't understand what she was looking at, then everything crashed into place as Sarah knew that there was no hope of going back to her old life.

Sarah's disembodied spirit was standing on the water.

"I need energy to stay in this world. The last thing you must give me, dear mother, is your soul."

Nobody heard Sarah's last scream as the dragon's teeth came down.

Erotica

ONE HELL OF A BAND

By J. T. Seate

It takes the right kind of groupies to get the load out.

*No matter how **Mr. Seate** starts a story, it inevitably turns to the macabre. It may be told with hard-core realism or erotic humor, but it gets his pulse racing enough to pull him from the grave to write something new. He is especially keen on stories that transcend genre pigeonholing. His stories and memoirs appear in numerous magazines, newspapers, anthologies and webzines.*

*You will find many of his works at **www.troyseateauthor.webs.com** and on amazon.com. J. T. currently reposes in Golden, CO.*

The Crimson Cowboys never sang before sunset. Their music was filled with dark words and sensual licks. The band had tapped into a disenfranchised collection of music lovers. It didn't hurt that their metal was heavier than any other country and western group. Listening to their concerts were many kinds of faces, each with a pair of hands, always moving. A thousand eyes were on them and hopeful smiles curved the mouths of the females.

Their followers had invented a hand symbol—a raised fist with the fingers curled over the thumb. The first and fourth fingers protruded forward just enough to symbolize canine teeth. To the beat of the songs, the fists bent like the strike of a snake. Whatever symbols and songs the eclectic mob took to their bosom was fine with the band.

They rocked and rolled and crooned, and even destroyed an instrument now and then. Wherever they appeared, they could count on a cluster-fuck of Goths, cowgirls, and biker-type chicks who toked on doobies, did liquor and stronger drugs, and cut themselves—a nice, schizophrenic mix that guaranteed a lot of exposed breasts and a broad selection of hot-pants at the after-parties.

The band members had long flowing hair and wore modified C&W band garb—black ten-gallon hats, mirrored shades, crimson-red shirts, blue jeans and shit-kickers. They played a few country standards such as "All my Exes died in Texas," "I've got Friends in Cold Places," "Even Vampires get the Blues," and "Looking for Blood in all the Wrong Places." But most of their music was original. "Bloodlust Country," some called it. Their fans would tell you they put on a hell of a show and always clamored for more of the Cowboys.

Kane was the band's leader. It was his dark vision and his musical genius that had made the Crimson Cowboys what they were—a red-hot, country-western vampire band. For Kane, the lead guitarist, it was always night. He was a bit of a risk, being blind and a spaz, but he could lay down riffs and hot licks that charmed many of their following right out of their panties. His long thumbnail served as his guitar pick and he was most calm when he was picking and singing. His shortcomings didn't seem to matter then.

During their intermissions, while a canned cacophony of sounds rattled though the concert hall, there was any number of girls waved backstage by security who were happy to suck the band members' dicks. The Cowboys made a point of restricting the antics to that

405

activity even though the hunger was always there. Keep things clean and neat, until later.

Then they would ramble out for their second set. A session drummer pounded the skins and the band jumped in. The Cowboys always ended their concerts with their classic, "Chug Another Beer then Blow Me." When they came to their final refrain, of "Momma, just chug another beer," repeated three times, the four musicians pulled their cocks out of their blue jeans, and finished the song with a screaming, "And blow me!"

A cheer went up and bodies moved haphazardly, repeating the final stanza along with the band. The crowd roared and hooted. They cried, they screamed, they jumped up and down in apparent rapture—young, old, drunk, and sober. It was an event to encourage unfettered pagan fun and frivolity. Fans screamed wildly with the joy of their own liberation as well as the band's dangling organs.

When the bright lights and colors dimmed, and the multitude began to disperse, it was time to get down and dirty. Badass bouncers assured the Cowboys' escape. They shuffled the band through to their idling, customized motor coach detailed with heavy drapes. Soon a smaller, but no less passionate crowd formed on one side of the mobile hotel. Slick, the fiddle player, was in charge of chick procurement. He popped open a soda, licked his lips and scanned the crowd.

He pointed at a group of four similarly dressed, well-appointed girls who were abundant with superficial attractions in all the right places. He motioned for them to come to the bus's door. They grinned, looked at each other then made their way through the crowd. Rock helped them up the steps while the Cowboys' driver held back the rest of the wannabes.

The giggling girls were ushered past Slick and Rock to where Kane and Animal were drinking soda pops. A blonde dressed in fishnet, black lace, and an ass-twitching leather skirt identified herself as Tish. A brunette, dressed from head to toe in a bright pink ensemble so tight it looked like it had been sprayed on was called,

Candy. There was also a redhead named Stormy. Her top was a dazzling floral, see-through that blended her large nipples into the pattern just enough to avoid an X-rating. The fourth girl's most outstanding feature was her long hair, the color of unfinished oak, that fell to her cute-ass miniskirt. Her name was Honey. Slick had selected well. All four girls were brutally hot and they knew it.

A great thing about celebrity was that you could be dog-shit ugly like Alice Cooper, or have leathery crags like The Stones, but the hottest little tits on the planet would line up to fuck you like you were spiritual guides into the party world.

"You ladies ready to party?" Animal asked with a cockeyed grin.

"Oh, hell yes. Our motto is 'keep in shape, have a blast, die anyway,'" said Tish.

"Not necessarily," Rock said.

The girls took inventory of the interior. "This is downright decadent," Honey said.

"Thanks," Slick answered. "Do you all love the Cowboys?"

"Let me show you how much," Candy said. She unzipped her leather top. A red and blue tattoo adorned her left breast, the letters CC intertwined inside a heart. The Cowboys whooped. Slick bent over and laid a sloppy kiss on Candy's symbol of devotion.

"What the fuck's she got?" Kane asked.

"Candy here's got our initials tattooed on her tit," Animal told him. "Our kinda girl."

"Fuckin' A," Kane agreed.

"You girls want a snort? A little toot? What?"

"We're up for anything," the redhead replied. "We've dreamed about getting in the Cowboy wagon. We just want to experience you guys."

"Want to be a part of the legend, huh?"

"Un huh," they answered in unison. "We know what you're all about. The rough stuff, I mean."

"Whoa, darlin'," Rock, the bass guitar player, said. "We might leave a few bruises, but in all the right places, that's all."

407

The girls looked at each other. "Cool," Tish said.

"Then let's get the show on the road. Hey, Billings," Rock called to the driver. "Time to get this pile of tin outta here."

Gears shifted and the bus began to move.

"Better get high, ladies. It might make our party go a little smoother," Slick advised. As the custom-made motor coach moved slowly away from the auditorium, muffled shouts and the sound of fists against the bus could be heard. "Don't worry about your wheels. We'll ride for a while then we'll bring you back," Rock told the girls.

"God, I can't believe we're actually with the Cowboys," Stormy gushed.

"Believe it," Kane said.

The bus rumbled out of the parking lot and onto the dark city streets. Like most bands, the Crimson Cowboys had their assortment of drugs and booze. But what really got them off was blood—the crimson elixir that kept them going. That's where all the groupies came in. If you partied with the Cowboys, expect to get bitten.

The girls slipped out of their clothes like snakes shedding skin then sat on the Cowboys' laps and allowed the musicians' hands to get acquainted with their bodies. Free of their leathers, lace and thongs, the groupies were on their knees in less time than it took to belt out a tune.

"It's awesome when you guys pull out your dicks onstage," Honey said while Animal pulled off his jeans so she could have a closer look. "How come you don't get busted?"

"We got a deal going. Everyone and everything has a price," he told her.

"Oh." She looked at Animal's cock up close. "Ohhhh, gee. You've got a big one. Is this why they call you Animal?"

"Start sucking it and I'll show you."

"Drop our jeans and socks, and grab hold of our cocks," Rock chimed in.

A Cowboys song called, "My Lovin' left with the Dawn," boomed through the bus at a decibel level that discouraged conversation. Kane's guitar led into his bass vocal.

"Oh, Kane. That's one of my favorites," Stormy said, then went back to work on his thick, slick shaft.

"Mine too, darlin'. Let me feel what you look like." He ran his palms over her face and then reached down further to feel her breasts. Her image burned through his hands to his dead eyeballs and into his brain. He grinned at the vision and unsnapped his shirt. His chest was wide and hard, covered with a thick mat of dark hair that trailed down his stomach and disappeared into the waistband of his jeans. "Come and get it," he said.

Stormy lowered her face to Kane's chest and dragged her mouth slowly down his belly. She set upon the task of freeing his penis. Her tongue found its tip, shooting heat through his veins.

The alcohol and drugs were having their affect. In a semi-circle of plush chairs, all four girls took to their assignment with gusto. Not only did they take the Cowboys' cocks down their throats, they ran them between their lips and gums, manipulating them as if they were cheek implants.

While the girls worked them, the Cowboys sang a ragged chorus of "Chug another Beer then Blow Me" with their ten-gallon hats and sunglasses still in place.

The suck-fest continued until Rock complained to Candy, "Easy, baby. My rod will only bend down so far."

"Oh, am I hurting you?" she stopped to say.

"That's actually one part of us that can be damaged. Sort of our Achilles Heel."

She looked at the thick, slick dick she was holding. "How about if I sit on it instead?"

"Yeah, ride the pony." He grabbed Candy by her armpits and lifted her onto his boner. "It's our turn now ladies. We'll swallow first."

That pronouncement was a signal to the other three guys. They pulled their girls' mouths off of their pricks. Slick lifted Tish from the floor and pulled her breasts against him. Crunch. His teeth bit into the soft flesh of her neck. Blood flowed over his upper lip as his mouth suckled at her throat. Tish gasped once and rested the weight of her body against his, surrendering to his thirst.

After a few moments of tonsil hockey, Animal did the same to Honey. Kane, being a bit of a spastic, jutted his jaw against Stormy's shoulder. He couldn't find the exact spot he desired on her neck. Instead he traced the underside of a large breast with his thumbnail and made an incision. "Let me drink," he instructed her.

She lifted the sliced, pendulous tit over his parted lips. While he imbibed on her crimson flow, he strummed her ass and corded her back like a human guitar. A dark pink shade stained the teeth of all four musicians while they dined on blood. The girls occasionally winced or moaned as the transfusions took place. Their throbbing hearts forced their blood, hot and thick, more rapidly through their veins. The Cowboys' hunger came with the fierceness of a special kind of caress, touching their deepest instincts, igniting a response as involuntary as the pounding in their loins.

Rock lifted his mouth from Candy's neck without losing a drop of her most precious elixir and licked his lips. "That takes the edge off, doesn't it, boys?" he intoned in a reverent voice.

"Ahhhh. America, the land of opportunity," Slick answered. "Where the buffalo roam and the hottest little cowgirls and punkies come out to play."

Candy managed to smile at Rock, not at all sure she wanted to be bitten again. She needn't have worried. The Cowboys never took too much. They didn't want to kill their groupies or take their souls. They just wanted some blood and ass.

"Now let's give these little fillies more of what they came for," Kane said.

"Amen to that," Animal answered.

While the bloodmobile continued its leisurely journey around the outskirts of the city, Rock got up, walked to the john, and came back with disinfectant, medical gauze, and tape. As the steel guitar player and onboard *medico*, he patched the girls' wounds and served them a round of whatever they'd chosen before to help dull their pain.

With their primary hunger satiated, the Cowboys returned to their secondary desire. This time, Slick partnered with Stormy and her taped tittie. Animal grabbed hold of Tish by her blonde, short curlies. Rock had designs on Honey, and Kane happily accepted Candy.

In the back of the bus, beyond the lounging area, was the bathroom, a kitchenette with two fridges—one for food and one for the boys' frozen specialty drink—and four sleeping compartments, but the hot-to-trot eight-some didn't make it that far.

The Cowboys tossed their headgear and removed their wraparounds. All four sets of eyes were the same—pinkish white around fiery red, piercing pupils. Even Kane's blind gaze burned crimson.

Animal admired the pink petals of Tish's vaginal lips. His tongue and lips turned hard. He gobbled at her rosebud mound then found the little man in the canoe. She trembled in exaltation and begged him not to stop.

Kane lifted one of Honey's feet off the floor. "I promise not to bite off your toes," he told her. In addition to lead guitar, he played a mean harmonica. He worked her piggies back and forth between his lips like he was running the scale.

He accidentally brought a little blood from her pinky toe, but it was Kane, the Crimson Cowboy, after all. "You want to play the other one?" she asked.

He returned her foot to the floor and pushed his cock into her love canal instead, like a hand slipping into a velvet glove. "I'd rather strum your cunt."

Individual proclivities were cool as long as the end result was red rather than dead. The Cowboys always appreciated a little initiative on a girl's part. They were especially happy to oblige any chick who could handle all four of them at once—one in the front, one in the back, and two in her mouth. That achievement would garnish more reward than just a group photo.

The music wailed as the sex continued. Four fannies bounced irregularly as each Cowboy and his partner had sex to the beat of his own drum. They played women like they played their instruments— long and hard. The spent semen they shot into their condoms was almost as red as their eyes. A couple of the girls cried out in rapacious glee at the strength and voracity of their masters' probing, insatiable cocks.

"We're back, boss," Billings called from the dark recesses of the driver's seat.

"That's it ladies," Slick announced. "Time to get your cute little asses dressed and outta here."

"Can we get autographs?" Stormy asked while looking for her top.

"Sure you can," Rock told her. Glossy 8x10s with pre-printed signatures appeared.

Tish took them. "Can't we at least get an original signature?"

"C'mere, girl," Animal said. He found a Sharpie and signed his name on her bare ass, next to where he'd bitten her. The other three decided they wanted the same thing, so the other Cowboys signed their bite marks as well.

"I think all of us should get a permanent reminder to commemorate the evening," Honey squeaked. "Get the name of our favorite blood-sucking band member tattooed over our wounds in tribute to this fabulous night."

"Once a blood-sucked groupie, always a blood-sucked groupie," Kane said.

It was getting early. The horizon would be losing its darkness soon. "All ashore," Billings called to the girls.

Honey wiggled to the front of the bus. "Don't open the door just yet. We have something for you as well," she told the driver. She reached over and placed her hands on the sides of his head. Her breasts dangled in his face for a moment. With a lightning quick move, she twisted Billing's neck. The pop could be heard all the way in the back of the cabin.

Animal saw Billings slumped over the wheel. "What the fuck? Open up so these broads can take off," he ordered.

Honey strolled into the lounge. "He won't be opening up. And I'm afraid we won't be leaving either."

"What in—"

"You picked the wrong bushel of titties tonight, cowboy."

Before the satiated Cowboys could protest too much, the girls were on all four of them like magnets as they turned into what they truly were—lustful succubi from Hell. They ripped open the throats of the Cowboys, tearing past vocal chords and muscle, twisting their necks until the four heads pulled free.

While blood spurted, the foursome held the mementos aloft in victory. "They were easy pickings, full of blood and emptied of their love juice," Stormy said victoriously.

"Guess it never occurred to them that someone might be looking for a little more than their peckers and a nibble," Tish added.

"We did what the master told us, so now it's our turn to rock the music world," Candy said.

"You go, girl," Honey said gleefully. "The Four Brimstones can play like hell. And we have better curves and better voices than these guys."

"We've only just begun," Stormy sang. She rubbed her hands along her arms. "Let's get some clothes on. I'm fucking freezing my tits off."

Tish drove the bus while the others dismembered the bodies. When they were finished, they observed the pile of not-so-human flesh and mockingly flashed the Cowboys' hand gesture. By the time the girls finished tossing body parts along the highway, the Cowboy flesh would be shriveled by the sun to the point where it could pass for deadwood. Bloodsuckers' remains didn't hold up well.

In the distance, a teasing palette of pastels signaled the approaching dawn. The captivating devil's imps planned to drive the bus to Mexico where it would be painted and rechristened "The Brimstone Express." Perhaps the master would drop in and play a lick with the hot, new band now and then. The girls preferred to run their own show, however. The master could be such a grouch, no matter how much he was accommodated.

LESTER'S OMINOUS GIFT

By Eva Hore

**There's nothing like a holiday in the country
to get the old juices flowing**

*Erotica writer **Eva Hore** has been published worldwide. Her work is seen in magazines such as **Hustler, Forum, Desire, Penthouse, Newcummers, Leg Sex, XL Magazine, Naughty Neighbors, Scared Naked Magazine, For Women, Adult Spy FRM, Playgirl, In the Buff, Hot Spot, Grass Roots** and **Swank Magazine**.*

Slamming on the brakes I cursed as I missed the turn off. Reversing quickly, the car fishtailed before I turned sharply and headed down the winding track, surrounded on all sides by flowering gums and eucalyptus trees. Lowering the automatic window I breathed in the wonderfully fresh air. The wind had picked up, tossing the leaves wildly, swirling them through the air before lashing out at my windshield.

I hoped Mary had informed the caretaker I was coming. The last thing I needed was to be bothered and the old guy, Lester, was creepy. I'd been up here once before, many years ago, while my husband was still alive. We'd come up for a romantic weekend but Lester bothered me so much we only lasted one night.

Now as the old shack loomed before me I wondered why I allowed my sister-in-law Mary to talk me into this. She said they'd done it up, that it had a homey appearance now, with a manicured and flower-filled garden that would cheer me up, would make me forget all of my problems.

My mouth dropped open as I broke through the clearing. There seemed to have been no work done at all on the outside of the shack, and the garden was overgrown with weeds. The lawn, if there was one, was buried under a mass of old car parts, weeds and rubbish.

Pulling up at the porch steps I hesitated. With the motor running I debated whether to turn around and go back but suddenly there in the rear view mirror was an ugly face, a face I'd hoped had changed, had somehow become less sinister, but alas that was not to be. If anything Lester looked uglier, scarier.

His face was deathly white with a tinge of grey. Eyes yellowed with blackened pupils that recessed so far back into his skull they were almost insignificant. His lips too were a stony grey, the color continuing down his neck into his probably equally revolting torso.

I shuddered, sickened by him. He seemed almost skeleton, his grey flesh hanging off his face.

My heart began to pound as suddenly loud splats of rain hit the roof of the car. My eyes were still locked on him and he smiled, a smile that showed his rotting teeth but did not reach his yellowed eyes. He shuffled over to my door in his baggy clothes, opened it and turned off the ignition.

"Nice to see you again," he chuckled.

Instinct told me to push him away, slam the door shut and take off, drive anywhere, be anywhere but here. Instead, I allowed his leathery old skin to touch my elbow as he guided me out. His flesh was reptilian, cold and crinkled. He had a hypnotic way about him; once he touched you it was as though his will became your own.

"Hi Lester," I whispered, trying hard not to show my revulsion.

416

"I've collected firewood and taken the liberty of stocking the fridge. Mary told me you were coming," the words whistling through the remainder of his teeth. "I've even left you a small basket of goodies, something to keep you amused," his chuckle had the hair on the back of my neck prickling with fear.

He popped the boot and retrieved my suitcase, carrying it effortlessly up the steps. He reminded me of an Auschwitz survivor, all skin and bones under his clothing. Considering his size he appeared quite strong and kicked open the door, to peer over his shoulder and, with a nod, beckoned me to enter.

I climbed the steps on shaky legs, terrified and yet unable to take my eyes from him. His clothes had a smell of rusty iron, like old blood and as I passed him the distinct odor of feces and urine assaulted my senses. I circled him, not wanting to contaminate myself with his scent and found myself in the lounge room.

The carpet was still the same and the dark furniture old and dusty. Why had Mary told me she'd renovated when clearly she hadn't? The slamming of the front door had me practically jumping out of my skin. I turned to see my suitcase standing by the door and hurried to peek out of the window, just in time to see Lester shuffling off, but as he did he stared back at me as though knowing I'd be looking after him.

What was I doing here, every instinct told me to go? My sixth sense screamed at me, "Leave before it's too late!" I pulled back, away from his lecherous stare and leaned against the wall trying to hold on to my emotions.

Locking the door I breathed a sigh of relief. I went from room to room, checking that all windows were locked and the house was secure. I was pleased to find both the bathroom and one of the bedrooms had indeed been fitted out luxuriously. A large spa and shower had been installed, as well as indoor plumbing. Thank God, for that. I'd almost forgotten about having to go out to the toilet the last time we were here.

I shuddered, remembering how whilst I was emptying my bowels, Lester had taken it upon himself to change the pan. How long he'd been out there, watching and listening, I did not know but I did know that he'd had the small door open for quite a while, catching me right in the middle of straining downwards.

It was the last straw for me. I had demanded John take me home but he just laughed it off, told me I was over-reacting. John had a way about him where he could only see the good in people. And one year, when they'd been younger, Mary had fallen into the lake. It had been Lester who'd saved her and the family had been grateful ever since.

And ever since they'd shared a special bond. You'd see them whispering together, laughing at what I couldn't imagine. Mary I'd always thought a bit strange too. She also was quite pale with darkened eyes, her pallor more accentuated by her long, stringy hair, which she insisted leaving loose.

Making him the caretaker had been Mary's idea. She said she felt secure with him around. Funny, how we differed on our views of him. I decided that perhaps I had over-reacted and I should give Lester a chance to prove himself to me too, after all it wasn't his fault he'd been born ugly.

I threw my suitcase onto the bed and began storing things away. The boom of distant thunder had me back in the lounge, lighting the kindle that Lester had so thoughtfully placed in the hearth. As the fire blazed to life lightning flashed and the rain began to fall at a steady pace.

With the room warm and the fire glowing, the eeriness of the old shack became more rustic. I lit some candles and headed off to fill the spa. As the water filled the tub, I pulled out my favorite pair of satin pajamas, threw some bath bombs in the water and padded to the kitchen to inspect the fridge.

True to his word, Lester had it stocked not only with food but bottles of expensive chardonnay as well. Pouring myself a large drink I carried the glass to the bathroom and stripped out of my clothes. Easing my tired body into the warm water I hit the jets, sculled half the contents and leaned back to relax. The wine warmed my insides while the water soothed my tired body.

A powerful crack of thunder jolted me awake. I must have nodded off. The water was cooling and I had the unnerving sensation that I was being watched. Glancing towards the window I was sure to see Lester's hideous face staring back at me, but thankfully he was not there.

Rising from the water I caught a glimpse of myself as I grabbed for the towel. Not bad for a forty-six year old. I'd had two children and my body showed no signs of stretch marks or cellulite. I'd been lucky. My breasts were full and my body toned from hours of exercising. After John's death I took refuge at the gym, exhausting myself to forget my loneliness.

Just before wrapping the towel around me I stared hard at my body. A cool breeze passed me and it was as though icy fingers tweaked my nipples and ran over my mound. My nipples stood rigid as I broke out in goose bumps. I gasped, securing the towel and hurrying back to the bedroom to dress.

The fire had the shack at a comfortable temperature. Filling a plate with cheeses, dry biscuits and fruit, I grabbed the bottle of wine and, placing everything I needed on a tray, carried it to the low coffee table where some magazines were neatly stacked.

Picking at the light meal I drank more wine, pleased with the inner glow I was feeling and the peace that came with it. I hadn't noticed before but there, on a side table, was a basket. Must have been the one that Lester had spoken about...

Placing it on the couch beside me I began to unwrap the parcels stacked inside it. You can imagine my horror when I uncovered a large black dildo, a packet of condoms, love beads, anal probes and an assortment of sexual enhancers.

What had he said? Something to keep me amused... I scanned the room expecting to see him standing there but fortunately I was still alone.

What on earth had Lester been thinking? The thought of his disgustingly stained fingers wrapping these gifts had me rushing to the bathroom to wash my hands. When I returned the basket was back on the side table. I was sure I'd left it on the couch. I couldn't remember moving it. I decided I was tired and perhaps I'd drunk too much wine and that was why I couldn't remember.

With the rain falling steadily I decided to take a nap. That was what I'd come here for. Since John's death, four months earlier, I'd had so little peace. There'd been so much to do. John's export business was booming and I had to learn very quickly all the ins and outs of it until one day last week where I'd collapsed on the floor.

My children and Mary had decided I needed this break. There were no phones, no passing traffic, nothing but peace and quiet. Taking my glass I headed off to the bedroom, pulled back the doona and slipped between the sheets. I fell asleep almost instantly.

My subconscious was dreaming. Erotic images of men and women fucking and sucking each other had my hand stealing its way between my thighs. Mary's face suddenly loomed before me as her fingers tore at the buttons of my pajama top, ripping it wide open.

I lay there staring up at her. She was dressed in a long robe which she shucked from her shoulders. It dropped to the floor and she stood there naked before me, her body almost waif-like, her bones protruding through taut white flesh...

Her breath was warm on my breasts as she lay upon me, suckling me like a child. I moaned in my sleep, enjoying what I obviously was craving in my real life: The touch of another person. Somehow she managed to remove the pants and was snuggling in between my thighs, her hot tongue lapping at my slit, licking down to my puckered hole before flicking amongst the folds to tantalize my clit.

All around the bed were strangers, standing there in their long robes watching. Lester too was there, sitting high on a throne with two naked women at his feet. Even in my sleep I sensed revulsion of him but couldn't tear my emotions away from what Mary was doing, loving every second of it.

I squirmed back into the bed, my legs falling further apart as she nuzzled in, parting the folds to lavish me with attention. My silky juices began to ooze and my clit throbbed, begging to be rubbed, to bring me to a climax I hadn't had for so long.

Her hands kneaded my breasts, her long fingers tugging the nipples, drawing them out. Oh, how wonderful it all felt and soon I was coming, exploding into her mouth, my sweet nectar gushing from me to pool onto the sheets.

I stared fleetingly at the people surrounding my bed. They seemed to be whispering something, chanting, and Lester, one hand on each of the women's breasts, was leaning forward, spittle drooling from his mouth.

Something was tugging at my subconscious as she rammed a strap-on dildo into my saturated cunt. She slammed into me. I caressed my own breasts before pulling the hood back from my clit and rubbing it crazily as she continued to fuck me. Her voice was loud and edgy, demanding of me, commanding me to lift my legs, to drop them further apart, to rub harder, faster until I was screaming in ecstasy, coming over and over again, only to fall back into the pillows, exhausted and sated.

I wanted to wake but couldn't open my eyes. It was as though I was drugged and I let go of the feeling and allowed myself to sink further into a deep and much needed sleep.

A shaft of light, creeping from the split in the drapes knocked at my eyelids. I knew I should get up, see about dinner, but I was still glowing in the aftermath of that wonderful dream. I'd never dreamt of having a woman make love to me, and why Mary, why not someone more, more sexually appealing? I wanted desperately to go back there, in my dreams, and relive that powerful orgasm but the growling of my stomach reminded me of how hungry I was.

Still feeling groggy I threw off the doona and pulled back alarmed.

I was naked.

Hugging the doona to me I thought back to my arrival. My head pounded as I tried to remember just how much wine I'd drunk. Surely no more than three quarters of the bottle. I certainly never opened another. What had happened to my pajamas? I peered about the room but couldn't see them.

Enfolding the doona to me I cautiously left my room. The fire still burned brightly in the hearth. The rain had stopped and a faint rainbow of light broke through the window. I walked quietly into the kitchen. It was spick and span. Nothing out of place. I opened the fridge door and there in the shelf was the nearly empty bottle.

What was going on? Had I removed the pajamas myself?

Deciding I would accomplish nothing by staring blankly at my surroundings I made my way to the bathroom, turned on the shower and adjusted the water temperate before stepping into the cubicle. My hands ran over my body and down between my thighs. There had certainly been some sort of sexual activity going on down there. The lips were swollen and sensitive. I inserted a finger and sure enough I was wet.

Remembering the dream had me feeling horny. My nipples became rigid as my memory gave me flashes of Mary between my thighs, her hot tongue probing me, her fingers groping and caressing my flesh. I pulled the hood back over my clit and noted the nub was swollen.

I began to rub and very quickly my desire built up. I leaned against the shower wall, lifted a leg and placed my foot flat against the tiles and began to rub vigorously as sharp stabs of water from the jets pounded onto my sensitized clit.

Within seconds I was coming, gasping for air as the convulsions overtook. That was what was wrong with me. I needed sex, lots of sex and if I couldn't have it then I'd have to pleasure myself. The thought of that black dildo, slamming into my pussy had me coming again, until my legs shook and I realized the water was begging to cool.

Drying myself quickly and with my head now cleared I dressed in warm clothes, made myself a hearty breakfast of scrambled eggs and bacon and then set off for an early morning walk.

Two hours later, my mind alert and my body invigorated. I rustled up a light salad and stoked up the fire, enjoying a glass of red wine whilst eating. Sitting at the dining table, my eyes roamed the walls, floors and windows. Everything was in order and yet I still had that uncomfortable feeling as though someone was watching me.

Rummaging through my bag I pulled out my latest novel and settled on the couch to read. My mind was drifting, my thoughts erratic until finally I lowered the book. Something was nagging at me. What? My eyes spied the basket and I pulled it towards me.

On inspection I found one dildo, a black strap-on like the one in my dream, condoms, an anal probe, nipple clamps and an assortment of other paraphernalia. What was it all doing in here? Surely Lester hadn't left this for me. Why would he? I shuddered as I placed the basket back on the table and as I did I noticed something shiny lying on the floor.

It was a condom packet. The condom was still inside, as though someone had changed their mind. I dropped it back in the basket, pushing it away with my foot. Images, like snippets from a movie crowded my sight. Lester, the two women, the people chanting around my bed... Surely it had all been a dream, what else could it have meant? The blazing fire had my eyes drooping and my head lolling back on the couch. Within minutes I was sleeping peacefully.

Intuitively I knew something was amiss. I tried to open my eyes but the lids were too heavy. A cool breeze kissed my body alerting me to the fact that I was cold. Had the fire gone out I wondered? Eventually, my eyelids fluttered open. I looked down to find myself naked once again, only this time I was lying on the dining table, my legs splayed open, my wrists pinned down by some imaginary force.

I struggled against whatever held me tight. Frightened, I tried to scream but something covered my mouth before a cold, eel-like presence slipped in between my teeth. I tried to scream but my voice froze as a cold manifestation settled over me.

My eyes searched the room for some sort of explanation. Cold finger-like sticks attacked me, searching out my nipples, tweaking them between what could only be fingers. I screamed, my voice piercing the stillness of the room. The fingers now roamed downwards, over my mound, caressing my slit before probing my pussy to pull apart my flaps.

I attempted to pull my legs together, to once again scream, to alert anyone to my frightening circumstances, but the cold weight across my ankles held firm as other hands seemed to roam all over me while I tried to struggle against my invisible captors.

Nipple clamps attached themselves to my breasts and the dildo that I'd been thinking about earlier rammed into my pussy. I was terrified as hands tore at my flesh, scratching at the soft skin of my inner arms and thighs while my breasts were crushed and played with.

My head thrashed from side to side as I tired to buck whatever was holding me away, but they, whatever they were, held me firm. Suddenly I was lifted upwards as though levitating from the table. My screams died in my throat as I hovered over towards the fire. My fear escalated as the front doorknob turned. Some sort of poltergeist was holding me up from the floor and as the door creaked slowly open I struggled vainly as Lester and his lecherous stare filled the room.

"Lester, please," I begged, "do something. Please, help me."

He stood there staring at me, his disgusting fur-coated tongue slipping from his mouth to drool over his bottom lip. His fingers fumbled with the buttons on his shirt, then his trousers as he shucked off his clothing. His stench over-powered the small room and before long he was standing naked before me.

"No, please don't. Please help me," I begged, repulsed by him yet unable to tear my eyes away.

He laughed; a sinister evil chuckle that bounced over the room. His ugly saggy body, grayish and bruised with long thick body hair nauseated me. Fearfully, my eyes stole down his torso and I struggled for breath as my eyes feasted themselves on his ugly cock. It hung over his saggy balls, flaccid and thick, half way down his thigh with something else, perhaps another disgusting testicle, hanging behind it. The knob was covered with a long membrane of skin and dangling from it was a slimy trail of precome.

Struggling against the hands that held me so tightly I begged yet again for help. Lester laughed as he made his way closer, his gnarled and knobby fingers probing my pussy flaps. I recoiled back from his touch, cold like ice; I was petrified of not knowing what was going to happen. The realization that this was not a nightmare, that it was real, that something evil was going on here and there was no way I could see of escaping.

He lowered his head and I jerked backwards, disgusted by his pock-marked face. His bulbous nose drooled snot and he sniffed loudly, sucking it back up through his nostrils, phlegm building in the back of his throat before he coughed it up and spat it into the fire.

"Please, Lester. Don't! Please help me. Please," I begged.

He lowered his head, his nose only inches away from me and sniffed in my scent. Looking up at me through sleep-encrusted eyes I saw the yellow of his eyes. Snot was dripping down his lip. His tongue snaked out and licked at it before he lowered his head further and tentatively lapped my slit.

"No, don't touch me," I screamed. "Someone help me."

He nuzzled in, his bulbous nose wiping his mucus against my pubic hair, leaving trails of silvery, yellow snot to continue further down where it rubbed against my slit. His disgusting tongue flickered over me. I began to scream and scream again but this only seemed to excite him and in a moment he was greedily devouring my pussy, his tongue digging in deeply, slathering me with his revolting saliva.

Tears fell as I screamed and attempted to buck away from him. It was as though a hundred hands all held me tight. His fingers were gripping onto my arse cheeks, pulling them apart as a dirty fat finger probed my puckered hole. For what seemed an eternity he had his way with me, his broken teeth nipping at my clit, electrifying it not with passion but pain.

I closed my eyes tight, hoping I'd wake to find it all a bad dream. Finally he stopped. I peered at him as he stepped backwards. Unable to stop my eyes from traveling downwards I spied his ugly wrinkly cock. Still flaccid, secretion flowed from it, a thick yellow discharge, to leak onto the floor.

A group of people had formed a circle and we were the centre of it. Mary was there with the two women from last night. They were naked and looked almost zombie-like with their graying skin and deathly features. Mary dressed in her robe reminded me of a priestess from one of those scary novels I usually read.

I willed myself to faint. To obliterate this all from my mind...

"Your pussy tastes delicious," he breathed, the rank odor emitting from his mouth threatening to knock me out. Death, that's what his breath smelt like. Was he too a zombie, were all these people in this room dead? Was I, would I be? Oh, God, please let this be a dream I begged.

"Lester, don't … please make this stop."

"Stop! You don't want me to stop," he laughed. "Not when you see what I have hiding in here."

He lifted his left arm. His right hand fumbled about the elbow and suddenly his forearm dropped to the ground. I screamed, louder than before, wishing fervently that I'd stayed home, in the security of my own fortress.

A long thick serpent-like cock, if you could believe that, slithered over my abdomen. His other hand pulled at the cock between his thighs, pummeling it to no avail. My eyes were riveted to the monster, hanging where his arm should be, and I watched in

426

terror as it began to grow. Within seconds it was hard, firm, and making its way up my body, over my breast and towards my mouth.

My head shook from side to side as it inched over my chin. I pressed my lips closely together as this monster, smelling like a rancid piece of meat, forced my lips to part. Cunning fingers pinched my nose until I gasped for breath and as I did he slipped the disgusting knob into my mouth.

Bile rose within me and spewed forth from my mouth.

"Oh, yeah," he leered. "Hmm, yeah that feels so good. All hot and juicy just like your pussy will be when I fuck your cunt with it."

"Get away from me you disgusting maggot," I screamed biting down on it. The image of the condom flashed before my mind. It would at least be some sort of protection against this vile entity, against disease and God knows what else.

"Maggot am I? You'll be sorry you said that?" he threatened.

"Please at least put a condom over it," I begged.

"Oh, so you want it now? Want it filling up your cunt do you?"

I didn't have time to answer. He laughed as he pulled back and rammed his serpent deep inside me. I screamed, cried and begged but all to no avail. He fucked me hard, slamming into me as my body swallowed him up to the elbow. He pumped harder, his eyes glazing over as he watched my pussy lips stretching to accommodate this ugly appendage of his.

My body was shaking, the hands that were still holding me so securely pinching into my flesh. Mary came closer, her face shining, her interest in what he was doing evident as she caressed his withered shoulders. Then suddenly he screamed and I felt a hot burning liquid fill my insides, and he pumped deeper, making sure his seed was in as far as it could go.

"Oh, yeah, baby. Your cunt is so hot, so fucking hot, just like I knew it would be."

"I told you it would be," Mary gushed happily.

"Get away from me, you bastards," I cried.

"Oh, I've not finished with you yet," he laughed.

The hands that were holding me now pulled at my flesh, pinching and nipping. Cold tongues slithered over me like cold-bellied snakes as fingers probed every crevice. Not only did I feel violated and debased but I was terrified as to what would happen next.

Lester lifted the cock he had hanging between his legs and another popped out beneath it.

"See what I have for you, what pleasures I can give you?" he said.

I didn't want to look. Didn't want to see but I had to. My eyes stared in disbelief. He was jiggling two ugly cocks at me. How was that possible? How was any of this possible?

Mary laughed maniacally. "You gave your life for me and now I give you her."

What? What was she talking about?

He lay back on the couch and what could only be mouths sucked at the limp pieces of flesh, pulling and tugging at the wrinkled flesh. An anal probe that had been in his basket of goodies was making its way towards me.

"No," I struggled, uselessly against them. "No, please no more."

He laughed hideously as my arse was pulled apart and the probe inserted. In and out they fucked me with it and all the while Lester's drool dribbled onto his sunken chest, the skin yellow and wrinkly as the mouths sucked him harder and before too long the cocks stood rigid.

"Flip her over," he demanded.

"No, no," I shrilled.

In a flash I was facing downwards, my hair hanging to cover my face. My legs were spread and his disgusting fingers slipped inside my pussy while his tongue rimmed my hole.

"Hmm," he said, licking my arse as though starved. "Just like I knew you'd be. Delicious."

I said nothing from then on, allowing him to have his way with me. His hands groped forward and latched onto my breasts, squeezing hard he milked my nipples enjoying himself when I whimpered in pain.

Finally, he stopped. He stood and they lifted me so I was level with his waist. He held onto my hips and in one quick motion both cocks entered me, one sliding deep into my pussy, the other spearing my hole while he shrilled with delight.

I passed out at some stage and when I came to I was lying face down on the floor. Liquid was oozing from my pussy and hole. My body was bruised and battered. I opened my eyes cautiously hoping he'd gone. Not moving my head, my eyes darted about. I could hear nothing. When a minute or so had passed I carefully maneuvered myself to my knees.

How long I lay there I don't know. I crawled, unable to stand, to the bathroom where I cowered into the shower. Hitting the taps I allowed the water to cascade over my hair and body, trying desperately to wash away the horror of this ordeal.

My teeth chattered and my body shook as my eyes darted about fearfully. What was I to do? I needed to get out of here, to leave in case they all returned. Lester! What was he? A monster! A zombie! Living here, ingraining himself into John's family. And Mary? What was she? He gave his life for her, what did that mean?

I didn't care; I had to get out and now.

I scrubbed my flesh, trying to wash out the semen that was trickling from me. It oozed over my fingers, thick and green in substance and I retched over my legs, unable to stop the bile from rising and spewing from my mouth.

I cried, cried for all I'd lost. Anger surged through me as I tried to plan my escape. How on earth would I be able to outrun them, out smart them when I didn't even know what they were? I had to try though. Had to get away from here as quickly as possible...

Weak but determined I dressed, not bothering to take my bag in case they were watching, and rushed from the house. Shaking fingers eventually managed to insert the key in the barrel and the car roared to life. My eyes darted about like a frightened rabbit's as every second I feared Lester's return. The horror of my ordeal had me driving like a madwoman, the car sideswiping trees, denting the panels in my haste to leave this nightmare behind me.

Just as I rounded the first bend I saw a red jaguar partially hidden behind Lester's dwelling. I gasped with fright. It looked like Mary's car. The dream about her mortified me. Had she made love to me, had she really been in bed with me? Had my wanting of her brought this on? Revulsion consumed me.

"Oh, John," I cried, tears blurring my vision. "What," I blubbered, "am I to do without you? Who will believe me?"

Pushing my foot hard on the accelerator I sped off through the bush vowing never to return and hoping beyond hope that there was no way I'd be pregnant to that fucking freak. Lester and Mary and all their scary friends could have the cabin and anything else they wanted as long as they left me and my family alone.

THE GATHERING
By Madeleine Swann

**Come along, come along,
to the castle hug and song.**

Madeleine Swann has had several articles published by various magazines including Bizarre, ranging in subject from church restorations to the toe wrestling championships. She writes and performs as part of comedy group Braintree Ways and writes fiction in numerous forms from her home in deepest, darkest Essex, England.

Elena, the housemaid, had been kind to her from the first moment. They had grown up in the same town and reminisced over things that reduced them to fits of giggles while the rest of the staff looked on.

The old castle had not been in use for kings or queens for several hundred years but, in typical Gentry fashion, Lord and Lady Symon had bought it and done their best to recreate its old aesthetic. The staff joked privately that a Knight was certain to wander from one of the rooms instead of a modern nineteenth century couple.

Elena's presence to Maggie was a miracle. Maggie had been lucky enough to find employment after her previous misdeeds, and had expected to live out her duty in plain servitude. Elena tried often to get her expand on the details but the shame of it made her blush. Secretly, however, she would revisit it at night in her room and feel horribly guilty the morning after. Her gratitude to Lord and Lady Symon for employing such a wayward girl was always in her thoughts.

She and Elena had been changing the sheets in the master bedroom when the other girl first mentioned it, excitement lighting her eyes like sulphur. "Surely the Master and Mistress wouldn't be involved in such things?" Maggie asked, pretending to be horrified at once.

"Oh but they are, they and their friends, the same night every year." She paused. "They wish me to bring you." Maggie was uncertain whether to believe her, trying to put it from her mind as she continued her daily rounds. That afternoon she couldn't help eyeing the overweight, middle aged cook as she leaned heavily over the range oven and wondering if she too attended the strange gatherings.

A week passed and its urgency faded in Maggie's thoughts. She was dusting the rooms when she entered the study without knocking. She was horrified at her faux pas when she saw the Master and Mistress leaning over an enormous slab of a book on the table. "Please, do not concern yourself," said the Master, "carry on as though we were not here." Maggie's eyes flicked uncertainly from husband to wife, but both seemed in very good spirits. She continued dusting self-consciously, specks tickling her nostrils as she tried not to sneeze on their fine clothes.

"How have you enjoyed your time here so far?" the Master asked in the confident baritone that came from a high society position.

"Oh wonderful," enthused Maggie, "I'm most grateful –" she stopped short, blushing furiously at her own mention of her past.

"Oh nonsense," he continued, "'t'is the hypocrisy of society that punishes mere high spirits, do you not agree my good wife?" The Mistress smiled, exposing her complete set of white teeth. Maggie fidgeted, uncertain whether she was expected to speak or continue cleaning. She opted for the latter as questions flamed against her head. The couple had returned to their book, however, and she was left dusting vaguely at shelves.

That night her sleep was uneasy as she dreamed of snakelike figures twisting and writhing over and around each other. In her half-waking confusion she could still feel the smooth lips and warmth from Mr. Cooke and reached out to him, waking fully and seeing nothing but white moonlight shining on the empty pillow. The heat from between her legs was too strong to ignore and her mind drifted back to the time his tongue had wandered down there. Involuntarily she let her hand take its place. When he had first done it she had laughed, thinking he had gone mad, but had soon moaned in surprise. He had looked so pleased with himself as he continued, tracing soft circles over the little nodule buried in her wet lips.

He was doing it now, slowly building up the fire that began at her groin and spread like little sparks down her legs and her arms. Her hips began to rock gently against her fingertip as the nodule grew bigger, the scent of the wood-smoke in his hair filling her nostrils. She sighed heavily, almost feeling his hand stroking her inner thigh. The flames built up higher and his tongue moved with greater speed as he slipped a finger inside, allowing it to slowly slide upwards and crook forwards, tickling the part deep inside her that made her moan her loudest. Her rubbing became furious and the release made her tip forwards in her bed. She rocked her hips still as her entire body was engulfed, and slumped down into the mattress. The gathering had lost its sinister edge; she didn't relish the idea of only her digits for company and she would be hard put to find a husband who didn't mind her unwholesome past. The month was closing in, soon she would have to decide whether to act or stay locked in her room.

The day in question began without ceremony. She rose as always, ran her washcloth over her skin as always and chose fresh garments. For hours she scrubbed windows alone, wondering if everything inside the castle was a dream. Everything changed when Elena scuttled past carrying fresh towels. "I'll see you later," she said in a low voice, winking lasciviously. Maggie was desperate to run after her and ask whether she meant at the staff dinner table or much, much later.

The Mistress drifted into the bedchambers while she swept the floor. Maggie tried to decipher the look she was given; was it an inviting, secret look or the usual empty glance the rich bestowed on their servants? When evening drew in Maggie was far more exhausted than after a usual day's work but the thrilling tingle coursing inside her cut through it. She suffered through the evening meal, trying to catch Elena's eye as they said grace. The other girl's face was serene and Maggie began to feel concern; surely a person who expected such an evening wouldn't be so calm. She tried to sneak a word with her afterwards but Mrs. Milne insisted on talking about her rose bed.

The candle flickered late in Maggie's room. She had been so terrified of falling asleep and missing the whole thing that she had remained upright in her wooden chair. Her hands shook with either anticipation or cold from the lowering fire. When the clock chimed midnight her heart surged; she removed her nightgown and slip and changed into her best outfit, a dress she wore for church. She picked up the candle lantern and departed into the dark.

The hallway was silent and the shadows skulked across the walls. Every footfall had her straining her ears for followers. Only now did she consider how wrong it all seemed, the danger of such activities. She arrived after a very long journey through the stone corridors.

Maggie heaved aside the wooden door, almost dropping her lantern. She bit her lip fearfully; Elena could have spun a pretty story, and with each minute she became more and more certain she was the subject of a practical joke.

Now, as she stood in the dark hallway, Maggie's corset suffocated her as she realized she had indeed been made a fool of. Candles surrounded the walls of the vast ballroom and eerie melodies strained from a violin, cello and piano. Men in expensive suits and women in elaborate gowns danced and drank from goblets of wine, and the air was laced with musky perfume. It was precisely the sort of gathering her mother had always warned her against.

All eyes turned to her and she opened her mouth, mortified. "I'm terribly sorry, I have the wrong room," she muttered, turning to leave.

"On the contrary, do come in," a male voice slithered from the crowd. She turned but couldn't tell its owner from the multitude of pale faces.

As she stepped forwards she noticed the strange markings painted on the floor in sticky dark red. The owner of the voice took the candle lantern from her and replaced it with a goblet of wine, and she smiled at the need of the upper classes to appear shocking. "You are beautiful," he told her, and she laughed. He didn't seem offended and danced with her, winding in and out of the other couples. He wasn't a man she would have chosen for herself, though his dark hair and brown eyes were pleasing. The situation was as intoxicating as laudanum and she allowed herself to be led.

The shadows stretched over the walls and after an hour of dizzying movement she saw Elena dancing with a man and another woman, he in the middle with his arms around both. This was unusual enough but the gentleman's hands also caressed their breasts. "My goodness," Maggie laughed. "Just look at what they're doing."

"They seem to be enjoying it," said her partner after a quick peek.

"Yes, they do," she agreed, her eyes growing wider as she watched. Despite her private vow to appear unruffled she couldn't quite hide her surprise. Talking about it and seeing it were such different things.

His hands had moved from stroking their fleshy breasts to the nipple area, covered as they were in the dark velvet of their ball-gowns. The two women smiled, slightly self-consciously, but did not push him away. They sighed as he began to circle the now hard nipples with his finger. Elena's gaze drifted to Maggie, who was now watching intently. Elena's pupils were so dilated her eyes appeared black and her lips were flushed bright red. Maggie gripped the shoulder of her companion.

Elena lifted her long skirts as the other dancers circled around them. Maggie herself had stopped moving, unaware now of her partner's presence. The man's hand fell from Elena's breast downwards to the hem of her dress. Her lace underwear was visible to all yet nobody seemed to notice. His fingers reached for the rim of the lace next to her white thigh and tugged gently at it, drawing a deep sigh from her. Slowly they crept inside the fabric and inched towards her private lips, tracing along them confidently.

Elena was now biting her lip and closing her eyes, and Maggie felt hot and wet between her legs. Turning her gaze she noticed the other guests in various acts that should have made her leave indignantly, but she stayed. Her heart thudded and her nerves jangled as her partner pulled down the material at her chest and found her nipple with his lips. She moaned softly, shivers of pleasure reaching her groin as she surveyed the scene around her. Many couples were already sprawled over the floor, some entwined with others to form a bundle of stroking, sighing, half-naked bodies.

She lowered herself to the ground, shaking with excitement but frightened of somehow making a mistake. He unbuttoned her dress and let it fall away, and she lay on the ground in her undergarments. A girl in a complete state of undress crawled over to them, candlelight playing over her skin. "You don't mind?" she asked the man coquettishly, resting on her knees, and he shook his head vigorously. She took Maggie's hand and placed it on her soft belly.

Maggie's fingers nervously fell downwards until she reached the girl's wetness. At first it felt strange, but when she saw how much the other enjoyed it she began to explore more confidently. The blonde girl gasped softly and from the corner of her eye Maggie noticed the twitch of the man's erection inside his suit.

"You should massage her clitoris," he explained. Maggie looked up at him questioningly, but allowed him to guide her hand to the right place until she found the little nodule. She was delighted she wasn't the only one who had it. "How does it feel to you?" he asked as she gently circled her finger over it.

"It is getting harder," she answered, and the girl's mouth opened as her breathing grew heavy and her lashes were low over her blue eyes. "She likes it," Maggie continued, watching in wonder as the girl's hips began to move along with her. As if in reply, the girl's moaning grew louder. Maggie felt the man's smooth hands slide over her shoulders and reach down for her breasts, squeezing them once before releasing them from her corset. He clasped her nipples, carefully teasing and rubbing them. Maggie cried out in shocked arousal, and the blonde girl shuddered and did the same.

Maggie turned now to the man, who kissed her briefly before removing her clothes entirely and reaching for her own soaking private lips. She made no effort to stop him, a tinge of guilt mixing with her pleasure and heightening it. His fingers felt hot and she lifted her pelvis slightly to meet them, focusing on his tense jaw-line. He smiled at her eagerness, locating her clit and doing for her what she had done for the girl now lying content on the ballroom floor.

Where he rubbed she became hotter and wetter. Her nerve endings slid downwards as her hips moved against his finger, and she gripped his shoulder as he inserted a finger inside and curled it gently forwards. To her slight annoyance he stopped and removed his own clothes, but she knew it would begin again soon. She stared at his erection nervously, she had had one before but the thought of another made butterflies tickle her stomach. She put out her hand as he placed a sheath over it but before she could feel it he flipped her onto her knees.

When the surprise had passed she enjoyed the scene of writhing figures; directly in front of her two men nibbled the ecstatic body of a woman, while elsewhere another took one man in her mouth and another behind her. Maggie shook her head at the strangeness of it all, squealing when she felt a familiar hand on her wetness. She turned briefly to face him, smiling, to reassure him as he hesitated. A moment later she felt something very different press at the opening of her quim; with a wry smile she felt him push his way in. She had not expected the sensations it would bring, the tingling as it slid inside, filling her up as its tip tickled against her innermost point. She gripped it with her muscles as tightly as she could, drawing a low moan from him.

His hand felt for her wet lips once more at her front, massaging her clit again. She rolled her hips with his as he pushed in as far as he could and withdrew, again and again, until she realized his finger was waking all of her senses once more. The feel of his cock along with his stroking finger made her feel dizzy and hot; she moved quickly against his outstretched finger, rubbing herself against it faster and faster, feeling something build up and up until she sighed and moaned along with the rest of the room. A rush of intense pleasure washed over her and her muscles stiffened. As she shook, he pressed himself into her with greater urgency until he too tensed over her.

His weight pressed down gently as she lay sprawled over the cool floor. Sounds of people lost in their private worlds surrounded her and the scent of flesh and sexual fluids filled the air. She looked up to see them entwined over the red paint of the pentagrams. The candlelight illuminated various body parts and Maggie smiled to herself. Whilst the Devil may not have made an appearance to this particular party, she still wouldn't mention it to her mother.

WOMB WITH A VIEW
By Reina Sobin

More boys in the hood.

*Reina Sobin is 30-year-old writer of Bizarro and erotica from Milwaukee, Wisconsin. Her work appears in **Collaboration of the Dead: Putrid Poetry & Sickening Sketches**.*

The quiet girl, who was not a girl, ate her dinner as she walked. She dug into her cart for another portion, constant hunger gnawing at her belly. Sharp teeth bit into the morsel and juices ran down the technological wasteland that was her arm.

She was a rebuilt child, a mechanized wonder, with a bloody heart encased in glass. A crimson robe wrapped her form, the hood of which was pulled over the terrible beauty of that flesh and brass face.

A fierce wind blew though the oxidized trees, the whistle reminiscent of a poorly-played flute. Shards of rusted leaves littered her way, crushed with ease under her booted feet. The conveyance whined like a temperamental child, its wheels spoke of a lack of oil.

The road was long, her way deserted, as she traveled further into the thickening copse. The townspeople told tales of this place being haunted, of grim specters that chased the unwary. She had cackled when she heard this and wondered how a dead thing could cause such fear.

She hummed to pass the time and, before long, her sweet voice emerged with limericks more suited to a common whore or a drunk.

"Your cock is hard, your balls are blue. Since I'm on my knees, I'll swallow you too."

"Her breasts are round, her labia thick. I'll bend her back, and take a lick."

She rounded the bend, her rhymes each more vulgar and carnal than the last, and jerked to a halt. A man appeared before her, a grin twisting his lips. In a smoke-grey suit and leaning against a fallen rowan, he appeared comfortable with the bitter air. A gold watch gleamed on his wrist and a briefcase dangled in his hand. She could smell him even at a distance-- a curious combination of expensive cologne and desperation.

"What have we here? A child shouldn't have such a filthy mouth."

The girl eyed him cautiously but continued her walk. A lone man in the woods was always a sign of trouble. This one's good looks made him even more dangerous.

Her hunger rose.

"I am far older than my looks convey."

He trailed her as she knew he would. Graceful stalking that trampled the dry leaves.

"How old? 15? 16? A virgin yet, I wager."

"Much older than that." She let him get close, close enough that she could smell the animal in him. "And my fucking habits are none of your concern."

"Perhaps I would like to make it my concern. A mechanical girl with a bewitching face makes one wonder what is beneath the cloak."

Wolves thought themselves cunning at seduction, but women were the true manipulators.

"You wouldn't know what to do with me."

He strutted up to her, his briefcase bounced with each step. She allowed him to press her against the cart, his golden eyes narrowed on her face. He dropped the case at his feet and revealed what parts of her were still woman.

He saw the beating heart, the blood that trickled in the glass. He licked his lips and she saw his hunger. His fingers poked at the copper plating over her ribs and slid lower.

"At least the good parts of you are still human."

"I don't have time for this." She shoved at the solid chest. "My grandmother's waiting."

"Waiting where?" His fingers toyed with the copper rings that ran through her nipples.

She jabbed a thumb behind her. "Just down the road. She's been ill, so I brought her some sweets to cheer her up."

In an instant, he stepped back and opened his case. He rifled through until pen and paper was in hand. "Was she injured at work? I can have my aide look into unsafe working conditions at her place of employment."

A lawyer. And one involved in personal injury. It was worse than she feared.

"She mentioned something about some kind of jelly and a vibrating curiosity that her and the neighbor were testing. She seemed embarrassed so I didn't ask anything further."

"Did she say who owned this 'curiosity'?"

"I believe that they were sharing the cost."

"Well, damn." He tossed his implements back into the case and closed it. "It doesn't sound like negligence."

She closed her robe around her bared breasts and turned back to her cart.

"Sorry to have lost your interest." The cart groaned as she continued her walk.

He danced up to her, cavorting like a puppy who needed attention. "Oh, I'm still interested in your charms but my concern for your grandmother took hold. I apologize."

He is slick. I'll give him that.

"I must see to grandma's needs first." She slid a metal finger to his waist. "But then we'll see about meeting yours."

"Some flowers might cheer her up."

She could see his eyes on her welded face, her metal arms and body. *He is probably wondering where to file the lawsuit. Bastard.* "That's a kind idea."

She grabbed a set of cutters from her vehicle and bent to task. Silver roses were clipped and thorns meticulously trimmed away, the metal shavings dropped between her feet. She tied the rigid bundle and turned back to her lupine pursuer.

He was nowhere to be seen but she could guess his location.

She snatched a bulging sack from her cart and strolled down the path. An elaborate marble structure came into view. Intricate columns lined the porch and a tangle of briars climbed the walls. She stepped over a scatter of weathered bones as she walked through the door.

"Grandmother?!" She called through the maze of hallways. "Grandmother?!"

"Red? In here, child."

"Ah, well, I see you two are becoming acquainted." She entered the bedroom to see the old woman bent over the unconscious wolf, a broken jug beside her. Red dumped her bag onto the table with a wet plop. "Thank you for watching her while I was gone. I've brought something for you."

The old crone's lips curled back and revealed her wicked yellowed canines. Red gestured to the table and watched as the woman pounced on the sack. Her hand dug inside and emerged with a chunk of dripping meat, which was instantly shoved between her lips.

442

The girl turned back to her bed and dropped her cape to the floor. She climbed over the creature and straddled him, one of the few parts of her still organic squeezed against his groin. His eyes opened, groggy and bewildered.

"So you thought an elderly woman and her granddaughter easy prey?" She gripped his wrists with inhuman strength.

The wolf, no longer in lawyer's clothing, shook his head. Her free hand around his throat prevented speech..

"My, my, what big eyes you have." She ran silver-capped fingertips down his furry chest. "The better to see what I'm going to do to you."

The man whimpered.

"My, my, what a big cock you have." She ground against him. "The better to fuck you with."

The erection that rose under her let her know that he wasn't nearly scared enough.

She leaned down and spoke against his ear. "My, my. The scent of your blood entices me. All the better to drink you."

Her teeth sank into his neck as he struggled for breath. He tried to shove her but the weight of her metal-infused body kept her seated. Hot blood slipped into her mouth and she gulped, starved for any fluid that he could provide.

"Red, don't drain him yet, dear. We need him."

She yanked herself from his throat and growled. "Meet my grandmother."

A young woman stepped up to the bed, her beauty such that any man would be helpless to resist her. At least until one saw the feral nightmare of her eyes. She caught a bit of the lawyer's blood and brought it to her lips.

"Clean, a bit of a dark taste, heavy meat-eater… You have found a good one."

"Actually, he found me. Wanted to take me right out there in the woods."

"Eager, is he? Good." The grandmother turned away and grabbed the old woman, who was still gnawing on a bit of liver. "Come, let's take our meal and give them some peace. Our Red can handle this one alone."

The man's eyes darted between her and the closed door, his brow wrinkled.

"You're confused by her looks." She rubbed her well-lubricated sex against his shaft. "Not to worry. You will not be thinking about it for long."

She sank on his hardness and released her hold on his throat. "You were excited by the thought of claiming me earlier... I'll tell you what- show me the wolf and I'll let you go when we're done."

His golden eyes narrowed to slits. "You want the wolf? Alright, you metal tease, let's play."

He gripped her copper-infused hips and surged upward. She could feel the way he stretched her pussy, gaining thickness and length as he changed. His face sharpened into a muzzle and long canines flashed each time he groaned. His body stayed human, but the hair covering it turned black and long.

Red rocked against him, delighted with his stamina. She released his wrist and scraped her nails through his chest hair. Her tongue rasped over his nipple and he howled behind clenched teeth.

"You liked that, did you?"

"I've never...ugh... had a woman play with my nipples."

She lapped at the tiny bud and slid her tongue up over his collarbone. She drank in his salty flesh and hummed in appreciation.

"That's a shame. Sensitive little things they are."

His hands found her breasts and teased them to nubs. He thrust up into her as she sucked at his earlobe. He growled and panted heavily.

"I want you under me."

Red stared into his eyes and saw nothing but his lust. She flipped them over, without breaking their connection, and wrapped her human leg around his thighs.

"Take me."

His thrusts were powerful, deep and full. She eased a hand between their bodies to fondle her clit as he moved. A series of whirls and clicks sounded as her mechanical arm worked her to peak. She tightened and cried out, milking his cock as she came.

"Ugh… come on, lawyer boy…mmm… come for me."

Sweat dripped from his face onto the tubing in her neck. She could see his struggle to control himself, the way he tried not to bite at her neck. Her fingers slid down his slick back and eased between his buttocks. Before he could protest, she drove one finger into his ass.

Birds squawked in answer to his strangled cry and she bit her lip when her grandmother whooped from downstairs. He jerked spasmodically as his balls emptied then collapsed onto her chest.

She eased her hand from his ass and pet him like a favored lapdog. "That's a good boy."

When his breathing finally slowed, her teeth sank into him once more.

She swallowed his memories of her and this house, then pinched a nerve in his neck until he passed out. She pushed his weight from her and capped the precious fluid inside her before it could escape. Her grandmother and the servant were called to make quick work of dressing him and carrying him downstairs.

Grateful for the twilight sky, they doused him with liquor and dumped him into their car.

"Drop him on the edge of town. He will wake up, think himself drunk, and stumble home."

The old servant nodded, long used to the ritual, and drove off.

"Perhaps, we should have taken care of him. He would have make a tasty roast."

The grandmother smiled at the hunger of youth. "That he would have, but we may have need of him again soon."

"Not for awhile yet." She opened the metal corset over her abdomen.

The translucent flesh revealed the intricacies of her body. Copper tubes meshed with organic structures, trails of wiring interlaced throughout. Her womb sat at the forefront of it all, luminous and pulsating with every heartbeat.

Even as they looked on, the swirl of fluid from their guest swam and danced around the egg within her. Its coloring shaded to red and the invader was pulled inside.

The grandmother touched the clear flesh, her canines emerged. "Our modifications finally worked. Ah, the wonder of machines."

The metal girl gazed at the glass marvel in her chest. No longer a trickle, but flowed to the top. "My heart is full."

"New life will do that, my dear."

LOVE BITES
By Andrée Lachapelle

**When you find a woman who likes fishing
and camping as much as you do,
you better hold onto her.**

*Originally from Québec, **Andrée Lachapelle** grew up near the
highway that ran through her small town, past the strip-mall, the
strip-joint, and the old movie theatre…*

*Before finding her true home, she wandered the world. She climbed
a volcano in Guatemala; museum-hopped in Vienna; had her
chakras realigned in Mexico; and swam with sharks in Turks &
Caicos.*

*Andrée enjoys reading, snorkeling, luxurious bubble baths, and
meat-flavored potato chips. She likes to wear bikinis year-round,
and takes great delight in all things taboo. Her work has appeared
in numerous publications including **Broken Pencil**, **Canadian
Woman Studies**, and **Hustler Fantasies**.*

*She lives in Toronto, Canada, with the most wonderful man in the
world and a ferocious savanna huntress masquerading as a calico
cat.*

When I heard a knock at the door of my trailer, I knew it had to be Dale. I grabbed my hairbrush and ran it through my hair to try to make some sense of the tangled mess. I looked like crap. I knew this. Dale walked in and stood in the doorway for a few seconds, six feet tall and dirty as sin, his t-shirt covered in dust and mud and what looked like specs of blood. It probably was.

He stared me down, closed the door behind him and took a few steps toward me, his face sombre. He was drop-dead gorgeous, when he got all serious.

I looked up at him and tried to smile.

We'd been sleeping together for three days.

We had known each other for four.

Without so much as a greeting, Dale reached out, grabbed a handful of my hair, and pulled me toward him. I started to melt, and my legs gave out from under me.

He pushed me down to the ground – not really violently, but quickly enough for me to gasp as the hard ground hit my newly bony ass. It felt as if something splintered off my hip but I ignored it, focusing instead on the bulge struggling against the threadbare fabric of Dale's jeans.

My mouth filled with saliva and I swallowed, hard. Dale unzipped his pants and his thick cock slipped out easily; he didn't bother with underwear, anymore. I licked my lips.

Dale grinned down at me and pulled my shorts halfway down my thighs. The little jewel in my labia glimmered in the moonlight, and Dale's thick cock stiffened.

"Turn around," he said.

I grunted, and got on my hands and knees.

Dale pulled me up a bit and then pushed me face down on the orange bench – the one that turned into a narrow bed, when you bothered to pull it open. He unhooked my dirty pink bikini top, now so clammy with stale sweat that it stuck to my breasts, grabbed my chin, and stuck his thumb in my mouth to keep me from making any noise; I sucked on it gingerly.

448

The rough upholstery brushed against my cheek as Dale slipped his cock between my legs and found my pussy. My skin felt alive with tiny flames. I spread my legs further apart as Dale rubbed the head of his dick on my swollen clit, teasing me; when he put his full weight on me and pushed his dick deep inside me, I started to moan.

"You're mine," Dale said, and I nodded, thinking of nothing but his smooth flesh on mine, how his cock moved in and out of me and how good it felt to be taken that way, rough and fast. No man had ever fucked me like that, even before – when I was still beautiful.

I spent every daylight hour waiting for this, Dale's nightly visit, that moment when he would come to me, hold me in his arms and make love to me, and make me feel alive again. When I was with Dale, the world around me melted away and there was only this. Him. Inside me.

"Let me hear you say it," Dale continued, his cock thrusting into me, a hard push I felt deep inside my belly, as if I were being ripped wide open. He rubbed his thumb on my lips, smearing the last of my raspberry lip-gloss.

"I'm yours," I tried to whisper, but I couldn't get the words to come out. I lost track of time, of space, of everything when Dale moved in me.

"Again," he said as he slowed down to penetrate me a bit more gently; his cock, sleek with the wetness of me, pushing in and out of my pussy rhythmically as I fought hard to catch my breath and speak. "Again."

His warm hands rubbed my skin and caressed every curve and crevice of my aching body. I pushed back against him and focused on tightening my flesh around his cock to hold him inside me as long as I possibly could. Dale started to breathe fast, one hand pulling my hips close to his belly and the other still wrapped around my hair. His firm grip had turned to a sensual caress.

Dale pulled out just long enough to turn my body around to face him before sliding into me again, the thickness of him unbearable now, pushing me open, overfilling me. His eyes were wild and I could smell the last of the Canadian Club on his breath as he pinned my arms behind my back and kissed me for what seemed like an eternity. The taste of his tongue in my mouth was maddening; I wanted to eat him alive.

He nuzzled my neck and nibbled on old love bites before traveling down to my breasts, three-day stubble scratching my chest as his tongue and teeth moved on my nipples, biting hard this time, breaking the skin.

When another small moan escaped me, Dale pulled his dick out of my soaking wet pussy and shoved it in my mouth roughly, his eyes piercing mine, all gentleness gone again. Dutifully, I started to suck on his cock, my mouth filled with the taste of oak and moss that seemed part and parcel of Dale's genetic make-up, like the sandy hair that refused to behave and blue eyes you could drown in.

He tilted my face up and we stared at each other as he moved in and out of my mouth. I ran my tongue along his shaft, exploring the length of his erection and lapping at the head of his cock, drawing small circles around the pearl of semen glistening at its tip until Dale took a deep breath, gasped, and filled my mouth with cum. His eyes, half-closed now, never left mine.

I tried to swallow it all, but semen dripped down my chin.

"I came here to mark my territory," Dale whispered, rubbing my face dry with his dirty fingers and bringing them to my lips, making me lick them clean.

I obliged. The man tasted very fine, indeed.

He adjusted himself, zipped up the filthy jeans he had been wearing since I met him, and sat on the floor next to me.

"I need to know that you're mine," he said, "no matter what. I can't do this half-assed. Not after everything that happened here. You're either with me, or you're not."

I tried to nod while struggling to keep my eyes open against a descending veil of darkness.

"Don't let those assholes get to you," Dale said.

The assholes in question had joined the camp the day after I came. One was your typical beer-swilling, sports-loving suburban idiot while the other – the Number One Asshole, the first one to have crashed our party – was more of the same with a bit of sexual molester added for good measure. He'd started off by trying to get into my pants, and was now taunting Dale, urging him to fight for what was his. The two men had hated each other from the start.

In these troubled times, relationships moved fast. People quickly became friends – or enemies – and the person who was your buddy yesterday could kill you tomorrow for a piece of stale bread, or a piece of ass. Food was scarce and so were women, and belonging to Dale was not the worst thing that could happen to a girl.

Outside, I could hear the two assholes arguing as they tried to come up with a plan. Asshole #1 – the one with the wandering hands – was telling his friend that he should be the one to take care of me while Asshole #2 – the more congenial of the two – argued that #1 should do it. I could see his point: Asshole #2 had already killed me once.

I absentmindedly swathed a fly off my shoulder while Dale got dressed. When he was done he helped me get back into my shorts and top, and lifted me onto the orange bench without bothering to open it into a bed. It didn't matter: I wasn't going to sleep, anyway.

Propping me up against the old pillows, he adjusted the soiled sheets around my wasted body and cocooned me in the old fleece blanket – once incredibly soft against my bare skin, but now stiff with blood and semen.

He smoothed my hair, and kissed my forehead.

"Don't worry about them, ok?" he said.

I struggled to hear his voice, a soft whisper like butterfly wings against my ear. I was so tired. Nothing made sense anymore.

"Just hang in there. I'll bring you something to eat when I come back tomorrow, I promise…"

Dale left, turning off the lights before closing the door behind him. And I sat alone, staring into the darkness.

***

I had been driving for a long time when I found the camp, and I hadn't seen another human being in weeks – nobody who hadn't already changed, that is. The few people I saw were dark figures hunched over in the cover of the night, hungrily ripping the flesh off god knows what and devouring it brutally, all traces of humanity long gone.

Some days, I saw no one at all. Those were the good days.

But that day, I thought I had finally gotten lucky. Constantly in need of supplies, I had stopped in the town of Leemansville, population 910 – in itself a good sign. How many goons could there be, if less than a thousand people had lived there to begin with?

I had no food but enough gas left over from my last pit stop to make it through town, and enough daylight hours left to try to find a store or a house that looked reasonably untouched, and quiet enough for me to do some looting in peace.

Near the edge of town there stood a little mom-and-pop shop that doubled as food market and fishing supplies store. This too, was a good sign: where there was fishing, there was water, and water was what I most desperately needed. I grabbed an old bag of Doritos and the few remaining dusty cans of Diet Coke and French-style seasoned green beans off the shelves and ignored the loud buzzing coming from the back room. Flies. They were everywhere.

On my way out I saw a little display by the door, advertising the hidden charms of Leemansville and the surrounding area: "Camp Tomago: A Fisherman's Paradise." The hand-drawn picture on the flyer showed a fisherman with an unnaturally large grin and equally unnaturally large trout. The back showed a detailed map on how to get to this pastoral paradise. I grabbed the flyer and stuck it in my back pocket.

I walked out and sat in the cab of my camper for a little while, drinking warm Coke and eating stale Doritos, trying to figure out my next move. Where I came from, was gone. And I had no clue where I was going. Camp Tomago seemed as good a place as any.

I headed north, away from beautiful downtown Leemansville, population 0, and toward the unknown. I checked the rear-view mirror frequently to make sure I wasn't being followed by throngs of undead – or whatever the hell they were – but I wasn't too worried: there was hope in my heart. I quickly lost it.

When I finally saw the faded sign by the side of the road, "Camp Tomago, Keep Right," I kept right, until I came to an old dirt road, poorly maintained and barely visible through the brush. At the end of the road stood a little pup tent that had been set up near an old pick-up truck parked in the shade of large maple trees. A picture-perfect squirrel sat on a branch, calling his mate. Beyond the clearing, by the lake, I could see an old boarded-up log cabin. And in the middle of the clearing stood a tall, sandy-haired man with the broadest shoulders I had ever seen, and the bluest blue eyes.

"Well shit," he said.

I took a quick look in the mirror and walked toward him. He was the first real live man I had seen in a long time.

"You're the first real live human being I've seen in weeks," he said. "You ARE real, right?"

I smiled. "Yup, real as they come." I introduced myself.

"Dale," he said, extending his hand. "You look hungry."

I was hungry, and tired, and dirty, and all of a sudden, horny. Despite his sunburned skin, Dale cut a dashing figure. He looked pretty good, all things considered. Clearly the lake had served him well.

"I was about to cook this up. Want some?" He took a small fish out of a bucket that sat on the ground by his feet, and held it up. I had never seen anything that looked so tasty.

I grinned and nodded, and shielded my eyes from the sun.

"How's the lake?" I asked.

"Perfect," Dale said, "nice and refreshing. Go check it out. I haven't seen any goons out this far, I think it's pretty safe."

I headed down to the lake, took off my clothes, and waded into the cool waters. It felt amazing. I stayed in, enjoying the fresh air and the feeling of being clean, at last, until Dale called me back to reality.

"Hey, missy," he called out. "Dinner's ready!"

Feeling giddy, I got dressed and walked back to camp, where I was greeted by the smell of freshly cooked fish. I handed Dale what was left of my supplies and we sat together by the fire, quietly eating fish and French-style seasoned green beans, drinking Diet Coke and Canadian Club late into the night.

***

I had been awake for a few hours when I heard a car approach. Rays of sunshine were coming in through the little window above my fold-out couch, warming my bare skin. I felt wonderful, clean, fed, well-rested. I could see Dale standing in the clearing, looking up toward the road. He had his shirt off; I could see beads of perspiration on his smooth chest and a dark line that ran from his belly-button and past the belt of his jeans, into unknown regions. I was mesmerized. My eyes lingered on his body while I absentmindedly caressed my own skin.

I found the soft folds of my pussy and slipped my fingers inside. I was already wet: this guy did it for me. If not for the Canadian Club and hours of driving, I would have been climbing all over him the night before. Instead, we had talked about who we were and where we came from and when Dale said goodnight and headed to his tent, I came back to my little camper and soon fell asleep – all sexual thoughts gone.

This morning was another story. After so long on my own, I was used to pleasuring myself – but the thrill offered by Dale, firm and fit in the morning sun, was enough to make me come almost instantly. My heart raced as I shivered in the throes of a violent orgasm but I wanted more.

I licked my fingers and caressed my breasts, rubbing small circles on the pink areolas before moving back down to the soft, moist hair of my pussy. I fingered the ring in my labia and played with the little bead until I climaxed again, struggling to catch my breath as my body arched into orgasm. I tried to smother my cries with the old pillows that littered my bed, but in the end, I gave up.

Outside, a man had just gotten out of an old beat-up Ford, and Dale absentmindedly rubbed the smooth flesh of his lower back while talking to the newcomer. When a loud moan escaped my lips, the man turned toward the camper and grinned. Asshole.

***

The second man arrived later that day.

Dale and I had introduced ourselves to Asshole #1, making idle chit-chat. Asshole told my breasts how he stopped in Leemansville for supplies, saw the ads for the fisherman's paradise, easily located the dirt road, and then stopped by to see if anybody in these parts was still alive.

"I didn't expect to see the likes of you here," he said, never taking his eyes off my chest. "Don't see too many women anymore."

"We're a rare breed," I said, turning toward my camper.

"Huh-huh," Asshole said. And he smacked my ass.

I sat inside for a bit, fuming. After a while I put on my swimsuit, threw a pair of shorts over the bikini bottoms, and headed down to the lake for a quick dip. Water was a rare luxury, and I wasn't going to let anyone ruin this for me. I swam around for a bit, keeping my eyes on the shore and possible danger. But Dale had said he hadn't seen any goons since coming to Camp Tomago.

I was heading back to camp, wondering if lunch was even an option at this point when I bumped into the asshole. He came up toward me and kept pace as I walked. I could see Dale in the distance, fiddling with his fishing gear. Asshole was quiet until we passed the old log cabin.

One minute we were walking side by side in the sun and everything was going to be ok, and the next my world was turned upside down and my life changed forever. I didn't see it coming.

Asshole grabbed my arm and pressed my body against the wall of the old cabin, his hands reaching for my breasts before moving down to my ass, his dick pushing against me.

"Come on, honey," he said, "I know you want this."

He stuck his hand down my shorts and I stomped on his foot with all my might, and started to run.

I was aware of branches scratching my face, of him yelling and of an impact that made my head snap back and threw me full force into the bushes lining the road. The car that had just hit me screeched to a halt, and Asshole #2 got out.

"Oh my god holy fucking god, fuck, oh fuck oh fuck!"

Everything slowed down, and sights and sounds came to me from far away. I saw Asshole #2 run toward me and hold my wrist, feeling for a pulse. I heard him scream, "Oh fuck oh my fucking god she's dead!"

Asshole #1 came up to us and kneeled on the ground next to me.

"Is she breathing?" he asked the other man.

Without waiting for an answer, Asshole #1 loosened my bikini top and put his ear down on my chest. His palm covering my breast, he squeezed a nipple between his fingers. His penis had grown hard. He was breathing rapidly. The other man was weeping.

I tried to speak, but all that came out was a gargled moan. The two men jumped to their feet and stepped back. When I tried to move, I felt myself being picked up by strong arms and although I couldn't clearly see who was holding me, I could smell oak, and moss.

***

When I came to, night had fallen. I was lying on the sofa-bed in my camper, my legs covered in blood, one of them sticking out at a very odd angle. I couldn't sit up straight or hold my head high. Dale was sitting next to me, cleaning my wounds using an old towel and water from the bucket that had held a small fish when I first got to camp, so long ago. My blood-stained clothes were on the bench next to him, neatly folded.

Dale took the damp towel and rubbed the blood off my thighs, parting my legs slightly as he did so. A small moan escaped my lips and Dale started, and then continued to clean me up, hands edging higher and higher up my thighs until he was no longer bothering with the water or the towel. His warm hands traveled over my mound and past the softness of my pubic hair, slipping right into me. His fingers played in the wetness of my pussy and I shifted my weight to push my pelvis against him until his entire hand was engulfed in my womb.

He gasped and folded his fingers into a fist, and I was paralyzed by pleasure, the entirety of him filling me up, touching every inch of my insides. He slowly pulled his hand out and rubbed his thumb over my clitoris while his other hand undid his pants and I saw his gorgeous cock for the first time. I swallowed, hard, the copper taste of blood filling my mouth.

Dale pushed his fist back into me and this time my flesh parted for him willingly. I looked down to see his hand disappear, the soft curve of my labia wrapped around his thick tanned arm, pulling him deeper into my pussy. When he could go no further I started to move slowly, letting his arm, his fingers, his fist fuck me as I rocked back and forth on the little orange couch until my back arched into orgasm and I grew limp, spent, and Dale spilled his warm semen on my ravaged stomach and chest.

Slowly, he pulled his fist out of me and rubbed his sperm all over my breasts before bringing his hand to my mouth, to make me lick it clean.

We were lost in the moment until we heard a voice right outside my window.

"Holy fucking god," it said, "did you fucking SEE that?!"

Dale had come to see me every night since the accident and each time he left, I could hear the arguments picking up speed and volume.

"I know she's hot," Asshole #1 said, "she WAS hot, I get it. But we've got to put an end to it, Dale, she's gone. You gotta let her go. You gotta finish her off."

"Nobody's finishing anyone off," Dale said. His footsteps faded away. "Nobody touches her. You two assholes just stay the fuck away from her, understood?"

I heard him get into his tent and the other men's conversation turned to a whisper as slowly, smoothly, darkness fell over my mind, and I found rest.

The next evening, when I heard the knock on my door, I tried to prop myself up but I felt weak, depleted. I could hardly move. It's only when Dale opened the door of the camper and let in some fresh air that I became aware of my own stench.

He walked over to me, smoothed my hair and kissed my forehead.

"Don't worry, baby," he said, "everything's gonna be ok. You're mine, and I'm gonna take care of you til you get better."

He held my face close to his chest and I took in the scent of him.

"You hold on a minute and I'll be right back," Dale said.

He went out into the night, leaving the door open behind him. Flies rushed in immediately and descended upon me. I was afraid, all of a sudden.

I heard a single gunshot echo in the night, followed by a scream.

"Holy fucking god!"

Dale shuffled his feet outside my door, out of breath as if struggling with a heavy weight. When he came back in, his shirt was dirtier than ever and his face was red. He bent down to drag something up the stairs, and then lay the beast down on the floor, where a pool of blood started to form.

Without a word, Dale walked back to the sofa-bed and picked me up to bring me over to his kill, and gently put me down on the floor next to it. I lapped at the blood like an animal and then, feeling a little bit stronger, I slowly crawled toward the asshole and started to feed while Dale watched tenderly.

And I knew then that he was right: it was going to be ok. Everything was going to be ok.

POMEGRANATE MOTH

By Richard Godwin

Flavored to the max.

*Richard Godwin is the author of **Apostle Rising**, a crime novel in which a serial killer is crucifying politicians and recreating the original murder scenes of an unsolved case. He writes crime and lets it slip like wash into horror. He is also a produced playwright. His work has appeared in many magazines and anthologies, including **CrimeFactory** and **Needle Magazine**. His **Chin Wags At The Slaughterhouse** are his unusual interviews with fellow authors. You can see a full list of his published works at his website at **www.richardgodwin.net**. Apostle Rising can be bought at all good bookshops, and online at Amazon.com and www.blackjackalbooks.com.*

He lived in the residue of sin.

Maxim Moth knew how to shake a fork at an angler.

He reasoned beyond reason.

He shook the dust from the wings of moths into the dishes he served at his diner 'The Filthy Phlegm House.'

He knew the Heterocera of each breeding zone and lived in the ash of flavours.

His customers loved his food and chewed ravenously on the dusty flavours of his pomegranate sauce.

He would stretch the living forms of caterpillars like slugs and drop them in a sizzling pan.

He thought they tasted of clothes and Naphthalene once seasoned with the relish that made him salivate.

He was a silkworm spinner and layer of violets in costly sauces that made the men and women who flocked there chew insanely until they swallowed.

He found the midnight flappers matched the taste of pomegranate and he made his dishes from the combination.

Their wings would shake food into a powdered trance.

He imported them from the Iranian Plateau and he would tear their red flesh until the seeds dropped out. He ran his hands along their raised erotic surface.

He would separate the arils from the peel and eject them into a bowl watching them fly from their husk and land liquidly in the water.

They bobbed like nipples in sauce.

Maxim Moth found their red soft fleshy skin erotic and slid his finger into them feeling them ply their tradework desire for human ingestion.

He opened his pomegranates up and brought them to a moist froth and tasted their fluids with finger to his lips as his wife Alicia bent over the stove.

He could smell her and read the desire she held inside her like the secret sign on a bleeding leaf.

He would watch the juice rise from their flesh and add the sap to his sauces shaking the moth dust in and letting it settle there.

That day at 'The Filthy Phlegm House' Maxim Moth cooked his dishes and watched his wife moisten at the sound of the hissing in the pan.

He cradled her with his hands and let her taste of the fruit as she bent to massage him.

She tasted of sin and he took her juice and added it in.

The customers were arriving as the sun penetrated the glass that looked out onto the marauding street.

They sat and waited to be fed.

And as Maxim Moth fed Alicia and quickened her desire he felt her juices stir and he brought his sauces to a froth that he added as a Carpaccio to the meats he stewed.

He served his customers and watched them taste the food.

Alicia rubbed her hands across her body and found hysteria's mantel in her heart.

Maxim Moth watched his wife denude herself at the spectacle of the eating and she found with hungry hands the hole she feasted on.

The sound of chewing was relentless and it filled the room with the sucking noise of cows and lips on lactating nipples.

Alicia's hands slowed and she spent her liquid in a tide of intoxicated gasps.

And Maxim Moth saw the dust settle in the air and spiral in the sunlight as the pomegranate sauce passed down the smooth throats of his customers and they parted their wet lips.

SONATA FOR INSECTS AND VIOLINS
By Peter Baltensperger

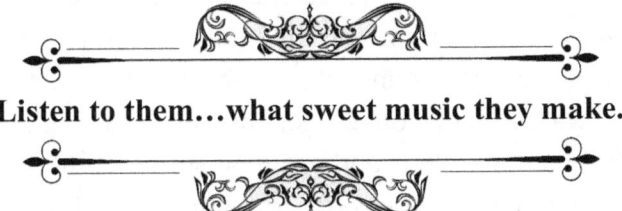

Listen to them…what sweet music they make.

*Peter Baltensperger is a Canadian writer of Swiss origin and the author of ten books of fiction, poetry, and non-fiction. His short stories, poems, and essays have appeared in several hundred publications around the world over the past several decades. His erotic stories, poems, and essays have been published in print in **The Mammoth Book of Best New Erotica, Sex in the City - Paris, Daily Flashes of Erotica Quarterly, The International Journal of Erotica,** and **In the Buff,** and appear on-line in **Clean Sheets, The Erotic Woman, Oysters and Chocolate, Black Heart Magazine,** and **Every Night Erotica,** among others. He makes his home in London, Canada with his wife Viki and their two cats and a tortoise.*

In the precarious uncertainty of a late night, charged hours barely held together by thin threads that could so easily tear, the fragile crescent of a waning moon hangs from invisible wires in a black sky, eclipsing a few stars close by. The rest of the sky glitters with myriads of pinpoint lights as if a giant hand had thrown them up and strewn them into the darkness like so many flickering beams, so many reminders of the tenuous transparency enveloping life.

A naked woman lies on a wooden table in the middle of an otherwise empty room, gripping the edges with her hands, her legs joyfully spread, her body shivering with blatant excitement, her mind delirious from myriads of minuscule feet, minuscule mouths, minuscule drops of acid stimulating her honey-brushed skin. A man stands by her side, his limp penis beginning to stir between his legs, quickening his own mind with the image of the prone woman exposed, the honey-covered breasts, the wide-open legs.

Their shadows sway in the flickering light of pillar candles arranged haphazardly around the room to illuminate them just enough to watch each other get higher and higher on their stimulations, bathing their bodies in a softly comfortable sheen. There are no windows in the room, shielding them from the delicate moon, the slowly rotating night, enabling them to fully concentrate on themselves and each other and the growing intensity of their mutual arousal.

A sophisticated sound system with the volume turned low softly plays a varied selection of sonatas for violins by different composers from different times, Bach, Beethoven, Mozart, Liszt, Brahms, Grieg, Debussy, masters all of the most complex compositions. The melodies wash through the room, intermingle with the candle light, enhance the sexually charged atmosphere for the two lovers in their intense arousal, mind to mind, soul to soul.

The woman is crawling with a colony of black ants grazing on the white landscape of her honeyed skin, scurrying all over her body in their single-mindedness, tickling her, nibbling at her, excreting their acid, stimulating her to distraction. Her body has morphed into one large expanse of shivering nerve endings, acutely sensitive pleasure centers, incredibly arousing sensations, feelings, emotions. She laughs delightedly between primordial moans and groans, cherishing the flood of sensory stimulation, then reaches out and grabs the man's penis, exchanging ants.

The more she writhes and moans on the table, the more ants venture across the synapse, the harder the man's penis becomes in her hand, the more tenuously fragile their tableau in the precarious night. Late night hours rotate slowly, enabling the mind to slowly submerse itself in the intricate physical pleasures derived from the ants, the string instruments, the hands. The soul joyfully saturates itself with the myriad of sensuous impressions flooding the body and the mind, penetrating the enchanted psyche all the way to the core.

The woman becomes increasingly aroused from the tireless ants crawling all over her and into her, nibbling at her, stinging her skin with their acid, tickling her with their busy multitudinous feet. Her breasts are tingling with excitement, her nipples big and hard, her pussy dripping with her fragrant juices, her mind a tumble of exquisite exhilaration, her psyche on fire, brightening the dimly lit room. She moans more and more throatily now, keeping tempo with the violins, with the rotating night, with the slow-motion journey of the moon.

And then, just as an errant cloud passes across the floating sickle in the sky, she arches her back, tightens her grip on the table and pushes her head against the wood. The rushes of her orgasm take hold of her, take over her shuddering body, wrap her into the night. She rocks through the rushes with total abandon, letting her orgasm fill every cell of her being, every nook and cranny of her mind, every recess of her soul. Screaming her absolute satisfaction into the room, she shivers with the delight of her release, the power of her gratification, the all-encompassing joy of her passion. Her whole body quivers, like so many butterflies in an afternoon breeze.

The man can hardly contain himself, watching her come again and again, listening to her scream and moan and groan, but he restrains himself. For him, all this has merely been the beginning, the slowly executed prelude to his own concerto, to his own fleeting participation in the night. As soon as the woman collapses on the table and lies quietly, gasping for breath and sighing contentedly, he releases his pulsing penis and reaches for an ornate box lying on the floor beside the ant farm. This is his culmination, his act of completion, his singular contribution and participation in the night.

Every night eventually comes to a point like that, when disparate currents line up in straight lines, the air suddenly becomes very still, and the mind can discern the distinct aroma of impending closure. The moon may still be hanging in the sky from its invisible wires or it may not, it's of little consequence at this point in time, and there may be clouds obscuring the stars or not. The strains of the violins are still filling the room with their soft persistence and the flickering candles continue to cast vague shadows on the ceiling and on the walls and the woman is still sighing on the table. She is sitting up now to watch him perform his own ritual and get aroused all over again from the spectacle he is about to provide.

And so the man opens the box in this extended moment of anticipation and carefully picks out two of the bees from his collection, one with each forefinger and thumb, attentive to their delicate nature. The woman watches wide-eyed as he places one bee on each side of his penis and lets them sting. He winces with the pain of the stingers penetrating his sensitive organ, but he grits his teeth so as not to disappoint the woman, then drops the bees to die on the floor and pulls the stingers out of his flesh. The night is gradually working up to a crescendo.

They watch intently as the head of his penis swells up from the acid injected into it until it reaches a formidable size. The man shudders with pleasure at the transformation, his arousal reaching a fever pitch from the mixture of intense pain and intense pleasure. He carefully takes his penis between two fingers placed well behind the swelling and holds it out to the woman to admire.

The woman moans. She reaches out and lightly touches the swelling, sending mutual shivers of delight through their bodies. She lies back down, still covered in ants, moves her rump to the edge of the table. Then she spreads her legs as wide as she can, pulls up her knees, steadies herself with her hands on her shins, exposing her receptive pussy to him. The night is at its fullest, the silence between them profound. They know exactly what to do.

The man steps up to the table between the spread legs, aims his swollen penis at her dripping opening, and pushes his enlarged head into her willing receptacle. They moan in unison, he from the pressure on his swelling, she from the engorged penetration, both from the incredibility of their fusion. The man digs his fingernails into her ant-covered thighs to alleviate the excruciating pain, grits his teeth as he pushes further and further into her. The woman moans and groans as she sucks the enlarged penis into her and clamps her muscles around him until he almost screams.

Yet he isn't to be deterred. This is what he has come here to do, drawn to her acidic cave, her ants crawling all over his exposed glans, intensifying his suffering, atonement under a star-strewn sky. In the final analysis, the excitement and the pleasure far outweigh the pain as he keeps holding on to her thighs and thrusts into her and she rocks against him until he shudders with his own orgasm and gushes into her. She reaches down and rubs her clit to treat herself to yet another orgasm while his swelling is still deep inside of her and he can feel her muscles expand and contract with the eagerness of her release.

The night has fulfilled itself. The recording of sonatas for violins is nearing its end, the candles on the floor are beginning to burn out, and the precarious moon in the sky has disappeared behind the horizon. A piece of sky breaks off the edge. The man and the woman, oblivious to the tenuous fragility of the night and everything that entails, wrap their arms around each other, he still buried inside of her, and slowly rock through the afterglow of their mutual completion.

The world has never been as good as this, despite the inherent ambiguities permeating the night. They, too, exist for legitimate reasons, just as the moon will always be somewhere in a sky, and something will always be taking care of the uncertainties no matter how precariously balanced everything might be in a late night with a crescent moon. Somewhere, a solo violin to keep the universe in place.

FROSTY

By Alice Jacobs

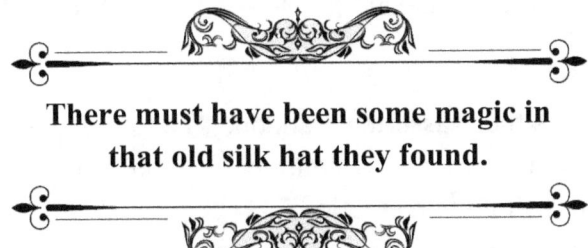

**There must have been some magic in
that old silk hat they found.**

Alice Jacobs works as a manager for a Canadian governmental agency. Long days are spent writing boring reports that nobody reads and going to endless meetings that decide nothing. It allows her semi-engaged mind to roam - to explore topics that are more bizarro than the effect of currency fluctuations on manufacturing output and the gross domestic product. Or perhaps it is just a different kind of bazarro - we'll leave you to be the judge.

The first time that Bill screwed a snowman, it was to win a drunken bet.

He had been out drinking with a group of friends. The discussion had turned into a series of lies about who had had the kinkiest sexual experience. Claims were advanced about partners, locations and practices that were too outlandish to believe, let alone waste time repeating here. All in all, it had been a convivial and harmless evening.

That is, until the bar closed. The group was walking back to the college dormitory. It was a cold December night. The snow crunched under their feet as they walked. They passed a small park in which children had built a snowman. Or, perhaps it was a snow woman. Weird as Bill's fetish eventually became, it was not driven by latent homosexuality.

"Did I ever tell you about the time I screwed a snowman," Bill said.

There was a groan from his companions.

"Is that why your pecker is so small?" George asked. "It got freeze dried?"

Bill hated George.

"It's impossible," asserted Landon. "The cold would cause the blood vessels in the penis to contract. It would be physiologically impossible to maintain an erection."

Landon was in pre-med.

"Ever get a blow job from one?" Riley wanted to know.

Riley was on the varsity football team.

"No, really. This one is true," Bill insisted for reasons that probably had to do with drinking.

"Fifty bucks says you can't," George said.

One reason Bill hated George is that George always had lots of money.

"You're on," said Bill. He took out his wallet and took out a twenty and a ten. Now it was empty. He dug in his pocket and got up to forty. With a ten-dollar loan from Landon (who was very curious – from a professional point of view, of course), Bill was set. It was easier for George to come up with his wager – he simply peeled off a crisp fifty from a large roll.

Riley held the stakes.

Bill approached the snowman.

"Better get her some chocolates," George called out. "She looks like a frigid bitch to me."

Bill's first problem was to get an erection with everyone watching. Fortunately for him, a few of the stories told that evening had struck a chord with him – never mind which ones. One fetish per story is enough to deal with.

Bill undid his fly and grasped his cock. He stroked it gently, thinking of some of the activity he'd heard described that evening. It worked. In a very short time, he was hard.

"Be careful Frosty," George catcalled. "Either he's got an icicle in his pants, or he's happy to see you."

Bill made a hole in the snowman with his finger. Then he slid his cock in it.

"Ohhhh. Up the ass," George hooted. "You are a dirty pig Bill."

But this time, George's wisecrack did not bother Bill. He was discovering, to his amazement, that he enjoyed the sensation.

Bill's sexual experience was limited, and generally solitary. He'd gone all the way with two girls – both at college. It had been fun, but the warm wetness of their insides had been faintly disgusting to him. Perhaps he had become too accustomed to the cooler dryness of the palm of his hand.

The snowman, however, was different than anything he had ever experienced. It was cold, to be sure, but a pleasant cold. It was neither wet nor dry. In all, it was a bit like using a cold damp cloth to clean himself off after making love – but in this case, he was still more excited than in need of cleaning.

Bill began to thrust. His cock was expanding the hole, compressing the snow so that he could get further and further in. The hotness of shaft, and the friction began to melt snow. He could feel the cold trickle of water down onto his balls. The sensations excited him. To be honest, so did the sheer weirdness of what he was doing.

Then he came. He slammed into the snowman as hard as he could, with a cry of joyous triumph. He felt the warmth of his cum on his cock, contrasting with the coldness of the snow. He sagged for a second, and then composed himself.

Pulling himself away from the snowman and tucking his cock back into his pants, Bill tried to be nonchalant.

"Easiest fifty I ever made," he said, trying to be as cool as his cock was.

"Quickest too," George replied. "No wonder Glenys never went back for a second helping."

Normally, this underhanded jibe about one of his two conquests would have enraged Bill. Tonight, he did not care. Riley handed him the money. Bill, with a flourish, handed ten back to Landon and put the rest in his pocket.

"Thanks for staking me even though you thought it was impossible," he told his friend. "Now you know something the physiology text books don't."

The group was silent the rest of the way to dorm. They seemed awed by what they'd witnessed. Even George was subdued.

As for Bill, he was simply pre-occupied. He was wondering where else he'd seen a snowman.

Thus began Bill's nocturnal wanderings. From that evening, every night that it was warmer than 10 below, Bill would walk the streets. He'd find a snowman or a snowwoman, and have his way with it. Sometimes, especially if it was in a more exposed location, he'd approach it like he did the first night – just make a hole in the large bottom ball of the snowman and enlarge it with his cock. Other times, he strived for new experiences. A few times, he found smaller snowmen – their heads were level with his cock so he imagined they were giving him blowjobs. A few times, he took off all his clothes so that he could get a fuller sensory experience. This was much more exciting to him, but only down to a certain point on the thermometer. He tried entering the snowman from the front and the back to see if it made a difference. It did not – although entering it from the side seemed to lend a new level of kinkiness that amused him for a few nights.

During the days, Bill found himself making snowmen and snowwomen. He retained enough common sense to do this off-campus only, since he knew that all those present that fateful evening would jump to conclusions if they saw him rolling balls of snow and piling them up. So too would the three hundred people who had heard the story of that evening.

Then Bill even found a way for a snowman to screw him. He had come across a snowman that had a large carrot for a nose. He converted this into a snowman's cock, dropped his pants and pushed against it with his ass. He gasped as the cold hard carrot entered him. Bill slid back and forth on the vegetable, his cock as cold and hard as the orange root inside him. But not even this was enough. A few days later, Bill made two snowmen very close together. One had a carrot for a cock. That night, Bill squeezed in between his two frosty friends and rocked back and forth. When he leaned backwards, he could feel the carrot penetrate deep inside him. When he moved forward, he imagined that the snowman was feeling his cock in exactly the same way. He felt strangely at one with the snowmen.

Then came spring.

Studies have found that 37% of first year college students are jilted by their lovers at the end of term. At least Bill had company in his misery.

FUN HOUSE
By Kimber Vale

Nothing like a clown to turn that frown upside down.

Kimber Vale is an avid reader, writer, and gardener. She worked as a registered nurse in a previous life, and more recently as a slave to three tiny people. A year ago she realized that her dreams of being an author would require actual writing and has been hammering away at the keyboard since. Thankfully her husband is supportive of her lofty ambitions. Currently, Kimber is armpit deep in a number of projects that span the genres of fantasy and sci-fi, to bizarro and erotica. She is thoroughly enjoying the "polluted stream of consciousness" that bizarro fiction allows her and has some deviant tales percolating right this second.

I had heard so much about the Fun House, and yet I had heard nothing. Like one of those old men's clubs my grandfather was involved with when I was a child. Elks or Masons or something. My brother once asked Pop what he did in his secret society. He gave no specifics, only told us "it'll change a man." Well, the Fun House would change a man or woman, it didn't matter which. With the coin and the desire, the Fun House would twist you permanently.

I longed to be twisted.

Once the war began and the bombs came raining down like a macabre hail storm, the world that had been Mason meetings and apple pies was warped as well. The shelters, scarce and underground, cost more than most could afford. And few enough could fit below to be 'saved.' But my family came from the few, the elite. The moneyed. And so down we went to salvation. And prohibition.

Lovelies we were christened. The unmarked and unscarred; the pale race that lives below the sun, subsisting on algae produced with eclipsing machines and rat meat from our free-loading friends. Had the vermin realized they would become cattle to our subterranean tribe, they might have taken their chances above with the Gritts. But once the hatches had been spun shut, only the coin would convince the guards to open them for a time. And rats had no coin.

If the Lovelies are ghostly pristine, we are still unfortunate in many ways. We live in darkness, cold and silent. Our skin glows white like the underbellies of dead fish recalled in flashes from my youth. We are locked in our cells and told we are blessed. And the privileged may be matched up for mating. But not all. Not many at all.

The barracks are crowded now; a small baby boom directly following our descent strained the capacity of our world. While the bombs still shook our ceilings and loosened rubble onto our heads, the scared rabbits fucked to stay sane. They fucked to recall the good old days and because life feeds on life. How could our world end when we still fucked ourselves silly?

But not me. I was only a child. And now fucking is a lottery for which I will never hold a winning ticket. Silliness I will never experience. My legs are too long, less than ideal for underground passageways. Our species will not stoop in future generations. I will never be allowed to reproduce in this shadow-filled world.

They did not sterilize me. They did not need to. No man would risk The Ostracizing. They would pull on their cocks and spew their juice into the running sewers of the Public Works tunnels before they would give it to me. I know. I have seen them. Strings of white exploding into the murky waters, wasted; and me watching with an aching vortex between my legs, coveting a taste of their raining spunk.

Above-living is considered too dangerous for us to move our people. Radiation readings have leveled off, but are too high to allow for non-mutated offspring. Cancer rates soar on the surface; the Gritts are grotesque and deformed from the heat.

Vile and unrefined but free and happy.

So some of us starve to stand in their seedy sunlight; to bask in their depravity. To be a snow white dove released from a tarnished cage and go forth to suckle at Gaia's disfigured teat.

Steady I scraped, working by day to recover the coin lost with the purchase of our passage. I worked to buy my trip back, harvesting algae in the sweltering containment chambers by day and sneaking to the sewer catwalk by night. After offloading my haul, I would run for a glimpse of the men offloading theirs. And I was reminded of the reason for my toil.

"How do you come to be at this hatch?"

It was the guard speaking. He was tall like me. I wondered if I had seen him with his hands stroking his hard shaft and grimacing as he reached his relief far above the rancid river.

I liked him better to think on it.

"I have coin for passage. My return will be at twenty-three hundred hours. I will tap with the iron pole above."

"Who told you of the pole? I am the one who will tell you what to do." He was scowling. I liked him less then. He would control me and stand before my well-deserved pleasure.

"I know people. I have coin for passage."

I repeated it. In the end, it was the only thing that mattered; the only language I would speak to this captor.

He took the purse.

"Twenty-three. If you do not tap at the designated time, you may try once more tomorrow. No more after that. The fall-out follows those who tarry too long. We do not want to suffer for your perversion."

"Would that I could throw my own perversion into the sewers," I glared at him, and he had the decency to look ashamed as I climbed up to the hatch and my freedom.

*

The clown had painted his face—candy-apple red with white surrounding his lips. He was naked but for the paint, and his radiation burns snaked across his body in angry pink welts.

"Why do you paint your face?"

He was rubbing up and down my length; raw, red phallus cocked like a gun. He dry humped my leg as a horny dog will.

"I would hate to show you my shame-faced shamefulness."

He turned to pinch my leg by separating the cheeks of his rear and squeezing them closed around the skin of my thigh.

"Do put on your outfit, my lovely lady. We will begin shortly in a short manner. Your coin will buy you such happy times here in our Fun House."

He disappeared through a small door, his scrawny ass sagging on his jutting bones and I noticed the slick black wings poking from his back. They were crumpled and defective, as a damp butterfly just out of a chrysalis. A shame he could not use them. Neither man, nor bird, nor truly clown, either; my heart bled for him.

The room was quite dark, but patches of lights, sconces upside-down, tossed blasts of prismatic color toward the ceiling. They illuminated a writhing collection of insects; pearly silver reflected the rays. They undulated to and fro above me. I watched their choreographed waving, liquid in unity, and wished Lovelies could work together with half the precision.

I peeled off my shift, white as my corpse skin, and tossed it aside. The black of my provided suit matched my mood, my desires; dark, inky things I veiled in my mind's recesses. Like these latex pants, skin-tight but for the gaping hole in the crotch; I would wear my depravity on the outside. Here my wickedness would be ordinary. My baseness the least base of my companions. I wore rubber and the devil's smile when my guide returned.

He circled me, snapping a finger under the strap of my suspenders. Rainbow striped and bedazzled, their elastic cracked against my otherwise naked breasts leaving them tingling with delicious anguish. I felt the dig of metal prongs behind the plastic jewels, biting my flesh.

His red-rod had grown larger. Near thick as my foot and twice as long, he slapped me with it as he spun. His giggle was childlike and sent a shiver pitching through my body. I would touch that stiff rocket, but the rules forbade it.

-Be touched, but never touch.

-Only suffering can birth satisfaction.

-Obey or go.

The plaque outside the crumbling stone building made my role abundantly clear. Did I know what consequence lurked behind disobedience? No, and I would not. Servitude was my lot below, but the demands of the Lovelies required my self-denial. Here service would stand before a mirror, and carnal gluttony would look back. Both would wear my face.

"To the next room, my Lovely? The Gorg awaits your face-making, make-facing. Already your attire has grown my man wand like magic, see?"

He poked at my open umbilicus with his fat stick, causing a flood of excitement to wet my lower lips.

"But not enough. The half-men like you in paint. They will show you their pleasure-poles, Lady, but hide your Lovely loveliness we must. Do not remind them to remember who you are!"

He pulled me through a door off the changing room. Well lit, spacious; my eyes squinted in the bright surroundings. A vanity covered in cosmetics hosted a set of chairs. On the far seat sat the peach-toned snake.

"Gorg, won't you Gritt this girl?"

"Of coursssse. Sssssit."

The snake, Gorg, gestured to the chair with a hand that was a smaller serpent sprouted on the side of her body. A matching appendage on the opposite side, and two legs lower down gave her five faces. She sat, thick bodied and bent, in a mockery of human posture. Her vertebrae were folded in a sitting position with a long coiled tail wound up under the chair. A hissing leg crossed over the other and she bounced it impatiently. The supporting limb buried fangs in the wood floor; a foothold held by a face-foot.

"Sssswiftly..." she beckoned me forward, the forked tongue of one hand gesticulating as a curled finger.

I moved and sat, my guide forgotten, so entranced was I by her sightless orbs. Lashes like horses' mane, thick and flowing, parted around each milk-white lens. Spider webs of blood vessels, no pupils, resided in those eyes.

"And yet you see."

"Ssshe sssells sssea ssshells..." Serpent heads spread before my face, imploring *me* to see. Eight eyes, beady black, sparkled like crystal. Eyed me up.

A small head snapped forward, biting a can of orange-yellow paint.

"Sssspread a ssssaffron ssssmile." Gorg's mouth moved, her sibilant tongue flicking with each consonant. I saw no teeth. Her mouth seemed puckered and shriveled with age; ancient as her eyes.

I took the pot of face cream from the jaws and dipped in a finger. Arrow-tipped limbs wove breezily about me, guiding, as I smeared the paste around my lips. They nudged my application wider and I complied, circling mouth and nose in a golden orange oval.

"Ssssapphire sssswirls sssurround the csssircle."

The blue was thicker, caking in my eyebrows and sticking in my pale hair. Gorg hissed encouragingly.

"Sssso nicsssse."

I watched a lump growing from what passed as her neck while I worked. It bulged bigger while I smeared the voluptuous cake through my hair. It clumped in a halo of midnight blue dreadlocks. The snake hands pushed me onward until my pot was empty.

By then the tumor was twice the size of my fist and something squirmed beneath the soft shell. A jagged white tooth pierced the skin from inside, slicing the covering in a smooth gash. A snake emerged. Head and body swayed provocatively as the serpent gazed with wonder through infant eyes.

Gorg spun her withered head toward the arrival and snapped at it with gummy jaws, opening and closing on the fresh flesh. She did not kill it with her toothless maw, but I could see the muscle and skin injured and crimped with each squeeze of her vice. The new snake fought back, sinking its egg-tooth into the murky eye of the mother.

But it was an act of dying desperation and as the upper limbs recognized the victor, they pounced, tearing into the wilting hatchling, ripping at it until it was no more than a patch of gore on the floor and a bleeding hickey on Gorg's diamond-dusted scales.

"A turtle-neck would cover that up, or is that reptile cross-dressing?"

The large head swiveled to me, the mutilated eye leaking bloody tears.

"Ssssillier. Sssso you may go."

I stood and noticed a wet spot where I had been sitting. A giggle, a high delirious trumpet passed my lips. The answering warble erupted from a door on the far wall. My wonderful guide stood waiting for me.

He would not slap me with that beet-red beat-stick now. A small woman, her trunk the size of mine, but her arms and legs half in length, stood before him. She faced me, her expression stoic as the firm sausage rested on her head. It was bigger than her leg, but she did not raise tiny hands to balance the swollen cock. I was reminded of the foreign women that carried ponderous vessels on their heads. Did they still live? And how about those jugs?

The two turned in perfect unison to lead me astray. My coin insisted, after all. The room I entered next was a never-ending corridor.

"Lay down if laying is what you crave, lovely lass." Clown stroked my stiff hair, trailing a skeletal finger down to my lips. I sucked in the tip and he did not scold me. He touched first, not I.

On the floor was centered a foot-wide conveyor. An outline marked my place and I molded to it.

From my perspective, the flood of nude males that marched down the aisle toward my prostrate form was astounding. Their cocks were heavy and hard, promenading proudly before the rest of their bodies. The first stopped, straddled above my face. He was a clown of sorts, tall, covered in raw welts. His two ass-holes stared at me, winking lasciviously. Others lined up down the hall, countless cocks and balls hanging above like bunches of tantalizing grapes. I saw a dew-drop form on the fat helmet above me and shivered, watching the clown stroke himself with a sneer.

The belt moved, began to pull me languidly beneath the bare bodies.

First they were clowns, decorated in motley paint, but their pricks were all scarlet, and not one was small. They dangled above me as their masters rubbed them with zeal. My face passed under a man as a jet-stream of cream flew off, missing me by the smallest margin. I craned my neck, snapping like a new-hatched bird toward brackish sustenance, but without reward.

On I slid, tears rolling down my temples and doubtless marring my gritty blue with rivulets of pasty white. The men were growing shorter; their bulging knobs teased closer and closer to my starved tongue. The legs surrounding me grew ever twisted by degrees, stunted and gorgeous.

Finally a beefy cock stroked my cheek as I rolled through. It slid over my lips and I stuck a tentative flick of the tongue to it. Salty manna greeted me and the half-man hopped to the side to allow me passage. My body would not fit between his legs. I watched him spend himself on the ground, screaming in agony at the game they played. Did they know that this was the same misery of my entire existence?

I howled in rage, gnashing feral teeth while my body lay in obeisance.

The lights died completely, but I felt myself rolling onward.

And then a sudden halt.

A match flared. At first I could not see beyond the wisp of flame, but my eyes adjusted to show another half-man. He lit candles on the floor surrounding us before picking one up and showing his face to me. Sandy hair fell over his neck and ears and his eyes were emeralds. His cheeks were sculpted and covered in sand-paper stubble. A god among small men.

"Come and bathe," he spoke, tilting his head to a steaming metal tub. I rose, peeling down elastic and rubber as I walked. I stepped in, and my beautiful dwarf sponged honeysuckle bubbles over me, washing away my colors and rinsing me clean. His fingers lingered on my breasts, pinching my small nipples to hard peaks. He slipped a diminutive hand under the foam; green tinged now, and found my clit. He worked it frenetically while he spoke. I trembled and tried to listen.

"Your roar touched me. I, too, burn to possess that which I do not. The masking entices the others. They have come to love our world, and themselves most of all. Not I. I am the Gemini to your deepest proclivities. I hold the keys to unlock you, and you me."

He bent and placed his lips to mine, his tongue, thick and strong, molested my mouth while his fingers entered my hot twat. I arched and groaned.

"The others cannot possess you as I can. Come."

I stood, dripping. My lover pointed to a bed of pillows nearby.

"Down."

I watched him strip. He was the only covered man in the Fun House. His pants dropped to reveal his double treasure. Two long cocks, one behind the other hung gloriously before me. I was wet from my bath, wet from his fingers, and wet from the sight of him.

Slowly the dueling members squeaked inside my coordinating holes. In and out they slid, brutally unhurried until I could expire from the torment. He knew. He pounded at me next, his two tools stroking each other through the slick wall that separated them. With hysterical laughter we climaxed together, him filling me up wholly in my holiest of holies. His thick jizz ran over my thighs when he pulled free of my clutches.

Tears distort my vision whenever I recall that sweetest pleasure of my life.

Now my belly swells and my breasts are puffy and sore. A small life kicks within me as I slave away in the food collection unit. But I have tasted the salt of the earth and my body has savored the seed of a half-man, more man by half than these clowns down below.

My babe may be the smallest Lovely ever born and will never want for gratification. And if not, I know where we will go. All wait to see if I will be Ostracized or become the Queen Bee, but either way it will not be the end of the world.

We have done that already.

BUTTERFLY KISSES
By Duncan Meece

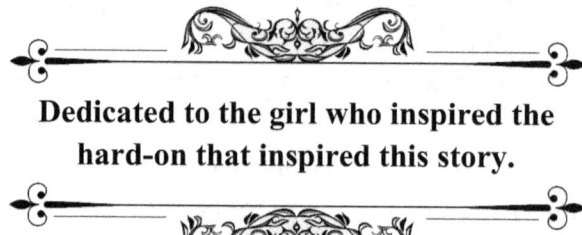

**Dedicated to the girl who inspired the
hard-on that inspired this story.**

*Duncan Meece is a fan of weird, dirty and violent shit. When not
getting drunk, he writes stories and makes films. He does this mostly
to entertain himself, though he doesn't mind if others enjoy the shit
he makes as well.*

On a hot day in June, Henrietta Mae Culbertson discovered a
family of fairies in a dead hornet's nest in her back yard.

She pulled her hands from her flower garden, knocking the dirt
from her late husband's tattered work gloves and wiped the sweat-
soaked tufts of gray hair from her brow as she struggled on wobbly
knees to stand. She was walking sluggishly through the thick brush
of her back yard towards her rickety, wooden porch when she saw
the nest, jutting out from the ceiling like a bulbous, mutant tumor.

She wondered how she managed to miss it when she walked
outside earlier. It was one of the biggest she'd ever seen. She
grabbed a large twig and proceeded to prod at it when a head poked
its way out from the entrance. She stepped back and blinked in

disbelief. A tiny man with blond curls. He immediately retreated into the nest upon seeing her.

"Hey. It's all right," she said. "Come on out. I won't hurt you."

He appeared again, cautiously.

"Hi there," she said.

"Hello," the tiny man said.

"What are you doing in there?" she said.

"It was abandoned when we got here," he said. "I'm sorry if we're trespassing but our village was attacked."

"Attacked?" she said, stepping towards the nest.

"Blackbirds. They brought death with them from the sky."

"My gosh! There's more of you in there?"

"Yes," he said. "Four of us. We managed to escape the massacre. There could be more survivors but... there was so much chaos..."

"How terrible. You must be awfully cramped in there. Why don't you come on inside where it's nice and cool?"

A relieved smile appeared on the tiny man's face. "I can't begin to express my gratitude."

The fairies fluttered their way into Henrietta's home. She watched them with wonder as her eyes began to glisten. Frail, transparent, kaleidoscopic wings. Tiny, naked bodies, no more than six inches high. She felt blessed to have these majestic creatures in her presence.

They landed atop the kitchen table and took in their new surroundings. It was a small, country home filled with various knick-knacks. A vast, alien world to the little fairies. Mrs. Culbertson kneeled forward as much as she could with her achy joints, a wide grin upon her face, observing every subtle twitch they made.

After several minutes, when she finally managed to break her fascinated stare, she went to the hall closet and retrieved an old fish tank. It had been years since she had fish but she figured it would make an appropriate residence for her new guests. She washed the tank in her sink and placed it on the table before them. "It's not much," she said. "But it's sturdy."

Henrietta's tabby cat was slinking around under the kitchen table. The commotion had roused him from his lazy slumber. The fairies settled themselves inside the tank. A solid, transparent barrier between them and the world of her home. The cat jumped onto the table, as enthralled by the visitors as Henrietta, pawing playfully at the glass. They looked upon the furry beast in awe and were grateful for the protection of the tank. Henrietta shooed the cat off the table.

"Do you have names?" she said.

"I'm Warren," the adult male fairy said. "This is my sister, Rose." He motioned to the female about his age. "The little one, Robin." The child was staring up at Henrietta, mouth agape and wide-eyed. "And Ella," he said, "the elder." He motioned to the oldest fairy sitting in the corner. She was a brittle thing, wings crinkled. It took every bit of her strength to fly as far as she had. Her eyes wandered farther than the rest of them.

"You poor things must be famished," Henrietta said. "I have some delicious, homemade pot pie in the fridge. I'll heat it up for you." She walked to the kitchen to prepare the food.

"Are you sure this is a wise decision?" Rose said to Warren, tapping her foot anxiously.

"Do you have to question every decision I make?" Warren said. "This is a safe place. How long do you think we would've survived in that nest?"

"Humans can't be trusted," she said. "This place gives me a bad feeling."

"Have you ever dealt with a human personally? All your assumptions are based on dark tales from foolish elders."

"*Foolish?*" she said with a laugh. "That'll be the day when you've earned the right to call anyone but yourself foolish. Anyway, you've never dealt with a human either. All I'm saying is we shouldn't let our guard down."

Mrs. Culbertson returned with a saucerful of pot pie. "Here you are, my darlings," she said, placing the steaming meal inside the tank. Robin rushed over and inhaled deeply, filling his nose with the unfamiliar but intoxicating scent of fresh cooked vegetables and chicken.

"Let it cool, Robin," Warren said, patting the little one on the back. "Thank you for all you've done for us," he said to the grinning giant before him. "What do I call you?"

Her grin grew wider. "Call me Henrietta."

Waking early the next morning, Henrietta gathered the biggest plants from her garden and constructed a faux oasis inside the tank. She filled a plastic container with water from the tap and placed it on a leafy bed so they could bathe.

She spent hours watching the fairies with an old magnifying glass she had found in a forgotten desk drawer in her bedroom. She watched Rose sit in the corner and talk to Ella while Warren roughhoused with Robin, the two of them laughing together for the first time in quite awhile since the village had been destroyed.

Most of Henrietta's attention was focused upon Warren. His body was lean and tight. And he was well-endowed, she noticed, relative to his diminutive stature.

Rose looked with disgust upon the colossal, veiny eye that monitored them. "Does it not disturb you to be put on display for that monster?" she said to Warren, keeping her voice low to escape the ear of Mrs. Culbertson.

"She's only curious," Warren said as Robin ran circles around him. "She's hardly a *monster*."

"We shouldn't have come here," she said firmly.

"When did you last see Robin this happy? Doesn't his laughter bring you any joy at all?"

"This place is a prison. Every time I look up at that *thing*, I expect it to grab me and gobble me up."

Warren laughed. "Rose, you are—"

"I am concerned for this family," she said, standing up to look him in the eye. "You don't know the intentions of this human. You're as reckless as you've always been."

"I made a decision to take this family out of harm's way," Warren said, clenching his fists in frustration. "This human hasn't been anything but welcoming to us. And yet, you call her a monster and condemn me. I didn't see you turn down the hot meal she gave us yesterday. If this shelter is unacceptable to you, you can leave any time."

"I would never leave this family," she said. "You know that."

"Then unless you have a better alternative..."

"I have an alternative," she said. "We leave this place and seek out other survivors. We regroup and rebuild."

"We can't go out there with the children and Ella again. It's a wonder we survived as long as we did."

Ella let out an exhausted moan from the corner of the tank. Rose and Warren turned to see her drooling and slumped over on her side. Rose rushed over and set her upright, wiping the drool from her shriveled lip.

"It's all right, Mama," Rose said, smiling. "I know you don't like it when Warren and I fight."

"She's getting worse," Warren said, crossing his arms and stepping forward.

"It's this damn place," Rose said under her breath.

"It's not the place, it was the move," Warren said. "And now you want to bring her *back* out there to roam around some more and get attacked again? Do you think *that* will help her mental state?"

"Of course we can't bring her and Robin. But one of us should still go and try to find others."

"And which of us might that be?" Warren said. "I suppose *I* should go, yes? It wasn't enough that I found this heavily fortified shelter, now I have to leave to find survivors that may not even remain."

"I can go find survivors!" Robin said boldly from the other side of the tank, thrusting a small leaf into the air like a sword.

"I know you could, my boy," Warren said with pride. "But I need you here to stand guard."

"I'll stand guard!" Robin went back to rushing around the tank, weaving in and out behind plants and diving into leafy piles.

"What would you have us do then?" Rose said. "Stay here forever?"

Warren looked up at Henrietta's massive face, still watching over them. "I'll think of something."

Warren couldn't get to sleep. Leaves rustled underneath him as he tossed and turned. He rolled onto his back and noticed the massive silhouette of Henrietta, watching him from the darkness. He sat upright and she stepped into the light, revealing her smiling face. He stood and fluttered his way to the top of the tank as she opened the lid to greet him.

"Hello, Henrietta," Warren said to the giant.

"Can't sleep? Would you like to visit for awhile?" she said hopefully.

"Sure," he said, after a quick glance at his sleeping sister.

Her bedroom was overwhelmingly blue. Blue walls, blue bed sheets, blue curtains, blue carpet. All different shades, all just as blue. It was cold.

She plopped down on her bed and placed Warren on the headboard shelf next to hand-painted clay figurines about his size. He looked curiously into their hollow eyes.

"I made them myself," she said picking one up. "They can be your little friends."

Warren chuckled awkwardly as she placed the figurine next to Warren. Its painted grin. Its sightless, dead eyes. A friend it was not.

"Your sister doesn't like me too much, huh?" Henrietta said.

"She's just protective," Warren said. "She's always been cautious, even as a child."

"I can see why she'd be protective of a cute little thing like you."

"Yes. I suppose. But not just of me," he said. "She's protective of the family." The dead eyes of the statues became increasingly disturbing to him.

"Did you have a wife?" Henrietta said.

"No, I didn't."

"Girlfriend?"

"There was no one like that," Warren said, eyes pointed down. "I took care of my mother with my sister. We stayed together. No one else."

"And the little one?" she said.

"Robin isn't our blood. He was orphaned after the attack on our village. But I look after him as if he were my own."

"Do you get lonesome?"

"It doesn't bother me. I've got enough to worry about."

"I know what it is to be lonesome," Henrietta said. "I've been alone for a long time since my husband passed."

Warren didn't notice Henrietta's finger until it brushed lightly against his thigh. Startled, he took a step back.

"It's okay," she said, scooting closer to the headboard shelf. "Relax."

"What are you–?" Warren backed himself against the headboard.

Henrietta spread his legs open with her index and middle finger. "It's okay," she said softly. He did not resist, keeping himself pinned against the headboard, arms out, palms flat. She began stroking his cock with her pinky. His heartbeat quickened. She licked her lips, watching as he slowly became hard.

She stroked from his balls to the base of his cock. He kept his head turned to the side, away from her, eyes shut tight. Her face moved closer. He could feel her hot breath against him. "It's okay," she said, softer still. His eyes popped open wide in shock when he felt her warm, sticky tongue in-between his thighs. He looked down at it with disgust, pink and yellow undulating flesh.

It didn't take him long. He came for the very first time onto Henrietta Culbertson's colossal tongue. The tongue retreated into her mouth and she swallowed before looking down at him and smiling. "Wasn't that okay?"

Warren was petrified, frozen against the back of the headboard, Henrietta's hot saliva coating his lower body.

She laid her palm out flat before him. "Come on," she said.

He reluctantly stepped onto her palm. She brought him close to her face and began to lick all over his body, coating him good. She stopped and looked at him. "I want you inside me," she said.

"Please..." he said desperately.

"I want you to go down there and go inside me," she said. "It's only fair."

Tears began to run down Warren's face.

"Do it now," she said, "or I'll rip your goddamn wings off."

Mrs. Culbertson set Warren down on the bed between her legs. She hiked up her nightgown, revealing her underwear, crotch stained with a pale shade of yellow. She pulled her underwear down to her ankles. Warren stood before her pussy. The hair was very thick and very dark and very gray. The smell was overwhelming. He could taste the foulness in the back of his throat.

"Go on," she said. "I want you in there. You go in there and wiggle until I say you can come out."

Warren slowly stepped forward and, breathing through his mouth, reached through the matted hair and pulled apart the opening, releasing an even more intense stench.

"That's it," Henrietta said. "Go on in."

Warren shoved his right arm in and then the other. His eyes were clenched tight, tears dribbling down his chin. He took a last breath before plunging headfirst into Mrs. Culbertson's slit.

She grunted with delight. "Get all the way in, you little sonnavabitch. Fuck me!"

Warren wriggled his way inside her. He left enough of his legs protruding so he could maneuver his way back out. He started to wiggle around as best he could to please the giant, surrounded by the pink and purple undulating walls of this cramped, stink-filled tomb.

Henrietta closed her eyes, slack-jawed, and reached down to her crotch. She pushed Warren deep inside her until his legs disappeared. He was sealed in. The more he struggled, the more Henrietta moaned and tensed up.

The vaginal walls convulsed. Warren felt them closing in on him, ready to squeeze the life from his bones. They were getting more and more moist with each convulsion. He kicked at the sealed entrance, fighting for freedom. This stimulated his living coffin further.

As Warren began to lose strength and give up hope, a torrent of sludge washed over him, filling his mouth, his nose, everything. He closed his eyes, struggling to swim, but there was nowhere to go until he felt himself being pulled from the death trap.

He opened his eyes, looking up into a hazy, blue sky. The stench was still heavily upon him, but it was less intense. He coughed some of the goo out of his lungs as he sat there on the mattress in a puddle of sludge, catching his breath. Henrietta had her back against the headboard, breathing heavily.

Neither of them moved for quite awhile.

At dawn, Warren stood wide awake in the tank after a mostly sleepless night, trembling from head to toe with the crushing weight of shame and the still intense stench upon him. He had tried to scrub himself clean earlier in the night but to no avail.

He could hear Mrs. Culbertson beginning to stir in her bedroom. He stared at the door, a cold, hateful look in his eyes.

"How are you going to convince her to let you out?" Rose said.

"She will let me out."

"How can you be sure?"

"Trust me."

Rose hadn't gotten much out of Warren when Henrietta returned him to the tank earlier in the night. Right away, she had detected the stink. She knew something terrible had happened to him, but he wouldn't give her any information. All she knew was that his opinion on the hospitality of the giant had drastically changed.

"And what happens when you return?" Rose said. "What if you don't find anyone? And even if you do, what then?"

"If I can find some able-bodied survivors, I'll have them wait outside," he said. "When that *thing* in there goes to sleep, they'll sneak in and free us."

"And if you can't find anyone?"

"Then I'll try again tomorrow."

Mrs. Culbertson's door creaked open and she shuffled out into the living room, rubbing her tired eyes. "Good morning, my little dears," she said. The fairies watched as she removed the tank's lid and took the empty food bowl and the dirty bath water over to the kitchen sink.

Warren nodded to Rose before fluttering out of the tank and over to the giant.

"Well, hello there," she said.

"Henrietta," Warren said, nodding. "Last night–"

"Last night," she said as she scrubbed the food bowl with an already dirty sponge, "was a fair exchange for free room and board for you and your little family. You live under my roof, you live under my rules."

Warren felt a hate-filled sickness rising up through his guts. He did his best to keep it from showing on his face. "No, that's not it at all," he said. "I... enjoyed last night".

She stopped scrubbing. "You did?"

"Yes," he said. "I've never felt such a feeling."

Henrietta smiled. "You haven't?"

"When I was young," Warren said, "the elders told legends of giants. Stories of wondrous, erotic adventures. Until last night, I thought they were just stories. You've shown me a magical world, Henrietta."

Henrietta soaked in every word. Her eyes drifted up and down his tiny body, moisture building in her mouth. She could still taste him.

"I need to find others," Warren said.

"What?" Henrietta said, snapping out of her lustful gaze.

"My people," he said. "There could be dozens more out there, fighting for survival. I have to find them and bring them to you."

"You can't go out there," she said, firmly, turning back to the sink.

"Please, I have to. They need you. They need to know you exist so that they can worship you as I do."

Henrietta was stunned. "Worship...?"

Warren kissed his sister, mother and little Robin goodbye before fluttering out of the tank, out the back door and into the wilderness that was Mrs. Culbertson's yard. She watched him fly away, fantasizing about the swarm of miniature men that would accompany him upon his return. Their little hands. Cocks. All over her naked body. Inside her mouth. Her pussy. She shuddered and clutched at her collar with a trembling hand.

Henrietta stepped out onto her porch, the golden glow of sundown enveloping her. "Warren!" she said, calling out. No response.

She rustled through bushes and gazed into treetops, squinting to fight the piercing orange glow. Each time she called for him, each cry louder than the last, only deafening silence called back.

As she turned around, she almost ran face first into it, seeing it and stopping herself only at the last second. A colossal spider web in-between two oaks. When her eyes adjusted, her heart skipped a beat. There he was, tucked in the corner of the web. A gray, shriveled husk, blood and organs sucked clean out.

"Warren...?" she said as she stepped closer, her voice cracking.

He had been dead for hours. As he had fluttered from the house in a hurry, he found himself suddenly stuck, never seeing the silk death trap until it was too late. He watched in horror as the spider disemboweled and ate him alive.

Henrietta clenched her fists, tears streaming down her wrinkled face, flushed with anguish. With an agonized scream, she swiped the web down from between the trees and stomped it furiously into the dirt. She collapsed to her knees and began to sob.

Rose had been awake all night. There had been no meal that evening. After Henrietta had come back inside around dark, she retired to her bedroom and had not reappeared since. Rose could feel Robin's stomach rumbling as she held him close.

She missed Warren. Somewhere inside, she knew he was dead but she couldn't admit it to herself. Her vision fixed on that ember of hope, she closed her eyes.

The water hit fast and hard, slamming Rose and Robin against the wall of the tank. She looked up and saw the source of the torrent; a garden hose fed through the lid of the tank. The giant shuffled back to her chambers, leaving the fairies to their fate.

Rose threw Robin on her back and rushed towards Ella. She plunged her arms into the water, grasping for her mother, buried under a pile of wet foliage. Finding a frail arm, she pulled. Ella's body came up from beneath the steadily rising water, eyes empty. With tears welling up in her eyes, Rose let the body sink back down.

Her wings were too wet to fly. She grabbed onto the base of the tallest plant in the tank and began to shimmy her way to the top, turning her head to shield her eyes from the stinging spray of the hose. Once at the top, Robin climbed onto her shoulders and slid out through the crack where the hose had entered. He made his way onto the roof of the tank, followed closely by Rose.

The hose ran down from the table to the floor. Robin wrapped his tiny, trembling arms around her waist and she slid down the hose until her feet touched the floor. She scooped Robin up in her arms, her eyes darting to the malicious giant's door. Still closed. She followed the hose with her eyes to the cat door. That was their escape route. *The cat door.*

Before the dreadful realization hit her, a pair of green eyes lunged at her from the darkness of the house. The feline was on top of her in an instant, claws tearing her breasts open, as it sank its teeth into her shoulder. Robin was thrown from her arms, tumbling across the kitchen floor. This caught the cat's attention and he turned to the tiny morsel.

Rose watched, bleeding out, as the cat pounced and munched down Robin. The bones cracking in the furry beast's jaws. Screaming. Gurgling. Echoing forever in her head.

With her final breath, she prayed. *May Henrietta Mae Culbertson live forever.*

SEXUAL MADNESS
By Rose de Fer

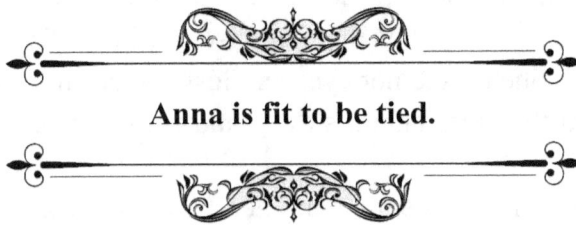

Anna is fit to be tied.

Rose de Fer sees the sensual in the strange and she loves the view from the edge. She lives in England with her husband, who feeds her wine and raw meat and keeps the chains tight when the moon is full.

Anna gasped as Dr. Rawlinson's strong fingers pulled the laces tighter, pressing the steel bones of the corset even harder against her ribs, so tight it felt as though she would be crushed. There was a momentary flash of panic as she realised she could no longer inflate her lungs fully, but that was merely another element of the absolute control he had over her. He controlled her shape, her breathing, her fear. Everything.

The steel cage forced her soft curves into the dramatic contours of an hourglass, pinching her waist while accentuating her bosom and hips. Across the room she could see her chambermaid's uniform, folded neatly on a chair, her own plain and functional corset on top. She had never seen, let alone worn, such a fine garment as the one her master was lacing her into now. It was of rich blue silk, accented with delicate pink blossoms.

She stood in the centre of the room, naked but for the beautiful corset. Her wrists were bound with soft cords and secured to the iron coat tree just in front of her. To keep her still, he'd said. In this way her body was presented for the demonstration.

"You see, gentlemen, how eager she is to please, how willing to endure discomfort merely for my approval."

"Very like a well trained pet, Rawlinson."

"Indeed," he said with pride. "She is the ideal specimen."

Anna's face grew hot as the men discussed her. There were eight of them in all. She closed her eyes and lost herself in the moment.

He pulled the laces again, slowly and firmly, cinching her waist ever smaller.

"As you can see, gentlemen, her breathing has become very shallow. Were she to be exposed to some fright, she would likely swoon. We are all aware, are we not, of the link between fear and arousal? Such constriction of her body is both frightening and arousing for her. Indeed, she is quite flushed."

He laid his cool fingers against her face and she trembled at his touch. But she would not disgrace herself by fainting as delicate ladies did. She would do her best to earn her master's praise.

"Compressing the female body in this way inflames the lower organs, overheating the blood and thereby exciting impure desires. Little wonder our good Reverend Chatham is so opposed to the practice, eh?"

The men chuckled in agreement and Anna braced herself as the laces were pulled tighter. Each tightening made her feel as though she were shrinking, as though her entire body could be laced down to the size of a tiny creature her master might hold in the palm of his hand or tuck away inside his pocket. She was grateful for the bonds. Without them she would not have been able to stand.

One of the older men frowned at her and then turned his glowering countenance on Dr. Rawlinson. "But sir, surely these women are merely following the dictates of fashion. They can't possibly be aware of anything as complex as sexual desire, nor can they possess the mental capacity to actively seek it out. That is the sole province of the male."

The statement sparked some discussion amongst the group. Half of the men insisted that the female of the species was not designed to experience sexual pleasure while the other half argued that it was possible but abhorrent to the sensitive female nature. None of them sought the opinion of the only female present.

"Gentlemen," Dr. Rawlinson said, "this is a debate for another time. For now let us focus on the subject of this demonstration. Namely, the observable effects of extreme corsetry on the female body. Our Anna is proving a most agreeable specimen, don't you think? Quite aware of the irregular nature of these proceedings and yet entirely trustful and obedient."

The older man who had spoken before snorted at that. "As I said earlier, Rawlinson, a well trained pet. She can't possibly understand the risks involved. Why, Reverend Chatham only last month published a pamphlet warning of the dangers of tight-lacing. It is a proven fact that it produces insanity."

Dr. Rawlinson smiled. "It is an argument I have heard, my good man. But I suggest to you that this 'insanity' is of a purely sexual nature. A temporary madness, if you will, which passes once the lady is freed from the constricting garment."

As he spoke he drew his fingers down the front of the corset to illustrate its constriction. Anna could barely feel his touch through the material, but it was enough to send a little thrill of arousal through her. She felt light-headed.

His hand moved down to the base of the corset, where he rested his palm gently against her bottom. Then he deftly slipped a finger between her legs and she gave a little cry as she felt him touch her sleek wetness. It was as though a light had flared within her. Her entire body came wildly alive in that moment and she felt the pleasure in every inch of her flesh. Her legs threatened to buckle as she clung to the coat tree, gasping until her master leaned in to whisper in her ear.

"Calmly, my girl," he urged. "Slow your breathing."

She obeyed, blushing at his nearness. She had felt the scratch of his whiskers against her cheek, smelled the hint of brandy on his breath. Delicious. Unable to stop herself, she pressed her thighs together, desperately craving his touch again and not caring if she made a spectacle of herself.

"Sexual madness," Dr. Rawlinson repeated for his audience. "She was a chaste young lady before this little demonstration and look at her now. As wanton as any harlot."

One of the men approached, standing before her and peering closely at her face. The evidence of her wantonness must be plainly visible, for he shook his head with disapproval and stepped away again. "My own wife is herself deceived by this scandalous practice of tight-lacing," he grumbled.

The gentleman nearest him, the youngest of the group, smiled at that. "I take it then, sir, that you are not the beneficiary of it?"

"Why, you impertinent—"

Dr. Rawlinson interrupted before the flustered man could complete his oath. "I believe there can be little harm in the practice if the lady is closely watched."

"But what of this resultant sexual madness you speak of? Are we to allow our women to succumb to such – such wickedness?"

"Perhaps one might provide the lady with an outlet for it?" Dr. Rawlinson suggested mildly.

The younger gentleman laughed. "That's what our friend here is afraid of!"

Anna ignored their jest and focused on the exquisite confinement of her body. Dr. Rawlinson had trained her well. Inch by slow inch he had accustomed her to the rigours of tight-lacing, first in the privacy of his laboratory and now here before his guests. But it wasn't merely the compression of her ribs that brought on the sexual madness. She experienced a similar madness whenever she brought her master his tea. Or his morning paper. In fact, she felt flushed and discomposed whenever he was near. Her mind would fill with unchaste images and impure thoughts. And although she had never confessed this shameful secret to him, she sensed that he knew it anyway.

She imagined him stitching her permanently into a corset, the long needle piercing both her skin and the corset as it bound the two together. She dreamt of the pain she would feel with each sharp penetration and with every movement thereafter. The euphoric suffering she would surrender to as she became a living statue of flesh and steel and silk. He would position her in an alcove in his bedroom and gaze at the perfection he had inflicted on her. There she would stand, day after day, driven to a pleasing madness by her desire. At night he would carry her to his bed and defile his creation, taking her in unspeakable ways. His violent exertions would tear the stitches and blood would stain the fabric like roses. Perhaps in time her body would absorb the corset, making it a living part of her. Then he would cut new laces from her skin. Pulling them tight would induce such a frenzy of lust that she must remain confined for the rest of her days, treated by him with the most extreme methods at his disposal. . .

"Are you ready, Anna?" he said, startling her from her reverie as he gave the laces a final pull, fully closing the silk panels around her torso like a cage. Her sex pulsed hungrily as he encircled her waist with his hands, the fingers meeting with room to spare. With a nod of approval he untied her wrists and turned her to face the group. His eyes met hers and she knew he could smell her desire. The wetness must be obvious to all. She couldn't have felt more exposed if she had been naked.

"But how can the poor creature breathe?" came a querulous voice from the back, "let alone go about her duties?"

"She is fully able to breathe," Dr. Rawlinson explained patiently, indicating the pale curves of her breasts. They rose and swelled with each shallow inhalation, faster now that she knew he was watching.

"As for her duties, well, of late her duties have been rather specialised. You see, she is more than just my chambermaid. She is both my subject and my assistant."

"A female assistant," scoffed the older man. "Next you'll be giving her the vote!"

Even the younger man laughed at that, clapping his companion on the shoulder as he turned to go. "I thank you for your hospitality, Dr. Rawlinson. It has been a most. . . intriguing display."

Dr. Rawlinson sighed and shook his head. "Gentlemen, you disappoint me. Here I had hoped to disabuse you of the notion of the delicate, asexual female this evening. A pity."

"You would have our wives and daughters embrace such indecency."

"Utter lunacy, sir!"

"There's a reason you were asked to leave the university," one of the men said darkly. "Your theories have no place in a civilised society. Good night, sir!"

Muttering like-minded sentiments, the men filed out, leaving Anna standing in the centre of the room.

Dr. Rawlinson turned to her with a shrug. "Perhaps the world is not yet ready for my ideas."

"Nor mine," she said and immediately blushed. She hadn't intended to voice her thoughts aloud.

"Oh dear. Has this public display had an unnatural effect on my little specimen?"

She lowered her head as her master approached her. He led her to the desk and turned her around, bending her forward at the hips. She placed her hands on the cool expanse of mahogany and spread her arms out to either side, lowering her face to the red leather inset.

"Let's see, shall we?"

He edged her legs apart and she whimpered softly as her dampness was exposed to the cool air. Her insides throbbed while she waited for him to touch her. It seemed an eternity before he finally pressed his fingers into her soft folds. Again, her body felt jolted and she cried out, pushing back against him to force him deeper.

"Goodness me," he murmured, and she could hear the smile in his voice. "If only I could submit my findings to the Royal Society."

His fingers described lazy circles around her sex and she clamped her legs together against his hand, begging him to go further. He didn't make her wait long. She heard the rustle of cloth as he removed his trousers and then something hard was pressing against her sex, demanding entry. Then he held her by her tiny corseted waist as he drove himself into her, again and again. She hadn't known such ecstasy was possible. Each penetration sent waves of excitement through her entire body and she cried out as she abandoned herself fully to the pleasure.

A deluge of images spun through her mind as her master fucked her. She saw herself naked and bound to the table in his laboratory, obscenely splayed for him as he penetrated her with cold steel instruments and commented on her unnatural response to such violation. She saw him towering above her as she knelt at his feet, a collar around her neck and attached to a chain he held in one hand as he fed her morsels of food with the other. She saw herself suspended via a series of elaborately looped leather straps from an iron frame, her body exposed and helpless as he stimulated her to madness.

Suddenly his body tensed and he clutched her tightly with a low deep moan. She felt the tiny spasms of his cock deep inside her and she realised that he had climaxed. She knew it was something that happened to men, although Dr. Rawlinson believed it was also possible for women. "Hysterical paroxysm," he'd told her it was called. She didn't know what such a thing would entail but as he pulled her to her feet and turned her around she suspected that he was about to show her.

His face was flushed and his hair dishevelled, but he suddenly seemed more dominant than ever. His authority brought out a natural submissiveness in her and she chewed her lip nervously, awaiting further instructions. She was panting for breath and her legs trembled, barely able to support her after the onslaught her body had endured.

"Remember your breathing, Anna," he said. "We don't want you passing out." He lifted her easily and sat her on the edge of the desk and then he eased her onto her back. "Shall we test another one of my theories?" he asked, smiling.

She closed her eyes, knowing he didn't require an answer. There was the sound of a desk drawer sliding open, followed by the rattle of items inside. Anna tensed in anticipation as he spread her legs wide apart. Something metal pressed against her sex and she gasped at the sudden chill. There was the whir of gears, as though someone were winding a clock, and then a series of fast and intense vibrations began to race through her entire lower body. The sensation was overwhelming and she cried out wildly at the powerful stimulation.

She could just hear her master's voice over the hum of the device. He murmured encouragement along with amused observations, objectifying her as he had during the demonstration. His little pet, his experimental subject, his specimen. The words bound themselves up with the physical feelings and before she knew it her body was entirely out of her control. At last the rising swell of ecstasy overtook her and for a moment she thought she would burst out of her skin. It lasted so long it was nearly unbearable. Stars exploded behind her eyes and she found herself crying with joy by the time the throbbing had subsided. Her whole body felt alive, exhilarated, devastated.

When she returned to herself she saw that Dr. Rawlinson was smiling at her. She covered her face, blushing furiously. He peeled her hands away.

"Don't be silly, girl," he laughed. "There's no reason why ladies shouldn't have as much fun as gentlemen do."

"But I'm not a lady, sir," she said shyly. "I'm just your chambermaid. It wouldn't do to be getting ideas above my station."

"Nonsense. You're my research assistant and my greatest achievement. My findings will change the world one day, you'll see."

He helped her up and she got shakily to her feet. Her body was still buzzing from everything he'd done to her that evening and she was sure she could even feel the vibrations through the steel bones of the corset. She closed her eyes, remembering. As she stroked the blue silk, a flurry of terms came to her: impure desires, hysterical paroxysm, sexual madness.

"Here," he said. "I should probably release you from that."

But she drew away. "Oh, please may I keep it on, sir?"

He looked both pleased and puzzled by her resistance.

"You said the madness was only temporary, that it would pass as soon as the corset was removed. And – well, I don't think I'm quite ready to be cured yet."

TERRA CUPIDUS
By Robin Tiergarten

See a doctor for an erection lasting more than four hours.

Robin Tiergarten lives in Southern California and loves playing in the mud and getting filthy. The outdoors are especially appealing to Robin who enjoys hiking, camping, and trail running in the local mountains. When not sleeping under the stars, Robin writes strange stories.

Hatchet-face and I have this deal. Used to be with Mallet, but she got burnt out, actually dried right up, like she was an old shriveled-up puss or some schoolmarm snatch who couldn't work it for fuck anymore. Just broken down, withered, but not Hatchet-face. She's my number now and has been for a while. She's all juicy like a watermelon, squirt right in your eye like a lemon. So refreshing, too. She can entice anyone. See we use that to our advantage. But you know that, huh?

Hatchet-face isn't just juicy; she's a piece too. Has a tight body with all the right curves and straights that she accented in just the right way. I don't know what I'd do without her. Anchor of the game. Most powerful piece. If I am king on the chessboard, she's the queen.

506

And I need her. Without her, it would be not worth living—none of it. Can I tell you why? Promise you won't tell anyone else? Not that you have the energy for that, huh? All right, here's the deal:

I lost my passion. I know what you think; you think everyone loses his passion for stuff, for everything he ever cared about. But that's not it. I really didn't lose it; it was stolen.

Let me be upfront. I have, well, interesting tastes. I like the exotic in certain areas, and sex was one of those areas. I'd tried most things you've heard of, the typical garden variety stuff—you know multiple partners, sex toys, all the orifices, tying up, tying down— until I was exhausted. Still I wasn't satisfied.

Then I met this woman—Joyce Janus. I saw her at this well-known bar for people like me. Had a few drinks with her, typical shit small talk. After the drinks and the small talk, she moved in close to me. She had one of those mouths I can only describe as dirty. Her lips were full and sensual. The lines in them were pronounced and deep. The lipstick clung in them and made little dark spots on her lips. Her teeth were slightly stained and a little crooked, but her tongue was deep red and it moved behind her lips and over her teeth like koi in a pond. That mouth wanted to eat not just me, but the entire world. Damn, if I didn't want to be part of that glorious meal, but something told me she would just consume me, leave me nothing but a husk. I didn't care enough; I wanted what I wanted and that mouth with its dirty promises of fleshly consumption couldn't be denied.

It whispered in my ear, "I have something you've never seen. Would you like to see it? Feel it?" I felt the heat of those lips. Imagined them licking the edge. "It's not what you think. I promise you have never felt something like it."

Joyce led me to a grimy backroom where there was a bed that only special customers could use. It was a really crappy bed that sagged in the middle. It had a thread-worn blanket on it. I normally wouldn't get near the thing, but Joyce Janus started kissing me. Then she went down with that dirty mouth of hers that seemed to work black magic. I could have been satisfied with that. I should have been, but she pulled me out of her mouth and said, "Ready for your new experience?"

I was so full of passion, so throbbing and hard, I could only manage a nod. I was stupid with desire.

She reached into a black shoulder bag. She had probably left it in the dirty backroom before she met me. She pulled out a mason jar. I looked at her like she was nuts. What was in there? Moonshine? Some kind of cheap high? Was she trying to get me to huff some industrial cleaner? When she brought it into the light more, I could see it was dark and muddy looking. Did she shit in a jar or something?

I was about to forget about this new thing even after that dirty mouth had worked its magic, but she grabbed my arm and stopped me.

"Look," she said. She held it as close as she could to a 25 watt bulb hanging near the door. The bare bulb threw grimy light on it. "See it?" Inside the mason jar, gold, purple, and red veins of light glowed and moved in a brown substance. Little sparks shone up and down the veins.

"What is it?"

"Terra cupidus."

I stared blankly at her.

That dirty sensual mouth of hers cracked a smile. "That's Latin for this rare substance. It is a special mud that can only be found in very rare and special caves. The best translation for it in English is 'desirous earth.' When you rub it on your skin...let's just say...it is like nothing you've ever experienced." Her smile grew. She licked her lips with that red tongue. Then she reached down with her free hand and stroked me.

The glowing mud, her smile, her lips, and her hand got me going again. Got me ready for anything. Made me agree when she asked if I wanted to try it.

"The best way to apply it is thickly on your most sensual spots." She pulled my pants down all the way and helped me sit on the edge of the cheap sagging bed. Then she sucked me a little. She got my full attention before she reached for the jar.

She opened it. A smell of earth, flowers, honey, and something slightly sickly wafted my way. She poured the muddy substance on my erection. Then she rubbed it over my skin, covering all of it. She took the mason jar and placed it underneath, waiting to collect it as it dripped off me.

It took a few seconds before the terra cupidus took effect. At first I felt heat and then intense humid sensual wetness. Suddenly it seemed to pleasure every part it covered, sucking from it the energy.

Imagine every pore having an orgasm at the same time. Now imagine every orgasm as the most intense one you have ever had. Now imagine the orgasms going on and on. Imagine that tired feeling you have, that contentment after a good orgasm. Now imagine you have nothing left—no passion because it was actually all spent. Imagine being so satisfied and tired that you didn't care if a strange woman who suddenly looked like a witch to you collected the muddy reason for this feeling by scraping it off you with a plastic spatula until you were nearly clean again.

Imagine her smiling as she held the mason jar aloft—the substance inside was glowing purple, gold and red. It was hard to look at, it was so bright. Imagine yourself helpless, so unable to move because you have no desire to do that or anything. That was me. I was just like that as she closed the mason jar and shook the contents. But then you can totally relate to that, huh?

"You certainly were a passionate fellow," she said. "I love a good horny man. So easy. So predictable." She studied the contents. Then she looked at me. "You'll live, just not the same way ever. You won't feel that rush again. It's gone. Told you you'd never experienced something like this."

I lay there and listened to her. On that crappy saggy bed, I could barely lift my head.

Then she did something cruel. She kissed me with that dirty mouth, held the jar against my cheek and opened it. That smell permeated the room this time. It was so strong. She breathed it in and sniffed at the air a few more times. Shudders of pleasure moved through her frame.

"Delicious."

Then as if to taunt me, she dipped her fingers into jar and covered them with the glowing substance. She moaned as she brought the hand under her dress and masturbated with it. She placed the jar on a table next to the bed and dipped her other hand inside. This one also moved under the dress. She moaned and gyrated beside my exhausted form. She stared into my eyes.

"Oh baby, you feel so good." She rubbed and rubbed herself with her muddy glowing hands. She showed it all to me by placing one knee on the bed. "Consider this your lovely parting gift." She rubbed frantically and slapped her flesh.

"Ahhh...ahhh...oh..."

But something happened. Right then, she just fell over. If I were a curious person, I would have asked myself, "Was it a massive heart attack or stroke?" Thankfully, I didn't give a shit. All I cared about was the hand with the glowing mud.

I struggled to lift my hand and reach for it. It took a few tries, but I managed to flop my hand on top of hers. The energy of the mud moved through me. I had the desire to rise and the energy to do it. Moments later, I stood over Joyce Janus' dead body. I reached for the mud, sat on the bed and poured the entire glowing contents on my cock. I felt the surge of returning energy; it was a huge rush of orgasm. As the mud ran off me, I took the mason jar and collected it. I'm not sure why I did. Perhaps it was because Joyce Janus did. I didn't want to break the effect of the terra cupidus. I even used the spatula to get it all off of me. When I looked at the mud, it was no longer glowing; it just had those purple, red and gold veins again.

Now I wish I could tell you I was all back to normal after that, but it just isn't so. I felt pretty normal for a day or two, but then, I started feeling drained again. A few days after that, I felt weaker and weaker. I knew what I had to do. I had to use the mud.

I cruised through the pages of Craig's List. I found a couple looking for a male third. I met them at a motel. We played around a little. I asked them if they would like to experience something new. Just like Joyce Janus, I spread the mud, but I did it to both of them. I left them exhausted on the bed. Perhaps they died.

I found I had to use the terra cupidus every few days. Once when I had a little extra energy, I spared Mallet. She reminded me of a girl I had a crush on in elementary school. She became my bitch who lured horny men to me. She spread the mud and collected it. I loved her.

But she touched the mud too much. Got all dried up. Finally, I left her on a bed with the last guy we drained. Some dumb fuck with a huge beer belly and a little cock. Not much energy there.

Later that night, I ran into Hatchet-face in the middle of the night at a Circle K. She was looking for a bite. I went in. Came back to the parking lot with a pile of food. Gave it to her. She had sex with me as a thank you. We enjoyed it and kept doing it. She's my number. Tight and juicy. She collects the mud now. Gets better guys than Mallet ever did. These young assholes from the local club want to fuck her or at least get a hummer. She leaves them drained in their driver's seats. Brings me the mud. She spreads it on me. She takes the spatula and cleans it off. Then she washes me carefully and completely. The whole time, I make her wear gloves. I don't want her to become another Mallet. When I'm fresh, clean and ready, Hatchet-face and I go at it all night long.

So now you get it, huh? Why you can't move from that bed. Why the last thing on your mind is fucking. You know I like you. I think Hatchet-face does too, young fella. I think we'll put on a show for you. Who knows? Maybe she'll put her stuff in your face. Maybe you like that. Doesn't really matter, huh? You get it whether you like it or not. You know if you had any energy left, you could scream. You won't. Not even if we decide to fuck you like a love doll. One more thing before we start. Look at Hatchet-face. She is so lovely in those garters, that leather bra and panties, ain't she? And don't you like how the glow of that mason jar lights up them titties?

"Hatchet honey, come on over here. Give Daddy his smear. Let's get this night started."

Other Great Titles From

Burning Bulb

PUBLISHING

www.BurningBulbPublishing.com

"This is a book that will keep you intrigued to the very end!"
Christine Soltis – Author of *Final Moon*

"Woo Hoo! ... I had a hard time putting it down."
Kimberly Bennett – Author of *Twisted Delights: A Thrilling Short Story Anthology*

PASSAGEWAY
BY GARY LEE VINCENT

When an archeological dig goes horribly wrong, the team is trapped in an alternate world where evil awaits them at every turn. Find out who will survive the Passageway! Part H.P. Lovecraft and part Indian Jones, this deadly tale will keep you guessing and wondering which path to take.
Paperback. ISBN: 978-1-4609-2478-5

GARY LEE VINCENT
Presents

DARKENED
The West Virginia Vampire Series

DARKENED HILLS (BOOK I)
DARKENED HOLLOWS (BOOK II)
DARKENED WATERS (BOOK III)

DARKENED HILLS
BY GARY LEE VINCENT

A tale of gripping psychological horror! When evil descends on a small West Virginia town, who will survive? Jonathan did not start out his life to become a rambler, it just worked out that way. William was a troubled youth with something to hide. Both were from Melas, a small town tucked away in the West Virginia hills... a town where disappearances are happening more and more frequently. After the suicide of a wanted serial killer, the townsfolk thought the nightmare was over. But when a centuries-old vampire is discovered they find out the hard way it's just getting started. Dark secrets can only stay hidden for so long and when the devil comes to collect, there will be hell to pay. Can Jonathan and William find a way to stop the vampire before it's too late? Find out in Darkened Hills! Darkened Hills is a gothic vampire novel written in the spirit of Dracula with much more sinister characters and eroticism then the old Victorian classic. Paperback. ISBN: 978-1453844854.

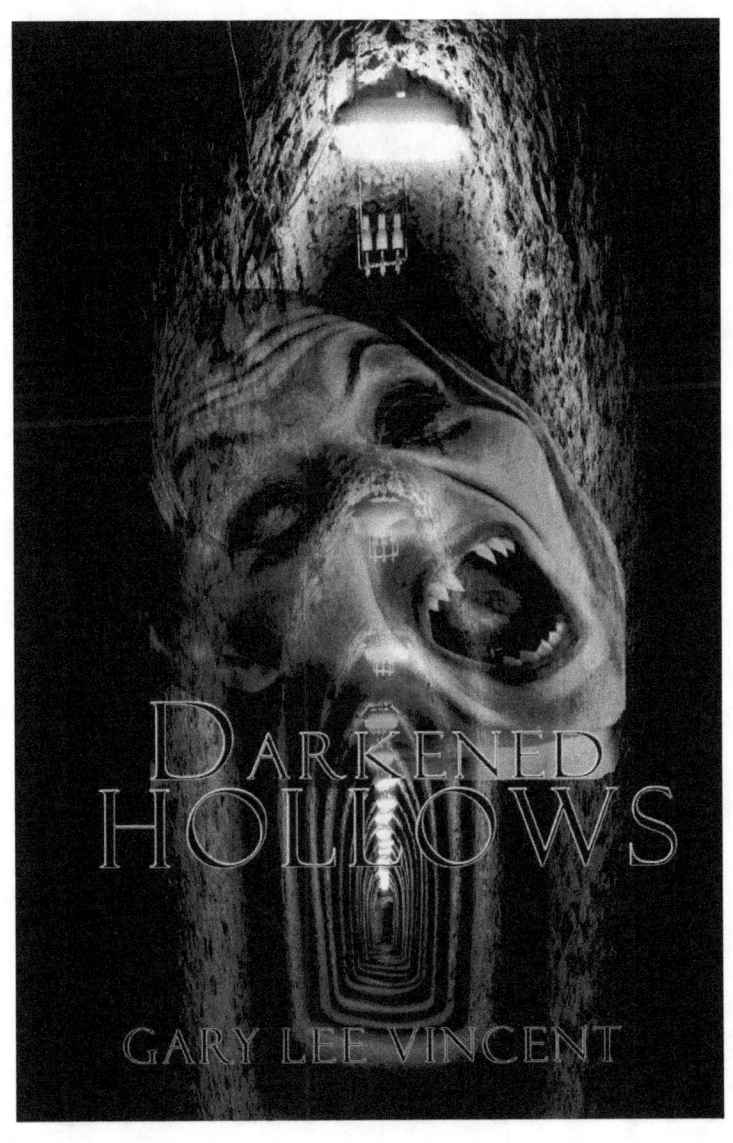

DARKENED HOLLOWS
BY GARY LEE VINCENT
Coming Fall 2011

DARKENED WATERS
BY GARY LEE VINCENT
Coming Summer 2012

RICH BOTTLES JR.

LUMBERJACKED

LUMBERJACKED
BY RICH BOTTLES JR.

Deliciously demented to say the least - two enthusiastic thumbs up! If you are easily offended or do not possess a truly depraved sense of humor, this story may not be the light summer reading fare you desire. As for the four feisty female freshmen stranded on top of West Virginia's third highest mountain, they have no choice but to experience the sick, twisted debauchery and perverted mayhem described deep inside the tight unbroken bindings of this horrific missive. Lumberjacked takes the reader to a nightmarish world where character development and aesthetic integrity are prematurely cut short by the swinging axes of maniacal lumberjacks, who are hell bent on death and destruction in the remote forests of Appalachia. And at the climax, when paranoia crosses over to the paranormal, Lumberjacked makes Deliverance look like a family raft trip down the Lower Gauley. Paperback. ISBN: 978-1453750278.

**HELLHOLE WEST VIRGINIA
BY RICH BOTTLES JR.**
Coming Fall 2011

THE ANONYMOUS WITNESS
BY THE ANONYMOUS CHRISTIAN

It was on an otherwise uneventful Sunday morning in early Spring when the minister of a small Methodist church in Appalachia provided a sermon based on the 23rd Psalm of the Holy Bible. He reminded his meager congregation that they should not fear the act of witnessing for Jesus Christ, even if it takes them into the proverbial Valley of Darkness. Little did the pastor realize that his routine sermon would result in the creation of this book - a revolutionary approach not only to witnessing, but to modern day Christianity itself. As a curious reader, you will soon recognize why this manifesto was written anonymously and you may even come to the conclusion that you too can be considered an "Anonymous Witness." Paperback. ISBN: 978-1448688777.

THE BIG BOOK OF BIZARRO
QUICK ORDER FORM
GET ADDITIONAL COPIES FOR ONLY $19.99

Email Orders: Orders@BurningBulbPublishing.com

Fax Orders: 270-477-4512

Web Orders: BurningBulbPublishing.com (click "Titles")

Postal Orders:
Burning Bulb Publishing
P.O. Box 4721
Bridgeport, WV 26330-4721
USA

Please send the following books:

_____
_____
_____

Name:_____

Address:_____

City:_____State:_____Zip:_____

Telephone:_____

Email Address:_____

Shipping:

U.S.: $4.00 for first item and $2.00 for each additional product.
For international orders, please go through the website and order
via amazon.com.

Credit cards accepted:

Number: _____

Exp.:_____   CV2: _____

Signature: _____

Offer subject to end without notice.

THE BIG BOOK OF BIZARRO
QUICK ORDER FORM
GET ADDITIONAL COPIES FOR ONLY $19.99

Email Orders: Orders@BurningBulbPublishing.com

Fax Orders: 270-477-4512

Web Orders: BurningBulbPublishing.com (click "Titles")

Postal Orders:
Burning Bulb Publishing
P.O. Box 4721
Bridgeport, WV 26330-4721
USA

Please send the following books:

_____
_____
_____

Name:_____

Address:_____

City:_____State:_____Zip:_____

Telephone:_____

Email Address:_____

Shipping:

U.S.: $4.00 for first item and $2.00 for each additional product.
For international orders, please go through the website and order
via amazon.com.

Credit cards accepted:

Number: _____

Exp.:_____   CV2: _____

Signature: _____

www.ingramcontent.com/pod-product-compliance
Lightning Source LLC
Chambersburg PA
CBHW071335020726
47502CB00001B/106